KU-561-394

Viktor's kiss took Maddie by surprise. It shouldn't have. Wasn't it natural to kiss to seal an engagement?

But the kiss did surprise her. And then it overwhelmed her, his lips coaxing a response that radiated throughout her body. They took possession of hers, insisting on the two things she'd said only that morning she wasn't capable of.

Submission and trust.

But then, like with so many other things in her life, the rules did not apply to Viktor Beck.

She found herself melting into him, no thoughts for self-preservation or holding anything back.

And he accepted her surrender with a forceful masculine desire that belied any claim for a lack of passion between them.

He devoured her mouth, his arms coming around her, his hands pressing her body flush with his.

Maddie's knees would have given out, but Vik's hold on her was too tight.

The kiss was Viktor Beck staking claim to the woman who promised to marry him and give him his dreams.

Lucy Monroe's

RUTHLESS RUSSIANS

Passion is in their blood

As boys, they came from Russia to America to make
their fortunes. Now formidable opponents in the
boardroom, Viktor Beck and Maxwell Black are
about to make the biggest acquisitions of their lives
by marrying two of San Francisco's most notorious
heiresses! Beneath their suave American exteriors
beat the passionate hearts of fearsome Cossack
warriors—and their intended brides are about to
give them the battle of their lives!

In AN HEIRESS FOR HIS EMPIRE
October 2014

A tabloid sex scandal means Viktor Beck can put his
plan in motion and marry heiress Madison Archer—the
key to taking over her father's business and building
his empire. But even this ruthless Russian is not
prepared for his wild bride to be a virgin!

In A VIRGIN FOR HIS PRIZE
November 2014

Formidable CEO Maxwell Black is about to
make his ultimate acquisition—
socialite Romi Grayson! She has something he wants,
and his need for control—in all areas—means he
won't rest until his ring is on her finger and the
innocent Romi is warm and willing in his bed!

AN HEIRESS
FOR HIS EMPIRE

BY
LUCY MONROE

MILLS & BOON

All rights reserved including the right of reproduction in whole
or in part in any form. This edition is published by arrangement with
Harlequin Books S.A.

This is a work of fiction. Names, characters, places, locations and
incidents are purely fictional and bear no relationship to any real
life individuals, living or dead, or to any actual places, business
establishments, locations, events or incidents. Any resemblance is
entirely coincidental.

This book is sold subject to the condition that it shall not, by way of
trade or otherwise, be lent, resold, hired out or otherwise circulated
without the prior consent of the publisher in any form of binding or
cover other than that in which it is published and without a similar
condition including this condition being imposed on the subsequent
purchaser.

® and TM are trademarks owned and used by the trademark owner
and/or its licensee. Trademarks marked with ® are registered with the
United Kingdom Patent Office and/or the Office for Harmonisation in
the Internal Market and in other countries.

Published in Great Britain 2014
by Mills & Boon, an imprint of Harlequin (UK) Limited,
Eton House, 18-24 Paradise Road, Richmond, Surrey, TW9 1SR

© 2014 Lucy Monroe

ISBN: 978-0-263-24997-2

Harlequin (UK) Limited's policy is to use papers that are natural,
renewable and recyclable products and made from wood grown in
sustainable forests. The logging and manufacturing processes conform
to the legal environmental regulations of the country of origin.

Printed and bound in Spain
by Blackprint CPI, Barcelona

Lucy Monroe started reading at the age of four. After going through the children's books at home, she was caught by her mother reading adult novels pilfered from the higher shelves on the bookcase... Alas, it was nine years before she got her hands on a Mills & Boon® Romance her older sister had brought home. She loves to create the strong alpha males and independent women who people Mills & Boon® books. When she's not immersed in a romance novel (whether reading or writing it), she enjoys travel with her family, having tea with the neighbours, gardening, and visits from her numerous nieces and nephews.

Lucy loves to hear from her readers:
email LucyMonroe@LucyMonroe.com
or visit www.LucyMonroe.com

Recent titles by the same author:

SHEIKH'S SCANDAL *(The Chatsfield)*
MILLION DOLLAR CHRISTMAS PROPOSAL
PRINCE OF SECRETS *(By His Royal Decree)*
ONE NIGHT HEIR *(By His Royal Decree)*

Did you know these are also available as eBooks?
Visit www.millsandboon.co.uk

For Judy Flohr, a very special reader
who I have long considered an honest friend.
It's sort of amazing to me that you've been reading and
sharing your love of my books since the very first one,
THE GREEK TYCOON'S ULTIMATUM, back in
2003. When I'm doubting myself, or the story,
I know I can re-read your emails or online reader
reviews and remember why I write and that
maybe I'm not so bad at this after all.

THANK YOU!!!

Hugs and blessings, Lucy

CHAPTER ONE

MADISON ARCHER SET her morning coffee down, hot liquid spilling over the rim, as she read her Google alerts with growing horror.

Madcap Madison Looking for New Master?
Archer Heiress into Heavy Kink
San Francisco Bad Boy Dumps Very Bad Girl

The articles made lurid claims about a lifestyle and relationship between Maddie and Perry Timwater. A completely nonexistent relationship.

The fact that Perry was the source caused the coffee to sour in Maddie's stomach.

His supposed exposé of their fictitious relationship claimed she was a submissive with a serious pain fetish and need for multiple partners. She gritted her teeth on the urge to swear as she read it was her inability to remain faithful that forced Perry to end things between them.

Maddie wouldn't mind ending Perry right that minute. Betrayal choked her.

How could he have done this?

He was her *friend*.

They'd met their freshman year at university. He'd made her laugh when she'd thought nothing could. Not after her epic fail trying to get Viktor Beck's attention. She'd started university with a broken heart and Perry had helped her paste over the cracks with friendship.

She'd helped him pass his accountancy courses. He'd played platonic escort for her and she'd provided him entrée to Jeremy Archer's world—an echelon above his own.

But never, not once, had their friendship ever taken a turn toward something heavier.

Pounding sounded on her front door. "Maddie! It's me, don't freak." Then barely a second later, the double snick of locks sliding back was followed by the door swinging wide.

Holding a bag from their favorite bakery aloft, her black bob swirling around her pixie face, Romi Grayson kicked the door shut behind her. "I come bearing the panacea for all ills."

"I'm not sure even chocolate and flaky pastry can make this situation better." Maddie slumped against the back of her chair.

Eyes the same vibrant blue as Maddie's glittered with anger. "So, Perry's lost his mind, right?"

"You saw the articles?"

"Only after reporters woke me from a dead sleep demanding my opinion of my best friend's darker sexual proclivities." Romi's mouth twisted wryly. "Proclivities I'm pretty sure you wouldn't have even if you *weren't* still a virgin."

"You've got that right. I've never been able to trust one man enough to have sex, much less multiple partners."

As ridiculous as that might seem at twenty-four, it wasn't going to change anytime soon, either.

"If you ask me, it's got less to do with trust and more to do with the fact you imprinted on Viktor Beck like a baby bird when you were a teenager and you've never gotten over him."

"Romi!" Maddie was in no mood to hash out her unrequited feelings for her father's dark-haired, dark-eyed, to-die-for-bodied golden boy.

"I'm just saying…"

"Nothing you haven't said before." Maddie's stomach grew queasier by the second.

Along with the rest of the world, Vik would see the articles, but she couldn't afford to think about that right now, or she really was going to lose it. "Father is going to kill me."

This new scandal was bound to crack even the San Francisco tycoon's icy demeanor. And not in the way Maddie had always craved.

He'd sent her away to boarding school months after her mother's death and Maddie had courted media attention in the hopes of gaining his. It had worked for her mother, Helene Archer, née Madison, the original Madcap Madison, but Maddie had come to realize the strategy had backfired pretty spectacularly for her.

In the nine years since Helene's death, Jeremy had developed a habit of thinking the worst of his daughter. When he wasn't ignoring her existence all together.

"If he doesn't die of a stress-related heart attack first." Romi put a chocolate-filled croissant in front of Maddie.

"Don't say that."

The other woman grimaced. "Sorry. Stuff just comes out. You know what I'm like. Your dad is wound pretty tight, though."

Maddie couldn't argue that.

"I think this time, Perry's diarrhea of the mouth has me beat anyway." Romi chewed her pastry militantly. "What was he thinking?"

Morose, Maddie stared at her friend. "That he wanted the money the tabloid paid him for the story?"

She'd had no idea that turning down his latest request for a loan would result in her utter humiliation. How could she? Friends didn't do that to each other.

"Jerk."

Maddie usually played peacemaker between her two closest friends, but she wasn't about to stand up for Perry this time. "What am I going to do?"

"You could threaten to sue and demand a retraction."

"Based on my word against his?"

Romi made a sound very close to a growl. "You two have never even kissed with tongue."

"But we have kissed, for the cameras." Perry had always made a joke of it.

He had been Maddie's go-to escort for years and more than one article speculating on their relationship had been run, often quoting anonymous sources and always accompanied by the joke kissing pictures.

"Do you think he's done this before?"

"Sold *confidential details* of your supposed relationship?" Romi asked.

"Yes."

"You know what I think."

Maddie sighed. "That he's a leech."

"Always has been."

"He was a good friend." Maddie couldn't make herself claim he *still* was.

Romi just gave Maddie a disbelieving look, no words necessary.

Ignoring it, Maddie said, "I probably can't prove we never had a relationship, but I can sue them for libel in the details."

"His word against yours."

"But he's lying."

"This is something new for the tabloids?"

Feeling hopeless, Maddie pushed her croissant away.

"You could always sic your dad's dogs on Perry. That media fixer of his could be cast in Shark Week on the Discovery Channel."

"I should." Even supposing her dad cared enough to assign his media fixer's precious time to helping Maddie.

Romi's expression turned knowing. "But you won't. Perry was your friend."

Maddie opened her mouth, but Romi put her hand up, forestalling words. "Don't you dare say he still is."

"No." Maddie swallowed back emotion. "No, it's pretty clear he's not my friend and maybe he never was."

"Oh, sweetie." Romi came around the table to hug her.

Maddie fought down stress-induced nausea. "I thought he was real."

"Instead, he turned out to be just another one of the plastic people." Romi's tone reflected her own experience with that. "All looks and no substance."

Maddie choked out a morbid laugh. "Yeah."

A bugler's reveille sounded from her smartphone.

With a snicker, Romi moved back to her seat. "Daddy's PA?"

"I thought it was appropriate." Maddie clicked into her text messages, unsurprised to see that there were dozens.

While she checked her phone periodically throughout the day, Maddie only had sound alerts set for certain people: Romi, Perry—who was going off the list today—Maddie's father, his personal assistant. Viktor Beck.

Not that her father's business heir apparent contacted Maddie these days. But still, if he did…she'd get an audible alert.

Ignoring the numerous messages from *friends*, acquaintances and the media jackals, Maddie clicked into the one from her father's PA.

Mtg w Mr. Archer @ 10:45—conf rm 2.

Mr. Archer. Not Mr. A, even though the PA had used text speak for the rest of the message. Not *your father*. That might have been too personal.

"He wants to meet this morning." Maddie bit her lip, considering what she'd have to change to make that happen.

Romi nodded. "Are you going to go?"

Maddie considered putting off her morning plans for the meeting with her father.

"No." It wasn't as if her showing up when he called was going to make Jeremy any less angry.

She shot a quick text back to the PA offering to come anytime after noon-thirty.

Fifteen minutes later, Romi was gone after a final pep talk when the strains of Michael Bublé's "Call Me Irresponsible" sounded from Maddie's smartphone.

Her father was *calling* her. Personally. Not texting.

Any other time, she would be thrilled. But right now? The crooner's smooth voice was as ominous as the sepulchre tones of a Halloween horror flick's sound track.

Maddie put the phone to her ear. "Hello, Father."

"Ten forty-five, Madison. You will not be late."

"You know I have a standing morning appointment." Not that he knew what it was.

Maddie had tried to tell him once, but Jeremy had mocked the very idea of his flighty daughter doing anything worthwhile. Worse, he'd made it clear how useless he thought it was to spend time volunteering at an underfunded public school predominantly populated by the children of poverty-level families.

Since then, Maddie had kept her two lives completely separate. Maddie Grace, nondescript twentysomething who loved children and volunteered a good chunk of her time, had nothing in common—not even hair and eye color—with Madison Archer, notorious socialite and heiress.

"Cancel." No give. No explanation. Just demand.

Typical.

"It's important."

"No. It is not." His tone was so cold it sent shivers along her extremities.

"It is to me." She wished she could be as unaffected by his displeasure as he was by hers. "Please."

"Ten-forty-five, Madison." Then he hung up.

She knew because the call dropped.

Wearing the armor of her socialite Madison Archer persona, Maddie got off the elevator at the twenty-ninth floor of her father's building in San Francisco's financial district.

None of the nerves wreaking havoc with her insides showed on her smooth face.

Makeup applied to highlight, not compete with, the blue of her eyes and gentle bow of her lips, she'd styled her chin-length red hair in perfectly placed curls around her oval face so like her mother's. No highlights had ever been necessary for the natural copper tones.

Her three-quarter-length-sleeved Valentino black-and-white suit wasn't this year's collection, but it was one of her favorites and fit the image she intended to convey. The wide black banded hem of the straight skirt brushed a proper two inches above her knees and the Jackie-O-style jacket with a statement bow was a galaxy away from slutty.

She'd opted for classic closed-toe black Jimmy Choo pumps that added a mere two inches to her five-foot-six-inch height. Maddie carried a simple leather Chanel bag, her accessories limited to her mother's favorite Cartier watch and diamond stud earrings.

Maddie didn't look anything like the woman described by Perry in his "breakup interview" with the press.

She walked into Conference Room Two without knocking, stopping for a strategic pause in the doorway to allow the other occupants a moment to look their fill.

She wasn't going to scurry in like a mouse trying to avoid the cat's attention.

The brief moment had the added benefit of allowing her to take her own *lay of the land*.

Seven people sat around the eight-person conference table. As to be expected, her father occupied one end. Maddie was equal parts relieved and worried to see his media fixer at the other end, but not happy at all to see the man seated to the right of her father.

Romi was right that Maddie had had a crush on the gorgeous Viktor Beck since he started working for Jeremy Archer ten years ago. The unrequited feelings had evolved from schoolgirl infatuation to something more, something that made it impossible for other men to measure up.

That first year, Maddie had still had her mother and Helene would tease Maddie for her blushes in the tycoon-in-the-making's presence.

Maddie had learned to control her blushes, but not the feelings the handsome third-generation Russian engendered in her.

Having him here to witness her humiliation tightened the knot of tension inside her until she wasn't sure it would ever come undone.

Less understandable, but not nearly as upsetting, was the presence of two of her father's other high-level managers in the remaining chairs on that side of the table. Her father's PA sat to his left, with an empty chair beside her.

The final man at the table had a powerful presence and a familiar face, but in her current state of highly guarded stress, Maddie couldn't place him.

Everyone had a stack of papers in front of them. It took only the briefest glance to see what they were: printed-out copies of the news stories Maddie had seen earlier on her smartphone. Underneath them was an individual copy for each person in the room of the actual tabloid the original story had run in.

Vik's pile was different. It had what looked like a contract on top. Looking around the table, Maddie realized everyone else had a copy of that as well, but on the bottom of their pile—the stapled corner was the only thing visible in the other piles.

She looked at her father and gave him the sardonic expression she'd been using for years to mask her vulnerability. "I don't suppose it occurred to you to discuss this with me privately before bringing in a think tank."

"Sit down, Madison." He didn't even bother to respond to her comment.

Which should neither surprise, nor hurt. So why did it do both?

She waited a count of three before obeying his brusque order, deliberately ignoring the stack of papers in front of her. "I assume we've already drafted a letter demanding a retraction?"

When her father didn't answer, she stared pointedly at his media fixer.

"Is it likely your ex-lover will recant his commentary?" the fixer asked in a flat tone.

"First, he was never my lover. Second, he doesn't have to recant his lies for us to sue the tabloid for libel." Though her chances of winning the suit weren't high without Perry's honesty.

"I am not in the habit of wasting time or resources on a hopeless endeavor," her father said.

"The story is out there and that can't be changed," she agreed. "But that doesn't mean we leave Perry's lies unchallenged."

Her father's eyes were chips of blue ice. "If you wish to challenge your ex-lover's *lies*, you may do so, but that is not my concern."

"You don't believe the stories?" she asked with a pained incredulity she couldn't quite hide.

"What I believe is not the issue at hand."

"It is for me." There were only two people in that room whose opinion Maddie cared about.

Her father's and Viktor Beck's, no matter how much she might wish that wasn't the case.

Her gaze shifted to Vik, but nothing from the stern set of his square jaw to the obscure depths of his espresso-brown eyes revealed his thoughts.

There had been a time when he might have tried to encourage her with a half smile or even a wink, but those days were gone. There'd been no softening in his demeanor toward her since her first trip home after going away to university.

And while that might be her own fault, she didn't have to like it.

Her father cleared his throat. "Those tawdry stories may have precipitated this meeting, but they are not the reason for it."

Maddie's attention snapped back to her only remaining family. "What do you mean?"

"The issue we are here to address is your unacceptable notoriety, Madison. I will not sit by while you attempt to rival other heiresses for worldwide infamy."

"I don't." Even when Maddie had tried to court her father's attention by gaining that of the media, she hadn't gone that far.

Okay, so she and Romi were known for their participation in political rallies of the liberal variety, which included a well-publicized sit-in protesting cuts in local school funding. That Maddie had gone further, bungee jumping from the Golden Gate Bridge with five others and unfurling a giant banner that read Go Green or Go Home, was beside the point.

There were videos online of her bungee jumping in less politically motivated and slightly more risky circumstances. The snowboarding had been a total failure, but she'd always loved downhill skiing and learning to jump had been fantastic. Of course, only her tumbles made it into the media.

But she hadn't done a thing to get herself in the papers in over six months. Not since hitting the headlines with a nighttime adventure in skydiving that had resulted in her hospitalization with a hairline fracture to her pelvis.

Her father had not only ignored her exploit, but he'd also ignored Maddie's injury. And not only had he refused to take her phone calls from the hospital, but he'd also made it clear, through his PA, that Maddie was not welcome at the family mansion for her recovery.

She'd been forced to hire a nurse to help during the weeks of her limited mobility. Romi had offered to stay with her, but Maddie refused to take advantage.

"Am I to understand you didn't read Madison in on the contents of this contract?" Vik asked, unexpected disapproval edging his deep tone. "Do you actually expect her to agree?"

"She'll agree." Her father gave her a stern glare. "Or I will cut her out of my life completely."

The words were painful enough to hear, but the absolute conviction in her father's voice stabbed straight through Maddie's carefully cultivated facade to the genuine and all-too-vulnerable emotions underneath.

"Over this?" she demanded, waving her hand toward the printed articles. "It's not true!"

"You will not continue to drag my name and that of my company through the mud, Madison."

"I don't *do* that." While she'd managed a certain level of media notoriety, it had never before been because of anything even remotely like the lies Perry had spewed to the tabloids.

Her father began reading the headlines out loud and weak tears burned the back of her eyes. Maddie refused to give in to them, wishing she could be as genuinely emotionless as the steel-gray-haired man flaying her with other people's words.

"I told you, *he lied*."

"Why would he?" the media fixer asked, sounding interested in an almost clinical way.

"For money. For revenge." Because she'd turned him down one too many times and compounded that by refusing his latest request for a loan. "I don't know, but he lied."

How many times did she have to say it?

"It is time for definitive measures to be taken," Jeremy said, as if she hadn't spoken.

"On that at least, we can agree, beginning with the demand for a retraction. I can do my own interview." Even though she hated that kind of direct contact with the media.

She considered offering the ultimate sacrifice of integrating her Maddie Grace life with that of socialite Madison Archer in order to combat the negative image that clearly concerned her father.

Jeremy dismissed her offer with a slicing gesture. "I believe I've made it clear that the current scandal is not my primary concern."

"What is your concern?" she asked, confused.

"The capricious lifestyle that has resulted in your unacceptable and notorious reputation."

"You want me to come work for AIH?" she asked with zero enthusiasm and even less belief.

The last time the issue of Archer International Holdings had come up, her father had made it clear he no longer harbored dreams of her one day taking over.

His harsh bark of laughter was all the answer she needed. "Absolutely not."

"You want me to get a job somewhere else?" She could do that.

She preferred using her education as a volunteer teacher's aide, but if it would help her relationship with her father, she would get a paying job—which hopefully wouldn't conflict with her volunteering schedule.

More derisive laughter fell from her father's lips. "Do you really think any reputable charity or business would hire you right now?"

Heat climbed up her neck, ending in a very rare blush. She'd become adept at hiding her emotions, even suppressing her blushes of embarrassment a long time ago.

But suddenly, she realized that if it *did* become known that Madison Archer was Maddie Grace, the school might be forced to disallow Maddie's volunteering. All because a man she'd thought was a friend had turned out to be a lying, manipulative, opportunistic user.

"He wants you to get married," Vik informed her, no indication in his tone or demeanor that he was joking.

Her father did not jump in with a denial, either.

For the first time, she looked around the room to see how the other occupants were reacting. Her father's media fixer and PA were both busy on their tablets, ignoring the conversation now, or giving a pretty good pretense of doing so.

One of his managers was looking at her with the type of speculation that left Madison feeling dirty, but the fact he had the articles about her spread out in front of him could have something to do with that, too.

The other manager was reading through the paperwork and the man who Maddie did not know was looking at her father, his expression assessing.

Vik's expression was enigmatic as always.

She met her father's gaze again, finding nothing there but implacable resolve. "You want me to get married."

"Yes."

"Who?" she asked, unhappily certain she already had an inkling.

"One of these four men." Her father indicated Vik, the two other managers and the man she did not know. "You know Viktor, of course, and I am sure you remember Steven Whitley." Jeremy nodded toward a manager she was fairly certain had been divorced once already and was nearly twice her age.

Maddie found herself acknowledging both men with a tip of her own head in some bizarre ritual of polite behavior. Or maybe it was just the situation that was so bizarre.

He indicated the manager whose look had given her the willies. "Brian Jones."

His expression was benign now, almost pitying.

"I thought you were engaged," she said, her voice almost as tight as her throat. But that couldn't be helped.

Hadn't Maddie met his fiancée at the last Christmas party?

"Are you?" her father asked, annoyance clear in his tone. "Miss Priest?"

His PA looked up from her tablet with a frown. "Yes, sir?"

"Jones is engaged."

"Is he?" Miss Priest didn't sound concerned. "He is not married."

"But I will be." Brian stood. "I don't believe I'll be needed for the rest of this meeting, if you'll excuse me, sir?"

"Did you read the contract?" her father demanded.

"I did."

"And you are still leaving?"

"Yes, sir."

A measure of respect shone in her father's eyes even as he frowned. "Then go." He nodded toward the stranger on the other side of Maddie as if the introductions had not been interrupted by the defection of one of his candidates. "Maxwell Black, CEO of BIT."

Maxwell smiled at her, magnetism that might actually rival Vik's exuding from him. "Hello, Madison. It's good to see you again."

He wasn't overtly sexual, but there was a vibe to him that made Maddie wrap her arms protectively around herself. This man carried power around him the same way Vik did, but with a predatory edge she hadn't experienced from her father's heir apparent.

Then, she'd never been his business rival.

"I don't believe we've met?" She forced her arms to fall to her sides.

"I saw you at the Red Ball last February."

She remembered going to the charity event that raised money for research into heart disease, but she didn't remember seeing him.

"I would have remembered."

"I'm glad to hear you say so." His teeth flashed in a blinding white smile. "But I meant what I said. I saw you there. We were not introduced."

"Oh."

Her father cleared his throat in that disapproving way he had, but if he expected Maddie to say it was a pleasure to meet the man—under these circumstances—he didn't know her very well.

But then that had been her problem most of her life, hadn't it?

CHAPTER TWO

THE MORNING HAD gone according to Viktor's plans so far, but the spark of temper in Madison's brilliant blue eyes threatened to derail it.

If Jeremy had evinced even one iota of the concern Viktor knew the older man felt for his daughter's current predicament, she would be reacting very differently. But then if father and daughter got along perfectly, or even very well, Viktor's own plans would by necessity be very different.

"You know, I never even entertained the fantasy that you called me to help me, to take *my side* for once, to protect me because I mattered to you." The beautiful redhead offered the emotionally laden words in a flat tone Viktor almost envied.

She would be one hell of a poker player.

She was lying, though. Madison wouldn't have shown up if she didn't think her father would help her.

"You never were a child taken with fairy tales," Jeremy said.

Viktor could have reined in the older man's prideful idiocy, but that wouldn't further his own agenda. However, he felt an unexpected pang of guilt at Madison's barely there flinch and flash of pain in the azure depths of her eyes.

She recovered quickly, her expression smooth—almost

bored. "No, that was always Mom's department. She lived under the fallacy that you cared about us. I know better."

It was Jeremy's turn to flinch and he wasn't as fast at hiding his reaction as his daughter, but then he had to be in shock. Madison didn't go for the jugular like that. In fact, in all the arguments between the tycoon and his daughter Viktor had been privy to, he'd never heard Madison use her mother's memory against her father before.

No triumph at the emotional bloodletting showed on Madison's porcelain features.

Instead, she looked like she wanted nothing more than to get up and walk away. The fact she stayed in her seat was proof the heiress might be criminally flagrant in her personal life, but she wasn't stupid.

She knew her father well enough to be aware that Jeremy's arsenal of threats wasn't empty.

"You have five minutes." Madison's words verified she did indeed realize her father had more *encouragement* to lay on the table, but also that she had little patience in waiting to find out what it was.

Color washed over Jeremy's face. "Excuse me?"

"She wants the other two prongs to the pitchfork," Viktor informed his boss.

Jeremy's scowl said he knew that's what she'd meant, but he didn't like the time limit or implied ultimatum that Madison would get up and leave if it wasn't met.

"Pitchfork?" Black asked.

Viktor could have answered, but he didn't. Giving Maxwell Black any kind of information wasn't on his agenda for the day. Viktor had ignored the presence of the other *candidates* at the table as superfluous, and planned to continue to do so.

Madison wasn't so reticent. "Jeremy never enters a fight he isn't sure he can win. To that end, he stacks the deck.

He'll have three scenarios in the offing, none of which will I want to eventuate."

"You call your father by his first name?" Black asked.

Madison flicked a meaning-laden glance in the tycoon's direction. "As he pointed out, I'm the not the one in the family to wallow in sentimental fantasy."

What she didn't say was that until that morning, Madison had called Jeremy Archer *Father* and sometimes even *Dad*. That she would no longer do so could be taken from her words as a given.

No question that the company president had seriously messed up in his approach to his daughter.

Viktor might have suggested the current course to protect AIH's interests and future, but he would not have blindsided Madison with it during a meeting with strangers.

He'd been angry when he realized Jeremy hadn't even bothered to brief his daughter about the meeting's agenda before her arrival. She might be flighty and prone to inauspicious, risky behavior, but she deserved more respect than that.

Viktor had no doubts that Jeremy would ultimately get what he wanted, not least of which because Viktor would make it happen.

However he had a nascent suspicion that the personal cost for that success might be higher for Jeremy than the president of Archer International Holdings anticipated.

Madison flicked a glance at the Cartier watch on her wrist. "Your time starts now, Jeremy."

"Golden Chances Charter School."

"What about it?" Madison asked with caution, the barest crack in her calm facade finally showing.

"Over the last three years, you have donated tens of thousands of dollars from your Madison Trust income to school improvements and projects."

"I am aware."

But Viktor hadn't been. He began to wonder what else he didn't know about Madison.

Jeremy's eyes, the only feature truly like his daughter's, reflected subtle triumph. "The school's zoning is under scrutiny."

"It wasn't as of yesterday."

"Things change."

"I see." Madison glanced pointedly down at her watch.

"Are you pretending that does not matter to you?"

"No. You have two more minutes."

Viktor was impressed. Madison would have done a better job negotiating a recent deal with a Japanese conglomerate than the project manager they'd sent to Asia.

Jeremy frowned. "Ramona Grayson."

"What about her?"

Viktor would be crossing his legs protectively if that tone and look had been directed at him.

"Her father is a drunk," Jeremy pointed out with well-known derision toward a man Madison had made no bones about considering a second father.

"And mine is a conscienceless bastard. I guess we both lost in the masculine parent lottery, though given a choice I'd pick Harry Grayson. His emotions might be pickled with alcohol, but at least he has them."

Viktor had seen Madison angry. He'd seen her hurt, embarrassed and even seriously disappointed. He had never seen her this coldly furious.

The Madison that Viktor had known for ten years was in no way reflected in the harshly dismissive woman in front of them.

Despite the implication of her words, she loved her father. In the past, she hadn't been able to hide her need for his attention and approval. Her mistake had always been how she went about getting it.

She'd followed in her mother's footsteps, not realizing

Jeremy Archer had been too traumatized by the loss of his wife to want to see her audacious nature reflected in their only child.

"Do you think Ramona sees it that way?" Jeremy asked. "Or perhaps she would prefer a father not lost in a bottle."

Madison shrugged. "It's not something we discuss."

"Nevertheless, the destruction of her father's business, followed by him losing everything to bankruptcy, would hurt her a great deal. Don't you think?"

Madison pulled her phone from her purse with an almost negligent move belied by the blue fire in her gaze. "You have exactly fifteen seconds to take that tactic for coercion off the table."

"Or what?"

"Ten."

And for the first time in Viktor's memory, infallible businessman Jeremy Archer made a mistake in negotiating. He silently called his daughter's bluff.

He believed that because she had no interest in business, Madison was not capable of the same level of ruthlessness as he was.

Viktor knew from personal experience that just because a parent and child lived very different lives, it did not mean that they shared no common personality traits.

Madison pressed her phone to her ear.

"Don't," Viktor said.

Madison just shook her head. "I'm sorry, Viktor."

There would be only one reason for her to apologize to him. Whatever she had planned would have a detrimental effect on AIH and, by default, Viktor's job and livelihood.

The possible implications were still firming in his brain as she made contact with the lawyer in charge of the Madison Trust. "Hello, Mr. Bellingham. I need you to draw some papers up for me. I'm texting you the instructions now."

Seconds later the lawyer's agitated tones came through her phone.

Madison listened for a moment in silence and then replied. "Yes, he knows. He's sitting right here. In fact, he's the one who put this in motion."

The fact the unflappable Bellingham was still speaking loudly enough for Viktor to almost make out his words said something about the nature of Madison's instructions.

"I am absolutely certain, and Mr. Bellingham? If your firm wishes to keep the Madison Trust as a client in sixty-five days when it falls under my control, I suggest you have those papers ready for me to sign when I stop by your office later this afternoon."

Another spate of conversation, this time quieter.

"Thank you, Mr. Bellingham."

Madison tucked her phone back into her purse and faced her father, her expression daring him to ask what she'd done.

Jeremy remained stubbornly silent, or maybe he was in too much shock to react. He had to realize the likely content of those papers, or maybe he didn't.

Maybe Jeremy Archer was under the mistaken impression that Archer International Holdings was important enough to his daughter that she would not do what Viktor was almost positive she had done.

"What do the papers say?" Viktor asked, unwilling to make decisions based on assumptions.

"As you know, because of the financial deal Grandfather Madison made with Jeremy upon his marriage to my mother, the Madison Trust holds twenty-five percent of the privately held shares in Archer International Holdings."

"Those shares are your heritage," Jeremy said.

"Romi is my friend."

"So you gave her some of your shares?" Viktor asked with no real hope it could be that simple.

"If Mr. Grayson's company is under threat from AIH or any company remotely affiliated with it, at one minute past midnight on my twenty-fifth birthday, all of those shares will be signed over to Harry Grayson personally. Not his company."

"You cannot do that!"

"I can." Madison looked more like her father in that moment than at any other time Viktor had known her.

"And if his company is not under threat?" Viktor asked, suspecting that Jeremy's calling his daughter's threat had precipitated some kind of permanent action on her part.

"Half of my shares will be signed over to Romi."

Jeremy stood up, his face flushing with color, his eyes narrowed in fury. "You will not sign those papers."

"I will." Conversely, Madison relaxed back into her chair. "You had your chance to take my friend's happiness off the table as a negotiating point, but you refused to take it."

"That's insane," Steven Whitley said, speaking up for the first time since his introduction to Madison. "Even half of your shares are valued at tens of millions."

"Romi won't have to worry about her drunk of a father ruining *her* life, will she?" Madison asked her father, as if he'd been the one to bring up the point of the shares' value.

Jeremy slammed his hand on the table. "I am not ruining your life, Madison, you've done a fair job of that yourself."

"No, I haven't, but I don't expect you to believe me."

"You are not giving away twelve and a half percent of my company!"

Viktor didn't know if Jeremy realized he'd just effectively taken the third prong of his threats off the table. No way was he going to allow Harry Grayson Sr. to own twenty-five percent of AIH.

Jeremy and Madison were too much alike. Both would

go to extreme measures for what was most important to them. The problem was that while Madison was very important to Jeremy, she did not believe it and Jeremy was willfully blind to what Madison needed from him.

Beyond that Archer International Holdings came first with Jeremy, and the people she cared about came first with Madison. Right now, those two priorities were in direct conflict.

Things were going to go completely pear-shaped if Viktor didn't take control.

"Sit down, Jeremy," Viktor instructed the older man in a tone that was respectful, but firm.

With a glare for his daughter, Jeremy returned to his seat.

"This meeting has derailed and I believe it is time to regroup."

Jeremy nodded.

Viktor stood and straightened his suit jacket before walking around the table and offering his hand to Madison. "Come with me."

"What are you doing, Viktor?" Jeremy asked, his expression considering.

The man knew that AIH sat near the top of Viktor's priority list, too. The company was the conduit for his own plans and no chance was he starting over because of the father-daughter issues of its owner.

"Madison and I have some things to discuss."

Steven frowned at him. "You are not the only candidate, you know. This contract was offered to four of us."

"I am the only one who matters."

An infinitesimal quirk of his boss's mouth said he knew that was true, but he said, "I believe that is up to Madison."

The lady in question made a sound of disparagement. "Right. If the decision is mine to make, I assume it's to be from the men you included in this meeting. One of whom was already engaged, another is old enough to be my father with a history of failed marriages and the other a complete stranger. And then there is Viktor."

"Maxwell Black is a man worth knowing."

While it might be true, Viktor didn't appreciate Jeremy pointing it out. Two half-Russian boys, raised to appreciate a culture not fully American, Maxwell and Viktor had grown up together, their families close, their goals similar.

Friends of a sort, but too alike for comfort, both men were determined to make their mark on the world, to be at the top of the food chain.

Because of the different paths they took to dominant positions in the business world, Viktor's and Maxwell's interests had not conflicted before today.

Thankfully, Madison didn't look impressed by her father's words.

She shifted so she could make eye contact with the CEO of BIT. "Mr. Black, do not be fooled by Jeremy's mistaken ignorance. Those articles are lies made up by a man I believed was my friend. Perry and I never had any sort of sexual relationship, much less a BDSM one."

The pain underlying her measured tones prompted Viktor to make some plans in regard Perry Timwater.

"I believe you." Maxwell's assurance proved he was every bit as intelligent as Viktor had always known him to be.

Madison relaxed infinitesimally. "Good."

"Regardless of the reason for our meeting, I would like to get to know you, Miss Archer." Maxwell, damn his hide, smiled charmingly at Madison. "You seem like an interesting person."

She inclined her head. "Thank you, but—"

"Don't dismiss the possibility of our compatibility out of hand," Maxwell interrupted her with another of his lady-killer smiles. "I bet I could teach you to like some of the things you've been accused of needing."

Madison's gasp said she was shocked by Maxwell's words.

Whether the words themselves or where he chose to speak them, Viktor didn't know and it didn't matter. *He* wasn't surprised. Maxwell played to his strengths and exploited the weakness of others.

Turning the lurid headlines into something forbidden but potentially exciting was a solid tactic for handling the current situation and the humiliation Madison had to be experiencing. Though she'd done nothing to let it show.

Unfortunately for Maxwell, Viktor wasn't going to let the ploy succeed.

Nothing was standing between Viktor and control of AIH. Not even Madison herself, but particularly not Maxwell Black.

Clearly upset with Maxwell's words, Jeremy made a sound of protest.

Before the older man could say anything Viktor was in front of Black, blocking his line of sight with Madison. "That is not something you are going to discuss here, or with Madison at all."

"You think not?" Black challenged back.

"I know not."

"I don't need your protection, Viktor," Madison said quietly from behind him.

He turned to face her, but didn't move so Black would have to stand and sidestep to see her. "Nevertheless, you have it."

She shook her head, whether in denial, or frustration, he didn't know.

"I'm nowhere near taking him up on his offer. I'm pretty sure even the mildest form of that kind of relationship requires trust and I don't have any. Not for men, particularly men with the same priorities as Jeremy Archer. *Businessmen.*"

She made the word sound like a slur.

Viktor didn't believe her regardless. Madison trusted *him*. She always had; even if she no longer realized it.

And while Maxwell's words hadn't surprised him, Madison's willingness to meet them head-on did. But then maybe it shouldn't have. She'd already shown her willingness to stand against her father.

Maxwell got up, his pose too damned relaxed for Viktor's liking. Even less did he like the way the other man moved around him to face Madison. "I see."

"Good."

"Nothing in the contract states we must share a bedroom."

Madison's eyes flared with...was it interest?

Viktor cursed under his breath. "In order to receive the shares stipulated, Madison and her husband must provide an heir for Archer International Holdings."

Madison gasped, anger shimmering around her like electric currents.

Before she could say anything, Maxwell shrugged. "There is always artificial insemination."

"While we live two entirely separate lives?" Madison asked in a tone Viktor recognized, but from the reaction of both Maxwell and her father, they did not.

Jeremy puffed up with renewed anger while the other Russian-American nodded with smug complacency. "Exactly."

"We would be married in name only?" she asked, the disgust levels rising enough that the others should have recognized them.

They didn't.

"No." Viktor was done with the verbal games.

Madison gave him a look like she was questioning his right to make the pronouncement.

"That sort of relationship would be too uncertain for the health of Archer International Holdings," Viktor pointed out.

Disappointment dulled the blue of Madison's azure gaze, but she masked the emotion almost immediately. Viktor cursed silently.

Her father, however, nodded vigorously. "Precisely."

"I think your daughter has already proven she is more than capable of her own decisions." Maxwell's admiration was annoyingly apparent.

"I won't sign the contract," Jeremy said in implacable tones.

The BIT CEO didn't look worried.

Madison's features had gone smooth with a lack of emotion once again as she stared at her father. "You believe I would agree to that kind of marriage?"

For once Jeremy seemed incapable of speech, perhaps realizing finally how little interest Madison would ever have in such a cold-blooded bargain.

"But then you believed the lies Perry spewed, didn't you?"

"I never said that." Jeremy's voice had an alien quality.

Realization of his colossal error in judgment in the handling of his daughter must be settling in, but being who he was, Viktor's boss wasn't going to back down, either.

Madison pulled her copy of the contract from the stack of papers in front of her and stood. "I assume you aren't going to do anything to mitigate Perry's lies."

"I have done it. Do you think this agreement is only about AIH? This is as important for you as it is the reputation of my company." Jeremy clearly believed what he said, but then Viktor had made sure his company's president saw things exactly that way. "Once you are married to a powerful man with an impeccable reputation, you can begin to live down your youthful excesses."

"My life has nothing to do with your company."

Viktor wasn't about to let the conversation degenerate further and there was only one direction it was headed if the two kept talking. Down.

"Conrad will put out a press release categorically denying all of Timwater's allegations," Viktor inserted before another word could be said.

The media fixer looked up from his tablet. "I will?"

Severely unimpressed with the man's lack of dedication to the protection of the company president's daughter, Viktor let Conrad see his displeasure. "You will do a hell of a lot more than that. If you'd been doing your job properly to begin with, this situation would not have happened."

"Protecting Miss Archer from her own excessive behaviors has never been in my job's purview," Conrad claimed in snide tones.

"Did you notice the loss of confidence in AIH articles in the online press this morning?" Viktor asked. "The first of which went live within thirty minutes of that tabloid hitting newsstands. Or did you think that was just a coincidence?"

The media fixer swallowed audibly and shook his head.

Jeremy didn't look too happy, either. He'd been too focused on using the current situation to bring his daughter into line, and had ignored the bigger picture. Something that was anathema to him.

"Your job is to protect the image of this company and anyone affiliated closely enough with it to impact our reputation in the financial community," Viktor reminded Conrad in a hard voice.

"Yes, sir."

"Maybe it's too much for you. Perhaps you'd prefer to move to a PR position working for a nursing home?" Viktor allowed the implication that was the only type of job Conrad would be able to get to hang in the air between them.

The usually unflappable media fixer paled, showing the man still had some of the intelligence he had originally been hired for. "I'm on it."

"You should have been on it at four-fifteen this morning after the scandal sheet went on sale."

Conrad didn't argue. He'd screwed up.

"I don't know what you spent this meeting doing on your tablet, but whatever it was, it wasn't as important as getting ahead of Madison's situation."

"I was writing the engagement announcement."

"I see. Not nursing homes then. Maybe you should be writing puff pieces for online dating sites," Viktor opined.

Nervous laughter filled the room and Jeremy made a sarcastic sound of approval, but it was Madison's genuine amusement that Viktor enjoyed the most.

"I'll need your signature on a civil suit against Perry Timwater," Conrad told Madison.

"No."

Viktor wasn't surprised by Madison's answer and forestalled any arguments from the media fixer or Jeremy. "The man was her friend. She's not going to sue him."

"Some friend." Conrad snorted.

The tiny wounded sound that Madison made infuriated Viktor. "We have other avenues of influence to bring to bear. I want a retraction from Perry in time for this evening's news. Play it off as a joke perpetrated by one friend on another."

Viktor turned to Madison. "For real damage control, you are going to have to do an in-person interview for one of the big celebrity news shows and meet with a journalist with a wider readership than the original article."

"Whatever I can do," she said with more conviction and none of the disagreement he expected.

Viktor's brow wrinkled in thought. Something about this scandal concerned Madison enough that she'd come to her father to ask for help.

While Jeremy might not see Madison showing up for this meeting as that, Viktor was certain of the truth.

Unlike her other escapades, Madison wanted this one cleaned up and her father's refusal to take it seriously had bothered her. A lot.

Viktor needed to figure out why it meant so much to her.

He put his hand out to her again. "Come with me, we'll talk your father's plan through and make some decisions from there."

She looked ready to argue.

He smiled at her. "Is that really too much to ask? I've got Conrad working on fixing this for you."

"Are you going to tell him to stop if I refuse?"

"No." Madison needed an act of good will.

It was important she realized that she could trust Viktor to watch out for her. He had to be the only candidate for her fiancé that she seriously considered.

Because her husband was going to take over AIH eventually and Viktor had every intention of that man being him.

Madison tucked her purse under her arm. "Okay."

"Just a minute," Jeremy said.

Viktor turned to face him. "I know what you want."

"But—"

"Have I ever neglected your interests in a negotiation?"

"No." Jeremy got that implacable look he was known for on his face. "Just remember that Madison's cooperation isn't the only thing on the line right now."

Viktor wasn't surprised by the threat, or even bothered by it.

He'd spent ten years working for this man and his ultimate goal was finally in reach. Viktor wasn't about to let it pass him by.

CHAPTER THREE

MADDIE FOLLOWED VIK into Le Mason, not at all surprised when the maître d' found them a table in a quiet corner in the perpetually busy restaurant, popular with tourists and locals alike.

"Did you eat breakfast?" he asked.

She shook her head, not even pretending to herself that shredding Romi's offering of chocolate pastries counted as actually ingesting calories.

He ordered the restaurant's specialty pancakes for her and coffee for himself.

"Did you bring me here to remind me of friendlier days?" she asked, sure she knew the answer.

"I brought you here because you used to crave their banana pancakes and I hoped to tempt you to eat." His six-foot-four-inch frame should have looked awkward in the medium-sized dining chair, but he didn't.

With his dark hair brushed back in a businessman's cut, his square jaw shaved smooth of dark stubble and a body most athletes would be jealous of covered in a tailored Italian suit, nothing about Viktor Beck could be described as awkward.

Doing her best to ignore his sheer masculine perfection, Maddie adjusted her napkin over her lap. "How did you know I hadn't already?"

"I guessed."

"I used to stop eating when I was stressed." She was surprised he remembered.

"Are you saying that's changed?"

"No." Too much was the same, but she wasn't about to tell him that.

She had to remember that Vik's interests here were aligned squarely with her father's. Not Maddie's. He'd made that clear six years ago and nothing had changed since.

Yes, Vik had gotten Conrad focused on curtailing the media frenzy around Perry's supposed breakup interview, but he'd done it for the sake of the company. Again...not Maddie.

Whatever his agenda now, it had the welfare of AIH as the end goal, she was sure of it. And if she got swept along with the tide, so be it.

"Give me the bullet points of the contract." She was morbidly curious about what her father had done to entice a man like Viktor Beck, or Maxwell Black for that matter, to marry her.

Vik's dark brows rose. "You trust me to tell you everything important?"

Answering honestly wouldn't just make a lie of her earlier words, but it would make her a fool. "I'll read it later to make sure."

"Your father accepts that you will not be his successor."

"What was his first clue?" She'd refused to get a degree in business and had fended off every request, demand and even plea for her to take a job at the company.

"Do you really need me to enumerate them for you?"

"No."

"Suffice it to say, Jeremy has finally accepted you are never going to be CEO of Archer International Holdings." Vik's deep tones were tinged with more satisfaction than disappointment at that pronouncement.

"It would certainly set a roadblock in your own career path if I were."

His espresso eyes flared with quickly suppressed surprise.

She smiled, pleased that he hadn't realized she knew. "You don't seriously think your desire for that office is a secret?"

"It's a family-owned company."

"That you plan to run one day and if Jeremy doesn't realize it, he's being willfully blind."

"That is one of his failings."

"You think?"

"He does not see you for who you are or what you need from him."

"You tried to tell him, once." The year before her clumsy attempt at seduction.

She'd thought Vik standing up for her meant he cared. But looking back, she had to conclude the friendship he'd offered her had been in pursuit of his own goals. Gaining Jeremy Archer's unmitigated trust.

She could have told Vik befriending her wouldn't do anything for him. Her father would have had to care about her for that to be the case. And he didn't.

The only thing that mattered to Jeremy Archer was the company. He'd married her mother to gain the necessary infusion of capital to make AIH a dominant player in the world market. His only interest in Maddie had been as a potential successor.

"He's given up on me personally because he realizes I'm never going to be his *business* heir." As much as it hurt, it also made sense of how unconcerned he'd seemed to be by "Perrygate."

"The only thing Jeremy has given up is his plan to try to lure you into the business."

Maddie shook her head, not buying it for a second. "You

heard him. He had no intention of having Conrad help me until you stepped in."

"Your father can get tunnel vision."

"And all he could see was the endgame." He hadn't even noticed that her scandal had adversely impacted AIH's reputation.

"Yes."

Maddie waited for the waitress to place her pancakes on the table and walk away. "Which is?"

"You married to a man who can and will be groomed to take over as Jeremy's successor."

"If my father can't get what he wants out of me, he'll use me to get it, is that right?"

"That's a very simplified view and not entirely accurate."

She wasn't going to argue something she knew to be true, as did Vik, even if he was too loyal to admit it.

"Jeremy wants his successor to be family." Hence the marriage. "How old-fashioned."

"It ensures his grandchildren will inherit his legacy intact."

"And that's important."

"To him."

The smell of pancakes, fresh bananas and syrup had her mouth watering. "What about you?"

"You need to ask?"

"AIH is your life." As much as it had always been her father's.

"Say rather AIH is the vehicle for my own dreams."

"I didn't know men like you dreamed."

"Without visionaries at the helm, companies like AIH would atrophy and eventually die."

"So, you think my father is just a very dedicated dreamer." Sarcasm hanging thick from her words, she took a bite of her pancakes and hummed with pleasure.

Vik laughed. "That is one way to put it."

"And your personal dreams include being president of AIH one day."

"Yes."

His easy honesty surprised her and charmed her in a way. She'd always thought of men like him as having goals. Solid, steady, unemotional stepping stones that marked their success.

"Wow. I guess the heart of a Russian really does beat under that American-businessman veneer."

"My grandparents like to think so."

She offered him a bite of pancake with a slice of banana. "And your parents?"

Vik took the bite just like he used to and memories of a time when they'd been friends, and all *her* dreams had centered on this man, assailed Maddie.

"My mother has been out of the picture for all of my memory. My dad is like a computer virus. He keeps coming back."

She smiled. "I should say I'm sorry, but having a father who drives you nuts makes you more human."

Vik shrugged, but she couldn't help wondering if he'd told her about his dad on purpose. To build rapport. She thought Vik had outclassed her dad a long time ago in the manipulation department.

After all, Jeremy Archer still thought he ran AIH. However anyone with a brain—not blinkered by willful blindness—and access to the company would realize it was actually Vik's show and had been for a few years.

"Whose idea was it to offer Steven Whitley and Brian Jones up on the chopping block?"

"It's hardly a sacrifice to be offered this kind of opportunity." Vik drank his coffee, his expression sincere if she could believe it.

But then what was to say she couldn't?

"Marriage to the prodigal daughter for an eventual company presidency?" That might well be worth it to a man like Vik.

"You don't exactly fit the distinction of prodigal."

"Don't I?"

"You haven't blown through your inheritance. In fact, you are surprisingly fiscally responsible."

"Thank you, I think."

"You haven't abandoned your family to see the world."

"I moved out of the family home."

He winked at her. "But stayed in the city."

"What can I say? I love San Francisco."

"And your father."

"I'd rather not talk about that."

"Understood." He smiled and her nerve endings went *twang*. "Your media notoriety isn't even of the truly scandalous variety."

"Until Perrygate."

Vik waved his hand, dismissing the importance of Perry's lies. "That will be handled."

"Thank you for that." The thought of being forced to give up her volunteerism because of an unsavory reputation hurt deeply, compounding her pain at Perry's betrayal.

He knew how important working with the children was to her.

"But seriously?" she asked, refocusing. "Whitley and Jones?"

Vik shrugged, but his lips firmed in a telling line. "They're the most likely men within the company to do the job."

"Marrying me?"

"Becoming the next president."

"Besides you."

"Besides me," he agreed.

"You're the only *real* candidate."

"I would like to think so."

"And then there is Maxwell Black."

Vik's eyes narrowed, the brown depths darkening to almost black. "Your father is never going to approve the kind of marriage Black suggested."

"And if that is the only kind of marriage I'm willing to agree to?" she taunted.

"Jeremy will hire a surrogate and have his own child in hopes of succeeding with him where he failed with you."

Wholly unprepared for that answer, several seconds passed before Maddie felt like she could breathe again. "He's not a young man any longer."

"He is fifty-seven."

"He would not be so cruel." And she did not mean to her.

No child deserved to be born merely as a player on the chessboard. She should know.

She'd taken herself out of play, but she'd had the strength of the memory of her mother's love to bolster her own courage.

This child would only have Jeremy Archer.

Maddie shivered at the prospect. "I'm not having a child simply for him or her to be put in the same position."

"You want children." There was no doubt in Vik's voice.

"Someday."

"Whenever you have them, or whoever you have your children with, Jeremy will want the company to ultimately pass on to them."

"I know." Her father's role in her life and that of any children she might have was something she'd already spent several hours talking to her therapist, Dr. MacKenzie, about.

"That is not a bad thing."

She'd come to realize that. While Maddie's feelings about AIH were too antagonistic for her to ever want to be a part of it, as she'd always seen it as the entity that kept her father from her, it did not automatically follow that her children would feel the same way.

"You said something about me having a child being necessary for the man I marry to take over AIH."

"Upon the birth of our first child, my succession to the presidency will be announced. Your father will shift into a less active role as chairman of the board on his sixtieth birthday."

"And if I haven't had a child by then?"

"My becoming company president will not happen until we have had our first child."

"What if we can't have children?"

"We can."

"You sound very certain."

"I am."

She remembered the ultrasound her doctor had ordered as part of her last physical, at the company's request. She'd thought it was odd, but since her medical insurance was through AIH, Maddie hadn't demurred.

"Jeremy had them run fertility tests on me."

"Just preliminaries, but enough to know that aside from something well outside the norm, you should have no trouble conceiving."

"That's so intrusive!"

Vik didn't reply and, honestly, Maddie didn't know what she wanted him to say. She wasn't entirely sure the test had been all her dad's idea. If Vik had suggested them, she wasn't sure knowing would be of any benefit to her.

"What else?"

"The contract gives five percent of the company to me on our five-year anniversary. Another five percent on the birth of each child, not to exceed ten percent."

"How generous, he'll allow me to have two children." She'd always dreamed of having, or adopting, at least four and creating a home filled with love and joy.

"The contract does not limit the number of children you have, only the stock incentive to me for fathering them."

She ignored the way Vik continued to assume he was her only option. "What else?"

"On your father's death, if we have been married for ten years, or more, I will get another five percent of the company. The remaining fifty percent of the company will be placed in trust for our children with voting proxy passing only to our children actively involved in the executive level of running the company. I will hold all outstanding family-voting proxies."

"But the other children will receive the income from the shares."

"Yes."

"It sounds complicated." But then her father wasn't a simple man, not by any stretch.

Vik took a sip of his coffee. "Jeremy wants a legacy and you've made it clear you won't be part of it."

"So he wrote me out of the will."

"Only insofar as his ownership of Archer International Holdings is concerned."

"I see." Honestly, she didn't care.

The Madison Trust provided all the income she needed to live on. That income would decrease once half of her shares in the company transferred to Romi, but Maddie didn't mind.

The biggest expense she had was keeping up her appearance as Madison Archer, socialite. As far as she was concerned, that part of her life could go hang. If her father wanted her to keep up appearances, he could pay for the designer wardrobe and charity event tickets.

"Is there anything else pertinent to me in the contract?"

"Your father would like us to live in Parean Hall."

The Madison family mansion, named for the pristine white marble used for flooring in the oversized foyer and the risers on the grand staircase, had stood empty since the death of Maddie's grandfather from a massive coronary upon hearing of his daughter's accidental death nine years ago.

"I have plans for the house." It was part of the trust and would come to her when she turned twenty-five.

"What plans?"

"That is none of your business."

"Indulge me."

Maddie didn't answer, but concentrated on finishing her pancakes. Vik didn't press.

His patient silence finally convinced her to tell him.

She said, "I want to start a charter school, this one with boarders from the foster-care system."

"An orphanage."

"No, a school for gifted children in difficult family circumstances." A place the children could be safe and thrive.

Vik sipped at his coffee pensively for several moments.

"How will you fund it?"

"A large portion of my trust income will go to it annually, but I also plan to raise funds amidst the heavy coffers of this city. I've learned a lot about fund-raising since my first volunteer assignment on the mayoral campaign when I was a teenager."

"Your father has no idea how full your life is."

"No, he doesn't." And Vik had barely an inkling as well.

She'd stopped telling him about her plans and activities when he'd rejected her so summarily six years ago.

Vik relaxed back in his chair. "The Madison family estate is a large house, even by the elite of San Francisco standards, but hardly the ideal location for a school. Either in building architecture or location."

"Oh, you don't think poor children should live among the wealthy?" she challenged.

He didn't appear offended at her accusation. "I think it will cost more than it's worth to get zoning approval."

"That section was zoned for the inclusion of a local school, but none was ever built."

"And you think that zoning will remain once your neighbors learn of your plans?" he asked in a tone that said he didn't.

"I don't intend to advertise them."

One corner of his lips tilted just the tiniest bit. "A fait accompli?"

"Yes."

"You have to apply for permits, hire staff…it's not going to stay a secret long."

"And then the fight begins, you are saying?"

"Yes."

"But why should the residents care if there's a school in their neighborhood? The city planners clearly intended there to be one."

"And the fact there isn't should tell you something."

"But—"

"I can find you a better building."

She didn't want to sell her grandparents' home. Her memories there weren't the greatest. Her Grandfather Madison had often made Jeremy Archer look warm and cuddly by comparison, but Maddie's mother's stories of her own childhood had been filled with delight.

Maddie always wished she'd had a chance to know her grandmother, Grace Madison.

"I'll have to sell the mansion to finance another purchase." No matter how much she might not want to do it.

The school was too important to give up and Vik was right, as he so often was—the opposition to a boarding school in that neighborhood for the underprivileged was bound to be stiff.

Vik shook his head decisively. "I'll buy the other building."

"In exchange for what?"

"Consider it my wedding gift to you."

"Presumptuous."

"I'm the only man I will allow you to consider." Dark brown eyes fixed on her with unmistakable purpose.

She ignored the way his words sent shivers through her insides. "You're assuming I'll agree to marry."

"Your father doesn't realize it, but I know he didn't need anything beyond his first threat to convince you to fall in with his plans."

"You don't think so?"

"Are you in another relationship?" Vik asked, the words clipped, something like anger smoldering in the depth of his gaze.

"No." Maddie saw no reason to hedge.

"Dating anyone?" he pressed.

"No." She frowned. "Why are you asking about this now?"

"Because if you were in a relationship with someone who mattered to you, no pressure your father brought to bear would sway you into marrying someone else."

He was right, but it rankled. "You think you know me so well."

"I know that your dad means more to you than you want him to believe."

"It's not a matter of what I want." Her father didn't think he mattered to Maddie because she wasn't all that important to *him*. Not in a personal way.

"Jeremy isn't going to back off on this."

"Why now?"

"You need to ask?"

"Yes." Her father had been too unconcerned about

Perry's scandal for it to be what tipped him into must-get-my-wayward-daughter-married mode.

"Jeremy has been worried about what will happen when you come into your majority for the Madison Trust for a while."

"Now he knows."

"I don't believe he saw that one coming."

"No. It wouldn't have occurred to him that I would purposefully put Archer International Holdings at risk."

"No."

"But apparently the idea that I might marry someone who might do that had already occurred to Jeremy."

"Yes." Something about the quality of Vik's stillness said he might have had more to do with that than her own father's paranoia.

"So, he was already considering how to get me to marry the man of his choice?" Maddie surmised. "He's using Perrygate as a vehicle for his own agenda."

She wasn't surprised by her father's mercenary motives, but she didn't have to like them.

"You would have to ask him." Vik indicated to the waitress to bring their bill. "I think the reality is more that he is afraid you'll end up with Mr. Timwater. Your father will do anything to prevent that."

"To protect the reputation and future of the company." Considering Perry's poor luck with his own business ventures, she could understand her father not wanting him to get even shallow hooks into any part of AIH.

"Sometimes, I think you are as willfully blind as your father." Vik shook his head. "He wants to stop you from marrying a man who would go public with the kind of claims Perry made in his interview."

"And Jeremy believes you're a huge improvement."

"You don't?" Vik asked, his tone more than a little sardonic.

She wasn't about to answer that. "Perry has never been in the running."

"Several articles in the media over the past six years would suggest otherwise."

"And the media *never* gets it wrong."

"You've never denied it, not publicly and not to your father."

"That's where you are wrong." And she had no satisfaction in that truth. "I told my father that Perry was just a friend, but he never believed me. He's always been more interested in his own interpretations and those of the media than anything I might have to say."

"I don't think that's true, but he is stubborn."

"So are you, in the way you defend him."

"Would you respect me if I had no loyalty for *my* friends?"

"Is my father your friend?"

"Yes." The single word wouldn't let her doubt his sincerity.

She used to think Vik was her friend, too.

Then things changed.

Now, she was facing the reality that it wasn't just that her father wanted her to marry Vik, but so did the man himself. Both had their reasons, but while different those reasons all centered around AIH, not Maddie.

She wasn't sure where, if anywhere at all, she came into the picture, other than as a minor piece on the chessboard. She certainly didn't feel like the queen.

CHAPTER FOUR

"I'LL BE BACK at three to take you to the lawyer's office," Vik informed Maddie as she unlocked her door and stepped inside.

"Are you sure that's not a conflict of interest?"

"Would you rather go alone?" he asked, a mocking twist on the masculine lips she'd spent far too much time studying as a teenager.

"No." Especially not after witnessing the media circus outside her building.

The paparazzi had always found her interesting, but it had never been like this.

And it was only getting worse as the morning wore on.

She'd managed to sneak out of the back entrance earlier, but the story and her location had spread in just that amount of time. There were almost as many media leeches haunting the other entrances to the building as in front now.

Even the parking garage hadn't been free of their presence.

She'd expected Vik to have his driver drop her off, but she could only be grateful he had insisted on getting out of the car and escorting her all the way to her apartment door.

He'd kept his body positioned protectively between her and the reporters stalking her. Vik was also very good at remaining silent no matter what was thrown at them and Maddie found it easier not to react with him as a buffer.

"Security will have the parking garage cleared," Vik said after a short text conversation on the elevator.

"Thank you."

They stepped off the elevator into a thankfully empty hallway.

Vik looked both ways before leading her toward her door anyway. "You need a security detail."

She shrugged, not wanting to get in to this argument right now, and not at all sure she would win it.

"When was the last time you had this lock changed?" he asked as she opened the door.

She looked up at him, wishing it didn't feel like all the oxygen got sucked out of the air every time she did that. "Why would I have it changed?"

"At least tell me you had new locks installed when you moved in."

"Why would I?" she asked again. "I'm sure the building management took care of it when the previous tenants moved out."

His expression said he didn't share her confidence. "You don't own the apartment?"

"No." She'd always planned to move into the mansion once she'd turned it into a school after she got control of her Madison Trust inheritance.

"Who has a key to this door, besides any previous tenant?" he asked with sarcastic emphasis on his last words.

Maddie leaned against the doorjamb when he showed no signs of following her inside. "Romi." She grimaced. "Perry, but he's not going to show his face."

Vik just shook his head before pulling his phone out and making a call. "Get the building access cards affiliated with Madison Archer's apartment deactivated and new cards issued for her, Ramona Grayson and myself."

He listened in silence for a moment. "Yes, have Ms. Grayson's delivered to her and the others to my office. I will pass Miss Archer's on when I see her later this afternoon. I want a security system installed, along with high-grade safety locks while we are gone."

The day before, Vik's high-handedness would have made Maddie livid. Today? It just felt like someone was watching out for her.

"You know, for a corporate shark, you're pretty good at this white-knight stuff," she observed as he tucked his phone away.

"I make a good ally."

"But a terrifying enemy, I bet."

"You'll never have to find out."

"Even if I refuse my father's ultimatum?" She didn't bother to point out that if she did agree, she could still choose to marry a different man.

They both knew how unlikely that was.

Her youthful affections notwithstanding, she wasn't about to marry a stranger or a man who had multiple divorces under his belt.

Vik reached out and cupped her nape, stepping forward until mere centimeters separated their bodies, the heat from his surrounding her in a strangely protective cocoon. He didn't say anything, just caught her gaze, his dark eyes compelling her to some sort of belief.

Her breath escaped in a whoosh, unexpected and instant physical reaction crackling along her nerve endings while her heart started a *precipitando*. "Viktor?"

"You will never be my enemy, Madison."

"You're so confident I'll do what you want?"

"I'm confident *in* you, there's a difference."

There so was. He couldn't have said anything more guaranteed to get to her. People who believed *in* Maddie were a premium in her life. And less by one after this morning.

Dark espresso eyes continued to trap her even more effectively than his hand on her neck. "Trust me."

"Do I have a choice?" she asked with an attempt at sarcasm.

"No." His reply held no responding humor. Tilting his head, he stopped only when their lips almost touched. "You don't, and do you know why?"

"Tell me," she said in a voice that barely registered above a whisper.

"You already do." Then his mouth pressed against hers and the drumbeat in her chest went to the faster paced *stretto,* while electric pleasure sparked from his lips to hers.

A sensation she'd only known once before despite the fact she'd tried kissing other men. Six years ago when she'd thought the best way to celebrate becoming an adult would be to tell the man she'd been infatuated with for years that she loved him.

Even the memory of that old humiliation could not diminish the feelings of ecstasy washing over her from this elemental connection.

The kiss didn't last long, just a matter of seconds, but it could have been hours for the impact it had on her. When Vik pulled away and stepped back, Maddie had to stop herself from following him.

"Three o'clock. Turn your phone ringer off. I'll text."

She nodded, her mind blown by a simple kiss. Which did not bode well for her emotional equilibrium.

She fought acknowledging the possibility that tycoon Viktor Beck might well be more dangerous to the almost twenty-five-year-old Maddie as Archer business protégé Vik had been to her as a teenager.

"Go inside and lock the door, Madison."

She nodded again, but didn't move as she tried to rec-
oncile the present with the past.

He shook his head, a curve flirting at the corner of the
usually serious lines of his mouth. "You're going to be
trouble."

"That's what my father says."

"I was thinking of a very different kind of trouble." Vik
traced her bottom lip. "Believe me."

"Oh, really." Her lip tingling from his touch, warmth
infused her that corresponded to the heat in his voice.

His smile became fully realized, and it was almost as
good as the kiss.

She wasn't the one who was going to be *trouble*.

"Oh," she said again, this time without intending to,
her body reacting to that warm expression in ways she
just *didn't* with other men.

Vik waited in silence, no sense of impatience in evidence, but Maddie knew every minute he spent with her
cost his tightly packed schedule.

She nodded to herself this time. "See you later."

Maddie stepped back into her apartment. Closing the
door on him was a lot harder than it should have been.

She threw the dead bolt and a second later there was a
double tap on the door. Vik's goodbye.

Using the pay-as-you-go cell phone she'd bought to provide Maddie Grace, volunteer, with a contact number, she
called the school and let them know she wouldn't be in for
at least a couple of days. She couldn't risk being caught in
her Maddie Grace persona and having the best part of her
life exposed to the media furor.

The next call she made was to Romi, who started curs-
ing in French when Maddie told her friend that Jeremy
Archer was using Perrygate to try to push Maddie into an
approved marriage.

Maddie didn't tell Romi about the threat to her own

father's company or Maddie's response to it. Romi would demand her friend not sign the papers.

"Are you going to do it? Are you going to marry the man you've been crushing on for the last ten years?"

"That was a schoolgirl crush. I'm twenty-four years old now."

"And still a virgin. Still avoiding relationships."

"I'm not exactly alone in that."

Romi's silence was as good as a verbal acknowledgment.

"Besides, I *could* marry one of the others."

"Right."

"Maxwell Black offered a marriage of convenience with children by artificial insemination." She couldn't help a small smile at the memory of her father's reaction to that offer.

She knew Romi would get a kick out of it as well.

"Max was part of your father's deal?" Romi demanded in a tone a couple of registers above her normal one.

All of Maddie's humor fled. "You know Maxwell."

Silence. "A little."

"More than a little if you call him *Max*."

"We went out a few times."

"You never told me."

"It's no big deal." But, threaded with vulnerability, Romi's tone said otherwise.

Maddie warned, "I think he found Perry's claims about our supposed sex life *intriguing*."

"I know."

"You what?" Maddie practically screeched, her own problems forgotten for the moment. "How do you know that?"

"Do you really need me to spell it out for you?"

"You're still a virgin."

Romi had said so and the woman might be a hyperactive, borderline political anarchist and more than a little eclectic in her dress style, but she never lied.

"Technically, that is true."

"Technically?" Maddie drew the word out.

"Look, Maddie, I don't want to talk about it." Vulnerability now saturated Romi's voice, defenselessness that Maddie could not ignore.

"Okay, sweetie. But I'm here for you. You know that, right?"

"Always. SBC."

"SBC." Sisters by choice.

Maddie's mom had called them that the first time when she was explaining to the elementary school principal why the girls would do better with the same kindergarten teacher.

He'd refused to change their assignments and Helene Archer had called in the big guns.

It was the only time Maddie could remember her father stepping foot in her grade school. Mr. Grayson had come down, too, threatening to withdraw his company's support from the prestigious private school.

Romi and Maddie had never been assigned different classrooms again.

They had shared everything, including their grief at the loss of the only mother either girl had ever known when Helene Archer's speedboat had crashed into rocks invisible under the moonless sky.

Maddie hadn't gotten her propensity for risky behavior from nowhere.

She understood now that her mother's increasingly erratic behavior had been Helene's way of crying out for help. Help neither Maddie, nor her father, realized Helene needed.

It was a failure Maddie was still coming to terms with.

Vik's text came in at ten minutes to three.

He was on a conference call he could not reschedule,

but two bodyguards would be at her door in a few minutes. They had AIH indigo-level security IDs and she was not to open the door unless she saw the familiar badges through her peephole.

Specially trained for protecting people rather than corporate property and secrets, the indigo team was her father's personal security detail. It used to be hers, too. Wanting to live as normal a life as possible, Maddie had refused to be assigned bodyguards when she moved out of the family mansion.

Her father had argued, but ultimately given in.

She didn't think Vik would be as easily swayed. If he thought Maddie needed a bodyguard for her security, she'd have one.

The same way the company's on-site security system had been upgraded because Vik deemed it necessary. Her father had been all for it, though.

Nothing was too good for Archer International Holdings.

The limo was waiting in front of the elevator bank in the parking garage. Thankfully, no enterprising reporter had managed to keep vigil. Which probably had less to do with the parking garage guards than the two additional indigo-badge bodyguards standing at attention on either side of the elevator doors.

One of them stepped forward to open the door to the limo and she stepped inside, only then realizing that Vik had taken the conference call on his mobile.

Every dark hair perfectly in place, his designer suit immaculate, he nodded at her while carrying on a conversation in Japanese.

His words did not falter, his Japanese smooth and unhesitating, and yet she felt the weight of his full regard. Like his attention was fully on her.

Like she mattered.

Succumbing to the desire to sit beside him, Maddie settled onto the smooth leather seat across from AIH's media fixer. Relieved that none of the bodyguards had instructions to join them in the back of the limo, she was still grateful the other occupant gave her an excuse to give in to the irresistible urge.

The need to be near Vik was verging on ungovernable, just like it had been six years ago.

Maddie wanted to chalk it up to the exceptional circumstances. She just wasn't sure she could.

Which was not enough of a caution to move to the other seat. There was simply no comparison between Vik and Conrad, who until that morning she had found slightly annoying but now considered flat-out obnoxious.

The PR guru took a break from typing madly on his tablet to silently acknowledge her. If his smile looked more like a grimace, she wasn't interested enough in interacting with him to call him on it.

Besides, Perry's fake exposé had triggered an ugly media frenzy beyond anything Maddie had ever experienced for her far more innocent escapades.

There was even speculation now that some of her riskier endeavors had been the result of orders from her *master*. That wasn't even the worst of it. Maddie did not know how a virgin could be labeled a sex addict with obvious intimacy issues, but she'd stopped reading her Google alerts after that headline.

The limo had exited the parking garage and pulled away from her building when Vik ended his phone call.

"Are you okay?" he asked Maddie.

Honesty would reveal a level of vulnerability she wasn't comfortable sharing with Vik, much less Conrad. She had no idea how her life had spun out of control so fast.

And Perrygate was only part of it. Her father's ultimatum and the realization their relationship would never be what she wanted had been followed too closely by the equally alarming, if for different reasons, acknowledgment that she was actually considering marrying her girlhood crush.

"I'm fine."

"Good," Conrad said, as if he'd asked the question. "Containing this media bloodbath is going to take serious effort and you need to be on your top game."

He didn't have to tell her. Maddie had spent the time since Vik had dropped her off earlier worrying about what would happen if she couldn't reclaim her reputation.

The all too real prospect of losing her dreams of opening a small charter school tightened Maddie's throat, so she just nodded.

Once the media started looking more closely at Maddie's life, her alter ego was bound to come to light and the probability of losing her volunteer position was pretty much guaranteed.

While she enjoyed the anonymity of her Maddie Grace persona, she'd only taken rudimentary steps to keep her two lives separate. She wasn't James Bond, after all, just a socialite who craved time contributing as a *normal* person.

The only reason no one had cottoned on to Maddie Grace and Madison Archer being the same person before was that the news simply wasn't all that interesting. Or it hadn't been.

Her notoriety as Madcap Madison had been of the innocent variety, good for filler pieces in the social columns, but not salacious enough to really impact circulation numbers. Therefore *she* had not been interesting enough to be targeted by any serious digging.

She'd no doubt reporters were getting out their sharpest spades now. Perrygate was all that and a bag of chips for the gossipmongers.

The most painful part of Maddie's predicament was

that it wasn't just her dreams on the line here; Romi was equally invested in the charter school.

Vik sent a text and then pocketed his phone. "Our lack of an immediate response opened the door to other spurious claims from supposed former lovers."

Vik gave Conrad a look that left no doubt exactly who the VP of Operations for AIH blamed for that mistake.

Maddie felt no smugness at the media fixer being so obviously in the doghouse with Vik. Her life was too out of control to harbor even a hint of that, but she couldn't help the small thrill of pleasure at him taking her side.

From the moment he'd stepped in and ordered Conrad's cooperation that morning, Maddie had known she wasn't alone in facing the painful consequences of her onetime friend's betrayal.

Conrad tugged at the collar of his shirt. "We're working on retractions, but the best strategy for solidifying the prank angle is to give the media hounds another story."

"What do you mean? Like a two-headed baby from outer space, or something?" Maddie asked as her phone chimed to indicate a text from one of her select group.

Thinking it was Romi, she pulled out her phone and checked the message. It wasn't from her SBC; it was from Vik and said, You are not fine. We will talk. Later.

She texted back. If you say so.

Vik pulled his phone out and replied to her text while speaking. "Or something. A glossy celebrity gossip magazine has already offered a two-page spread announcing our formal engagement in exchange for exclusive photos of a lavish, well-attended wedding reception."

"We're engaged now?" Had she missed something between the text convo and their in-person discussion?

Vik didn't answer, but waited in silence for her to come to her own conclusion.

"It's the best way to stop any more dirty snow falling in this avalanche," Conrad said unctuously.

"Dirty snow? Really?" she asked sarcastically.

"Do you have a better word for it?"

"Perrygate."

"Appropriate, but don't use it on your social networks," Conrad instructed her. "It implies a negative rift between you and Mr. Timwater. We're dismissing all this as a joke gone wrong."

"Then you can play it off as the bad joke that ruined a friendship. I won't play nice with Perry." She couldn't.

Conrad frowned thoughtfully. "It would be better for you to be seen as the forgiving friend. Waiting a few months to cut the man from your life will increase your popularity."

"I don't care."

"Timwater isn't coming within a hundred feet of Madison, not even to apologize." Vik's voice brooked no argument.

And Conrad proved he was more intelligent than other evidence to the contrary because he didn't make one. "Fine. Fine." He started taking notes. "'The Prank That Ended a Friendship.' I can use that. We can spin the angle even. 'The Bad Joke That Almost Ended an Engagement.'"

Maddie looked at Vik. "Is he for real?"

Part of her knew this was the way things had to be, that Conrad was just doing his job, but having her life reduced to clichés and headlines was not fun.

"It's going to be okay, Madison." Vik pulled her cold hand into his own. "Trust me."

He had never hesitated to invade her personal space, or to touch her, though she'd never noticed him being so free with others. It was one of the reasons she'd convinced her eighteen-year-old self that Vik might return her feelings.

She'd realized later that the small touches were probably the result of the way his Russian grandparents had raised him. Maddie had figured she hadn't seen him behave that way with others because he had so few personal relationships.

None but his grandparents and her father that she'd ever actually come into contact with.

That was one thing she and Vik had in common.

A very small inner circle.

She didn't comment on this now, just gave thanks for the fact he was willing to offer her the kind of comfort she needed and had never been able to ask for.

Vik squeezed her fingers. "Conrad is one of the best in the business. Before this morning I would have said *the* best."

Conrad flinched, proving he'd been listening even as he typed.

"And our engagement is the only way to restore my reputation?" she asked almost rhetorically.

She didn't see another way out, either.

Her father had more leverage for his plan than he could possibly comprehend. The realization of Maddie and Romi's dreams relied on a reputation Maddie could not afford to lose.

Vik frowned. "I'm sorry, Madison, but nothing is going to make the story go away completely."

"Why not?" Media fixers worked miracles.

Isn't that what everyone said? If they couldn't fix this, her and Romi's dreams were going to crash and burn. There was no way Maddie was going to let that happen.

Conrad looked up from his tablet. "Some people will always believe that where there is or was smoke, there had to be some ember of fire."

"But there isn't one."

The twist of Conrad's lips said he was probably one of *those* people.

Vik's hand moved to Maddie's thigh, bringing her attention careening back to him and him alone. "I believe you."

"No matter what the press has claimed, I've never even had a serious boyfriend," she admitted painfully.

Something flared in Vik's eyes, but he just nodded. "You've been too busy getting into trouble."

"Not *this* kind of trouble."

"I know."

"And not even my usual in the last six months."

Conrad's head snapped up. "Is that true?"

"I haven't done anything zany or even remotely news-worthy since I broke my pelvis in that botched skydiving landing."

Conrad narrowed his gaze. "What about parties? Random hookups?"

"Did you not hear her, Conrad?" Vik asked, dropping the temperature in the limo with the ice in his tone. "Madison does not do random hookups."

"She said she hasn't had a serious relationship, that the men claiming to have engaged in BDSM encounters are lying. Miss Archer never claimed to be celibate." Okay, so Conrad *had* been listening.

Vik didn't thaw even a little. "You can take *no random hookups* as a given."

"Can I?" Conrad asked Maddie, surprising her with his tenacity.

"Yes," she replied firmly. "I haven't been out in the evening except to attend charity events since my accident."

"With Perry as your escort?" Conrad asked, sounding unhappy by the possibility.

Which she could understand, in light of recent events. She wouldn't call the emotion she was feeling right now unfettered joy, either.

"A couple of times."

Vik's jaw hardened.

"Most events, Romi and I go together. Perry isn't all that interested in helping others." Maddie felt disloyal admitting that truth, but Romi had always said it.

Perry had never been as interested in the causes Maddie supported as the A-listers and potential business contacts he could meet at certain events.

"You've been at most of them, yourself," she offered to Vik.

He frequently represented AIH at that sort of thing, being an expert at making connections Perry only aspired to. Maddie knew that Vik also supported the causes in very tangible ways, both on behalf of the corporation and personally.

The gorgeous, corporate white knight nodded.

"That could work in our favor, unless you were photographed with your date for the evening," Conrad mused. "Even then, we could make it work."

"Vik hasn't had a date with him at one of these events in over a year." Knowledge that revealed how much attention Maddie paid to Vik.

A fact she'd done her best to hide even from herself, darn it.

His raised brow and knowing look said he realized that, too.

"That's good. We can back-engineer a budding relationship you've taken pains to keep out of the media spotlight." Conrad took more notes on his tablet. "This works."

Maddie turned toward Vik. "We're really getting married?"

"You tell me."

"Only it doesn't seem possible." Everything since her nearly spilled cup of coffee that morning felt like a dream, at times odd, unpleasant and bordering unbelievable.

"Believe it," Vik said, unconsciously answering her silent thoughts.

She narrowed her eyes, trying to read him. "How can you take this so calmly?"

"What am I supposed to be upset about?"

"Yesterday you were a free agent. Today you are engaged." Didn't that bother him, even a little?

Or was it something Vik had planned all along? Somehow, she couldn't quite dismiss that possibility.

"We are not engaged yet."

Something went tight in her chest. "But—"

"We will finish this discussion after you meet with the lawyer."

What did that mean? Did he think they were engaged, or not? *Were* they engaged? Had she said *yes?* She was pretty sure she hadn't. And she might know her choices were very limited, but did Vik? Really?

He returned his attention to his phone and sent a text.

This time she had no doubts it was to her.

Sure enough a few seconds later, her phone chimed. Trust me.

Trust him. Right. He thought it was that easy? "You aren't going to try to talk me out of signing the paperwork?"

"I told Jeremy threatening Romi could boomerang on him."

"He didn't believe you."

"He has a hard time backing off once he's set a thing in motion."

"Are you saying he's already started the wheels of destruction for Mr. Grayson's company? They used to be good friends."

Vik shrugged noncommittally. "He's done the research on how to make it happen."

"And he didn't want to waste his efforts?" Her dad could be so cold, but then that wasn't breaking news.

"You and I have agreed Jeremy could have no idea how spectacularly it would come back to bite him on the ass."

"But you aren't trying to change my mind."

Conrad stopped typing and listened as if he, too, was curious about what was motivating Vik's behavior.

Vik ignored the other man, his focus entirely on Maddie. "Those shares ultimately belong to you."

"My father doesn't see it that way."

"It never occurred to Jeremy that any child of his would consider AIH as a means to an end rather than the end itself."

What did he know? Did Vik realize she had always intended to use her income from the shares to run the school?

It wouldn't be a long stretch from what she'd told him that morning.

What he couldn't know was that Romi would do the same. She wanted the school as much as Maddie.

Vik's dream was something quite different, but obviously just as important to him. "You want the company."

"Like your father, I want to leave a legacy for my children." Some might think the lack of emotion in Vik's deep tones belied his words.

Maddie knew better.

His dark brown eyes burned with certainty. "Archer International Holdings will be that legacy."

"But we're not engaged." She couldn't help the small bit of sarcasm.

Maddie was unsurprised by Vik's lack of response.

CHAPTER FIVE

MADDIE'S TIME IN the lawyer's office went quickly, though the elderly man did ask if she was sure she knew what she was doing.

Maddie had no doubts.

Vik stood when she came back into the anteroom, no sign he was in any way upset about what she'd been doing. "All finished?"

"Yes."

"Do you have any plans for the rest of today?"

"No."

Vik put his hand on the small of her back and walked with her out of the law office. "Good."

"Why?"

"We have a photo shoot with the magazine photographer this evening. He'll join us for dinner at your father's mansion. My grandparents will be there."

"Playing happy families? Is that really necessary?"

"Yes."

When they reached the parking garage, he led her to his car, the limo and SUV full of bodyguards nowhere in evidence.

"Conrad is in the limo with a redheaded decoy." Vik opened the passenger door of the black amethyst Jaguar XJL for Maddie.

She settled into the luxury car. "Better her than me. I would have made a lousy celebrity."

"You think?" he asked. "Your father thinks you've been doing your best to become the next reality TV star."

"Just Madcap Madison, version two-point-oh."

Vik's expression went from smile to grimace, reflecting Maddie's own conflicting feelings about her mom's escapades in the light of adulthood. "In many ways Helene Madison Archer was an amazing woman and she raised a strong and impressive daughter, but the way she chose to cope with the things she didn't like in her life wasn't healthy. You must see that."

"I do." It had taken some time, but Maddie had come to that conclusion a while ago. The *Madcap* was something Maddie was doing her best to drop from her name. "Believe it, or not, I've always been very careful what part of my life I allow the media into."

"Perry isn't so choosy."

Vik was in the driver's seat, their identity obscured behind the Jaguar's tinted windows, when she replied. "Perry is an idiot who relied on our friendship to protect him from the consequences of his lies."

"It is."

"You think so?" She indulged in an old favorite secret pastime as he drove out of the financial district and through Chinatown toward Van Ness.

Watching Viktor Beck.

Memories of their recent kiss played over in her mind, a mental movie she could not seem to turn off and that caused a visceral reaction in her body. A reaction she wasn't sure if she should try to suppress, or not.

If they were getting married, reacting to his kiss was a good thing, right?

Thankfully, she didn't have to answer the disturbing question of whether she would marry him for the sake of her dreams if she *wasn't* attracted to him. How much of her father's ruthlessness colored Maddie's spirit?

She was sure Jeremy Archer would say the papers she'd just signed answered that question, but that wasn't how she saw it.

Vik shifted down, his car purring as it climbed the hills of San Francisco's streets. "You refuse to sue Perry despite his defamation of your character."

"Our friendship is over." Ultimately that would cost Perry more than any settlement she might get in court.

"Is it?"

"Yes."

"You sound very certain." Vik didn't.

"I am."

Vik turned onto Highway 101. "Good."

"And even if for no other reason than that he'll never get another loan from me, that's a serious consequence for Perry." One she really didn't think the other man had foreseen. He would have counted on her loyalty, but had made the egregious error of not giving her any. "He'll also never again be able to use being my escort as a way into events his own connections won't provide entrée."

"It sounds like it was a pretty one-sided friendship."

"That's what Romi always said, but it wasn't true."

"Yes?" Vik sounded genuinely curious, if doubtful.

"Letting people in isn't easy for me."

The business tycoon who had spurred more fantasies than any teenage heartthrob in her adolescent breast made a disbelieving sound. "You have a huge social network."

"And a total of two people I called friends, now only one."

"I think two still." Vik flicked her a glance with meaning. "Just not the same two."

Unexpected and not wholly welcome warmth unfurled

inside Maddie at the claim. Nevertheless, she admitted, "I'm glad to hear that."

She just hoped it was true. Chances were good. Viktor Beck might be a bastard in the business world, but he was no liar.

"He made me laugh," she admitted, falling back on old habits of sharing her uncensored thoughts with Vik.

"You have an infectious laugh," Vik offered. "I missed it."

It was weird to think of Vik missing anything about her. "You decided our friendship was over."

"Not over, just truncated."

"If you say so." But six years on, she could maybe share his point of view.

"I thought it for the best."

It was entirely possible it had been, no matter how much his rejection and subsequent pulling away had hurt. She hadn't thought so at the time, the combined loss of her mom, then her grandfather, what little attention she'd had from her father and then Vik's friendship had left Maddie with real intimacy issues. But if she and Vik had maintained their close friendship, she never would have gotten over him.

Nor would she have made her own way in life, building dreams completely independent of AIH.

"Looking back on it, it's kind of surprising I let Perry get so close." But then she'd needed a replacement for Vik at least.

"You loaned him money."

Which had taken their friendship into a different realm, she now realized—a realm where Perry saw Maddie as a resource rather than a friend. "In the interest of accuracy, we'll have to call them gifts, not loans."

"And that makes it better?"

She shrugged, though Vik's attention was on the road as

they joined the heavy traffic over the Golden Gate Bridge. "Perry's business ventures never seemed to work out."

"Selling this story to the tabloids is pretty stupid as a long-term plan if you were already bankrolling him."

"I wasn't. I turned him down the last time he asked for money." It had been a hard decision, but she'd had her own dreams to bankroll. "I'd come to the conclusion there were better places I could sink my money than down the rabbit hole of another one of Perry's unlikely business ventures."

"So, he betrayed you."

"Yes." She sighed sadly. "I had no idea my friendship was only worth a few dollars."

"Fifty thousand."

"That's how much he got paid?" She wasn't surprised Vik knew.

The man made it a habit to know everything of even peripheral importance to him. Maddie figured it would be a matter of days, if not hours, before he learned of her anonymous volunteering and even her therapist.

Uncertainty about his reaction to her secrets was the only thing stopping her from telling him herself.

"For the initial tabloid article. He planned to leverage the scandal into more paid interviews and even a book deal." Vik's voice was laced with disgust.

"That's ridiculous. I'm not exactly a celebrity." She hated this.

"No, but you are the Madcap Heiress."

"Madcap Madison. It's what they called my mother." She could still remember the first time one of the tabloids had used the moniker for Maddie.

It had made Maddie feel like maybe Helene was still with her in some small way. Only later had her own maturity and help from her therapist helped Maddie to see how distorted that thinking was.

"You share her penchant for making it into the press,"

Vik agreed. "Perry's book wouldn't have made him a million dollars, but someone would have paid him a hefty advance for it."

"That's just stupid."

"That's our reality-television, celebrity-drama-obsessed society." Vik shifted into the higher gear as they finally made it over the bridge.

San Francisco's gridlock could get really ugly, though it was better than the freeways that became parking lots during high commute times in and around L.A.

"I suppose. You talk about the book deal like it's in the past."

"It is." Definite satisfaction colored Vik's two-word answer.

She shouldn't be surprised Vik had worked so quickly, but she couldn't deny being impressed and only a little apprehensive. "What were Perry's terms?"

"Timwater didn't set the terms, trust me."

She had no trouble believing that, not when Vik was involved. Perry had no hope with the power of AIH brought to bear against him at the instructions of its VP. "What did Conrad get him to agree to?"

"Do you think, after his screwup this morning, I would trust this negotiation with Conrad?"

"*You* met with Perry? Wasn't that overkill?" Putting Vik and Perry in the same room was like pitting an alley cat against the heavyweight champ.

The cat might be wily and street smart, but he was still going to get pulverized.

And she wasn't entirely convinced of Perry's street smarts.

"From now on, anything to do with you goes through me personally." Vik exited the freeway, downshifting the powerful Jaguar.

"That's not how my father operates."

They were headed toward the Marin Headlands. Maddie recognized the route, though she hadn't been there since her school days, on the obligatory field trip to the Golden Gate Bridge and to view the city vista.

"I am not your father."

"But you're a lot alike."

"In how we do business? Yes. But you share more personality traits with your father than I do."

"You're kidding."

"No."

"I know we're both stubborn, but…"

"It does not stop there, believe me."

"So you say." She was *nothing* like her father.

"I do."

Typical. Vik felt no need to explain himself, or convince her, which only made her want to hear his justifications all the more. She wasn't going to ask, though.

Not right now.

Right now, she was far more interested in what they were doing in the parking area near Battery Spencer. "Is the magazine photographer here to get some color shots, or something?"

"No."

Vik pulled neatly into a parking spot and turned off the car, but made no move to get out.

He unbuckled his seat belt and turned to face her. "It is a good thing the friendship is over from your side. Timwater signed a nondisclosure agreement that covers every aspect of his association with you. The penalties for breaking it are severe."

"But he's going to talk about our friendship." It had spanned the same six years as the dearth of Vik in her life.

"No, he is not."

She had no desire to see the man again, but she wasn't sure how she felt about their friendship disappearing as if it had never been, either. "It isn't going to help with what he's already done."

Vik's eyes bored into hers. "He's signed a retraction, admitting everything he told the tabloid was a lie."

"Won't that leave him open to a lawsuit from them?" And why was she worried about someone who had so very blatantly not been worried about her?

"They don't get a copy of the confession…unless he screws up again." The threat in Vik's words would have been spelled out to her ex-friend in no uncertain terms.

"And that will protect him?"

"Do you care?"

"I probably shouldn't."

"You would not be you if you didn't," Vik said with something like indulgence and no evidence of judgment.

"I'm not a pushover."

"No one witnessing you facing your father down in the conference room this morning would ever question that."

"Okay."

Vik smiled. "You are a strong woman whose strength is tempered by compassion. My grandmother Ana is such a woman."

"And you love her."

"Yes."

Did that mean he might love Maddie one day? She did her best to quash that line of fantasy thought. Like she'd told her father earlier, Maddie wasn't the fairy-tale believer her mom had been. She had no expectations of marrying for undying love and irresistible passion.

So, she couldn't understand where the tiny ember of hope burning deep in her heart despite Maddie's strictest self-talk came from.

Unaware of the war going on inside of Maddie from that simple admission, Vik added, "Timwater will make a public apology for his prank after our engagement is announced."

Even though they *weren't* engaged, according to Vik.

It suddenly occurred to her that they hadn't come to the overlook for privacy to discuss Perry.

Even so, she needed to know one thing. "How much?"

"Did we pay him?"

"Yes."

"The way his apology will play, he'll get to keep his fifty thousand from the tabloid." Vik didn't sound particularly happy about that fact.

"And?"

"The only thing I gave Timwater was my word not to destroy his name in the business world. The nondisclosure agreement guarantees we will not sue him in civil court, either—so long as he keeps his side of it."

"He never would have believed I would do that."

"I would. Regardless of if it was on behalf of the company rather than you, Timwater would be just as screwed."

"You're ruthless."

"It's not just an Archer family trait. We do what we need to get what is important to us."

"Like marrying the owner's daughter to take control of a Fortune 500 company."

"Yes."

"Thank you."

"For?"

"Not trying to pretend this is something else." No matter what her heart wanted.

"What exactly do you think this is?"

"Necessary."

He nodded. "Yes, but it will be a marriage in every sense of the word. You do realize that?"

"You mean…"

"Sex. We will not be living celibate lives."

"No affairs?" Not that she would be willing to take this step if she thought he was a womanizer, if she herself had plans to look outside the marriage for that kind of companionship.

"No affairs," he repeated, making no attempt to suppress how disgusting he considered the idea.

Vik wasn't that guy.

He *was* the grandson of a very traditional Russian man. Vik would never do anything that would disappoint the old man. He thought his father had done enough of that.

He'd shared that, and a lot more she hadn't expected him to, when they were friends during her teen years. He'd never been like a brother, but he had been one of the few people she'd believed she could rely on back then.

Could she rely on him now?

"Be very sure you understand what I am saying here, Madison." Vik reached across the console and cupped her nape in a move that was becoming familiar. "I am not Maxwell Black. My children will not be conceived in a test tube."

"Of course not." Whatever their feelings for each other, this situation was very personal for him.

He nodded like that had settled everything still left unsaid between them. She wasn't so sure she agreed, but she didn't hesitate to get out of the car with him.

They took the path to the overlook, Maddie grateful she'd worn the sensible pumps and that the ground was dry. Neither of them spoke while they walked, but he kept his hand on the small of her back, moving it to her elbow in the uneven patches of terrain.

When they stopped, they were at one of the favorite overlooks that gave a view of both the famous bridge and the San Francisco skyline. A few tourists dotted the area, but none near enough to hear any discussion she and Vik might have.

Vik maneuvered them so he stood only a few inches from her, his body acting as a barrier against the incessant winds off the harbor. The close and clearly protective positioning felt significant.

"My grandfather gave my grandmother her first view of San Francisco in this very spot," Vik said after a moment of silent contemplation of the vista before them. "He promised her a future with food to put on the table for their family. A future without oppression for their Orthodox beliefs."

"He kept his promise."

"Yes." Vik went silent for several seconds of contemplation. "Grandfather brought my dad up here as a child. Misha told Frank he could be anything he wanted to, a true American with no accent, his name just like all the other boys'."

"Your grandfather gave your father the freedom to be anything he wanted to."

"Even a failure."

She couldn't argue that assessment, not when she knew Frank Beck had spent his adulthood running from responsibility. Unless something had changed in the last six years, Frank only contacted Vik when he wanted something. Usually money.

Placing her hand on his forearm, Maddie said, "He didn't fail when he fathered you."

"Misha and Ana raised me to be who I am."

"An undisputable success."

Vik turned to face her. "You believe that?"

"I do."

"That is good."

She smiled, not sure why she felt the need to reassure Viktor Beck, but determined to do it anyway.

"*Deda* brought me up here, too, when I was boy. Frank could not be bothered, but I made promises to myself, commitments to the children I would one day father. Promises *I* will keep."

"I have no doubt."

Vik's gaze warmed, his expression filled with unmistakable determination. "My grandparents were not in love when they married, but theirs is one of the strongest marriages I have ever witnessed."

"They are devoted to each other."

"And to their family, even my dad."

"I believe it."

Vik nodded, his dark eyes reflecting approval of her words. "That kind of dedication runs in my veins right along with the ruthlessness."

"I know."

Vik laid his big hands on her shoulders, creating a private world of two for them. "I believe our children will share those traits."

"No doubt." There was nothing she could do about how breathless her voice had become.

He was touching her, and even through the fabric of her Valentino suit jacket and the shell she wore under it, she felt the connection intimately.

"Considering it will come from both their mother and their father, our children have little hope otherwise."

"I'm not ruthless," she said, shocked by the accusation.

"The paperwork you signed today would say otherwise."

"You know that isn't the way I usually do things." It just had been…necessary.

"Ruthlessness does not have to be the dominant trait in your nature for you to have it."

"And it doesn't bother you?"

"That you'll fight for those who deserve your loyalty, even those who do not? No."

"You expect to deserve my loyalty."

"Yes."

"And will I get yours?"

His expression said her question surprised him. "Do you doubt it?"

"Six years ago…"

"You kissed me and I pushed you away."

"That's a simplified way of looking at it and not entirely accurate."

"No?"

"No. I told you I loved you. You told me I was too young and you didn't just push me away, you pushed me out of your life completely. Our friendship ended with one kiss."

"It was necessary."

"We could have stayed friends."

"No."

"Why not?"

"You were an eighteen-year-old, barely a woman."

"But I was a woman."

"I know." There was a message in his voice she couldn't decipher.

"You were also the daughter of a man I admired and who trusted me with you."

"Not to mention he was your boss," she reminded him a little snidely.

"Yes, my boss. The president and owner of a company I intended to run one day."

"A relationship with me would hardly have gotten in the way of *that* goal."

"It would have. Six years ago."

"But not now." No, *now* it was the opposite.

Marriage to her would give Vik exactly what he wanted.

"No, not now."

"I loved you." She wouldn't call it a crush; it hadn't been by then. She'd gotten over it, but at one time she *had* loved him. "Your rejection hurt me."

"I am sorry."

But he wouldn't change his past actions, even if he could. She knew him.

"Look on the bright side," he said almost teasingly.

She didn't remember anything bright about that time. "What?"

He smiled like a shark. "It should be easy for you to learn to love me again."

"Emotion doesn't work like that." And she was pretty sure falling in love with this man, even if she married him, wouldn't be the smartest thing she could ever do.

"Doesn't it?" He pulled something out of the inside pocket of his coat. A small lacquer box that fit in his palm. "My grandmother brought this *Palekh* over from Russia when she and my grandfather defected during the Cold War."

"It's beautiful."

"It is a reminder."

"Of what?"

"The beauty they left behind and the life they hoped to build. *Deda* always said *Babulya* was his frog princess."

The top of the box was decorated with an image from the Russian fairy tale where Prince Ivan ended up married to an industrious and lovely princess who had once been a frog. The magical princess outdid her aristocratic counterparts set to marry Ivan's brothers in every way.

Maddie thought maybe she understood why Vik's grandmother Ana had told Maddie the story of the frog princess the first time they'd met.

"Does this make you my frog prince?" she asked tongue in cheek.

Vik traced the rich image painted in egg tempera on black. "Perhaps it does."

"You know I don't believe in fairy tales."

"Maybe you should."

Now, *that* was definitely *not* something her father ever would have said to her.

"Your grandfather's promises seem to fly in the face of Russian pessimism." But then Misha Beck had never struck her as a pessimist.

The man who had changed his last name to reflect his new country and life had a decidedly forward-thinking attitude.

Maddie had only met Vik's grandparents a few times, but she liked them.

A lot.

Despite the fact Misha and Ana had raised their grandson, Maddie had always considered them the epitome of a *normal* family. The kind of family she'd always wanted.

The kind she wasn't sure Vik was offering with whatever was in that small lacquer box.

"*Deda* never believed the old adage that to speak of success cursed it." Though his shoulders didn't move, there was a shrug in Vik's voice.

"His life and yours prove his skepticism."

"That is one way to look at it."

"The other?"

"*Deda* gave up being a Russian and embraced the way of his new homeland."

"The American ideology does tend toward the positive."

"Remember that."

"You think I have to be a dreamer because of where I was born and raised?" she demanded.

"No. You have your dreams. I have mine. It is not about where you were born, but who you were born to be. I want you to believe in both of our dreams."

"And that takes some of the idealism this country is known for."

"Yes."

He wanted her to believe in his dreams.

It might be love between them, but this was more than a business proposal—no matter what had prompted it.

CHAPTER SIX

"AND THIS?" SHE pointed to the *Palekh* that had to be at least fifty years old. "Is it a reminder for *me* now?"

No matter how unmoved she tried to appear about that possibility, it touched her deeply.

"Yes."

Her breath hitched. "Of the successful legacy you promised your unborn children?"

"Among other things."

"That kind of success is more important to you than it is to me." Maddie wanted promises of other things.

She wasn't naive. She wasn't looking for undying love, despite the odd feelings deep in her heart she was doing her best not to acknowledge. Even Helene Archer had been too pragmatic to promise her princess a knight in shining armor that would *love* Maddie. But there was more to life than building a company that dominated the world market.

"You think so?" he asked, sounding amused.

Though she didn't understand why. Maddie could only nod.

"It will take the *significant* results of that type of success to make your school a reality."

She couldn't deny it.

"You think money means little to you, but then you have never lived in fear of want." If he had sounded even a little condescending, she would have been angry.

He didn't.

"And you have?" she asked, wondering if there was something about his past she didn't know.

"Not like my grandparents, but let's just say the year between my mother's death and *Deda* deciding I would come to live with him and *Babulya* was not one I would ever allow my own child to endure."

"I'm sorry."

"Frank's inability to make anyone's needs as important as his own, including the basic need to eat of his six-year-old son, taught me as much about who I did not wish to be as *Deda* taught me about the man I would become."

"Your grandfather is a good man."

"He and *Babulya* raised me with an appreciation for the difference between working to provide and working an angle."

"Like your dad."

Vik grimaced. "Frank is very good at angles."

"You want your life to matter."

"It already does."

She couldn't argue that. Didn't want to. "I want my life to matter, too—we just have a different way of going about it."

"Yes, we do." He didn't sound bothered by that fact. Why was she?

She wanted to tell him about Maddie Grace, but wasn't sure how she would handle it if Vik had the same attitude about her efforts as Jeremy had had.

"I have already promised to help you see your dream of a charter school realized," Vik pointed out.

Yes, he had, which put Vik miles ahead of her father in that regard already. Maybe their differences would make both of their lives better, rather than tearing them apart.

"What kind of promises are you making with that box,

Vik?" she asked, almost ready to believe in the possibility of the complete family she'd never had.

His handsome lips tilted a little at the nickname she hadn't uttered in six years, keeping it strictly private to her thoughts. Something she had not been able to let go of, but would not share with others, either.

"If you accept my proposal, I promise fidelity."

She nodded.

"I will expect the same," he said, as if there was any chance she didn't already realize it.

Interesting that he'd led with that one, though. Was that because he thought she needed it after Perry's betrayal, or was it more personal for Vik?

Either way, she said, "That's a given."

"I am glad to hear that."

When he said nothing else, but looked down at her with an expression that seemed to see into her soul, Maddie prompted, "And?"

"I promise to continue to grow AIH, leaving our children a legacy worthy of both my family and yours."

It was a promise meant more for and to himself and their future children, but she didn't dismiss it is as unimportant. Not after he pointed out her own dreams required money just like his did, if not on the same scale. "All of our children?"

"Yes." His brow furrowed. "Why would I distinguish?"

He could be one of those men who considered their eldest their only important child, or only their sons. But she knew he wasn't.

Her concerns were a lot more unpredictable.

"I am willing to have two children with you, but I want more and they will be adopted." This wasn't a deal breaker for her.

Not if she could have her school, but it was something she desperately wanted to do. Be open to the possibility of bringing children into her life that they could offer a family, not just support, encouragement and help.

Vik's brows drew together in thought, not a frown. "You want to adopt?"

"Yes."

"Babies or children?" he asked.

"Does it matter?"

"No."

Happy with that answer and the speed of it, she offered, "Most likely children."

"All right."

"That's it? You agree?" Shock coursed through her.

"I assume we will make any decisions in regard to bringing more children into our lives—both those born to us and adopted by us—together."

"Of course, but you're open to it?"

"Nothing would delight Misha and Ana more than a house full of grandchildren to spoil."

"There are a lot of bedrooms in Parean Hall." Which was her acquiescence to living there as a married couple.

His satisfied smile said he recognized that as well. "I do not anticipate filling them all with children, but have no objections to our family inhabiting half of them."

It was a ten-bedroom mansion.

Could it really be this easy? "You'll put that in the prenup?"

"If you insist, but I assure you it is not necessary." He placed the antique Russian keepsake against her palm. "Any promises I make you here will not be broken."

"So long as it is within your power."

"Yes." His tone and expression implied Viktor Beck considered very little outside his power and influence.

"And you will be a father to our children, not just the man with that title." He wasn't the only one with memories of neglect after the death of a mother.

Hers might not have been to her physical needs, but Jeremy Archer had let Maddie starve emotionally.

"I cannot promise to make every Little League game or sit-in your daughters organize, but I will make our children a priority."

"*My* daughters?"

"Mine will be too busy trying to take over the corporate world for social activism."

Tickled, she laughed like she hadn't with him in too long, but grew serious again quickly enough. "I won't have my child forced into dedicating his or her life to AIH. That has to be a personal decision."

"Agreed." But clearly Vik had no problem believing his children would be as dedicated to AIH as he was.

Who knew? Maddie herself might have wanted a career in AIH, at least in some capacity, if she'd had a different relationship with her father.

"I think we will have to accept that our children will be influenced by both of us," she told him.

"I can think of much worse things."

"I'm glad you said so," she replied cheekily, secretly touched by his sincerity.

"Open the box," Vik instructed.

"Are you done making promises?"

"Any other commitment I make to you would fall under the three I've already made."

"Three?"

"Fidelity. Dedication. Family."

Inexplicable emotion clogged her throat, but he was right. He'd promised the things that mattered most to her. With a few words he'd committed to building a *family* with her and all that entailed.

She took the lid off the box, incapable of hiding the way her fingers trembled.

Inside, nestled in a bed of black silk, were two rings.

One she recognized as a traditionally inspired Russian three-strand wedding band. Each diamond-encrusted ring interwoven with the others was a different shade of gold: yellow, white and rose.

It was beautiful, but not ostentatious. Perfect for her. Beside it rested a diamond engagement ring set in the pink-tinted gold that would sit flush against the curved wedding band when he put it on her hand.

She didn't ask how he knew the rose tint that used to be known as Russian gold was her favorite. Vik was scary like that.

She didn't ask if she would be able to wear the ring beside the wedding ring after they were married. She could see the curve in the band that would make that possible.

He'd melded the traditions of his homeland with that of his grandparents and taken her own preferences into consideration. It was so Vik. She might not still be in love with him, but it was no wonder she'd never been able to accept a substitute.

"It's beautiful," she breathed, the moment feeling unexpectedly profound.

"As is the woman it was designed for."

"You didn't have this designed for me." He couldn't possibly have.

This kind of custom work wasn't done in a few hours.

He cupped her hands with his own. "You will have to accept that my plans for the future have included you for much longer than you considered me in the same regard."

"I sincerely doubt that." He'd been *it* for her since she'd had her first real thought about boys and girls and how their lives came together.

Even when she hadn't realized she was still comparing every man to Viktor Beck. Darn Romi being right all these years anyway.

He shook his head. "You had a schoolgirl crush, but have not thought of me in that way for six years."

So, he *wasn't* all-knowing. "That shows how much you know. Romi always says I hold other men up to your example and they pale in comparison."

"And what do you say?"

"I always denied it."

"See, I told you."

"I've begun to realize she might have been right." No other man had a chance with Maddie.

Not Perry, not anyone.

Vik's expression dismissed her words as an exaggeration.

"I never forgot you." He'd been too deeply embedded in her psyche, if not her heart.

Maddie had honestly believed her issues with trust had prevented intimacy with another man, but now realized memories of *that guy* had been enough to keep others at bay.

"You avoided me like the plague."

"You did your own avoidance."

"For about a year," he acknowledged. "I missed our friendship. I thought enough time had passed that we'd gotten past the awkward incident."

And he'd approached her. She'd rebuffed him, doing her best to never be put in a position where they could speak privately again. She'd stopped coming home unless her father demanded her attendance and that happened rarely enough.

For at least two years, Maddie had turned down every invite that might put her and Vik in the same sphere.

"I wasn't on the same page." What had been awkward for him had been humiliating for her.

"You made that unmistakable."

"I was angry with you." She'd felt betrayed.

Perry's treachery hurt; Vik's rejection had devastated her.

"And now?" Vik asked.

What did he want her to say? She'd stopped avoiding him at social functions before she graduated from university, but she'd still made sure there was no opportunity for them to renew the old friendship.

"The world looks like a different place from twenty-four than eighteen." It was the best she could do.

"You will forgive me for hurting you?" he asked, like it really mattered.

So, she told him the truth. "I forgave you a long time ago, Vik."

"It did not feel like it."

She looked up into his espresso-brown eyes. "Do you forgive me?"

"For kissing me?" he asked, sounding genuinely confused.

Not a usual circumstance for him. She would take a moment to savor it and even tease him if the discussion wasn't so important.

She explained, "For mistaking your kindness for something more and making our friendship impossible."

"I never held it against you." His tone implied something else altogether.

"You thought you should have known I was falling in love with you," she realized.

"That wasn't the way I termed it, but yes."

Right. He'd thought her love was a crush. But if it had been only a crush, it would have taken months, not years, to get over.

"You're not omniscient, Vik."

"If I'd been paying better attention, I could have headed you off gently."

She wasn't sure that was true. Vik was right that she

and her father shared a stubbornness that resulted in a tenacity of purpose almost impossible to derail.

"If we'd remained friends, Perry would never have gotten the hold on you he did."

"You think you would have stopped us becoming friends."

"I would have prevented him from using you as his personal bank and he would have known that you had people looking out for you."

"People scary enough to abandon his plans for the phony exposé before he ever put feelers out for the first reporter?" she asked with a smile.

"You think I'm scary."

"To men like Perry? Oh, yes, definitely."

"But not to you."

"No, Vik, you don't scare me."

"Good."

He frowned. "Perhaps you would not have taken the chances you have in the past years if you'd had the stability of my presence in your life."

"You're pretty arrogant."

"Do you deny it?"

"Actually yes," she said firmly. "My actions are not your fault, or your responsibility."

He shrugged, clearly disagreeing.

"You really have a God complex."

"No, but I know my responsibilities."

"And I'm one of them?" she demanded, frustrated more with herself for seeing that as romantic than Vik for his arrogance.

His smile sent heat through her, reminding her of that lack-of-celibacy thing he'd taken pains to make clear. "I hope more than that."

"Friends again?"

"Yes, definitely."

"But you want more." Maybe not passionately and personally, though she was beginning to see that Vik *did* desire her, but to make his dreams come true, Vik was going to marry her.

"Yes."

"Okay."

"To?"

"Everything."

His expression turned even more heated and predatory. "Be careful what you promise."

"This is a special place. Promises made here stick, right?"

"Yes." No doubts.

"Then I promise to do my best to make both our dreams come true."

"I make this promise as well."

That was way better than him promising to build AIH into some world superpower, in her opinion. "Thank you."

His kiss took her by surprise. It shouldn't have. Wasn't it natural to kiss to seal an engagement?

But the kiss did surprise her. And then it overwhelmed her, his lips coaxing a response that radiated throughout her body. They took possession of hers, no longer coaxing, but insisting on the two things she'd said only that morning she wasn't capable of.

Submission and trust.

But then, like with so many other things in her life, the rules did not apply to Viktor Beck.

She found herself melting into him, no thoughts for self-preservation or holding anything back.

And he accepted her surrender with a forceful masculine desire that belied any claim for a lack of passion between them.

He devoured her mouth, his arms coming around her,

his hands pressing her body against his, one thigh pressing between her legs as far as her skirt would allow.

Maddie's knees would have given out, but Vik's hold on her was too tight.

She'd thought the kiss this morning had been hot, but it was nothing like Viktor Beck staking claim to the woman who promised to marry him and give him his dreams.

Viktor knocked impatiently on Madison's door thirty minutes before they needed to be at Jeremy's ostentatious home in Presidio Heights.

Viktor had not given himself time for a drink or idle chitchat on purpose. After the kiss at the overlook, he did not want to risk his self-control before the dinner.

If his grandparents weren't going to be there, as well as the photographer from the magazine, he would never have left Madison that afternoon. But she deserved to show up to her engagement dinner on time and *not* looking like she'd spent the hours before in bed.

He'd told her the truth earlier. Six years ago he'd seen her as barely a woman when she'd kissed him.

He'd been shocked by his own body's response to her overtures, realizing for the first time that she was an adult and *not* a child. Not that he'd given that revelation much credence.

Not at first, but after a year of avoiding her and indulging in more liaisons than his workaholic regime usually allowed for, two things had become obvious.

He missed Madison and she was the only woman he wanted sharing his bed. She was still too young and Viktor's plans didn't include marriage for at least a few more years.

Anything else with the daughter of AIH's president and owner was out of the question. And not just because Viktor considered the older, driven businessman a friend.

Viktor wasn't sure when he realized his own business ambitions included marrying Madison, but it was well before he broached the subject in any oblique way with Jeremy. The older man's concern regarding what would happen when Madison inherited full control of the trust gave Viktor the traction he needed for Jeremy's approval of his own future plans.

He'd had the rings commissioned and intended to launch his courtship of Madison in the coming weeks when Timwater sent a spanner into the works with his "breakup interview."

If Viktor had started his pursuit of Madison earlier, the opportunistic man would not have had a chance to hurt her with his lies. It was unacceptable bad timing that had left Madison vulnerable.

It angered him. Viktor did not do bad timing. And he did not get caught by surprise. But he had not anticipated Timwater's betrayal of his long-standing friendship with the heiress.

While it had not precipitated long-term action on Viktor's part that he wasn't already planning, the intolerable situation had brought things to a head before he intended. *And* it had forced him to work around Jeremy's knee-jerk response to his daughter's misadventure.

While that might have ended up working in Viktor's favor, it had come with additional emotional cost to Madison.

He might be ruthless, but that was not okay with him. Her well-being was his responsibility now.

The door opened and Viktor's thoughts scattered.

Madison's copper curls flirted around her face, her blue eyes vibrant and flashing with a response to his presence that found a corresponding reaction in his body.

Lips entirely too kissable despite the dark color staining them in a perfect scarlet bow curved in a smile of welcome. "Hi, Vik. Are you coming in?"

She'd encased her tempting body in a 1950s-inspired couture cocktail dress in a shiny dark blue that rustled as she moved.

The skirt was full, nipping in at the waist, and the bodice fitted, the artistically cut neckline dipping to reveal the hint of cleavage he found more sexually alluring than any woman he'd seen in a dress that revealed most of her breasts.

"You..." He cleared his throat, finding it unaccountably dry. "You look beautiful."

Only after he spoke did it occur to him that he had not answered her question.

"Thank you." She blushed, something she rarely did anymore. "It works?" The nerves that slipped in to tinge her smile were something else she didn't show others. "Only I wanted your grandparents to see *me,* not the..."

She didn't have to finish. "It will be all right. *Deda* and *Babulya* are eager to see you and welcome you into our family."

"They know we are engaged? Have they seen the articles?"

Ignoring his own best intentions, he pushed into the apartment and right into Madison's personal space.

She gasped and looked up at him, eyes wide, breath hitching. "Vik? What?"

He curved his hands around her waist, enjoying the soft slide of the fabric and the heat of her skin under it even more. "They know we are engaged and they are delighted."

"Oh."

"They know about the stories and they are furious with Timwater."

"They don't believe them? You told them he lied, didn't you?"

"I did and they don't." Viktor reveled in the implicit trust in his ability to make things right that could be read into her questions.

"Thank you."

Mindful of the crimson color on her lips, he bent down and pressed a soft kiss to the side of her neck, staying to inhale the subtle fragrance of honeysuckle mixed with orange and a hint of vanilla and her own unique scent. "You smell good."

"It's my perfume."

"It's you. Rosewater would smell just as delicious against your skin."

She trembled against him, her hands pressing into his chest. "Vik."

That was all she said. Just his name. But it was a plea, whether to step back or to do something about the electricity arcing between them, he did not let himself contemplate.

He stepped back. "We need to go. Everyone is waiting."

"Including the photographer."

"He has his instructions to be as unobtrusive as possible."

Madison grimaced, her opinion of how unobtrusive that could actually be very clear.

He looked around and spied her coat over the back of an armchair. Viktor had always enjoyed Madison's efficiency and was glad to see that she had not developed the habit of keeping a man waiting that he always found more irritating than intriguing.

Grabbing the coat, he offered it to her. "We need to head out."

"You cut it a little close." But she didn't hesitate to let him help her into the fitted wool trench coat the same crimson red as her lips.

He saw no reason to hide the truth. "Protecting us both from how much I want you."

"What are you talking about?" she asked, sounding genuinely confused as she did up the oversized black buttons and tied the belt on her coat.

"You must realize the prospect of having you in my bed has my libido in overdrive." The truth of that was never more blatant to him than in how hard he found it to lead her out of the apartment without once mussing the color of her lipstick.

However, nothing said he had to curb his desire to touch her completely. They made their way to the elevators with his arm around her waist.

"But why would it?" Could she sound more innocent? He didn't think so.

"You are an incredibly beautiful woman." But more importantly, she was the one woman who sparked desire hot enough to do his ancestors proud.

"You didn't want me before."

"We discussed this. You were barely more than a child." And he *had* wanted her.

"You're right," she said distractedly. "But—"

"Nothing. Trust me. I want you. Six years ago, the timing was wrong, but I will gladly offer you all the proof you desire later tonight, *after* dinner with our respective families."

"You want to come back to my apartment tonight?" she squeaked, charming him.

The elevator doors closed, giving a false sense of privacy he had to once again fight taking advantage of.

"You have no reason to be nervous," he assured her. "I am not an animal in the bedroom."

Even if he wanted her with heretofore untapped primal mating instincts.

"Vik…" She blinked up at him, her lips parted slightly. "I told you, I'm a virgin."

"What?" The elevator doors opened but he didn't step out, his brain short-circuiting.

"I told you—"

"That you hadn't been in a serious relationship." But that didn't mean she hadn't had sex. Things happened. She was twenty-four. This was not possible.

"No random hookups."

"Ever?" he asked in disbelief.

"I told you I had no experience."

"In BDSM."

"In anything."

"That will change." Viktor was not above using whatever means necessary to ensure the future he planned. Including being Madison's first lover.

The fact he wanted her more than any woman he had ever known was beside the point.

She stepped off the elevator into the parking garage. "I don't think being engaged to you is going to be anything like I was imagining."

"If you thought it was going to be without sexual intimacy, I'd have to say you are right," he said as he helped her buckle into the passenger seat of his car.

He gave in to the urge that had been riding him since the moment she'd opened her door and kissed her. He reined in his desire. Barely. And stepped back.

He closed her door and took several deep breaths before moving around the car to slide into the driver's seat.

Her eyes glowing with blue fire, she asked, "No pretense of waiting for our wedding night?"

"We made our vows at the overlook this afternoon. Nothing said later between us will be any more profound." He started the engine, but didn't back out of the parking spot, waiting with an odd feeling in his chest for her reply.

"I thought it felt that way…like it was profound."

"It was." He put the car in gear.

"So what? You consider us married now?" She sounded like she didn't believe her own words and yet he knew she had felt the weight of the promises they'd made earlier.

"As good as, yes."

"You make your own rules, don't you?"

"You are just now figuring this out?"

CHAPTER SEVEN

THE ENGAGEMENT DINNER was a lot more enjoyable than Maddie had expected it to be.

Especially considering the fact the guest list had grown to include some Archer second cousins, a Madison great-aunt, one of Misha's nephews and his wife, who just happened to be visiting friends who owned a vineyard outside of Napa, and Romi.

Maddie's father was all smiles, though underlying his bonhomie was an unfamiliar reticence with her that gave Maddie a certain level of comfort. He had not escaped this morning's debacle in the conference room unscathed.

Small winces indicated he did not like her new habit of calling him by his first name, either, but if he wanted her to stop, he'd have to ask. Nicely. And behave like a father. Somehow.

She hadn't started calling him Jeremy to hurt him, but because it simply hurt *her* too much to refer to a man who treated her like a stranger more often than not as Father.

Vik acted as a buffer between them, not exactly a new role for him, but one he hadn't played with any consistency in six years.

Taking it a step further than he used to, Vik actually physically stood between her and others in unconscious protection whenever she felt herself growing uneasy. While no one had the bad taste to actually mention the articles spawned by Perry's lies, family could manage intrusiveness in subtle ways strangers never could.

Thankfully, Vik seemed to recognize her moods—sometimes even before she did—and took steps to make sure the questions didn't get a chance to edge into being blatantly intrusive.

Tellingly, no one seemed to find it hard to believe they'd been carrying on a relationship outside the media's radar for months now. Not even Misha's nephew evinced surprise at the engagement.

Everyone was happy to congratulate Maddie and Vik, making her feel like maybe this thing could really work.

Regardless of what had precipitated the engagement, their friends and family considered them a good match. A big part of her agreed.

She only hoped she wasn't making a huge mistake… that Vik was the man she was discovering. More the white knight in Armani than the heartless tycoon following in her father's footsteps that she'd seen him as for the past six years.

Vik's grandparents were wonderful, as always.

Misha was a gray-haired, slightly stooped version of Vik with an exuberant warmth very unlike his more reserved grandson. A retired scientist, Ana was both highly intelligent and gently affectionate by nature. She wasn't as overt as her husband, but she would make a wonderful great-grandmother for Maddie and Vik's children.

The magazine photographer turned out to be extremely good at fading into the background and Maddie found herself relaxing and enjoying the first real family dinner she remembered since her mother's death.

"Your grandparents are such nice people." Maddie allowed Vik to remove her coat and his own before taking both of them and hanging them in the hall closet.

Such a simple thing to do. She'd done it hundreds of times for other guests, but never with the same homey feeling—or sense of irrevocability that washed over her as she closed the closet door.

Vik was staying the night.

And Maddie's heart was pounding in her chest like a bass drum.

Not from fear, though. No, nothing like it, though that surprised her. Shouldn't there be at least a little anxiety?

She'd never done this before, after all.

But all she felt was excitement.

Maybe it was because she knew Vik would leave if she asked him to. Only she didn't want him to leave.

She wanted him to follow through on the promise of passion in their kisses earlier. Besides, if they weren't compatible in bed, that could be a real problem.

Right?

Only what were the chances when his kisses turned her inside out. Self-justification much?

She made a sound of self-deprecating humor.

"Liking my family is a source of amusement for you?" Vik's hands landed on her shoulders before he turned her to face him.

His expression wasn't mocking or judging, just inquisitive.

She smiled up at the beloved handsome face as she shook her head. "No, I was thinking about the things we tell ourselves to justify doing what we want to do."

His look promised things she'd never experienced but was pretty darn sure she wanted to. "What *things* do you want to do?"

"Like you don't know."

He shook his head. "I'm still a little stunned you've never done them before."

"Pretty pathetic, huh?"

"In what way were you pathetic?" Vik asked in a tone that didn't bode well for anyone who might have used that word to describe her.

Including herself.

She liked the feelings his instant protectiveness engendered in her despite the fact she thrived on her independence.

Feeling a little odd about that, she moved away from him and crossed the living room, which was decorated in her favorite shabby chic. While she loved the perfect blend of distressed wood furniture, floral damasks, lifelike silk bouquets set in epoxy to look like water, the pristine whites and abundance of feminine styling screamed "single woman living alone" to her.

And while there was *nothing* bad about that, she wasn't as pleased by the fact she'd never even had a short-term relationship. She'd be happier if something in her home indicated the need to take someone else's preferences, or even needs, into account.

"What would you call a twenty-four-year-old virgin?" she asked, turning back to face him.

"Picky." His smile melted her.

She grinned up at him. "That's one word for it."

"You were waiting for me." She could tell by his tone he thought he was joking.

A sudden revelation hit her. Romi had definitely been right all along. "I was."

She might have been able to get over her first love, but Maddie had never moved on from thinking that Viktor Beck would be the ideal lover. And so she had turned down every other man.

Yes, trust was an issue for her, but right along with her lack of trust in other men had been a primal certainty of whom she wanted to share her body with.

A certainty she'd been consciously denying but living under for the past six years.

Espresso eyes darkened with unmistakable lust, blowing her mind. He wanted her. He'd said he did. He'd kissed her like he did, but that look?

It was imbued with the same primitive passion she'd acknowledged in herself. So predatory. It sent shivers chasing along her nerve endings.

"You were made for me," he said, confirming it wasn't her imagination.

The driving force between them was very mutual.

"A pity you didn't realize that six years ago." She regretted the words as soon as she said them and shook her head. "Forget I said that."

Maddie got why Vik had turned her down before. Wishing they'd already taken this step so she wouldn't be dealing with her public humiliation right now was both futile and borderline ridiculous. Because even if they'd gotten together then, there was no guarantee they would still be together now.

His jaw firm, his lips set in a determined line, Vik moved toward her with intent. "I was not ready for marriage and you were not ready for me."

"I—"

His finger pressing against her lips stopped the argument. "We both had living to do."

"You were really thinking about *this* then?" she asked with surprise she couldn't hide.

"Yes."

"But you weren't happy about it." Wasn't happy about the memory if his current expression was anything to go by.

"You were eighteen. I was still used to thinking of you as a child. It felt wrong."

"I was an adult, a grown woman." But even as she made

the claim, she knew that compared to Vik she *had* been a child.

"You could vote, join the armed forces and take on your own debt. That didn't mean you were ready for a relationship with a man like me."

"A relationship, or sex?"

"Same thing when it comes to you and me."

"Is it?"

"It has always been marriage or nothing between us, Madison." Vik reached out and traced the line of her bodice, his fingertip never straying from the sapphire-blue taffeta of her dress to the skin of her bosom.

Her breath hitched, but she didn't move away. "Because of AIH."

"Because my grandfather raised me to be a man with a sense of honor." The "unlike Frank Beck" went unsaid, but she heard it anyway.

Vik would never be like the father that had caused both him and his grandparents so much grief and disappointment.

"You may be a shark, Vik, but you're an honest one."

He smiled wryly, his fingertip resting on the point of the V dipping between her breasts. "And I don't eat guppies for breakfast."

"Am I a guppy?" she asked breathlessly.

"No." Satisfaction burned in his dark gaze. "You are a twenty-four-year-old woman."

The emphasis he placed on the word *woman* was a conversation all in itself.

"You planned to marry me before Perrygate ever happened."

"I did." Vik looked with significance down at the custom ring on her finger and she caught on.

There was no denying the truth in front of her eyes. "You really did have the rings made for me."

"I do not lie."

"No, but…" The scope of what he was saying left her grasping for words that would not come.

"Timwater forced me to move my plans forward, but only by a couple of weeks."

"You were going to ask me to marry you?"

"I planned to date you first," he said with some wry humor, almost self-deprecatingly. "We needed to rebuild the rapport we once had."

His thinking made him a different man than her father in ways she didn't feel like enumerating, but wouldn't deny. "You recognized before Jeremy did that the only way my father would have an heir to leave in charge of the business is if I married him."

"Yes."

"So, you made plans to play on my father's desire to leave his legacy to *family*." It was brilliant. And manipulative.

But he'd already shown that as important as his own plans for AIH were to Vik, he would not ignore Maddie's happiness. He'd offered to buy her a building for her dream as a wedding gift.

Calculated? Maybe, but *for* her benefit, not to her detriment.

Vik's silence was answer enough. Not only had he strategized, but he'd also started working on her father already. Jeremy had come to the whole "his daughter must marry to save herself and the company's reputation" pretty darn quickly otherwise.

"I'm not sure how I feel about this," she admitted.

She understood. To an extent.

But it still felt like she'd been maneuvered.

Vik's touch finally strayed entirely from her dress to the upper swell of her breasts, tracing the same path as before, only along her skin this time. "While you are deciding, take into account that if you had been a different woman, my plans would have taken a different direction."

She shivered, her breath quavering in her chest until another thought came to her. "You would have taken AIH out from under my father?"

Horrified because as much as she didn't get her father, she loved him, and she was certain Vik would have done exactly that. Rather than allow a stranger to come in and take over what he considered to be his.

Vik shrugged, neither confirming, nor denying. "It was not necessary."

"You said Jeremy is your friend."

"He is."

"But you would still take his company."

"I would not have betrayed him."

No. That wasn't Vik's style. "You still would have figured out a way."

"Does that upset you?"

"I said before that you're ruthless."

"This is not news."

No, it really wasn't. "My mind doesn't work like yours."

"Make no mistake, you have your own brand of ruthlessness, but if you were too much like me, we would not fit so well together." Both his hands moved to settle on her waist.

She was distracted by the sensation of his thumbs brushing up and down against her lower ribs. "You think we fit?"

"I know we do."

"So, you're saying you don't just want the company. You want me, too." Not just sex with her, but Maddie as a complete person.

At least the Madison Archer he knew about. What would Vik think of Maddie Grace?

"You will support my dreams in a way a woman of less strength could not do."

"Your plans would have been really messed up if I'd picked one of the other candidates Jeremy put forward." She gave in to the irresistible urge to poke at the bear.

Vik's gorgeous mouth twisted in disdain. "You were never going to choose another man."

"You don't think so?"

"I know."

"Another word for excessive confidence is arrogance."

"I prefer honest."

She laughed softly and then had a revelation. "You manipulated the choice of candidates."

"I was not expecting Maxwell Black."

"Neither was I." And she still wanted to know what the man had done to Romi. "He's intense."

"He's a good businessman."

"Is he honorable?"

"Yes."

"As honorable as you?"

Vik considered his answer for a second. "I would do business with him on a handshake."

"Good to know."

"Why? Considering your options?" He didn't sound too worried by the prospect.

"According to you, there are no other options."

"True." Vik looked like he was considering what he was going to say next. "We grew up together."

"What? Like in the same neighborhood?"

"Same Russian-American-dominated street, same school, same afternoons spent in activities sponsored by the Russian cultural center."

"Were you friends?"

"We still are...of a sort."

"You're too alike to be really close."

"We jockeyed for the top place in class until we went to different universities."

"No one else had a chance."

"No."

Maddie bit her lip, but finally decided she would be honest about her concerns. "Romi dated him."

Vik's gaze flared. "I see."

"He's intense," Maddie repeated.

"Are they still dating?"

"No."

"Then…"

"I don't need to be worried?"

"He is a good man."

When it was Viktor Beck making the claim, Maddie believed him.

"Are you really spending the night?" she asked, focusing on what mattered most in the present moment.

"Yes."

"After a single day." One day in which they had decided to get married, made that decision public and negotiated a future they could both live with.

"In one respect, but between us?" He pulled her body close so they shared heat. "Tonight is the culmination of ten years."

"We've barely spoken in six."

"When was the last time Frank was in town?" Vik asked her, like she'd know.

And she did. "Three months ago. He was in San Francisco for Christmas." Vik's father had attended Jeremy's holiday party along with Misha and Ana.

Vik nodded, his expression dour. "*Babulya* was pleased."

"But you couldn't wait for him to leave."

"You are the only person who knew that."

She found that hard to believe, but then…maybe not. Vik didn't wear his emotions on his sleeve.

But that wasn't the point, was it? "Just because I saw

your father at my father's home and knew he was in town doesn't mean you and I communicated in any meaningful way."

"Didn't we?"

Okay, so in the past two years, they'd had increasing numbers and depths of conversations. And it struck her. She'd thought she was just being grown-up about the past, but he'd been working on rebuilding that rapport he had mentioned earlier.

The man made Machiavelli look like a preschooler in the art of the deep play.

"Still." Not a brilliant comeback, but what she had.

Vik smiled that shark's smile. "When was the last time I took a date to an event?"

So, she knew the answer. She'd revealed earlier in the car with Conrad how closely she watched Vik without meaning to watch him at all. "That doesn't mean anything."

"Doesn't it?"

"Vik…"

"I believe both the fact that I have not had another woman on my arm in over a year *and the fact you know that* is significant."

"Really?" she drawled sarcastically even as she couldn't help wondering if he was right.

"I know that you haven't dated, either. I wasn't entirely sure about Timwater, but the way you two are together doesn't imply sexual intimacy."

"I should hope not."

"Besides, he was sleeping with other women."

She'd suspected, though Perry had always tried to play it like he didn't sleep around. She wasn't sure why. It wouldn't have mattered to her either way.

Vik knowing however, meant he'd been paying attention. "You have a file on him, don't you?"

"Naturally."

"And Romi?"

"Romi has been your friend for longer than me."

"You're saying you don't have a file."

Vik leaned down and spoke softly, right into Maddie's ear. "I'm saying I don't need one."

It wasn't exactly sweet nothings, but she still shivered from the sensation of his breath gently blowing across her ear.

"You know her well, too," Maddie said, not even sure why she was trying to keep the conversation going.

"Yes."

Curiosity and concern prompted her to ask, "Did you know she'd dated Maxwell?"

"No."

"Good. I don't feel like I was so oblivious."

Vik straightened, but didn't move back. "I'm sure if you did not know, they both took pains to keep it private."

"You're right." While Maddie was still worried, she didn't feel like a bad friend anymore.

She let herself fall into his deep coffee gaze, even as she relaxed more completely into his body. "I want to kiss you."

Bad friend, or good one, Maddie didn't want to think about anyone except her and Vik right now.

"What is stopping you?" He leaned down so their lips were a fraction of an inch apart, taking away the only barrier that mattered.

She moved toward him, speaking in a breath against his lips. "Nothing."

The first brush of her lips against his electrified her. It was the barest of caresses, but near unbearable in its intimacy. She was staking a claim with the featherlight touch and he was accepting that claim as surely as she'd accepted his promises earlier.

They were distinctly different, one set of lips masculine, the other feminine, and yet they fit with the perfection of molds aligned and cast simultaneously.

Vik's response was full-on alpha man, accepting her mouth with his and then turning it around and moving his lips against hers, driving the kiss to greater sensation and closeness.

Nipping oh-so-gently with his teeth on her lower lip, he demanded entrance. With no thought but to give it, she let her lips fall open.

His tongue swept into her mouth and just that fast Maddie was drowning in a sexual response only this man had ever brought out in her, thoughts and emotions overwhelmed by the onslaught of devastating sensuality.

Vik's hold on her tightened as he pulled her body completely flush with his, his big hands roving over her back and up to knead her scalp.

Her own hands slid of their own volition up his pecs, over his shoulders and to the back of his neck, pulling her body around so her breasts were crushed against his chest. Sparks of delicious sensation pricked her nipples nearly to the point of pain in their intensity.

It felt so incredible still dressed, she could not fathom what it would be like once they were naked skin pressed to naked skin.

Vik made a rumbling sound of approval in his throat before his body shifted and then she was being lifted into his arms as he stood.

The man was strong. Following on that thought came another.

They were really going to do this.

For the first time, Maddie was glad she was a twenty-four-year-old virgin.

She wanted no past experiences shadowing this moment with him. No memories of hands on her flesh but his.

Vik carried her unerringly into to her bedroom, lowering her back to her feet and pulling his mouth from hers. She didn't want to stop and used her hold on his neck to lift herself back up so the kiss could continue.

It was only natural to swing her legs up and around his waist, locking her ankles behind his back.

Something about her actions flipped a switch in Vik and the kiss went nuclear. His mouth devoured hers as he cupped her bottom through the rustling silk of her dress's full skirt.

Overwhelmed by sensation, Maddie lost her connection to anything but the kiss. She did not know how long their mouths ate at each other. Nothing registered but the sparks of pleasure he ignited in her rapidly fanning into a conflagration that consumed.

She wasn't even aware he'd moved them to the bed until he broke away from her and she didn't fall to the floor.

She mewled with her need to reconnect to his lips, a sound that would have mortified her if she was not too lost to desire to care.

"Vik!" she demanded, no other word coming to the forefront of her mind.

His smile was feral and hot. But the wink that came with it was hotter. "Clothes."

CHAPTER EIGHT

ONE WORD BUT it was all Maddie needed.

She sat up and reached back to unzip her dress. It was tricky at the best of times, the top of the zipper hitting her in the center of her back.

With her hands trembling from need, it was impossible. So frustrated she could almost cry, she struggled to unzip it.

All the while, she couldn't pull her eyes from Vik. He'd ripped his Armani sweater off and tossed it on the floor, the black T-shirt he wore under it joining the pile of cashmere a second later.

His belt made a whoosh as he pulled it out of his trousers and the buckle clunked against the wall when he tossed it. His tailored slacks were next, dropping to reveal a straining bulge behind dark designer briefs.

"Your body is beautiful," she breathed in awe.

Every muscle of his six-foot-four-inch frame was honed. Dark hair covered his chest, narrowing to a trail that disappeared into the waistband of his briefs.

She didn't know if it was the dark, clingy fabric or reality, or even her oversensitized emotions, but Vik looked huge.

Maddie's thighs clenched even as her fingers itched to touch. And she hadn't seen the actual package yet.

Vik looked back, his own expression filled with desire. "You're still dressed," he accused.

"I know," she said with pure frustration.

He winked again, the expression just as mind-bogglingly sexy this time as the first. "Need some help there?"

"Yes."

He stalked toward the bed like a big sleek cat, climbing on with the same grace. He reached around her and let his fingers trail down the shallow V of her dress to the top of the zipper. "Is this your problem?"

"I can't reach it."

"How did you get dressed then?"

"I wasn't hampered then."

"By what?"

"What do you think?" she asked, wanting to sound annoyed and only succeeding in revealing the need inside her.

"Me?"

"Desire," she clarified.

"Desire for me."

"Yes," she admitted, no real reason to pretend otherwise, but annoyed all the same at having to say it out loud.

"Good." He lowered the zipper inch by inch. "I like this dress."

"I'm never wearing it again."

"Please do."

"Why?"

"I have always enjoyed unwrapping my gifts. Just ask my grandparents."

"I'm not a Christmas package."

"No, you are something far more valuable." He kissed the corner of her mouth and then brushed her lips with his lightly. "You are the woman who will share my life."

"You're awfully good at romance for a corporate shark."

He wasn't kidding about enjoying the process of unwrapping. Time moved by in increments measured by her rising passion as he took off first her dress, removing it to reveal her body one slow inch at a time. His desire-filled gaze burned her with sensual appreciation.

The silk foundations she wore under the dress came next, but he took even more time with those than the blue taffeta, kissing bits of her flesh as it was revealed, sensitizing her body in ways she'd no idea he could do.

When he was done, she was a naked, quivering mass of sexual need.

And he still had his briefs on.

She tugged at the waistband, her voice husky with passion when she managed to force the words past the tightness in her throat. "Take them off."

"Not yet."

"Why?" she demanded, patience in another universe.

"You are a virgin."

"So?" He was going to change that, wasn't he?

"So, you need preparation and I'm on a hair trigger where you are concerned."

"You have to take your underwear off to make love to me," she spelled out slowly, like she wasn't sure he got it.

He bared his teeth in a smile that had no humor. "And before that happens I will make sure you are ready to receive me."

"But—"

"You will have to trust me on this." His eyes demanded her acquiescence.

She didn't know if she could give it. "I want you!"

"And you will have me."

Vik's hand slipped between her legs right then, fingers delving in the moist heat no other man had ever touched, and she cried out. He touched her in ways she'd only ever dreamed of being touched, caressed her to her first shattering climax before she even realized what that desperate feeling inside her was leading to.

She'd touched herself, but it had never felt like this. She was still trembling with spent pleasure when a single long masculine finger slipped inside her. Something shifted in her heart at the intimate intrusion.

He was not inside her, not the way she'd always imagined, but they were connected on a level that corresponded to a place inside her soul.

He pressed upward and she winced with pain.

"Hurt?" he asked, his own tone strained.

"A little."

"It will sting."

"Why?"

"I am going to break your hymen with my finger. It will make the actual penetration of my sex easier on you." The words were clinical, but his tone and the concern in his expression was not.

He'd thought this through and that touched her in the same place in her soul his intimate intrusion had.

He pressed a little harder.

A sharp shard of pain stabbed her. "It more than stings!"

"I am sorry." He grimaced. "It will be worth it."

She wasn't so sure about that, but trusted him enough to give him the benefit of the doubt.

That trust was sorely tested a moment later when the pain increased to the point that she felt like he was invading her with a hot poker, not his finger. She gasped and tried to pull away, surprised when she succeeded in dislodging his hand.

He leaned back on his haunches, the telltale traces of blood on his finger a testament to his success.

Grateful that the pain was already morphing to a low-level throbbing rather than stabbing, she asked, "Now?"

"Not yet. There is more to do."

The more included him stripping naked finally. In the bathroom, where he ran a very hot bath.

He looked even bigger jutting out from his body than he had with his erection tucked behind black silk knit.

He smiled at her with gentle humor. "Your eyes are as wide as saucers."

"You're as big as a baseball bat."

That startled a laugh out of him. "Not even close."

"Right."

"Your eyes are playing tricks on you."

Unsure where it came from, annoyance drove her stomping across the tiled floor and gave her the boldness to grope him in her fist. "My fingers are not touching."

The sound he made was not a word.

Viscous drops formed on the tip of the flesh in her hand. She touched it with her fingertip and brought it to her mouth, licking it cautiously.

Surprisingly it was almost sweet, with only a hint of the salty bitterness she'd heard about. "I like it."

He groaned and then jerked his body backward so his hard flesh slipped from her hand. "Bath. Now."

"Why?"

"Can't you just trust me?"

"I trust you more than any other man on this planet." He might be the only man on the planet she *did* trust. He had to know that.

"It will make it better for you," he explained.

"How do you know?" she demanded. "Have you had sex with many virgins?"

She found that possibility seriously disturbing.

"None," he practically snarled as he lifted her up and set her in the bathtub with surprisingly gentle movements, considering his apparent irritation. "I read up on it."

"Because you're a planner."

"Yes." He still sounded like a man ready to take someone's head off.

"Why are you mad?" she asked plaintively.

"I'm not angry!"

"You're snarling at me."

"I'm turned on." The low growl rumbled through her.

"So am I. The bath was your idea!"

"For your benefit."

Oh, man. "I'm sorry. This isn't easy for you, is it?"

"Waiting?" He stepped into the bath behind her, pulling her into his lap, his hands settling on her possessively. "No, my sexy little redhead, it is not easy, but you are worth it."

Another white-knight moment. "If you aren't careful, you're going to have me believing in fairy tales."

His only answer was one languid touch to her thigh. That caress was followed by another and another and another, all over her body and each touch accompanied by the ever-present presence of his hardness pressed against the small of her back.

Her nipples were aching and sensitive, her clitoris vibrating with pleasure, and her entire body melted over his by the time his hands stilled their insidious movements.

There were no words left in her brain when he drained the tub and lifted her back to the tile floor. They dried off in silence, bodies aware and straining toward each other.

She and Vik stripped the bedding back without acknowledging that was what they were going to do, and then together they fell to the mattress covered by the single sheet.

The lovemaking was everything she had ever dreamed it would be, his sex filling her so deeply she felt like they'd really bonded into one entity in that moment.

There was still some pain, but nothing stabbing and dark, and the pleasure pushed any lingering discomfort to the bottom register of Maddie's awareness.

This time when she climaxed, she screamed until her throat protested the strain. Vik grew impossibly hard inside her, his body going rigid just before he shouted his own release in the form of a single word.

"Mine."

She didn't even think about birth control until the next morning.

Viktor came to awareness in the dark, two things at the forefront of his mind. The woman he'd craved for years was now in his arms and they hadn't used birth control the first time they made love.

The former gave him satisfaction and the latter a twinge of regret. In a perfect world, they would have a couple years of marriage to enjoy their time together as a couple, to solidify their relationship.

In the real world, Madison had been forced into marriage by the actions of that bastard who had called himself her friend, and Viktor's grandparents were getting on in years. If his children were to have the time to enjoy them as Viktor had, they would have to come along sooner than later.

Viktor had taken advantage of Timwater's idiocy. He could deal with the consequences of other realities, too.

For him, family was everything.

It was the reason he'd been driven to succeed. The one thing that drove him most intensely was the desire to not only make his grandparents proud, but to also provide for his own family as his own father had not done.

Viktor had determined early in his life never to walk a single step in his own father's shoes.

When he'd first met Jeremy Archer, Viktor had believed he'd found the mentor he sought. And he had, but he had also come to the realization that as wrapped up in AIH as Jeremy was, his vision was still too limited.

Both in a business sense and when it came to family.

Jeremy had never understood that all of AIH's success

meant nothing in the face of his spectacular failure with his daughter.

Madison was Viktor's match in every way. They were not just sexually compatible, they were combustible. Just as he'd known they would be.

But equally important, they were friends with compatible, if very different, goals for the future.

Viktor felt an unfamiliar sense of having dodged a bullet with Maxwell Black's presence in the conference room that morning. Jeremy bringing in Maxwell—of all men— had precipitated actions on Viktor's part he hadn't intended to take until later.

But he couldn't complain about the outcome.

He in no way regretted making love to Madison and had every intention of showing her that no other man would be her match as Viktor was.

He wasn't just the perfect successor for AIH, he was perfect for Madison.

With that thought, he brushed his hand down her flank, leaning over to kiss the side of her neck and bring her to wakefulness for another example of how very well they meshed in bed.

For the first time in her life, Maddie had woken in another person's arms.

She lay, warm and secure as half of Vik's body covered hers, his breath still even and slow in sleep.

And she thought of babies and the possibility of family. Had he done it on purpose? Or had he been as lost to the final satiation of years' worth of unfulfilled desire that the idea of birth control hadn't even entered the picture?

Before she'd been made love to by a man who never seemed to get enough, she would have written the latter off as a complete improbability.

But Vik had woken her several times in the night and

pushed the boundaries of pleasure and her body on each occasion, his hunger for her something she would never again be able to doubt. There'd been no question when they *were* sleeping that they would do so skin-to-skin.

The one time she'd tried donning her sleep pants and tank top, he'd gotten this look in his eyes. Really intense, feral and determined. Her pajamas had been in a puddle on the floor moments later and her body humming the music of the Viktor Beck pleasure symphony.

Even now, his oversized sex…

No, she didn't believe him that he was no bigger than most men. She'd heard on one of those talk shows hosted by a group of interesting and mostly famous women that the average length was just about five inches erect. Well, she knew from five inches and his was nearly twice that. Average? She did not think so.

Right now, that not-at-all-average hardness was pressing against her hip, telling her that when he woke he'd be ready for more physical intimacy. Despite the twinges of soreness making her aware of muscles she hadn't known she had, nipples that ached from all the stimulation they'd enjoyed and a tender feeling in the flesh between her legs, she knew she wouldn't hesitate to respond.

Except…they hadn't used any form of birth control in the long night of passion. Not once.

"I can hear you thinking." Vik's early morning voice rumbled above her head.

"You said we would make any decision about children together."

Tension seeped into his big body, but he did not move away. "Yes?"

"We did not use birth control last night."

Oddly, he relaxed. "No, we did not."

"Vik," she said in warning.

He sat up, somehow getting pillows propped against

the headboard behind him and her sideways in his lap with a minimum of movement. It was a position he apparently enjoyed.

He tilted her chin up, bringing their gazes into alignment. "We made that decision together."

"I didn't make a decision at all. I didn't even think of it."

His eyebrows rose. "Neither did I."

She narrowed her eyes, trying to gauge the truth of his statement. She might be blind, but Maddie couldn't see the smallest flicker of deceit in the espresso orbs.

"It never once occurred to you that a condom might be a good idea?" she asked.

It was his turn for his eyes to narrow, but they glittered with anger not concentration. "You believe I would lie to you?"

"No, but you're ruthless enough to take advantage of an expedient situation."

He agreed, no sign of embarrassment at the truth. "Yes, but to what end would I ignore birth control?"

"You get five percent of the company when I give birth to our first child." Did she really have to remind him of that fact?

"Did you plan to wait to start a family?"

"No." She couldn't even claim not to have thought of it.

Dreams were something even a woman who didn't believe in fairy tales could indulge in. And Maddie's dreams included building the kind of family she'd always wanted to have.

"I did not think you did." Therefore, he had no need to take advantage of circumstance.

"Okay."

"Okay, what?"

"I believe you."

He kissed the tip of her nose. "As you should."

She wrinkled her nose. "It might be old-fashioned, but

I would still like to wait until we are married to conceive our first child." Though if she *was* pregnant, she would accept that as the gift she believed it to be.

"Agreed."

"So, from now on, birth control," she insisted.

"Agreed."

"You're being awfully compliant."

"The truth? I would prefer to wait a couple of years before having children."

"Oh." She hadn't considered he wasn't keen on starting a family right away.

"But my grandparents are in their seventies," Vik continued. "If my children are to have the benefit of *Deda* and *Babulya's* presence in their lives, we cannot indulge me."

"I see." Wow.

Once again, she was reminded that while she and Vik might be motivated by different hopes for the future, they both had them. And lucky for her, they dovetailed, as surprising as that might be.

"I hesitate to point this out," Vik said. "Because I *do* want to gift my grandparents with the next generation of our family."

"What?" Maddie couldn't believe how comfortable she was having this discussion naked and sitting in his lap on the bed.

"Won't it be difficult to start your school if we have a baby right away?" he asked.

She gave him a self-deprecating grimace. "I say all the time that money doesn't matter to me, but the truth is, I'm counting on it to be able to 'have it all,' as they say."

"You plan to have a nanny?" He sounded almost shocked.

And she loved him all the more for it. "Probably, but not to *raise* our children. However, if we are ever going to be able to leave the house, we have to have someone besides your grandparents we can trust to care for our children."

"Yes."

"So, we'll have a nanny, someone who fits into our family, preferably matronly in both appearance and age." So, sue her if Maddie didn't want a beautiful young woman living under Vik's nose in their house.

"What do you mean about the money then?"

"I have every intention of hiring qualified staff who share mine and Romi's vision to run the school."

Vik's dark brow furrowed. "But you will both still give a great deal of time to the school. You will have to."

"Yes, but we'll make it work. Romi and I already discussed what would happen in the event one or both of us had a family."

"I'm not surprised."

"My father would be." He'd always assumed she had no business sense if she didn't want to be part of *his* business.

"Jeremy only sees part of the picture when he looks at you," Vik agreed pragmatically.

"That's all he's interested in." Jeremy Archer had never wanted to give the time necessary to get to know who Maddie was, not before Helene's death and definitely not after.

"He *can* break out of his tunnel vision."

"So you say. I've witnessed no evidence."

Vik shook his head, clearly done with the topic. "You'll need an efficient and knowledgeable personal assistant."

"Exactly." A nanny for convenience, not necessity, but a PA? That Maddie would *need* to make sure things got done.

Vik's phone rang before they could continue their discussion. It was Conrad, excited about the opportunity for a live interview with the newly engaged couple on an evening celebrity-news show.

And so it began.

* * *

The next weeks passed in a whirl of activity. Interviews as a couple, interviews by herself. The media furor around Maddie and Vik's engagement was even bigger than the initial craziness Perrygate had spawned.

Vik slept at her apartment every night while decorators and contractors worked overtime getting Parean Hall habitable for them. Maddie interviewed domestic staff while overseeing the changes to the main rooms and the master suite. She did her best to make sure both her and Vik's design aesthetic was incorporated in their new home.

And could hear his voice saying "I told you so" when she realized she knew enough about his preferences to do that.

Maddie went back to her secret volunteering in her brown wig and contacts, dressed in clothes from the local superstore. Every minute spent with the children cemented her determination to do more.

She also scheduled a visit with the therapist she'd seen in the immediate months after her skydiving accident, when Maddie had realized the time had come to break away from her past. Dr. MacKenzie was vocal in her praise for how far Maddie had come in dealing with both her mom's death and her father's emotional neglect.

However the therapist evinced some concern about the marriage that Vik said he intended to be *real* and yet was connected to a very lucrative contract for him. Dr. MacKenzie asked Maddie to consider carefully her reasons for agreeing to the engagement.

So Maddie did and, even more importantly, she talked to Vik about it.

"Yes, the contract your father offered is beneficial to me, but getting married right now is important for you, too."

"You think I said yes to the whole marriage thing because of the school, don't you?" Had she?

She'd told herself on that crazy, surrealistic day that was exactly why she needed to consider the idea seriously.

But Vik just shrugged. "Even if the scandal had blown up like it could have, you would not have given up on the school. Romi would have been the public face to run it and you would have been the silent partner as I now will be."

She loved his confidence in her. The pleasure of it masked the full import of his words for a moment, but then it settled in.

"*You* will?" When had Vik offered to partner with her and Romi in founding the school?

"We made promises to see one another's dreams fulfilled. Marriage to you will give me AIH. I've told you that I will ensure it provides for your dreams as well."

Maybe she should have expected something like this, but she hadn't. "You really are my white knight."

"I thought you did not believe in fairy tales." His voice and expression were teasing, but something told her he liked her claim.

"Maybe I just believe in you." He had always been the exception, the one man she trusted—even when she hadn't thought she had a reason to.

Refusing to admit it didn't make it any less true.

"You do," he said with a mix of implacability and smugness that should have annoyed her.

It didn't. She liked it. "So certain."

"Of you? Yes."

Ultimately, it all came down to that simple truth. *She* trusted Vik to keep the promises he'd made at the Marin Headlands overlook.

The fact that she was falling in love with Viktor Beck all over again? Well, that was something she didn't bring up even to Romi.

How could she help it? The man spent more time masquerading as a white knight than a business tycoon.

The wedding was going forward. And soon.

For the ceremony itself, they planned a very small gathering, but the reception would be huge and attended by the cream of society, the scions of the business world and even a few celebrities.

When Maddie's follow-up therapy appointment conflicted with a meeting with the caterers for their wedding reception, she told Vik she didn't want to reschedule her time with Dr. MacKenzie.

"You are seeing a therapist?" Vik asked. "Why didn't I know this?" The latter clearly the only thing that bothered him about her revelation.

"Because I didn't tell you?"

He made a scoffing sound.

"No one knows except Romi."

"When did you start seeing him?"

"Her. And right after the skydiving incident." Maddie had realized she was taking the same self-destructive path as her mother and she wasn't going to do that. "I saw her weekly for a couple of months and then a few more times after that."

"I'm impressed."

"You are?" She had worried a little he would think she was weak for needing to see someone.

"You realized you couldn't help children if you didn't deal with your own childhood issues."

That had been exactly it. "How do you know me so well?" she asked, falling a little more in love with him right then.

"You know the answer to that."

"You make it a point to get to know everything about the people and businesses you plan to partner with, or take over."

"Our partnership will supersede all others. Of course, I will know everything about you."

She liked hearing that, even if it wasn't exactly true. "But you didn't know I was seeing Dr. MacKenzie."

"No." He sounded chagrined.

Maddie laughed. "Even you are not infallible, Vik."

"Miss Grayson knew."

"She's my best friend."

"What am I?"

"The man I'm going to marry. The man I'm falling in love with all over again." There, she'd said it.

What he did with that knowledge was up to him. But one thing she knew, it was time he met Maddie Grace.

Silence stretched between them.

"Vik?"

"I am...honored."

"Good." That was better than thinking she was a fool for believing in the emotion.

"You...I..." For the first time in memory, Vik didn't sound in complete control of his words or his thoughts.

"I don't expect you to say it back."

"Good." The relief in his tone was not complimentary, but she wasn't surprised by it, either.

"You'll never lie to me," she said, as if just making that revelation.

But maybe she understood the depth of his commitment to honesty between them fully for the first time.

"No, I will not."

That included not claiming to love her when he didn't, but it also meant that his promises? Were written in concrete as far as Viktor Beck was concerned.

CHAPTER NINE

MADDIE WAS SHOCKED when her father called and asked her to come to dinner. Alone.

They ate in the formal dining room. Even with the leaves removed from the table, it would easily seat six.

Maddie sat to her father's left and swirled her soup with her spoon, pretending to eat.

Her father didn't seem any more at ease than she felt.

Finally she gave in and asked, "Why am I here?"

"It's been a long time since we had a family dinner."

"There's a two-page magazine spread to prove otherwise."

He shook his head, an expression she couldn't quite decipher on his familiar features. "That is not the same."

"I'm not sure what you mean then."

"You and me. Family."

"We stopped being a family when Mom died." She didn't say it with accusation, or even anger.

He could thank the therapist he didn't know about for that, but it was still the truth.

"It was never my intention for that to happen."

She couldn't hold back a small scoffing sound. "You sent me to boarding school within months of her death. I'd say your intentions were pretty clear."

"That was a mistake."

Something inside Maddie cracked at that admission,

but she merely shrugged. What could she say? *Yes, it had been a huge, painful mistake.*

Somehow agreeing didn't seem like the thing to do, though. Not least of which because no acknowledgment now could change the consequences of his choice when she was fifteen.

"I didn't know what to do," he admitted with a candidness rare for Jeremy Archer. "I failed your mother and I was terrified of failing you, so I sent you away, hoping they could do for you at school what I was so clearly not qualified to do at home."

Maddie stared at him as an emotional maelstrom swirled inside her. "Who are you and what have you done with my father?"

It was an old joke, but *man,* was it appropriate.

Her dad barked out a laugh. "I told Viktor this wouldn't be easy."

"He wanted you to talk to me?" Why wasn't she surprised?

"Yes." Jeremy sighed. "Viktor thinks our relationship is salvageable."

"He's an optimist."

"He is."

Giving up on the pretense of eating, she set her spoon down. "You sound surprised by that fact."

"It's not a side of him I noticed before."

"You don't think his business world-domination plans take optimism?" she asked, only partially tongue in cheek.

Her dad laughed again, this time longer and with more real humor. "I suppose they do."

"I guess that makes you something of an optimist, too." Which wasn't something she'd ever acknowledged before.

"Enough of one to believe things could be different for you than Helene." He sounded like he meant it.

"We all have our demons. I'm learning to cope with

mine without jumping out of airplanes." Maddie could give him that at least.

Her father took a ruminative sip of his wine. "I used to think Helene got into trouble just to get my attention. She seemed to take a perverse pleasure in being written up in the media."

"She did."

He looked startled at Maddie's agreement. "But she was a risk taker before we ever met. You know that, don't you?"

"She used to tell me stories over her scrapbooks." It had all sounded so thrilling to a young girl.

Jeremy nodded. "It was one of the things I admired about her."

"You weren't the first important man in her life to ignore her." That was one of the things Maddie had come to realize.

Helene Madison had craved her own father's attention and only managed to get it when she acted out. By the time she married Jeremy Archer, the attention-seeking behavior was an already established coping mechanism.

"You're saying Helene wasn't adventurous by nature, but because her exploits got her father's attention."

"Oh, I think Mom was definitely adventurous, she just discovered that in giving in to that side of her personality, she got something she craved."

"She always said she understood the amount of time I had to give to my company."

"Would you have listened if she said she didn't?" He certainly hadn't responded to Maddie's verbal pleas for his time, or to return home from boarding school.

"Probably not," her father admitted with more honesty than she expected.

"Her death wasn't your fault." It was a truth that had been very hard come by for Maddie.

She'd blamed her dad for so long, but one of the first

breakthroughs she'd made with her therapist was the realization that Helene Archer had been responsible for her own choices.

"Wasn't it?"

"No."

He didn't look like he agreed.

"Do you think Mom went racing because she didn't love me enough to want to be around to raise me?" Maddie asked.

Her dad went pale with shock, his eyes dilating, his mouth going slack for a second before he nearly shouted, "No, of course not. She adored you, Madison. You must know that."

"But she still went racing on the water at night."

"Not because of you."

"And not because of you, either."

"But—"

"Mom was an adult woman who suppressed normal caution for the adrenaline spikes that made her feel alive." The fact it had the side effect of gaining her the attention she craved only made her mom's adventures doubly irresistible to her.

"You sound like a psychologist."

"A degree in early childhood development has its share of psych courses." Maddie wasn't telling Jeremy about her sessions with a therapist.

She wasn't ashamed of seeing Dr. MacKenzie, but Maddie didn't trust her father enough to share the more private parts of her life with him. Not even this *new and improved* Jeremy. She didn't know how deep the changes went or how long they would last.

Her dad's eyes—the same shade as her own, but without the vulnerability she saw in the mirror when she was alone—flickered with something between speculation and curiosity.

"Speaking of your mother," he said in a more familiar tone that revealed no emotion.

"Yes?"

"You and Viktor have chosen her birthday for your wedding date."

"Yes." A month before Maddie turned twenty-five, it had just felt right to speak their vows on a date connected in such a special way to her mom.

"Viktor said you wanted to honor her memory with the date."

"We do." Did her dad find that uncomfortable?

Neither she nor Vik had considered that possibility.

Her father smiled, the expression appearing genuine. "I was hoping you would be willing to honor her memory in another way as well."

"How?" she asked warily.

"Do not worry, I am not going to use your mother's memory to try to guilt you into withdrawing the paperwork giving company shares to Ramona Grayson upon your twenty-fifth birthday."

But he hadn't forgotten it, either.

"It wouldn't work anyway. Mom loved Romi and I personally wouldn't have survived boarding school if her father hadn't sent her there, too."

Maddie had desperately wanted her SBC to come to the school once she'd realized her father wouldn't budge about her going there. However she'd never asked. It wouldn't have been fair. Just like Maddie, Romi had a life in San Francisco.

But Romi had begged her dad to send her and he'd done so.

Jeremy nodded. "He sent her because I offered to pay the tuition and dorm fees."

"No." Wouldn't her father have told her that before this?

"Yes. He told me when Romi came to him and asked to

follow you. He didn't want to send her, but I thought you would both be better off with each other than your fathers."

Maddie's dad was sounding more and more human by the minute. She wasn't sure how she felt about that, but she thought it might be hope.

However, she felt compelled to say, "Mr. Grayson always loved Romi."

"But he was already drinking heavily by then. Do you think he was any more aware of his daughter's needs than I was of yours?"

No, the man who had fallen asleep drunk most nights had not been aware of what Romi needed.

"If she hadn't gone to boarding school, she would have become her dad's caregiver." Jeremy sounded very certain of that. "Romi needed to get away and Gray needed to pour *himself* into bed at night."

"You used to be his friend."

"I still am, as much as you can befriend a man intent on drinking himself into an early grave and his own business into bankruptcy."

Worry creased Maddie's brow. "It's not that bad."

"Yet. But it will be."

"Don't pretend threatening to take his company over was a favor you would do him."

"No, it wouldn't be a favor to Grayson, but it would be to Romi." Her dad sounded very sure of that assertion.

"So you say."

"You don't trust me at all, do you?"

"Not really, no." She couldn't even say that if she thought the welfare of AIH was a given that her dad would put hers next.

She wasn't convinced of that.

Rather than appear upset by her denial, her dad shrugged. "Maybe you are right not to."

"That's not a comforting thing for you to say."

He shrugged. "Would you rather I lied?"

"No, but you would, if you thought it would get you what you wanted."

"That's one of the primary differences between Viktor and I. Our business peers know it, too. If I want another company president to believe something, I make sure he hears it from Viktor."

"Has he ever lied for you unknowingly?" she asked, not sure she wanted to know the answer.

"No. I'm not saying I haven't been tempted, but while I may not feel the same compunction for truth that my successor does, I do recognize that if I did that and Viktor found out about it, he would find another vehicle for his ambition than AIH."

Well, she'd never considered her father to be stupid. "I think you're right."

"I know I am."

"So, about Mom's memory…" Maddie said, ready to get back to the reason for her presence at her father's dinner table.

"She always said she wanted you to wear her wedding dress when you married."

"You still have it?" Maddie couldn't hide the eagerness in her tone.

If she'd been with Vik, she wouldn't have even felt the need to try.

"Of course."

"But you got rid of all her things." Maddie would never forget coming home for the first time from boarding school to find most of the house redecorated and her mother's things gone.

"I kept her wedding dress and her jewelry for you." Her father's tone implied he didn't understand why Maddie wouldn't know that.

"Why? When you got rid of everything else?"

"The dress is a piece of history."

"Not business history." So, why would her dad care?

"Family history. A famous designer created it for your great-grandmother in 1957, the year after he did a similar dress for an actress in one of her more famous roles." Jeremy cleared his throat almost as if talking about this was making him emotional. "Every generation in her direct line has worn it since."

"I know."

"Oh, I thought maybe you'd forgotten. You didn't mention wearing it."

"I thought you'd gotten rid of it."

"I didn't."

"I'm so glad." It was a dream she'd thought would have to die with her mother.

"You're very much of a size with your mother. I doubt it will require much tailoring."

The beautiful ivory strapless gown with embroidery in champagne silk thread around the full skirt and on the bodice required no altering at all.

Though she and Romi agreed Maddie should wear a corset under the embroidered bodice for smooth lines. The champagne lining flipped over the hem as a contrast lay exactly as it was supposed to.

"You look so beautiful," Romi said with suspiciously shiny eyes.

The dress hugged Maddie's breasts and torso, nipping in at her natural waist and then flaring in a full skirt shorter in the front than the back, which had an understated train that swept the floor elegantly behind her.

"I look like my mom."

"But you have your dad's eyes." Romi twisted her mouth comically. "I can't believe he paid for me to attend boarding school with you."

"Me, either." But Mr. Grayson had confirmed Jeremy's claim.

"He loves you, I always said so."

"In his own way," Maddie agreed. "Just not the way I needed."

"Maybe he just didn't know how. From what you've told me about his parents, it doesn't sound like the Archers were a warm family."

Maddie had only a few memories of grandparents who were both dead by the time she turned five, but none of them included a hug, or a kiss, or any other sign of affection.

"You could be right, but Jeremy admitted he'd lie if it got him what he wanted."

"Well, you knew that."

"I did. It was just weird having him admit it. I guess he has his own personal brand of honesty, too."

Romi adjusted the folds of Maddie's skirt just so. "I suppose. I prefer Viktor's."

"Me, too," Maddie said fervently.

Both women laughed, and it felt good.

But then most things felt pretty amazing right now. Maddie was marrying the man she loved and even if he didn't love her, he'd promised a *real* family.

And Vik kept his promises.

Viktor walked down the elementary school's hallway behind an office aide who had agreed to escort him to Miss Jewett's first-grade classroom.

Unlike Madison, Viktor and Maxwell had attended public school, but in an area more affluent than this one. The mix of children and teachers here reflected San Francisco's varied population like the rarified social strata of the Archers did not.

Viktor wasn't sure why Madison had asked him to meet

her here. She'd said something about wanting to talk to him with the help of a visual aid.

He didn't know what that meant. He couldn't see how an overcrowded public school would work as inspiration for her charter school. Unless it was the success they had with their volunteer program.

He'd done a little research before leaving the office on this grade school and discovered that they had a significantly higher than usual rate of parent participation in the classroom as well as other volunteerism.

When he'd arrived at the office, it was to discover that he was expected. So, he was definitely in the right place.

Whatever Madison's reasons for having him there.

He noticed two things immediately after the aide opened the classroom's door—Madison looking very unlike herself and the absolute silence he did not associate with a roomful of children.

Wearing a mousy brown wig, contacts that obscured the Mediterranean blue of her eyes with brown and clothes clearly bought off the rack at a box store, his fiancée sat at a small desk in a circle with six students.

Tattered books with brightly colored pictures, large print and few words were open on the desks in front of the children. Madison held her own copy, a smile frozen on her face as she met his gaze.

Vik allowed one brow to rise in query. "Hello, Madison. It appears you have some friends I haven't met."

Her fixed smile morphed into a genuine grin as she jumped to her feet. "You're early."

He couldn't help noticing the cheap cotton top and denim jeans she wore showed off her curves in ways that affected his libido as surely as her designer dresses.

He didn't like the wig or colored contacts, though.

He shrugged away her comment about his timing. "Introduce me."

"Of course."

Not wanting to intimidate the children with his size, Viktor dropped to one knee and reached to shake hands with each child as Maddie introduced them.

A few returned his greeting with charming politeness. One small girl, clearly Madison's favorite from the way the small girl tucked herself behind his fiancée's legs, ducked her head, but wiggled her fingers in a shy hello.

Viktor met the teacher and the parent volunteer as well.

"Very nice to meet you," he said to Miss Jewett.

"The pleasure is all ours." She smiled, her eyes warm as they lit on Madison. "Your fiancée is a fantastic volunteer. She's so good with the children and could be a teacher with her credentials."

"I am aware." He just hadn't been aware that she volunteered in the public school system.

Did her father know?

Madison clearly didn't want to leave right away, so Viktor stayed, enjoying the time helping six-year-olds with their reading.

They were in his Jaguar and headed toward the other side of the city when she finally pulled off the offensive wig, exposing her red curls crushed in a messy pile. It reminded him of the way she looked after sex, the only time she was completely disheveled—Madison woke looking more tempting than ever.

She rubbed at her scalp and ran her fingers through her hair, causing some curls to bounce up again. "It's always such a relief to get that thing off."

"Why do you wear it?"

"Because *Maddie Grace* is a normal woman with a degree and desire to volunteer with children. She doesn't get written up in the tabloids or followed by the paparazzi."

"And that's important to you?"

"To be normal? It was when I started. Now, it's just

easier. Can you imagine what the media would make of the billionaire heiress as a volunteer teacher's aide?"

"I have a feeling we're going to find out."

"That's what I thought. With our marriage and the vestiges of Perrygate, I kind of figured it was only a matter of time before my secret got exposed."

"Some secret." She was even more wonderful than he'd always known. "How long have you been volunteering like this?"

"It started as a dare with Romi. Trying to attend a political rally incognito. It worked and I got the idea to volunteer at a soup kitchen the next weekend *dressed up*."

"Don't you mean dressed down?"

She laughed, the sound soft and more enticing than he was sure she meant it to be. "I guess."

"It might be a good idea to come clean before some enterprising reporter does it for you."

"I guess," she said again, not sounding nearly as amused or enthusiastic.

"As much as you enjoy being Maddie Grace, Madison Beck will be able to effect more widespread change and influence." Just giving Madison his last name verbally was satisfying in a way Viktor didn't understand or analyze.

"But will she get to teach a first-grader how to read?"

"Yes. That's what the charter school is about, right? Helping children one-on-one."

"It is." He could hear the smile in Madison's voice.

"So Grace for Romi Grayson?"

"No, my grandmother Madison."

"That's right." He'd forgotten.

"You don't mind?"

He pulled into a parking spot on the side of the road, wanting to have this conversation face-to-face. Cutting the engine, he turned to face her.

Brown eyes stared back at him and he frowned. "Can you take those out?"

"What? Oh…" Comprehension dawned.

She pulled a small case from her backpack, so different than the trendy designer bags he usually saw her wear, and proceeded to take out and store away the contacts.

"This persona, she's more you than the famous designer wedding dress?"

"Sometimes. Sometimes I just really love my Chanel, you know?" Madison's pretty bow lips twisted in a wry grimace. "I like to pretend that I couldn't care less about the latest fashions and keep up with them just to be Madison *Archer*, but the truth is? I like both."

He nodded. Not because he understood. He wore tailored designer suits as a sign of power, not because he thought about how they looked. But because he was glad Madison Archer, soon to be Madison Beck, wasn't someone she didn't want to be.

"So, the question was *do I mind?* Yes?"

Madison's beautiful blue eyes shone at him. "Yes."

"Do I mind that I am going to marry a woman who cares so much about helping others she has created an alternate persona so she can do it? No, Madison. I do not mind at all."

Giving in to the urge that seemed to grow with each passing day, Viktor leaned across the console and kissed Madison.

He lifted his mouth to say, "In fact, I think it's amazing."

Madison sighed and leaned back into the kiss, delight radiating off of her and twisting its way around Viktor's heart.

Viktor's *deda* and *babulya* had them over for dinner a couple of days later and dropped their own bombshell.

Stunned at his grandparents' request, Viktor could only ask, "You want us to what?"

"When we moved here, we gave up all the old ways," Misha said. "We changed our last name from Bezukladnikov to Beck—we even changed our baby boy's name from Ivan to Frank. Very American."

"I know all this." It was family history he had shared with Madison years ago.

Her lovely face expressed memory of the event too. Viktor just didn't understand why his *deda* felt the need to rehash those realities now.

"We did not speak Russian in our home. We encouraged our little Ivan to become fully American." *Babulya's* voice broke on his father's original name. "Frank, who spoke without an accent and did all the things the other children at school did."

"You wanted him to embrace and be embraced by his new homeland," Madison offered in understanding while Viktor reeled with alien confusion.

His grandmother smiled appreciatively. "Exactly, but we gave away too much and he became the man he is today."

"A flake. You can say it, *Babulya*." Vik frowned with frustration, really not liking the idea his beloved grandparents were trying to take responsibility for his father's lifetime of selfish and poor choices. "My dad is a deadbeat."

"Do not speak of your father that way," Misha said, but with little heat.

Viktor didn't argue, but he didn't promise not to, either. He couldn't.

Madison looked at him with something far more attractive than compassion. Her eyes glowed that way they did when she called him her white knight. Viktor had no clue what in this particular situation would put that look on her face, but he would not question the obvious lack of the one emotion he hated above all others.

Pity.

His *babulya's* eyes usually filled with a tranquility he'd always relied on, but now shimmered with regret. "We think we let go of too many traditions and he felt himself cast adrift."

"Oh, for..." Viktor clenched his jaw to bite back the first words that came to his mind. "Dad did not become a con artist because he didn't have a traditional Russian wedding. The one right and good thing he did in his life was his marriage to my mom."

"That is not true," Misha said in a deep voice so like Viktor's own. "He fathered you."

Viktor opened his mouth and shut it again without a word.

Madison grinned, a smug glint in her azure eyes. "I told him the same thing."

"You are a very good match for our grandson." His grandmother's answering smile was blinding. "It pleases Misha and me very much that you appreciate our Viktor as we do."

"He's easy to love."

Once again Viktor did not know how to respond to those words, though he liked hearing them. Very much.

But love was not something he had ever considered in the equation of his marriage to Madison and the life they would build together. Was it enough that she felt the emotion, or did she expect him to reciprocate one day?

Could he? Did he even know how?

He had never been in love before. The affection between his grandparents had grown over time and did not look on the surface anything like the passion that burned between Viktor and Madison.

The silence had stretched and it should have been awkward, but the three most important people in the world to him simply observed Viktor with varying degrees of understanding.

It was a strange experience, but not unpleasant.

"Thank you," he finally said to Madison, hoping that once again it was enough.

His grandfather winced, but patted Viktor on the shoulder. Misha didn't say anything, though.

Madison's smile turned soft in a way Viktor did not understand, but liked nonetheless.

His grandmother rolled her eyes. "Viktor, my dear grandson, you have much to learn about romance."

Viktor could not deny it.

She didn't seem to expect an answer. "Is it so much to ask you follow a few of our family's traditions?"

"I'm not answering before you tell me exactly which ones you're talking about." His caution was necessary.

Russian wedding preparations and celebrations could become extremely complicated and involved.

But his grandparents' requests weren't unreasonable, even if they did mean Madison had to spend the night before her wedding at Jeremy's home instead of Viktor's bed.

Five weeks after Perry's exposé, Maddie waited in the drawing room of her father's mansion the morning of her wedding.

She was wearing the gown her mother had worn, and her mother before that and *her* mother before that in 1957.

Her full-length Victorian-era veil of Brussels lace was even older than the dress. Romi had shown up with it a week ago. And it was the exact same ivory as the gown.

Romi adjusted the veil around Maddie's face now. "You are so beautiful."

Maddie couldn't answer. If she tried to talk, her emotions were going to get the best of her.

"Viktor is going to be here any minute. Are you ready?"

Maddie indicated herself with a wave of her hand and forced an even tone. "What do you think?"

"I already told you, beautiful. But, sweetie, that's not what I'm talking about. Are *you* ready?"

"According to Vik, we got married that day we made promises overlooking San Francisco's skyline."

"Pffft." Romi shook her head. "Men."

"Those promises were vows." Of that Maddie was very certain.

"So are the words you're going to speak today."

Maddie nodded. "I'm ready."

"You love him."

"I do." There was no point in denying it. Besides Romi could always tell when Maddie was lying.

"You always have."

Maddie wasn't so sure about that, but she couldn't deny she'd never fallen in love with anyone else.

"Perry didn't stand a chance."

"He didn't want one." Their friendship had never been like that.

"I'm not so sure about that."

"It doesn't matter."

"No," Romi said with finality. "It doesn't."

Maddie grinned at her sister-by-choice. "I'm getting married today."

"You are." Romi grinned back.

Their hug was fierce enough to crush silk and neither of them cared.

The sound of the doorbell came faintly from the hall. Then Vik's voice and Misha's laugh.

Oh, this was real. It was happening. Now.

More laughter and then the door to the drawing room swung in and bounced against the wall.

Her six-foot-two distant cousin James, wearing a distinctly masculine tuxedo and tulle veil, stumbled in first. "He figured out I wasn't you, cuz."

Maddie found herself laughing along with the others as they came in behind him. The first tradition had been observed. Her father had pretended to offer an alternate "bride" and Vik had shown his determination to only wed one.

Misha, looking dapper in his own tux, and Ana, beautiful in her rose-pink suit, came in behind James. Maddie's father wore a traditional morning coat and ascot, but Vik was in breath-stealing Armani.

James's parents were there, too, along with the second cousins who had been at the family engagement dinner. Vik's aunt, his father's younger sister by ten years, and her two teenagers had flown in from New York. Frank hadn't made it.

The cousins from Russia had extended their stay in California, though, so they were here as well.

Enough family to please Misha and Ana's need for traditions to be observed, Maddie hoped.

But really? As far as she was concerned, no one else mattered, not when Vik came to stand in front of her, his expression hungry, approving and supremely satisfied all at once.

"Ti takAya krasIvaya." Vik reached out to touch her, but his hand hovered in the air between them, not quite connecting.

"He is telling you that you are beautiful," Misha informed her.

Maddie nodded her understanding, but couldn't look away from the intensity in Vik's espresso gaze.

"I have come to ransom my bride," he said in formal tones clearly meant for her father, but Vik's attention never strayed from Maddie.

"Your father tried pawning this one off on us," Misha

said, pointing at James. "But my grandson is too observant to be fooled."

Because anyone would have mistaken her tall, *male* cousin for her.

But Maddie laughed because it was supposed to be in fun and she found she enjoyed this Russian tradition very much.

Vik offered an open Tiffany box with a sapphire-studded tiepin and cuff links resting on the cream satin.

Her father accepted it with what sounded like genuine thanks, but then he shook his head. "This is not enough."

And she knew that was part of the ritual Misha and Ana wanted to see observed.

Misha made a production of arguing the merits of the gentlemen's jewelry, but Vik never even cracked a smile. His powerful focus was entirely on Maddie and she felt a connection to him that was more spiritual than humorous.

Finally, Misha came between them, offering her another Tiffany box. This one contained a five-strand pearl necklace and perfectly matched pearl studs in a vintage inspired gold setting.

Her gaze flicked between the pearls and Vik and then to Romi, because Maddie's SBC had convinced her to go without a necklace. "You knew."

Romi nodded, her brilliant smile watery.

Maddie reached up and removed her mother's diamond earrings and handed them to Romi, who she now realized had left her own ears bare just for this. It was right that Romi would be wearing something of Helene's at Maddie's wedding.

Vik helped Maddie put on the earrings and the necklace, the moment unbearably intimate. When he was done, he bent down and placed a barely there kiss against her lips before carefully dropping her veil back into place.

"Now, there can be a wedding," Misha said with hearty satisfaction.

CHAPTER TEN

THEY TOOK TWO limos to the church.

Maddie didn't pay attention to who went where except that she had Vik on one side of her and Romi on the other.

The Holy Virgin Cathedral looked like it had been transplanted right out of Russia, with its cross-topped triple-domed spires and white facade. The inside was awe-inspiring, with its domed ceilings decorated with iconography and the ornate public altar area.

She lost herself in the beauty of the service, but nothing was as moving as the moment before the crowning ceremony when Vik sidestepped tradition and lifted her veil to kiss her again and whisper that now even God knew she was his.

The words might be considered irreverent by some, but they settled in Maddie's soul. He left her veil folded back so that when the crown was placed on her head signifying the sacrament, Maddie felt both bound and freed at the same time.

They skipped the civil ceremony that would have been required to make the wedding legal in Russia because it wasn't necessary in America. Consequently, they broke crystal glasses at the reception in front of a few hundred of her father and Vik's nearest and dearest.

Both glasses shattered into rubble, though there could

be no doubt that Vik threw his with an impressive force beyond what Maddie used. Everyone cheered.

"It will be a long and blessed union," Misha announced loudly.

She was a little surprised to discover the man hired to be toastmaster was a well-known Shakespearean actor, and one of her favorite up-and-coming performers sang for the guest's enjoyment.

They ate, cut the cake and toast after toast was made to the happy couple.

It was all sort of overwhelming and amazing. Nothing about this wedding felt like a business arrangement. When she mentioned that to Vik, he smiled.

"Because this marriage is *not* a business arrangement," he said firmly.

"But—"

"It's a marriage of dreams. Accept that for what it is."

Happier than she had ever been, Maddie nodded and did just that. She wasn't at all surprised when Romi caught her bouquet.

Maddie had been aiming after all.

What was surprising and even a little worrisome, was that Maxwell Black caught the garter. The look he gave Romi would have had Maddie running for the hills, but her friend just blushed. And looked more than a little interested.

Huh. That was something to think about.

After Maddie's own honeymoon.

She smiled so much during the reception that her cheeks hurt by the time the white Rolls-Royce arrived to take them away.

Maddie was surprised when the car pulled up in front of the Ritz-Carlton instead of Parean Hall.

She turned to Vik. "I thought we were going home."

"I like the sound of that."

"Going home?" she asked, confused and not minding a bit.

"Home. *Our home*," he emphasized.

Heat she did not understand crept into Maddie's cheeks. "But we aren't there."

"No, we are here. And this moment the only three people who know that are you, me and the driver." Vik sounded very proud of that fact.

"What about security?"

"Not even them. Not tonight. No friends. No family. No security. *No press.*"

Delight suffused her. "Tonight is ours."

"Yes."

"I like it."

"Good."

He carried her over the threshold of Suite 919, one of the two most luxurious sets of rooms on the club level.

Its beauty was lost on Maddie, though. She was way too focused on Vik to pay attention to marble floors and Chippendale furniture.

"Champagne?" he asked without putting her down.

She shook her head.

"Snack?"

A smile flirted at her mouth as she said primly, "No thank you."

His eyes darkened with primal intent. "Bed then?"

"Oh, yes."

He carried her into the bedroom and lowered her to her feet. "Did I tell you how lovely you are today?"

"You may have mentioned it, yes."

He nodded, as if in serious contemplation. "I can only imagine one circumstance in which you could be more breathtaking."

"Yes?" she asked.

"Let me show you."

"Okay," she breathed out.

He removed her crown and veil with careful, deliberate movements. Then he took off the jewelry he'd helped her put on earlier.

"I don't think I told you. The pearls are exquisite. Thank you."

"They are just little white beads until you are wearing them."

"Oh, wow...I don't know even know how to take some of the things you say."

"As truth. We've established I do not lie to you." He brushed his lips over the back of her neck.

She did nothing to suppress the shiver the small touch elicited. "Or at all, according to Jeremy."

Vik came around and faced her, and then leaned down to press their mouths together softly for only a brief moment. "Or at all." He kissed down her neck and along her bare shoulder.

Each caress of his lips left a trail of goose bumps in its wake and she was trembling with desire by the time he made it around to the back of her dress.

He undid the bodice, trailing kisses down her spine as he did so.

The silk of her corset was no barrier between his lips and her skin. He helped her step out of the dress and then took the time to carry it into the dining room and lay it on the table.

When he came back into the bedroom, she said, "Thank you."

He looked at her questioningly.

"For caring about my dress."

He shrugged as if his consideration wasn't important, or maybe rather that it should be taken for granted. "It is a living memory for your family."

She hoped she never stopped appreciating the big, but especially little things he did to take care of her.

"So, is this what you were talking about?" she asked with a sweeping gesture toward herself with her hand.

Maddie stood before Vik in her corset, panties, sheer silk thigh highs and glittery Jimmy Choo heels, but nothing else.

His smile was predatory when he shook his head. "Almost, but not quite."

She stepped out of her heels.

"Closer." Sensuality oozed through his voice.

She swallowed. They'd made love every night for the past five weeks, so nothing about this one should make her nervous.

But as much as he'd claimed to consider their promises at the Marin Headlands overlook to be enough to bind them, the look of possession in his eyes was about ten times more intense than it had been the past weeks.

She reached down to unhook her stockings, but he put a staying hand. "Let me."

"Okay." She straightened and waited.

With no consideration for the expensive fabric of his tuxedo trousers, Vik knelt in front of her. But rather than undoing the slide button holding her stocking in place, he settled his big hands on her hips and leaned forward to press a kiss between her breasts.

Her breath caught and her knees went weak. "Vik, please."

"Please what?" he asked, his voice dark with passion. "This?"

He nuzzled the slopes of her breasts, his tongue flicking out to taste her skin. Little sparks of pleasure chased the path he took with his mouth.

His hands slid around to cup her bottom and then fingertips teased the exposed skin between the bottom of her panties and the tops of her stockings.

She only realized he'd undone the hooks when the soft silk slid down first one thigh and then another—with a little help from Vik.

Over a month ago, she'd never been touched like this, but now her body knew the delight to be had. She felt empty inside in a way she never had before she'd known what it was like to be filled up.

Her thighs quivered with brush of his fingertips while part of her craved even more. Firmer touch, more intimate caresses.

Her nipples had already drawn tight in anticipation of his attention.

Images of what he'd done before melded with the present to intensify every brush of skin against skin.

Vik reached behind her to undo the corset and she was grateful she'd gone for one with a zipper rather than laces. It parted and came away from her overheated skin in a matter of seconds.

"Mmmm…" he hummed, his expression both pleased and predatory. "Almost there."

There was no surprise when he hooked his fingers in the waistband of her panties and tugged them down. Only a sense of breathless anticipation.

With one final kiss on each of her nipples, he stood. "Now, that is the most beautiful sight I could ever imagine."

Heat suffused her body; she'd lost her ability to suppress her blushes around this man.

None of her defense mechanisms came naturally around Vik anymore.

"You're still dressed." Her voice sounded like a croaking frog.

"Would you like to change that?" he asked, his tone filled with sensual challenge.

In answer, she stepped forward and undid his bow tie.

"I'm starting to understand how you feel about unwrapping gifts," she said as she pulled the tie slowly from the starched collar of his shirt.

"Yes?"

"Oh, yes." She took her time on the buttons as well, leaning forward to inhale his masculine scent and nuzzle the chest hair not covered by his white silk undershirt.

Maddie reveled in each new inch of golden skin revealed, taking her time to touch and kiss as he had done.

Funny how quickly she'd gained the confidence to do this, but then he'd never reacted with anything but all-out enthusiasm to any sexual overture she made. No matter how small.

When she had him completely naked, she stepped forward so their bodies were flush. He was so much bigger than her and yet they fit together like they'd been created as adjoining pieces of a puzzle.

They kissed for several very satisfying minutes, no sense of urgency, just pleasure as they connected as intimately as when he was inside her.

But there was something she wanted to do, something she hadn't yet tried, something that intrigued, but also intimidated her.

What better time to take the plunge but on her wedding night?

She pulled back to break the kiss, but he drew her back in. This happened a few more times before she finally managed to separate their lips and bodies.

"I want to taste you," she told him.

A supernova flared in his eyes. "I'm not about to tell you no."

"I didn't think you would." She dropped to her knees in front of him.

"Wouldn't you be more comfortable on the bed?" he asked, sounding like it really mattered to him.

And she knew it did.

She took his large erection in her hand and caressed up and down. "Maybe, but not yet." Maddie stroked him a second time.

Groaning, Vik swayed.

She loved the velvety smoothness of his skin here and knowing that small touch affected him in such a primal way.

Leaning forward, Maddie took her first real taste of Vik's straining sex. The skin should taste like any other skin on his body, but it was even more addictive to her taste buds.

Drops of preejaculate burst with flavor on her tongue and she thought how she would be the only one who got to experience this. Never again would another woman know him in this way.

Only Maddie.

Vik was hers.

She swirled her tongue around the spongy skin of his head and he made a sound between a growl and a groan. "Please, *milaya moya*."

He could deny it, but the wedding made a difference to Vik. He'd never spoken in Russian to, or around her, before today. He was bringing her into his inner sanctum.

And that was as alluring as the naked man in front of her.

"What does that mean?" she asked, tipping her head back to see his face.

Their gazes locked, his dark eyes filled with passion.

"My sweet." His hips canted forward, seemingly of their own accord, and the tip of his erection brushed her lips.

She took him into her mouth, bringing forth another deep sound of pleasure from Vik. Hollowing her cheeks, Maddie sucked, moving her mouth forward and backward, but never so far forward she choked.

His hands settled softly against her head, but he made no effort to hold her in place or guide her movements. It was like he was giving her silent approval, as if he thought maybe his sounds of pleasure weren't enough.

It was wonderful, but her jaw got sore faster than she expected and she had to pull back.

"That was amazing," he said with apparent sincerity.

She smiled up at him. "Short, you mean."

He laughed, the sound husky. "Much longer and I would have come."

"You're easy."

"For you? Definitely." Vik pulled her to her feet and right into a mind-numbing kiss.

Not just easy, but *hungry*.

She hadn't known that missing a single night of lovemaking would make him so impatient, so ravenous for her and the pleasure they created together.

But Vik lost no time backing her up to the bed. He ripped the coverlet and top sheet off with a single, powerful yank and then maneuvered them onto the center of the king-sized mattress.

He guided her legs apart, her knees bent and she expected immediate penetration. What she got was his mouth against her most intimate flesh.

In moments, she was writhing with the need to climax, but an even stronger desire to have him inside her.

"Please, Vik. Make love to me now."

His head came up, eyes nearly black with passion meeting hers. "What do you think I am doing?"

"Not like that."

"Oh, yes, like this."

"But I'm going to come." Desperation overrode her every inhibition.

"Yes, you will," he promised in a sexy growl.

"But—"

"At least once."

Then he went back to what he was doing, taking her to the edge and over, her cries echoing around them in the luxurious bedroom. His tongue laved her gently through aftershocks until her body went boneless, her legs flopping down to the bed.

He pulled the sheet from its tangle with the comforter and wiped his mouth on it before surging up and over her. "Condom, or no condom?" he asked.

They'd been lucky and their first time without protection hadn't resulted in pregnancy. He'd been very careful to use condoms since.

But they were married now and had agreed to start a family right away. Equally important to her, she wanted the intimacy of no barrier between them.

"No birth control."

He nodded, if anything, his expression turning even more feral with a voracious sexual need. His desire came off him in waves and he still managed to enter her carefully, giving her most sensitive flesh a chance to adjust to his granite-hard erection filling her.

After her recent explosive climax and the way he incited aftershocks until she simply couldn't respond anymore, she'd been prepared to share the intimacy with him and revel in the emotional connection. But not much more.

Maddie was not prepared for the way her body reacted to their joining. The physical ecstasy ignited again, as if it had never been banked, burning hotter with every movement of his body in hers. Pleasure that she should be too sated to feel rolled through her, making her womb spasm and the muscles around his hardness contract.

He set a slow, but thoroughly penetrating rhythm that built the ecstasy inside her until she was on the verge of another inconceivable orgasm.

As if he could read her mind, or maybe it was just the clues her body was giving him, Vik sped up, pounding into her, jolts of pleasure going through her on every thrust.

He stared down at her, his face a rictus of sexual ecstasy, his coffee-brown eyes burning with demand. "Come now, *milaya moya*."

And improbably…she did, screaming as rapture sent her body into tremors that could have toppled cities.

He went completely rigid and joined her in the ultimate sexual pleasure, their gazes as connected and intimate as the most passionate kiss.

"If that didn't make a baby…" she said breathlessly.

He pulled her close into his body. "We will keep trying with great delight."

Which they did for the rest of the night, falling into exhausted slumber after the sun lit the morning fog.

He woke her to shower at noon. Not alone. Showering together was one of her recently discovered perks to sharing physical intimacy with Vik.

They came out of the bathroom to find clothing lying across the freshly made bed.

A familiar black-and-white polka-dot set of hard-sided luggage was sitting against the wall beside a black fold over garment bag and matching leather duffel as well.

"How long are we staying here?" she asked as she donned her bra and then tugged on a black silk shell over it.

Vik flicked the suitcases a glance and then met her eyes. "We are checking out in an hour."

"Where are we going?" Not home.

Both their personal possessions had been moved to Parean Hall the day before the wedding. So, there would be no need for luggage.

He pulled on his briefs and then a pair of dark indigo designer jeans. "Palm Springs."

"Why?"

"Our honeymoon."

She stilled in her own efforts to get dressed. "But I thought we weren't going on a honeymoon."

"I do not recall agreeing to that."

"We never talked about it," she pointed out.

He pulled on a black-and-white Armani X polo. "It is traditional."

"Our marriage isn't exactly." The jeans she stepped into were a pair of her favorites.

"I disagree."

She shook her head, knowing he wouldn't budge on his outlook. Vik saw nothing odd in marrying a woman he didn't love so he could build a legacy for the children he most certainly would.

"So, Palm Springs."

His grin was knowing. "I saw little point in an exotic location when we are likely to spend most of our time in the bedroom."

Blushing, she ignored his assertion and shrugged into the burgundy-and-black color-blocked jacket someone had left out for her to wear. "I like Palm Springs."

In fact, the small resort city nestled in the California desert was one of Maddie's all-time favorite places. She used to visit with her mother every winter. There were enough celebrities that vacationed there, the Archers of the world were barely a blip on the media's radar.

Maddie had continued to travel to the desert when she needed to get away from being Madison Archer, notorious heiress.

Somehow, she thought Vik knew that.

He smiled. "It is a good thing you are as intelligent as you are, or the amount of school you missed traveling with your mother would have been a real problem."

"She always brought a tutor along and got my assignments."

Vik's expression turned heated. "I'll be the only tutor you'll need this week."

"After the last five weeks, and particularly last night, I'm pretty sure there isn't much for you to teach me."

"You'll be surprised."

Not "you could be" or "you might be," but "you will be" surprised. The man had no shortage of confidence.

And the following eight days proved how justified he was in that regard.

True to his word, they spent *a lot* of time in the bedroom of their suite at an oasis-style resort outside of the city. However, Vik also insisted on visiting Maddie's favorite spots, taking her to dine at some of the best restaurants in and around the city as well as shopping in the exclusive boutiques of top designers.

Maddie, who had always considered her socialite side something of a necessary evil, enjoyed herself in ways she hadn't in Palm Springs since Helene's death.

Vik was flatteringly enthusiastic about almost every article of clothing Maddie tried on, and even the growls that particularly revealing pieces elicited were flattering in their own way.

They returned to San Francisco to a list of possible properties for the charter school that Vik had his real estate agent compile.

Vik had too many things on his desk no one else could handle after a week's absence to accompany Maddie and Romi when they toured the properties. But he asked detailed questions each evening about what Maddie had seen, proving the sincerity of his interest in the project.

* * *

Friday morning, Maddie got a text from her father's assistant requesting she come to a meeting in his office that afternoon.

She was supposed to do another tour of the property she and Romi had pretty much decided was *the one* for the school. Feeling magnanimous toward the world in general, even her father, Maddie called and rescheduled the tour before texting the PA that she would be at the meeting.

Maddie was shown into her father's office by his secretary, who surprisingly did not stay to take notes. So, it was a personal meeting?

Only, why at his office?

Her dad stood and came around from behind his desk. "Madison. I would like you to meet Dr. Wilson, the director for..." Jeremy named a well-known institution that specialized in psychiatric studies.

It was then she noticed the other man in the room.

Gray-haired and distinguished-looking in a suit of good quality, if not an Italian designer label, Dr. Wilson was sitting in one of the armchairs that sat opposite a matching leather sofa on the other side of her father's office.

He rose now and walked to Maddie, putting his hand out for Maddie to shake. "Madison. It's a pleasure to meet you."

"Thank you. I hope I can say the same." Though she did not have a good feeling about this.

Why did her father have a psychiatrist in his office for their meeting?

"Let's all sit down and get comfortable," Dr. Wilson said, indicating he considered himself a key player in the meeting to come.

The fact that her father followed the doctor's lead without comment indicated he agreed.

Maddie wasn't feeling quite so acquiescent. She remained standing as her father took a position at one end of the sofa and the doctor returned to his leather armchair. "What is this about?"

"Sit down, Madison, so we can discuss this like civilized people."

"Tell me what we are discussing first," she demanded in a chilly tone she hadn't used in weeks.

Her father frowned. "You are being rude."

"And you are being cagey." When it came to her father? Cagey was way worse than rude.

"Do you see what I mean?" Jeremy asked the doctor. "Unreasonably intractable."

"You've asked Dr. Wilson here to evaluate me?" Maddie demanded, emotion cracking through the facade of cool before she reined it in.

Surprisingly, her dad winced, but he nodded. "It has come to my attention that you've been seeing a therapist."

"I did for a few weeks, yes. Half of America has at one time or another." And her choice to do so was a good thing, not a weakness.

"That is actually a bit of an exaggeration," Dr. Wilson said, like he was making note of Maddie's tendency to overstate things. "The number is closer to twenty percent."

"Who told you I was seeing someone?" she asked Jeremy, ignoring the doctor.

Vik wouldn't have told him. He might not love Maddie, but he was her white knight. Vik would never sacrifice her to the king.

"Does Vik know about this meeting?" she demanded.

Her father gave her his game face. "What do you think?"

"That you don't want to answer my question." She pulled out her phone.

"Who are you calling?" Dr. Wilson asked, his tone overly patient.

"My husband."

"You see? Shades of codependency and paranoia," her father said.

Maddie wanted to throw her phone at his head, but didn't want to know what the psychiatrist would make of that. Vik's phone sent her to voice mail.

He must have been in a meeting.

She left a message. "It's me. Jeremy called me in for a meeting with a psychiatrist. I need to talk to you. Call me."

Dr. Wilson was watching her with an indecipherable expression. Her dad's eyes were narrowed, but she wasn't sure if it was with worry or annoyance.

"So, you know I saw a therapist and you've brought Dr. Wilson here to observe me. Why?"

"No one said I was here to observe you," the doctor said.

"No one said you weren't."

Neither the doctor nor her father answered that.

Finally, Jeremy said, "I've told Dr. Wilson my concerns about your increasingly erratic behavior over the years."

"And while I applaud your positive action in seeking help," Dr. Wilson said, as if speaking to a child, or an adult whose reasoning ability was compromised, "I must concur with your father that your actions since your mother's death indicate a spiraling condition."

"I do not have a condition." What she did have was a brain and it was starting to work. "You aren't going to prove me mentally incompetent to sign the paperwork giving Romi half of my shares in AIH. It's not going to work."

Her father's expression said he disagreed.

Even more ominously, the doctor shook his head. "Signing such a document as the one your father described to me in and of itself is hardly a rational action."

"You think not?"

"You think it is?"

"I know it is and I also know what I do with my money

and assets is not your business, Dr. Wilson, or for that matter, Jeremy Archer's."

"You call your father by his first name. That indicates a level of dissociation to those closest to you."

Who was this guy? Popping off with psychobabble on the basis of nothing but her father's obviously biased assertions and a few seconds conversation was not in any way professional.

"I'm closer to my cleaning lady than my father. In fact, I'm closer to *his* housekeeper than I am to him." And that might have been an exaggeration, but she defied either of them to prove differently.

The psychiatrist gave her a concerned look. "Your lack of emotional intimacy with your one remaining parent is certainly something we can explore together."

"Dr. Wilson, you are not and never will be *my* doctor. Now, if you two will excuse me." She turned to leave the office.

"Madison!" her father barked.

She didn't stop. He could leave whatever threat he wanted to make on her voice mail.

CHAPTER ELEVEN

MADDIE WAS IN the parking garage when her phone rang. Vik's ringtone.

She answered. "My father found out I was seeing a therapist."

"I didn't tell him."

"I didn't think you did."

"Good."

"I'm just…" Frustrated. Confused. Upset. "He wants to prove me incompetent to sign the papers giving Romi half my AIH shares."

"I had n—"

"There's something he didn't think of, I bet," she interrupted, not really hearing Vik.

"What is that?" Vik asked, sounding both cautious and concerned.

"If he gets a judge to say I wasn't competent to sign those papers. I wasn't competent to say my vows, either, and *we* aren't married. What will that do his precious plans to marry me off to his heir?" she demanded.

Vik made a sound like a growl. "That is not going to happen."

"I thought things were getting better with him."

"They are."

"If anyone has lost their mind it is him."

"I agree."

She nodded.

"Madison?"

"You're on my side, right?" Vik wouldn't support his mentor and friend in this, would he?

"Of course. You are my wife and you are staying that way."

Because he wanted control of AIH. Because he wanted the future he planned with her. Right that second, Maddie wished desperately there was another, more emotionally compelling reason for Vik to insist their marriage stood in validity.

Love.

She needed her husband's love. More than she wanted her father's acceptance. A lot more.

She couldn't really care less about Jeremy sliding back into old habits. However, suddenly the knowledge that the man she loved more than her own life appreciated her feelings but didn't share them hurt in a way she couldn't ignore.

"I need some time to think."

"What? Madison, where are you? I will come to you."

"No. I just…give me some time, Vik." She ended the call and then turned off her phone.

She didn't want to talk to anyone. Not even Romi.

Maddie got into her hybrid car—not exactly what an heiress might be expected to drive, but it was environmentally responsible—and drove to her favorite coffee shop/bookstore.

How was she going to live the rest of her life in love with her husband and knowing he didn't reciprocate her feelings. She didn't know if it was *couldn't* or *wouldn't*, but it didn't matter.

Maddie hadn't been to the coffee shop since before Perrygate, but she needed time to think and a place to do it in that Vik wouldn't think to look.

She got her usual order and took it to her favorite table positioned between a book stack and the window. Since the lower half of the window was painted with a mural that looked like old leather volumes on bookshelves, no one would see her from the outside.

Not unless they got right up to the window and looked down.

Her thoughts whirled in a mass of contradicting voices and images as her coffee cooled in its cup, but one idea rose to the surface again and again.

Vik *acted* like a man in love.

He couldn't get enough of her sexually. Maddie's happiness was very important to him. Given a choice, he *always* opted to spend time with her rather than away from her. He wanted her to be the mother of his children.

Did the words really matter?

She'd been doing fine without them to this point. But being thrown back into Ruthlessville by her father had undercut Maddie's sense of emotional security.

Did she really need Vik to admit he loved her for her to feel secure in her happiness with him?

She still had no answer to that question when she heard her name spoken in a masculine tone she'd never planned to hear again.

She looked up and frowned. "Go away, Perry."

"You don't take my calls or respond to my texts."

He was surprised? "I blocked your number."

"I figured that out."

"You aren't supposed to be talking to me."

"Nothing in the agreement that bastard you married got me to sign said I couldn't talk *to* you, only about you." Perry sounded really annoyed by that.

"What did you expect?"

He put on the wounded expression that had always gotten to her in the past. "I didn't expect you to dump six years of friendship over one little mistake."

"It wasn't the first time you lied to the media about us." And that sad look wasn't tugging at her heartstrings anymore.

Perry jerked, like he hadn't expected her to have worked that out. "It was all harmless. I needed the money. We aren't all born with the silver spoon of Archer International Holdings to feed off of."

"Telling people I was a sexual addict who couldn't be satisfied with a single partner wasn't harmless. You destroyed my reputation."

"For exactly twenty-four hours. Viktor Beck saw to that."

"Conrad is good at what he does."

"Your dad's media fixer? Yeah, I kind of expected him to get involved, but he's a cuddly kitten compared to that vicious shark you married."

"Vik protected me when *you* fed me to the wolves. I'm not sure I'd label *him* the vicious one."

"You know I didn't mean it." Perry sounded like he really expected her to believe that.

What a jerk. And this man had been one of her dearest friends for *six* years. "I knew you were lying, that's not the same thing as knowing you didn't mean it."

"I needed the money. You knew I did."

"And I refused to give it to you." Which was what it all came down to, wasn't it?

"I asked for a loan. From a *friend*."

"When have you ever paid back even a single dollar of all the money you *borrowed* from me, Perry?" she demanded, the confrontation with her ex-friend unexpectedly bringing her current situation into clear and certain focus.

Perry was that guy. The user. The manipulator. The prevaricator.

Vik was her white knight. Full stop.

He might never say the three little words she most wanted to hear, but she wasn't going to spend the rest of her life lamenting that fact. Not when he gave her so much to rejoice about instead.

"You can't guarantee business investments."

"So now they were business investments." She narrowed her eyes at Perry. "Where are my contracts showing the percentage ownership I had in those business ventures?"

"We don't need contracts between us."

She thought of the agreement Vik had forced Perry to sign. "Apparently, we do."

"Come on, Maddie. Call off your attack dog."

"Vik?"

"Who else?" Perry did his best to look beseeching.

"We aren't friends anymore and we never will be again," she spelled out very carefully.

"This is because of Romi, isn't it? She finally turned you against me."

"*You* turned me against you, Perry. You lied about me and did your best to destroy my reputation."

He'd gone back to looking wounded. "No."

"Yes. And if you'd succeeded, my dreams of starting a charter school would have been dust." At least with her name on any of the paperwork.

Perry shrugged. "San Francisco doesn't need another school."

His ability to dismiss the dreams of her heart so easily took her breath away. "I don't agree."

"Well, it didn't happen."

"No thanks to you."

"Hey, I went public with an apology and a confession that it was all a joke."

Did he expect her to thank him? "But it wasn't a joke.

It was a big ugly lie. Nothing even a tiny bit amusing about that."

"Come on, Maddie. You have to forgive me."

"Yes, for my own sake. I have to let it go."

Triumph flashed in Perry's washed-out blue eyes. "We can be friends again and forget about that agreement Viktor forced me to sign."

"No."

"But—"

"No one forced you to sign anything. You signed that agreement of your own volition because you didn't want to risk being sued by both AIH and the tabloid you sold that story to."

Maddie's head snapped up at Vik's voice. What was he doing here? How had he found her?

He stood like an avenging angel over Perry. "You are not my wife's friend. She's convinced you were at one time, but that time passed long before this latest incident."

"Who do you think you are to—"

"I am the man who will *ruin* you if you come near *my* wife again." His jaw hewn from granite, Vik's eyes burned with dark fury.

Perry put his hands up. "No problem. Look, I just thought we could still be friends, but I can see you're not comfortable with that."

"I'm not comfortable with it," Maddie inserted. "Stop blaming other people for your screwup, Perry. You destroyed our friendship and Vik is right, that started a long time ago."

"But, Maddie…"

She shook her head. "No. We're over. If you see me at a function, walk the other way because I don't want to talk to you anymore."

"We aren't going to be at the same functions," he said bitterly.

Maddie didn't bother to reply. That was Perry's problem, not hers.

"Are you going to leave, or will you force me to call the police to enforce the restraining order we have against you?"

"I'm leaving," Perry said quickly, backing out of the alcove.

"We have a restraining order?" Maddie asked Vik.

"Yes."

"Didn't I have to sign something for it?"

"No. His malicious intent was in the papers for the world to see. We filed for it on behalf of AIH and its primaries, of which you are one."

"Oh."

He looked down at her untouched coffee. "You're not drinking that."

She shook her head. "How did you find me?"

"Are you sure you want to know?"

"Yes."

"The 'find me' function on your phone."

"I turned it off."

"As long as the battery is in it and holds any charge, the GPS function works."

"So, if I want privacy, I have to take out the battery. Good to know."

He had to have looked up her GPS signal right away to have gotten to the coffee shop so quickly. More evidence that she mattered to him in the ways that were truly important.

Her father never would have just dumped his schedule to go running after her mother, or Maddie, certainly.

Vik inhaled, opened his mouth to speak, closed it again and then said, "I would prefer you not do that."

"Okay." It was a matter of safety as well, as much as she might prefer to forget that fact. "You came after me."

"Of course. You were upset. What Jeremy did to you…"

She coughed out a laugh at the rare vulgarity that came out of her husband's mouth.

Vik put his hand out to her. "Will you come *with* me now?"

Maddie didn't hesitate. "Yes."

"Don't you want to know where?" Vik asked as she took his hand and let him lead her from the coffee shop.

"I guess I assumed we'd go someplace private."

Vik's expression turned hard. "Actually, we're going back to AIH to confront your father."

"Together."

"Yes."

Implying Vik and Maddie were on one side and Jeremy Archer the other. Nice. If she'd needed proof that she came first with Vik, her father couldn't have provided a better opportunity.

Which, okay, maybe having the proof *was* nice, but she wasn't about to thank Jeremy.

Her father was in his office when they arrived, Dr. Wilson gone. The PA tried to tell them that Jeremy was in a meeting, but Vik just walked through.

He reached across Jeremy's desk and ended the call, sending Maddie's father surging to his feet as he spluttered with annoyance.

Vik waited until her father had gone silent to speak. "Have you ever known me to lie to you?"

Jeremy shook his head, his expression instantly wary.

"Do I bluff?" Vik asked.

"No," Jeremy said shortly.

"Then you will know I mean every word I say when I tell you that if you attempt to prove Madison incompetent to forestall her giving half her shares to Romi Grayson, I will destroy Archer International Holdings until the very building we are standing in is leveled to the ground."

"You don't mean that," Jeremy said, his voice warbling with emotion for the first time in Maddie's memory.

She hadn't even seen him appear this distraught at her mother's funeral.

There was no give in Vik. Not in his expression. Not in the way he stood, towering over Jeremy's desk. "We have just established that I do."

Definitely not in his tone.

Her dad said something else, but Maddie wasn't listening. Everything inside her had gone still as she had her second major revelation for the day.

"You *do* love me," she said to Vik, ignoring her father completely.

That oh-so-serious espresso gaze fixed on her. "You are mine to protect."

"And to love." Giddy with joy that could not be tempered even by her father's machinations, she could hardly help the delight surfing every syllable.

She didn't even want to try.

Maddie beamed up at the man she'd crushed on since she was fourteen and loved since she was sixteen. "I love you, too, but you know that."

"Do you?" Vik asked. "Even now?"

"Especially now." He wasn't even remotely responsible for her father's actions.

"I meant what I said to your father." He said it like it was a warning.

"I know."

"I am utterly ruthless and without remorse."

She might argue that point, but understood that Vik believed it. And that was okay with her.

He used his powers for good, even if he didn't see it.

She smiled at him, letting her love show in her eyes.

"Your sense of honor is the shiniest and clearest facet of your nature. Everything else about you is filtered through the light it casts."

"I am not a nice guy."

"You just threatened to destroy my company," her dad said with feeling. "You sure as hell are *not* a nice guy."

Maddie's smile morphed into a full grin. "It's all a matter of perspective. I love that you would pull out every stop to slay my dragons."

"I'm not a dragon. I'm your father, damn it."

She flicked him a disgusted glance. "Who threatened to have me declared mentally incompetent."

"You can't believe I wanted things to go down that way, but you're giving away my company." Vik might claim to be remorseless, but Jeremy's expression and tone were soaked with regret.

"Don't exaggerate," she said, dismissing her father's words. "Twelve and a half percent with the voting proxy assigned to Vik and any successor he should formally appoint."

Vik jolted beside her. "I didn't know that."

"I trust you."

His gaze turned soft like she'd never expected to see. "You do."

"You knew that."

"I told myself you did."

"And me." He'd told her when she'd still been denying it to herself.

"Apparently it is different coming from you."

Her dad sighed. "You know, your mother and I never felt the need to talk our emotions to death."

Finally, Maddie gave Jeremy her attention. "Maybe if you had, things would have been different."

"I cannot change the past," he said with a pained expression.

"You spend enough time screwing up with your daughter in the present, the past is hardly what you need to be worried about," Vik told her father.

"I am sorry for ambushing you with Dr. Wilson, Madison." Jeremy looked at her with appeal. "It probably makes no difference to you, but I told Dr. Wilson I wouldn't be needing his services immediately after you left my office."

"That's hard to believe." Her father didn't back down once he'd set a course of action in motion.

He just didn't. And he *did* lie.

Jeremy said, "Call him. He'll tell you."

Bluffing or truth?

"He's telling the truth," Vik told her.

Maddie looked up at her husband. "How can you tell?"

"His eyes shift to the left when he's lying about something important."

"And this is important to him?" she asked with suspicion.

"It involves you and his company. There is nothing more important to him."

That she believed. At least the part about the company.

"Why did you tell Dr. Wilson to back off?" she asked.

Jeremy shifted uncomfortably in his chair. "I knew that if I followed through with my plan, you would never forgive me."

"Are you sure it wasn't because you realized that my marriage to Vik would be invalidated if I was deemed unfit to make legal decisions?"

Her father's eyes widened, his skin going pale. A reaction he could not fake. He *hadn't* thought of that. "No wonder Vik pulled out the rocket launchers."

"He wants to be married to me more than he wants to be president of AIH." Just saying the words gave her emotional satisfaction to the very depths of her being.

Jeremy nodded, his expression more vulnerable than

she'd ever seen it. "I hope you've worked out that I want to be your dad more than I want control of those shares."

It was her turn to nod, but maybe with not as much conviction.

"It might benefit you both if your father attended some sessions with you and Dr. MacKenzie," Vik said.

Maddie waited to see her father's reaction to that piece of advice before offering her own.

Jeremy Archer shocked her to the very marrow of his bones when he said, "I would like that very much. Are you willing, Madison?"

"I don't know." What if he used the time they had together with the therapist to compile ammunition against her?

"Do you believe Vik will destroy Archer International Holdings if I attempt to have you declared mentally incompetent?"

"Yes." There was not a single atom in her body that did not trust Vik to do just that.

"Then you have nothing to fear," her father said, showing he'd guessed correctly what had her hesitating.

"I'll talk to Dr. MacKenzie. If she thinks it's a good idea, we'll arrange the sessions."

Her dad startled her again, getting up from his desk and coming around to kiss her on the cheek and shake Vik's hand. "Thank you for watching out for her better than I ever have."

"I always will." It was another Viktor Beck promise.

And the places still cold inside from Maddie's unexpected meetings with her father, the psychiatrist and then Perry, warmed. "And I will watch out for Vik."

Starting with taking him home and teaching him how to say three all-important words.

"I believe you. You have your mother's loyalty and my stubbornness. He couldn't be in better hands."

Maddie surprised herself, accepting the compliment with the warmth it was intended. "Thank you."

Vik slid his arm around her waist. "It's time for us to go home, I think."

"What about your afternoon meetings?" she asked, not really wanting him to go back to work.

But now that she knew he loved her, Maddie could wait for the evening to hear him say it. Maybe.

"I canceled everything after your phone call."

"Because nothing is more important to you than I am," she said with satisfaction.

Vik could have shrugged. He could have tried to deny it. He could have grimaced in unhappy acknowledgment.

He did none of those things.

What he did was turn his big body to face her, blocking out her view of her dad and his office.

Vik cupped Maddie's cheeks, his hands trembling against her skin. "Exactly."

Oh, man. She was going to melt right there.

"Take me home, please," she said, her voice low with fervency.

Vik made a sound like something had broken inside him and then leaned down and kissed her. His mouth claimed hers with undeniable need. She gave in to it without hesitation.

Maddie didn't know how long the kiss lasted, but when her father's voice finally penetrated, she was pressed against Vik, his arms tight bands around her.

"Sheesh, you two need to go home."

"Kicking us out?" Vik asked with no evidence of embarrassment at what they were doing.

Her dad, on the other hand, had a definite ruddy cast to his cheeks. "What's coming next is not going to happen in my office."

Maddie's own cheeks heated at the implication of his words. He was absolutely right. It was time to leave.

The trip home happened in a haze for her and Maddie was glad Vik drove.

He surprised her by pulling her into the morning room, the shabby chic so like her former apartment and cheery lemon-yellow accents barely registering as he pulled her to sit with him on the deep sofa.

"I thought we were going upstairs." To make love.

That's certainly where their kiss in her father's office had been leading.

"We're going to talk." Vik winced as if the words pained him. "About the emotional stuff."

"Can't we do that later?" Knowing he loved her was making her desire for the physical proof overwhelming.

"No."

"Why not?" She wasn't whining.

She wasn't, but so far, her day had sort of sucked. Making love with her husband? Now, after learning he was in love with her, that would take this one into the "best days ever" category.

"Because maybe things would have been different for Helene and Jeremy if they had," Vik said, quoting her own words back at her.

"That was them. We aren't my parents."

"No, we aren't." Vik took a deep breath and let it out, his complexion just a little green. "I love you, Madison."

She didn't tease him for nearly being sick with stress over the admission, though the temptation was great. But she appreciated how hard this had to be for her usually single-minded, alpha business tycoon.

"Maddie."

"What?" he asked, like she'd strayed from the script.

"You love me. I love you. You call me Maddie, like Romi does."

"Perry, too." And Vik didn't appear happy about that.

"Not anymore. Perry doesn't get to call me anything. You saw to that."

"The restraining order lasts two years, but we'll renew it."

She shook her head. "I don't need the restraining order. Trust me, you're enough, Vik."

"He approached you."

"So, I'll stop going to that coffee shop."

"That won't be necessary. I'll buy it and have him banned."

"Can you say overkill here, Vik?"

"Nothing is too much to protect you."

"Oh, man." She saw a lifetime ahead of her of reining in Vik's impulses to keep even the hint of harm from her and the children they would have.

Honestly? The image had a pretty rosy glow.

"Do you want me to leave AIH?" he asked.

"What? No!" It was her turn to reach out and cup his face, meeting his eyes with an expression as sincere as she could make it. "I do not need you to give up your dreams to believe you love me."

Though knowing he was willing to heal wounds in her heart from twenty-four years as Jeremy Archer's daughter.

"I do. I did six years ago, but…"

"You didn't recognize what the feeling was," she guessed.

"No. I'd never been in love."

"I'm glad." The thought she could have lost him before she ever had the chance to catch his eye sent cold tremors through her.

"I didn't think I needed love."

"We all need love."

Vik frowned. "I'm not sure that is true."

He sounded so uncertain, so very unlike the man she was used to. But this was not his area of expertise.

Emotions were almost as foreign to Vik as they were to her dad.

"It's okay, Vik. We love each other and we are going to be very happy."

"Aren't we happy right now?"

Giving in to the urge, she threw herself into his arms with a laugh. "Yes, my darling, wonderful husband. We are very happy."

He caught her to him, responding to her kiss and holding her tight.

Oh, yes, *very* happy.

They made love, right there on the sofa, and practiced saying those three little words to each other.

EPILOGUE

VIK AGREED WITH Maddie and Romi on the property they picked out for the charter school. Declaring it the perfect location, he insisted on putting an offer in on it immediately.

Afterward, he took her and Romi out for champagne to celebrate.

"Isn't this a bit premature?" Romi asked as they clinked glasses. "The offer hasn't been accepted yet."

Maddie just laughed. "The sellers could be a business consortium of questionable pedigree and they wouldn't have a chance against Vik."

"We'll get the property," Vik said as if there simply wasn't another option.

Maddie was pretty sure with her tycoon on the case, there wasn't.

Romi grinned, lifting her glass toward Vik. "To business shark negotiators and dreams coming true."

They didn't go straight home after, but Vik took Maddie back up to the overlook at Marin Headlands. She didn't ask what they were doing there.

Maddie just held his hand as they traversed the path to what many considered the best place for viewing San Francisco's skyline.

He stopped in the same spot he'd proposed. "We forgot some promises when we were here before."

"Did we?"

He nodded. "You forgot to promise not to leave your security detail behind anymore."

That wasn't what she was expecting him to say, but it was so in line with Vik and his priorities that she grinned. "Duly noted."

"Promise."

She put her hand over her heart. "I promise to keep my security detail with me."

"Your days of volunteering anonymously are over." He leaned down and kissed her. "I'm sorry."

"It's okay. You'll just have to find me a detail that likes children."

"I think that can be arranged."

Suddenly she realized why they were dealing with this now. "If my detail had been with me when I went to the coffee shop, Perry wouldn't have gotten within ten feet of me."

"If that."

"Right."

Vik shrugged. "Do you think Romi would allow me to assign a detail to her as well?"

"What? Why?"

"She is your sister-by-choice."

"I didn't know you were aware of that."

"Your mother considered her another daughter."

"She did." Maddie smiled in memory. "But I'm not sure Romi needs security because I consider her my sister."

"In a few weeks, she will own twelve and a half percent of a multibillion-dollar company."

"No one but us will know that."

"You know better than that."

She did. "I don't know if we can convince her."

"Tell her security comes with the shares."

"She's not going to be happy."

Vik didn't look too worried about that reality. "She's part of my family now. She'll get used to it."

Maddie wasn't sure she agreed, but she loved the sentiment.

Vik pulled Maddie close, but kept eye contact. "I love you."

It didn't matter that he'd said it before, that she knew it to be true—saying the words here made them a vow for him.

Maddie's throat constricted, moisture burning hot behind her eyes and all she could do was nod.

"I will love you always," he promised.

She took a steadying breath. "Me, too."

"We *will* say the important stuff."

"Yes."

"We'll talk about the emotional stuff often." He still looked a little green around the gills at the idea, but he was making the promise.

And Maddie knew Vik would keep it.

"With our children, too," Maddie vowed.

Vik nodded. "When I forget, you'll remind me."

"Yes." Not that she was convinced he would ever forget the important things.

When Vik set his mind to something, he succeeded.

He looked like he had something he wanted to say, so she waited for him to say it. "Your father…"

"Yes?"

"I could have been him."

"No. You're different."

"I am, but I could have been. He never got that love and family made having the power and the business matter, not the other way around."

"But you do."

"I do." The absolute conviction in Vik's tone touched her to the core.

"Perry really played into your hands, didn't he?"

Vik shrugged. "We would have married, one way, or another."

"Because you loved me and could not imagine your life without me."

Vik's smile was brighter than the sun in the height of summer. "Exactly."

"Ditto."

Their shared laughter floated over the bay as their bodies pressed together in the most basic promise of all.

Shared love for a lifetime.

* * * * *

*If you enjoyed this book,
look out for Max and Romi's story in
A VIRGIN FOR HIS PRIZE by Lucy Monroe.
Coming soon!*

"Suit yourself," Nic had replied. He'd shrugged, but Mattie had been far too aware that every inch of him was hewn of steel, that he was himself a deadly weapon.

She'd felt the power he wore so easily like a thick, hot hand at her throat. Worse, she'd been aware of that part of her that craved it. Him. *More.*

"I have a very long memory, Mattie, and a very creative approach to retribution. Consider yourself forewarned."

"Be still my beating heart," she'd snipped at him, and then had tried her best to ignore him.

It hadn't worked then. It didn't work now.

"Will we reminisce all day?" she asked, injecting a note of boredom into her voice that she dearly wished she felt, while he continued to hold her immobile. "Or do you have a plan? I'm unfamiliar with the ins and outs of blackmail, you see. You'll have to show me how it's done."

"You're free to refuse me yet again."

"And lose my father's company in the process?"

"All choices have consequences." He shrugged, much the same way he had at that benefit dinner. "Your father would have been the first to tell you that."

That he was right only infuriated her more.

VOWS OF CONVENIENCE

Bound by duty!

The Whitaker name was once synonymous with power, wealth and control. But with the family business facing certain ruin, and its reputation turning into dust, the Whitaker siblings need to make the ultimate sacrifice to safeguard their futures…

HIS FOR A PRICE

Following the death of Mattie Whitaker's father, a merger with Greek tycoon Nicodemus Stathis's company will go a long way towards fixing her problem—but Nicodemus's help comes at a price…

October 2014

HIS FOR REVENGE

Chase Whitaker is playing his own dark game of revenge against Zara Elliot's father, the chairman of his board. He plans to replace him— but he has no defences against Zara's unstudied charm and natural beauty…

December 2014

HIS FOR A PRICE

BY
CAITLIN CREWS

All rights reserved including the right of reproduction in whole
or in part in any form. This edition is published by arrangement with
Harlequin Books S.A.

This is a work of fiction. Names, characters, places, locations and
incidents are purely fictional and bear no relationship to any real
life individuals, living or dead, or to any actual places, business
establishments, locations, events or incidents. Any resemblance is
entirely coincidental.

This book is sold subject to the condition that it shall not, by way of
trade or otherwise, be lent, resold, hired out or otherwise circulated
without the prior consent of the publisher in any form of binding or
cover other than that in which it is published and without a similar
condition including this condition being imposed on the subsequent
purchaser.

® and TM are trademarks owned and used by the trademark owner
and/or its licensee. Trademarks marked with ® are registered with the
United Kingdom Patent Office and/or the Office for Harmonisation in
the Internal Market and in other countries.

Published in Great Britain 2014
by Mills & Boon, an imprint of Harlequin (UK) Limited,
Eton House, 18-24 Paradise Road, Richmond, Surrey, TW9 1SR

© 2014 Caitlin Crews

ISBN: 978-0-263-24997-2

Harlequin (UK) Limited's policy is to use papers that are natural,
renewable and recyclable products and made from wood grown in
sustainable forests. The logging and manufacturing processes conform
to the legal environmental regulations of the country of origin.

Printed and bound in Spain
by Blackprint CPI, Barcelona

Caitlin Crews discovered her first romance novel at the age of twelve. It involved swashbuckling pirates, grand adventures, a heroine with rustling skirts and a mind of her own, and a seriously mouth-watering and masterful hero. The book (the title of which remains lost in the mists of time) made a serious impression. Caitlin was immediately smitten with romances and romance heroes, to the detriment of her middle school social life. And so began her life-long love affair with romance novels, many of which she insists on keeping near her at all times.

Caitlin has made her home in places as far-flung as York, England, and Atlanta, Georgia. She was raised near New York City, and fell in love with London on her first visit when she was a teenager. She has backpacked in Zimbabwe, been on safari in Botswana, and visited tiny villages in Namibia. She has, while visiting the place in question, declared her intention to live in Prague, Dublin, Paris, Athens, Nice, the Greek Islands, Rome, Venice, and/or any of the Hawaiian islands. Writing about exotic places seems like the next best thing to moving there.

She currently lives in California, with her animator/comic book artist husband and their menagerie of ridiculous animals.

Recent titles by the same author:

UNDONE BY THE SULTAN'S TOUCH
A SCANDAL IN THE HEADLINES
    (Sicily's Corretti Dynasty)
A ROYAL WITHOUT RULES *(Royal & Ruthless)*
NO MORE SWEET SURRENDER
    (Scandal in the Spotlight)

Did you know these are also available as eBooks?
Visit www.millsandboon.co.uk

To Megan Haslam, my wonderful editor,
for twenty great books together!
Here's to twenty more!

CHAPTER ONE

IF SHE STOOD very still—if she held her breath and kept herself from so much as blinking—Mattie Whitaker was sure she could make the words that her older brother Chase had just said to her disappear. Rewind them then erase them entirely.

Outside the rambling old mansion high above the Hudson River some two hours north of Manhattan, the cold rain came down in sheets. Stark, weather-stripped trees slapped back against the October wind all the way down the battered brown lawn toward the sullen river, and the estate had shrunk to blurred gray clouds, solemn green pines and the solid shape of the old brick house called Greenleigh, despite the lack of much remaining green. Behind her, at the desk that she would always think of as her father's no matter how many months he'd been gone now, Chase was silent.

There would be no rewinding. No erasing. No escaping what she knew was coming. But then, if she was honest, she'd always known this day would arrive. Sooner or later.

"I didn't hear you correctly," Mattie said. Eventually.

"We both know you did."

It should have made her feel better that he sounded as torn as she felt, which was better than that polite distance with which he usually treated her. It didn't.

"Say it again, then." She pressed her fingers against the frigid windowpane before her and let the cold soak into her skin. No use crying over the inevitable, her father would have said in that bleakly matter-of-fact way he'd said everything after they'd lost their mother.

Save your tears for things you can change, Mattie.

Chase sighed, and Mattie knew that if she turned to look at him, he'd be a pale shell of the grinning, always-in-on-the-joke British tabloid staple he'd been throughout his widely celebrated bachelorhood in London, where he'd lived as some kind of tribute to their long-dead British mother. It had been a long, hard four months since their father had dropped dead unexpectedly. Harder on Chase, she expected, who had all their father's corporate genius to live up to, but she didn't feel like being generous just now. About anything.

Mattie still didn't turn around. That might make this real.

Not that hiding from things has ever worked, either, whispered a wry voice inside her that remembered all the things she wanted to forget—the smell of the leather seats in that doomed car, the screech of the tires, her own voice singing them straight into hell—

Mattie shut that down. Fast and hard. But her hands were shaking.

"You promised me we'd do this together," Chase said quietly instead of repeating himself. Which was true. She'd said exactly that at their father's funeral, sick with loss and grief, and not really considering the implications. "It's you and me now, Mats."

He hadn't called her that in a very long time, since they'd been trapped in that car together, in fact, and she hated that he was doing it now, for this ugly purpose. She steeled herself against it. Against him.

"You and me and the brand-new husband you're selling me off to like some kind of fatted cow, you mean," Mattie corrected him, her voice cool, which was much better than bitter. Or panicked. Or terrified. "I didn't realize we were living in the Dark Ages."

"Dad was nothing if not clear that smart, carefully chosen marriages lead to better business practices." Chase's voice was sardonic then, or maybe that was bitterness, and Mattie turned, at last, to find him watching her with that hollow look in his dark blue eyes and his arms crossed over his chest. "I'm in the same boat. Amos Elliott has been gunning for me since the day of the funeral but he's made it known that if I take one of his daughters off his hands, I'll find my dealings with the Board of Directors that much more pleasant. Welcome to the Dark Ages, Mattie."

She laughed, but it was an empty sound. "Should that make me feel better? Because it doesn't. It's nothing but a little more misery to spread around."

"We need money and support—serious money and very concrete support—or we lose the company," Chase said, his voice flat and low. So unlike him, really, if Mattie wanted to consider that. She didn't. "There's no prettying that up. The shareholders are mutinous. Amos Elliott and the Board of Directors are plotting my downfall as we speak. This is our legacy and we're on the brink of losing it."

And what's left of them—of us. He didn't say that last part, but he might as well have. It echoed inside of Mattie as if he'd shouted it through a bullhorn, and she heard the rest of it, too. The part where he reminded her who was to blame for losing their mother—but then, he didn't have to remind her. He'd never had to remind her and he never had. There was no point. There was scarcely a moment in her entire life when she didn't remind herself.

Still. "This is a major sacrifice, to put it mildly," she pointed out, because the thoughtless, careless, giddily reckless creature she played in the tabloids would. "I could view this as an opportunity to walk away, instead. Start my life over without having to worry about parental disapproval or the stuffy, disapproving Whitaker Industries shareholders." She studied her brother's hard, closed-off expression as if she was a stranger to him, and she blamed herself for that, too. "You could do the same."

"Yes," Chase agreed, his voice cool. "But then we'd be the useless creatures Dad already thought we were. I can't live with that. I don't think you can, either. And I imagine you knew we had no other options but this before you came here today."

"You mean before I answered your summons?" Mattie clenched her shaking hands into fists. It was better than tears. Anything was better than tears. Particularly because Chase was right. She couldn't live with what she'd done twenty years ago; she certainly wouldn't be able to live with the fallout if she walked away from the ruins of her family now. This was all her fault, in the end. The least she could do was her part to help fix it. "You've been back from London for how long?"

Her brother looked wary then. "A week."

"But you only called when you needed me to sell myself. I'm touched, really."

"Fine," Chase said roughly, shoving a hand through his dark hair. "Make me the enemy. It doesn't change anything."

"Yes," she agreed then, feeling ashamed of herself for kicking at him, yet unable to stop. "I knew it before I came here. But that doesn't mean I'm happy to go gentle into the deep, dark night that is Nicodemus Stathis."

Chase's mouth moved in what might have been a smile,

had these been happier times. Had either one of them had any choice in this. Had he done much smiling in her direction in the past twenty years. "Make sure you tell him that yourself. I'm sure he'll find that entertaining."

"Nicodemus has always found me wildly entertaining," Mattie said, and it felt better to square her shoulders, to lengthen her spine, as she told that whopper of a lie. It felt better to make her voice brisk and to smooth her palms down the front of the deliberately very black dress she'd worn, to send the message she wished she could, too. "I'm sure if you asked him he'd list that in the top five reasons he's always insisted he wanted to marry me. That and his fantasy of merging our two corporate kingdoms like some feudal wet dream in which he gets to play lord of the castle with the biggest, longest, thickest—"

She remembered, belatedly, that she was talking to her older brother, who might not be as close to her as she'd like but was nonetheless *her older brother,* and smiled faintly.

"Share," she amended. "Of the company. The biggest *share.*"

"Of course that's precisely what you meant," Chase replied drily, but Mattie heard something like an apology in his voice, a kind of sorrow, right underneath what nearly passed for laughter.

Because his hands were tied. Big Bart Whitaker had been an institution unto himself. No one had expected him to simply drop dead four months ago—least of all Bart. There had been no time to prepare. No time to ease Chase from his flashy London VP position into his new role as President and CEO of Whitaker Industries, as had always been Bart's ultimate intention. No time to allay the fears of the board and the major shareholders, who only knew Chase from what they read about him in all those smirking British tabloids. No time to grieve when there were too many challenges, too many risks, too many enemies.

Their father had loved the company his own grandfather had built from little more than innate Whitaker stubbornness and a desire to best the likes of Andrew Carnegie. And Mattie thought both she and Chase had always loved their father in their own complicated ways, especially after they'd lost their mother and Big Bart was all they'd had left.

Which meant they would each do what they had to do. There was no escaping this, and if she was honest, Mattie had known that long before her father died. It was as inevitable as the preview of the upstate New York winter coming down hard outside, and there was no use pretending otherwise.

Mattie would make the best of it. She would ignore that deep, dark, aching place inside her that simply *hurt*. That was scared, so very scared, of how Nicodemus Stathis made her feel. And how easy it would be to lose herself in him, until there was nothing left of her at all.

But you owe this to them, she reminded herself sternly. *All of them.*

"He's here already, isn't he?" she asked after a moment, when there was no putting it off any longer. She could stand here all day and it wouldn't change anything. It would only make the dread in her belly feel more like a brick.

Chase's gaze met hers, which she supposed was a point in his favor, though she wasn't feeling particularly charitable at the moment. "He said he'd wait for you in the library."

She didn't look at her brother again. She looked at the polished cherry desk, instead, and missed their father with a rush that nearly left her lightheaded. She would have done anything, in that moment, to see his craggy face again. To hear that rumbling voice of his, even if he'd only ordered her to do this exact thing, as he'd threatened to do many times over the past ten years.

Now everything was precarious and dangerous, Bart was gone, and they were the only Whitakers left. Chase and Mattie against the world. Even if Chase and Mattie's togetherness had been defined as more of a polite distance in the long years since their aristocratic mother's death— separate boarding schools in the English countryside, universities in different countries and adult lives on opposite sides of the Atlantic Ocean. But Mattie knew that all of that, too, was her fault.

She was the guilty party. She would accept her sentence, though perhaps not as gracefully as she should.

"Well," she said brightly as she turned toward the door. "I hope we'll see you at the wedding, Chase. I'll be the one dragged up the aisle in chains, possibly literally. It will be like sacrificing the local virgin to appease the ravenous dragon. I'll try not to scream too loudly while being burned alive, etcetera."

Chase sighed. "If I could change any of this, I would. You know that's true."

But he could have been talking about so many things, and Mattie knew that the truth was that she'd save her tears because they were useless. And maybe she'd save the family business, too, while she was at it. It was, truly, the least she could do.

Nicodemus Stathis might have been the bane of her existence for as long as she could remember, but she could handle him. She'd *been* handling him for years.

She could do this.

So she held her head up high—almost as if she believed that—and she marched off to assuage her guilt and do her duty, at last, however much it felt like she was walking straight toward her own doom.

* * *

The worst thing about Nicodemus Stathis was that he was gorgeous, Mattie thought moments later in that mix of unwanted desire and sheer, unreasonable panic that he always brought out in her. So gorgeous it was tempting to overlook all the rest of the things he was, like profoundly dangerous to her. So gorgeous it had a way of confusing the issue, tangling her up into knots and making her despair of herself.

So absurdly gorgeous, in fact, that it was nothing but unfair.

He stood by the French doors on the far side of the library, his strong back to the warmth and the light of the book-laden room, his attention somewhere out in all that gray and rattling wet. He stood quietly, but that did nothing to disguise the fact that he was the most ruthless, wholly relentless man she'd ever known. It was obvious at a glance. The thick, jet-black hair, the graceful way he held his obviously dangerous form so still, the harsh beguilement of the mouth she could only see in the reflection of the glass. The menace in him that his smooth, sleek clothes couldn't begin to conceal. He didn't turn to look at her as she made her way toward him, but she knew perfectly well he knew she was there.

He'd have known the moment she descended the stairs in the great hall outside the library. He always knew. She'd often thought he was half cat. She didn't like to speculate about the other half, but she was fairly certain it, too, had fangs.

"I hope you're not gloating, Nicodemus," she said briskly, because she thought simply waiting for him to turn around and fix those unholy dark eyes of his on her might make her dizzy—and she felt vulnerable enough as it was. She thought she could smell the smug male satisfaction heavy in the air, choking the oxygen from the room as surely as if one of the fireplaces had backed up. It put her teeth on edge. "It's so unattractive."

"At this point the hole you have dug for yourself rivals a swimming pool or two," Nicodemus replied, in that voice of his that reverberated in her the way it always had, low and dangerous with that hint of his Greek childhood still clinging to his words and wrapping tight around the center of her. "But by all means, Mattie. Keep digging."

"Here I am," she said brightly. "Sacrificial lamb to the slaughter, as ordered. What a happy day this must be for you."

Nicodemus turned then. Slowly, so slowly, like that might take the edge off the swift, hard *punch* of seeing him full on. It didn't, of course. Nothing ever did. Mattie ordered herself to breathe—and not to keel over. He was as absurdly gorgeous as ever, damn him. No disfiguring accidents had turned him into a troll since she'd seen him at her father's funeral.

He was as smoothly muscled as he'd been when he was in his twenties and honed to steel-like perfection by the construction work he'd somehow catapulted into a multi-million-dollar corporation by the time he was twenty-six. The fine, hard lines of his face were nearly elegant while his corded strength was as apparent in the line of his pugilistic jaw as in that impossibly chiseled chest of his that he'd concealed very poorly today behind a tight, black, obviously wildly expensive T-shirt that made no concession whatsoever to the weather. He was too elemental. He'd always made the hair at the back of her neck stand on end, her nipples pull painfully taut and her stomach draw tight, and today was no different.

Today was worse. And on top of that, Nicodemus was smiling.

I am lost already, she thought.

Nicodemus was a sheer, high, dizzying cliff and she'd spent ten years fighting hard to keep from toppling off. Because she still had no idea what might become of her if she fell.

"You really are gloating," she said, folding her arms over her chest and frowning at him. It was more of a smirk than a smile, she thought as she eyed him warily, and that too-bright gleam of a warmth like honey in his dark coffee gaze. "I don't know why that surprises me, coming from you."

"I'm not sure that *gloating* is the word I'd choose."

He was lethal, pure and simple, and his dark gaze was too intent. It took everything she had to keep from turning and bolting for the door. *This day was always coming,* she told herself harshly. *Accept it, because you can't escape it.*

Though she'd tried. God, but she'd tried.

"The first time I asked you to marry me you were how old?" he asked, his voice almost warm, as if he was sharing a fond reminiscence instead of their long, tortured history. "Twenty?"

"I was eighteen," Mattie said crisply. She didn't move as he roamed toward her. But she wanted to. She wanted to bolt for her childhood bedroom on the second floor and lock herself inside. She made herself lock her gaze to his, instead. "It was my debutante ball and you were ruining it."

Nicodemus's mocking little smile deepened, and Mattie fought not to flush with the helpless reaction he'd always caused in her. But she could still remember that single waltz her father had insisted she dance with him that night. Pressed up against his big body, much too close to his fierce, demanding gaze, and that mouth of his that had made her nothing but…nervous. And needy.

It still did. Damn him.

"Marry me," he'd said instead of a greeting, almost as if he'd meant to let out some kind of curse, instead.

"I'm sorry," she'd said, holding Nicodemus's dark, dark eyes as if they hadn't bitten deep into her, making her chest feel tight. She'd been a brash girl when she'd wanted to be, back then, forever attempting to get her father's attention, but her voice had been small. He had terrified her. Or maybe that wasn't terror, that overwhelming thing that had swamped her, fierce and instantaneous, but she hadn't known what else to call it. "I don't want to marry you. Or anyone."

He'd laughed as if she'd delighted him. "You will."

"I will never want to marry you," she'd told him stoutly, some kick of temper—or self-preservation—in her gut making her bold. She'd been eighteen. And it hadn't been lost on her that Nicodemus was not one of the silly boys she'd known then. He'd been very much a man.

He'd smiled at her as if he knew her and it had connected hard to her throat, her chest, her belly. Below. It had made her toes cramp up inside her ferociously high shoes.

"You'll marry me, princess." He'd seemed certain. Amused, even. "You can count on it."

He seemed even more amused now.

Nicodemus closed the distance between them almost lazily, but Mattie knew better. There was nothing lazy about him, ever. It was all misdirection and only the very foolish believed it.

"Have we ever determined what was wrong with you that you wanted to marry a teenager in the first place?" she asked him now, trying to divert whatever was coming. But he only stopped a scant few inches in front of her. "Couldn't find a woman your own age?"

Nicodemus didn't reply. He reached over and raked his fingers through the long, dark hair she decided instantly she needed to cut off, then wrapped it all around his hand, like he was putting her on a leash.

Then he gave it a tug. Not a gentle one. And she felt it deep between her legs, like a flare of dark pleasure.

Mattie wanted to smack his hand away, but that glinting thing in his dark gaze dared her to try, and she didn't want to give him the satisfaction when she was already tilting her head back at an angle that made a dangerous heat kindle to bright life inside her. Then build.

"That hurts," she told him, horrified that there was a hint of thickness in her throat when she spoke. That gave him ammunition. It couldn't be allowed.

"No, it doesn't." He sounded as certain as he had when she'd been eighteen, and it was infuriating. No matter if it made everything inside her tilt again and then tighten.

"I realize I've been bartered off like chattel," she bit out. "But it's still my hair. I know how it feels when someone pulls it."

His smile deepened. "You lie about everything, Mattie," he murmured, the slap of the words at jarring odds with the way he crooned them, leaning in close. "You break your word the way other women break their nails."

"I break those, too." It was like she couldn't stop herself. "If this has all been a bid for the perfect, polished trophy wife, Nicodemus, you're going to find me a grave disappointment."

He laughed softly, which wasn't remotely soothing, and tugged again, and it wasn't the first time Mattie regretted the fact that she was both tall and entirely too vain. Five feet ten inches in her bare feet, and the gorgeous black boots she was wearing today put her at a good six feet and then some. Which meant that when Nicodemus loomed over her and got too close to her, that mouth of his was *right there*. Not miles above her, which was safer.

Within easy reach—and she imagined he was deliberately standing this close to her because he wanted to remind her of that.

Like she—or her shuddering, jolting pulse she could feel in a variety of worrying places—would be likely to forget.

"I told you a long time ago that this day would come," Nicodemus said now.

"And I told you that I wasn't going to change my mind," she replied, though it cost her a little more than it should have to keep her chin up and her gaze steady on his. "I haven't. You can't really believe that this grotesque, medieval form of blackmail is the same as me surrendering to you, can you?"

"What do I care how you come to me?" he replied in that low, amused voice of his that kicked up brushfires inside her as it worked its way through her and made her feel a delicious sort of weak. "You mistake me for a good man, Mattie. I'm merely a determined one."

And despite herself, Mattie remembered a long, formal dinner in Manhattan's Museum of Natural History for some charity or another and her father's insistence that she sit with Nicodemus, who, he'd informed her when she'd balked, was like another son to him. *A far-better-behaved one,* he'd added. Mattie had been all of twenty-two—and infuriated.

"I'm not trying to change your mind, princess," Nicodemus had told her in a voice pitched for her ears alone, at odds with the way he'd spoken to others that night— mighty and sure, bold and harsh. He'd shifted in his seat and pinned her to hers with that knowing dark glare of his she'd come to know far too well. "We both know how this will end. Your father will indulge you to a certain point, but then reality will assert itself. And the longer you

make me wait, the more I'll have to take it out of your rebellious little hide when you're where you belong. In my
bed. Under my…" He'd paused, his dark eyes had glittered,
and she'd felt it as if he'd licked the soft skin of her belly.
Like a kind of glorious, transformative pain. His lips had
crooked. "Roof."

"What an inviting fantasy," Mattie had retorted, aware
he hadn't meant to say *roof* at all. "I can't imagine what's
keeping me from leaping at the opportunity to experience
that great joy."

"Suit yourself," he'd replied. He'd shrugged, but she'd
been far too aware that every inch of him was hewn of
steel, that he was himself a deadly weapon. She'd felt the
power he wore so easily like a thick, hot hand at her throat.
Worse, she'd been aware of that part of her that craved it.
Him. *More.* "I have a very long memory, Mattie, and a
very creative approach to retribution. Consider yourself
forewarned."

"Be still my beating heart," she'd snipped at him, and
then had tried her best to ignore him.

It hadn't worked then. It didn't work now.

"Will we reminisce all day?" she asked, injecting a note
of boredom into her voice that she dearly wished she felt
while he continued to hold her immobile. "Or do you have
a plan? I'm unfamiliar with the ins and outs of blackmail,
you see. You'll have to show me how it's done."

"You're free to refuse me yet again."

"And lose my father's company in the process."

"All choices have consequences, princess." He
shrugged, much the same way he had at that benefit dinner. "Your father would have been the first to tell you that."

That he was right only infuriated her more.

"My father was misguided enough to consider you like
a son to him," Mattie said, and there was no keeping the

emotion at bay then. It clogged her throat, made her eyes heat. But she didn't care if he saw this, she told herself. *This* wasn't the emotion that would destroy her. "He adored you. He thought more highly of you than he did of Chase, at times." She paused, as much to catch her breath and keep from crying as for effect. "And look how you've chosen to repay him."

She'd expected that to be a blow to him, but Nicodemus only laughed again then dropped his hand from her hair, and it took everything Mattie had not to rub the spot where he'd touched her. The worst part was, she didn't know if she wanted to wipe away his touch or hold it in. She never had. He canted his head to one side as he studied her face and then laughed some more.

"Your father thought I should have dragged you off by your hair years ago," he said with such lazy certainty that Mattie flushed with the unpleasant understanding that he was telling the truth. That Nicodemus and her father had discussed her like that. "Especially during what he liked to call your 'unfortunate' period."

She flushed even darker, and hated that it hurt. And she suddenly had no trouble at all imagining her father discussing her regrettable, motherless and rudderless early twenties with Nicodemus, no matter how much it scraped at her and felt like a betrayal.

"I did the best I could," she bit out, and she broke then, because that was scraping a bit too close to truths she didn't dare voice, and that terrible guilt that lay beneath everything. She stepped back and would have put even more distance between them, but Nicodemus's hand shot out and wrapped around her upper arm, stopping her that easily.

She refused to think about the impossible strength in that hand, much less its dark heat, no matter that it blasted into her through the soft, black cashmere knit of her dress.

She wouldn't think about it and she wouldn't react to it. *She wouldn't.*

"You know very well that you did not do anything remotely like your best," he said evenly, with only the faintest hint of old tempers and half-remembered harsh words in his voice. "You made it your business to shame your father. I would say you shamed your family name, but we both know your brother had that well in hand. How a great man like your father managed to raise two such useless, ungrateful, overly entitled children remains one of life's greatest mysteries."

Chase was right. Her father might have agreed with Nicodemus while he'd lived, but Mattie couldn't let herself live down to those low expectations any longer. She could smell the leather again, feel the heat of the South African sun. Then the screech—

"Almost everyone is useless, ungrateful and overly entitled in their early twenties," she told him, forcing herself to face him, to hold that judgmental gaze of his, and not try to jerk out of his hold. She suspected he wouldn't let go, and then what? "The trick is not *remaining* any of those things."

"Some of us had far more serious things to do in our early twenties, Mattie. Like survive."

So pompous. So full of himself. But better that than he know anything real or true about her. That was the only way she was going to make it through this.

"Yes, Nicodemus," she said with an exaggerated sweetness he couldn't mistake for anything but sarcasm. "You're a self-made man, as you're the first to point out at every opportunity. Alas, we can't all be you."

His fingers flexed against her arm and she hated the arrow of fire that shot from that faintest contact straight into her sex. She hated that her body had never cared how dangerous this man was, no matter how panicked her brain might be.

He'd proposed again when she'd been twenty-four.

Mattie had been dancing for hours in a dress that was really more of a wicked suggestion with a few cleverly placed straps, a cheeky selection for a night out in London. Then she'd walked outside the club to find *him* waiting there at the private, paparazzi-free back entrance, leaning up against a muscular little sports car parked illegally in the alley with his arms folded over his powerful chest.

For a moment, Nicodemus had only stared at her, his mouth a sardonic curve and his dark, honeyed gaze alight with a fire that did not bode well for her.

But Mattie hadn't been a teenager anymore, so she'd dug out a cigarette and lit it as if his presence didn't bother her at all. Then she'd blown out a stream of smoke into the cool night air, like it was a defensive weapon she could use against him.

"Why bother with those pointless scraps of fabric at all?" he'd asked her, his voice a scrape against the night and a scrape straight down the middle of her, as if his words had their own claws. "Why not simply walk around naked?"

"It's cute that you think it's your business what I wear," she'd said with deliberate nonchalance. As if he'd bored her. She'd wished, not for the first time, that he had.

Nicodemus's gaze had slammed into her then, making her feel hollow. Dizzy. As drunk and as dangerously out of control as she'd been trying to remain during these blurry, pointless, post-collegiate years. It had reminded her who and what he was. Harshly.

"Oh," he'd said dangerously. "It's my business, Mattie. It's all my business. All the men you let touch you. All the nights you flaunt that body of yours for the world to see.

The courtesan's ring in your belly you show off every time you let them photograph you in various states of undress. That tattoo I warned you not to put on your body. Those filthy cigarettes you use to pollute yourself. Believe me, it's my business."

He'd straightened from his obnoxiously hot car while he spoke, and then he'd stood over her, one of the few men she knew who was taller than she was despite her dramatic heels, and she'd told herself she hated the way he made her feel—that shivery, panicky, out of control fire that had burned through her when his dark eyes had fixed on her.

He could take everything, she'd thought then. He could take all of her and she'd be lost, and then what happened when he discovered the truth? What happened when this fire was gone and there was nothing between them but the awful truth of what she'd made happen?

"If you were as smart as you pretend to be, you might realize that I don't care what you want or what you think," she'd told him while her heart had slowed then beat harder. Much harder. "Because I don't. You should find someone who does. I'm sure there's a website for compliant little girls looking for big, bad billionaires to obey. You could be playing lord and master of your own private castle in a week, tops."

His lips had quirked, which on any other man might have meant laughter, but it was Nicodemus, with those stern, dark eyes that had drilled into her with all of his disturbingly fierce patience. It had disrupted her breathing.

"Marry me, Mattie. Don't make this even worse on yourself than it already is."

"Why?" she'd asked, almost helplessly.

"Because I want you," he'd said, sounding very nearly grim, as if it was an imposition, that wanting. A trial for him. "And I always get what I want."

"I'd rather swallow my own tongue," she'd replied, a wave of a kind of despair swelling in her, because she knew better than to consider the things *she* wanted. What was the point, when she couldn't have any of them? "I'd rather impale myself on a—"

"You're a very foolish girl." He'd shaken his head, muttering something dark in Greek. "But you're mine."

Then he'd jerked her toward him with one hand on her shoulder, knocked the cigarette from her fingers with the other and slammed his mouth to hers.

And all of that dark wonder had simply *burst* within her. Hunger and heat. That damned harsh mouth of his like a kind of miracle against hers. Claiming her. Branding her.

Shaking her to her core.

But she'd kissed him back, despite everything. She'd tasted him until she'd thought she really was as drunk as she sometimes acted. She'd fallen apart in his arms as if she'd been waiting her whole life for him to taste her. As if she'd always known it would be like that.

On some level, she had.

Fire. Panic. An instant and impossible addiction that had already gnawed at her, even while he'd still been taking his lazy, devastating fill of her mouth, as lethal and sure in the way he'd kissed her as in everything else.

"I told you," he'd growled into her mouth when she'd been limp and useless against him. "You're mine. You always have been. You always will be. How long do you plan to draw this out?"

Mattie had stared at him, unable to speak with all of those dark and wondrous things moving in her, and he'd smiled then, as close to tender as she'd ever seen him. It had transformed his dark face. It had made him something far more dangerous than simply gorgeous.

So she'd run in the opposite direction.

"Play your games, princess," he'd said, harsh and amused as she'd fled from him. *Certain,* the way he always was. "When you come to me, I will make you crawl."

She'd believed him.

"No," he said, yanking her back into the dangerous here and now. His hand was on her arm, and that heat was stampeding through her and this time, there was no hope of escape. "We can't all be me. But you can certainly learn how to please me, Mattie. And if I were you, I'd learn it fast."

It was another threat. Or more of a promise, she supposed. Because despite everything, despite how long and how far she'd run from this man, he'd won. The way he'd always told her he would.

"I've never really been a quick learner," she told him with a kind of manic cheerfulness, because she couldn't let herself think about what *pleasing him* might entail. God help her, but she didn't dare. "Oops. One more disappointment for you to swallow, I'm afraid."

CHAPTER TWO

HE'D WON.

That was what mattered, Nicodemus told himself as he looked down into the lovely, rebellious face of this woman who had defied him and haunted him across the years, and somehow willed himself not to put her over his knee. Or under him right here on the library floor.

He took a breath, the way he would if this was as simple as the business deal he was pretending it was. Then another, and still she watched him like he was an animal, and she was half-afraid she might pick up a few fleas if she stood too close.

Nicodemus couldn't understand why he didn't feel jubilant. Wildly triumphant. Instead of this same dark fury that always beat in him when she looked at him like this, so recklessly defiant when the fact he would win could never have been in any doubt.

He made himself let go of her, though it was hard. Too hard, when everything inside him beat like a tight, taut drum and he wanted nothing more than to bury himself in her, at last. To ride out his victory until she screamed his name the way he'd always known she would, to taste her and learn her and take her, over and over, until this vicious hunger was sated.

Because he was certain it would be sated once he had her. It had to be.

But that would come later.

"Sit," he ordered her, jerking his chin in the direction of two deep, dark brown leather armchairs before the nearest fireplace. "I'll tell you how this will work."

"That doesn't sound like a very promising start to the marriage you've been threatening me with for years," she said in her usual flippant, disrespectful way that he really shouldn't find as amusing as he did. Like it was foreplay. "In fact, if you ask me, it sounds like the kind of marriage that will lead to a very big, very public divorce in approximately eighteen months, or as soon as I can escape and file."

"You won't escape," he said, nodding toward the chairs again, and less politely. "Though you're welcome to try. I'd be happy to chase you down and haul you back."

He was rewarded with that dark blue glare of hers that had been making him ache with a driving need for almost as long as he'd known her. He smiled and was rewarded with the faintest hint of a shiver that she tried to hide.

She settled herself in the far chair with that wholly unearned grace of hers that he'd found nothing short of marvelous since the day they'd met. Mattie Whitaker had never suffered through any awkward phase as far as Nicodemus could tell. She'd been a gleaming bright beacon at sixteen, with her half-American, half-posh-British accent she'd wielded like a sword, even then. At eighteen, she'd been magnificent, pure and simple. From her glossy blue-black hair to her rich, dark blue eyes, to that wide mouth that should have been outlawed. She'd had poise and elegance far beyond her years, a consequence, he'd decided long ago, of having had to play hostess for her father after her mother had died when she was only eight.

He'd walked into that silly ball, that leftover nod to some gilded-age American fantasy he couldn't begin to understand, and had been struck dumb. Like she'd been a lightning bolt instead of what she was, what he knew she was: one more pretty little rich girl in a sparkling dress.

But God help him, it was *how* she'd sparkled.

She'd been so careless—thoughtless and spoiled as only wealthy heiresses could be. He'd suffered through that once already back in Greece, with self-centered, deceitful Arista, who'd nearly taken him to his knees and to the cleaners when he'd been twenty-two and a trusting, stupid fool. He'd vowed he'd never trust so easily nor be so deeply foolish again.

But there was something about Mattie that had drawn him in despite that. He'd watched her careen through all her blessings as if she hardly noticed them. He'd studied the way she'd shrugged off her expensive schools and the featherweight jobs she'd taken afterward, in publishing companies or art galleries or the like that paid so little only heiresses could afford to work at them. Or only occasionally work at them, in her case.

Nicodemus watched her now as she leveled that frank gaze of hers at him, her dark eyes serious, though they were the precise color of after-dinner chocolates with that intriguing shimmer of darker blue. She could be flighty and reckless and sometimes attention-seeking, but she was also intelligent. He'd long suspected she liked to pretend otherwise, for her own murky reasons. Another mystery he looked forward to solving.

"I think it's time you told me what this is really about," she said, and she reminded him of her father then, with that matter-of-fact tone and her direct gaze. Nicodemus pulled in a breath. "I mean it," she said as if that had been an argument. "I don't believe for one second that there aren't parades of more suitable heiresses if an heiress is what you want. Prettier ones, if that's your thing. Richer ones, certainly. Far more notorious ones and one or two who might as well have spent their lives in a convent. You've always struck me as being particularly annoying—" and there was the faintest hint of that dent beside her mouth that he knew was a dimple, that he'd spent many a lazy hour longing to taste "—but there's no denying the fact that you'd be a nice catch. You're disgustingly wealthy. You're very powerful. You're not exactly Quasimodo."

"What a resounding recommendation," he said, torn between laughter and incredulity that she dared speak to him the way she did. She always had. Only Mattie, in all the world. Maybe that was why she haunted him. "Who *wouldn't* marry me?"

She eyed him for a moment that bordered on the uncomfortable. "Why me?"

And what could he tell her? That he'd been hit by something he still didn't understand? He didn't believe that himself. Nicodemus got what he wanted, no matter what it took. It was how he'd clawed his way to where he was today. It was how he'd first claimed Arista, then rid himself of her and her sharp claws. It was how he'd survived learning the truth about his stern, rigidly moralistic father and what his exposing that truth had done to his mother. It was what he did. Why should this woman be any different? He told himself that was all there was to it.

He'd been telling himself that for years.

He forced a smile. "I like you. That's why."

"If you do," she said drily, "then I suspect you might be mentally ill."

"Perhaps I am." He shrugged. "Does that make me less of a catch? A little more Quasimodo than you thought?"

He'd meant to simply outline what would happen from

here now that she'd finally come to him. Lay down the law with the supreme pleasure of knowing that this time, she'd do as she was told. Because this time, she had to do it.

And he hadn't lied to her. He never lied. He didn't care how she came to him. Angry or on her knees, whatever worked. Nicodemus didn't waste much time worrying about the cost of Pyrrhic victories. It was the victory itself that mattered.

It was the only thing that mattered.

"It makes you much more likely to find yourself committed to a mental institution by your devoted wife one day," Mattie was saying. She smiled that fake smile of hers. "Depending on the fine print of our prenuptial agreement, of course."

She was eyeing him with a certain mild arrogance, as if she was the one with all the power here. When he could tell—from the way she sat with her legs crossed tight and her arms over her middle, from the telltale fluttering of her pulse at her neck and that faint flush high on her cheeks—that she knew she was on precarious ground.

But then, so many things about this woman were an act. Smoke and mirrors. And he vowed he would find the truth beneath it all no matter how long it took him. He would take her apart and put her back together the way he wanted her.

He'd been waiting for this—for her—for years.

"We marry in two weeks," he said, watching her face as he said it. Something flashed through her dark eyes, but then he saw nothing but that polite mask of hers that he'd always known better than to believe. "It will be a very small ceremony in Greece. You, me, a priest and a photographer. We will honeymoon for two weeks at my villa there. Then we will return to Manhattan, where your brother and I will finally merge our companies, as was the wish of both your father and me." He smiled and let her see the edge in it. "See? Simple. Hardly worth all this commotion for so many years."

"And what is my part of this?" she asked as if she couldn't care less either way.

"During the wedding I expect you to obediently recite your vows," he said silkily. "Perhaps even with a touch of enthusiasm. During the honeymoon? I have a few ideas. And ten years of a very vivid imagination to bring to life, at last."

There was no denying the flush that moved over her face then, or that look of something like panic that she blinked away in an instant. Not touching her then very nearly hurt—though wanting Mattie was second nature to him now. What was waiting a little bit longer after a decade?

Besides, he suspected that his feigned laziness drove her crazy, and he wanted any weapon he could find with this woman he still couldn't read. Not the way he wanted to read her.

"I meant when we return in all our marital splendor to New York City," she said, and it occurred to him to wonder if it was difficult for her to render her voice so loftily indifferent. If it was a skill she'd acquired once and could put on whenever she liked or if she had to work at it every time. "I have my own apartment there. A life, a job. Of course, I'm happy to live separately—"

"I'm not."

She blinked. Then smiled. "I doubt very much you'd enjoy moving into my tiny little two-bedroom. It's very girlie and I don't think you'd look good in all that pink."

She reached into one of the pockets he hadn't realized she had in that dress of hers to pull out a cigarette and a lighter, then lit the cigarette, watching him blandly as she blew out a stream of smoke.

"Enjoy that cigarette, Mattie," he told her mildly. "It will be your last."

She let out another stream of smoke. "Will it?"

"I have very specific ideas about how my wife will behave," he said, and smiled when that coolly unbothered front of hers slipped slightly. "That she will live in my house and that she will not work, if that's what you call it, at that laughable excuse for a public relations firm in all those see-through clothes."

"I see. This will be a medieval marriage, to go along with the Stone Age courtship rituals we've been enjoying thus far. What a thrill."

He ignored her. "I have certain expectations regarding her behavior. Her style of dress, her comportment. The lack of cigarettes sticking from her mouth, making her smell and taste like an ashtray." He shrugged. "The usual."

She held the cigarette in one hand, not looking the least bit worried, though that faint tremor in the hand that held that cigarette told a different story, and stared at him. "I understand that this is all a big chess game to you, Nicodemus, with me playing the role of the most convenient pawn—"

"More the queen than a pawn. Unpredictable and hard to pin down, but once that's sorted, the game is over." He smiled when she frowned.

"I hate chess."

"Then perhaps you should choose a better metaphor."

"I'm a *person*," she told him, and he thought that was temper that made each word like a blade. Her dark eyes blazed with heat. And fear. And yet her voice was cool, and he wanted her with that desperate edge that made him loathe himself. The wanting was fine. The desperation was not. He'd thought he'd outgrown that kind of thing when he'd shaken Arista off. "And this is not, despite all appearances to the contrary, the twelfth century—"

"Then why are you marrying me?" he asked, making no attempt to keep that lash from his voice. "You don't have to do it, as you've pointed out. There's no gun to your head."

"A merger between our two companies will strengthen both, and bolster Chase's position as CEO," she replied after a moment, something shrewd and sad in her gaze. "It changes the conversation he's been having with the board and the shareholders, anyway. And of course, you'd become the COO, and you've proved you're very good at operating companies and making piles of money. But you don't have to marry me to make that happen."

"I don't." He shrugged. "I'm not the one crafting objections to this marriage and looking for explanations. You are."

"But you won't hold up your end of your business arrangement with Chase if I don't agree to do this." Her eyes darkened. "I want to be a hundred percent certain we're both clear about who's pressuring who in this."

"I'm perfectly clear about it." And practically cheerful, as he smiled at her obvious flash of temper. "But this is all more of these games you like to play, Mattie. We both know you're going to marry me. You've known it since we met."

She didn't like that. He could see it on her face, stamped across those lovely cheeks of hers. But it didn't change that simple truth. Nothing ever had.

"I haven't done it yet," she pointed out quietly. "I'm not sure I'd get carried away counting my chickens if I were you."

He laughed then. "I'm going to enjoy teaching you the

appropriate way to respond to your husband, Mattie. I really am." He leaned forward, took that nasty cigarette from her and tossed it into the fire without looking away from her. "I'm marrying you because I want you. I always have. More than that, I want to merge my company with your father's, and I want the link between us to be strong. I want to be part of the family, so there can never be any question about who deserves a seat at the table. That means marriage. Babies. A very long life together, because I don't believe in separations or divorce. Or secrets."

Especially the secrets, he thought, shoving those terrible old memories aside. The lies and the devastation they'd wrought.

Mattie held his gaze for a long moment, something slick and glazed in hers. The only sound was the storm outside, harsh against the windows, and the crackle of the fire. He fancied he could hear her breath below that, too fast and uneven, betraying her—but he doubted she'd let that show and assumed it was only in his head. More wishful thinking, and he should know better.

"What you mean is, I'm a pawn," she said evenly. "You can say it, Nicodemus. It's not as if I don't know it already."

"And you're marrying me because…?" His lips curved when she only glared at him. "You enjoy playing the martyr? You've always wanted to barter yourself? You have a deep desire to prostrate yourself before the ambitions of others?"

"Family duty," she said primly. Piously. "I don't expect you to understand that."

"Of course not," he said, and he wasn't laughing then. "Because everything I have I tore from the world with my own two hands. My father never believed I would amount to anything." *And he did his best to see that I wouldn't,* Nicodemus thought grimly, those same old lies like painful scars deep inside him. "My mother cleaned houses and worked in the factories. The only thing they gave me was life. The rest I worked for."

And held on to, despite the best effort of grasping materialistic little parasites like Arista.

"No one ever said you weren't an impressive man, Nicodemus," Mattie said to him. "But what does it have to do with anything? You've been chasing me for so long, I think you don't even know why you started."

"No, Mattie," he said gently. Too gently, maybe. He thought that might have been the trouble from the start. He'd treated her like she was made of glass, and she'd done nothing but cut him with her own sharp edges. It was time he remembered that.

It was time he took control of this.

Her cheeks were flushed and her mouth was so close, and he'd waited *so long*. He could see the panic in her eyes as she looked back at him, the rise and fall of her perfect breasts against that unfathomably soft dress she wore. He couldn't stop himself from reaching over and taking her hot cheek in his hand, holding her there and tracing her lips with a single restless movement of his thumb.

He watched her redden, felt himself tighten at once in reaction, and it was like that lightning all over again. A bolt, brilliant and true, burning him alive where he sat.

It had damned them from the start. It had made all of this inevitable.

And made it worth it. He'd been sure of that, too.

"I've always known why," Nicodemus told her, and it was as close to the truth as he could get. The rest hung around them in all that white-hot heat, wrapping them both in the same wild hunger. He could see it in her face, in that bright blue sheen in her dark eyes. He felt it in his own flesh. He smiled. "It's you who have been confused. But you won't be for very much longer."

They were high over the Atlantic Ocean with nothing but darkness on all sides before Mattie gave up on her internal battle and the magazine she hadn't read a single word of no matter how fiercely she'd scowled at it. She finally stopped pretending and looked down the creamy, gold-edged interior of the private jet to where Nicodemus sat, looking for all the world like the wholly unconcerned king of his very own castle.

He was sprawled out at the table, sheaves of papers spread out before him and his laptop at his elbow, looking studious and masculine and very much like the deeply clever, world-renowned multimillionaire she was grudgingly aware he was. His dark hair looked tousled, like he'd been running his hands through it, and despite herself, her breath caught.

And he either felt her gaze on him or he heard that telling little catch, because his dark eyes snapped to hers at once.

"Has the silent treatment ended, then?" he asked, dry and amused and so very, very patronizing. "And here I'd got used to the quiet."

Mattie had been doing such a good job of ignoring him up until then. He'd left her in her father's house that day with no more than an enigmatic smile, and that had been that. He'd simply…let her stew for the next week and a half with no further threat or argument or input from him.

Mattie had considered running away, naturally. She'd dreamed it at night. She'd gone so far as to plot it all out. One day she'd even booked a plane ticket to Dunedin, New Zealand, tucked away on the bottom of the planet, the farthest place she could find on the map. But despite her wildest fantasies and several more detailed internet searches involving far-off mountain ranges and remote deserts, when Nicodemus had appeared at her door to whisk her off to Greece earlier this evening, Mattie had been there.

Waiting for him, as promised, like a good little arranged bride. Like the daughter she'd never been while her father was alive, as she'd been too busy veering between acting out or acting perfect to get his attention. She'd even packed.

Nicodemus had shouldered his way into her airy, comfortable apartment, walking in that lethally confident way of his that had made a shiver whisper down the length of her spine. She'd assured herself it was anxiety and not something far more feminine and appreciative. Her apartment was in a prewar building on Manhattan's Upper West Side, replete with lovely old moldings, scrupulously maintained hardwood floors and soaring ceilings that made the place seem twice its actual size. And yet Nicodemus made it feel like a closet-size studio simply by standing in it. Like a tiny, claustrophobic box. He was too *alive. Too much.* He'd nodded at her bags, his people had whisked them away and then he was simply…standing there in a very small, enclosed space. *Her* space.

Like it was already his. Like she was.

Mattie had refused to entertain that crazy little part of her that had melted at the notion. It would all be so much easier if he was less brutally gorgeous, she'd thought furiously. He wore a dark, fine sweater that did marvelous things for his already too perfect torso and an open wool coat cut to add warmth and elegance, not bulk. And his dark trousers looked both rugged and luxurious at once. He was a remarkably attractive man. There was no getting around it. She'd hated the fact she couldn't ignore that truth. Even when she'd known perfectly well he'd been there, shrinking down her living room and making her skin feel two sizes too tight, for the singular purpose of towing her off to do his bidding.

The fact that she'd be married to him in a handful of days had felt impossible. *Ludicrous.* And every time she met his too-knowing gaze, she felt like he'd lit her on fire and tossed her headfirst into a vat of gasoline.

"None of this is pink or even particularly girlie," he'd said, his harsh mouth curved with that sardonic amusement that had made her feel much too jittery. She'd felt stretched thin between a reckless hunger and a driving panic already, and she'd been back in his clutches all of five minutes. His dark eyes had held hers, hard and mocking at once. "You really do lie about everything, don't you?"

"Are you really starting out our glorious Two Weeks of Love by calling me a liar?" she'd asked, and she didn't care how brittle she sounded. How cold and obvious. She'd let out a laugh that hadn't sounded any better. "That bodes well."

"I suppose it must be me," he'd said quietly, eyeing her in a way that had made her feel flushed and flustered while something deep in her gut knotted into a red-hot fist. "If I stood in the pouring rain you'd tell me the sky was the brightest blue you'd ever seen. I inspire this in people, apparently. Especially women. I think you should worry about what will happen, Mattie, when I figure out how to read the truth no matter what lies you choose to tell me. Because I will."

"I've worried about very little else since that delightful meeting at my father's house," she assured him.

"Another lie."

"That was actually the truth. Amazing, I know."

And he'd reached over and taken hold of her chin like that was his right, the way her body had seemed to think it was as it had burst into all those hectic fireworks and roaring brushfires, nearly knocking her from her feet where she stood.

"That's not what you're worried about," Nicodemus had said, much too close and entirely too sure, as if he could taste that humming need in her that she'd wanted so badly to deny.

Mattie had decided right then and there that she needed to stop talking to him. It was too dangerous. Especially if it led him to put his hands on her.

She'd told herself she was relieved when he let her go again without pressing the issue, but it wasn't quite that simple. There were the aftershocks to consider—the rumbling, jagged tectonics that shifted and reshaped everything inside her no matter that she didn't want any of it.

But Mattie was nothing if not pointlessly stubborn. She'd maintained her silence all through the car ride out to the private airfield in the suburbs of Manhattan, through the boarding of the sleek Stathis company jet that waited there and their several hours of flight en route to what he'd called *my small, private island in the Aegean Sea.*

Because *of course* Nicodemus had *an island*, the better to make absolutely certain that Mattie was completely and utterly trapped with him, truly forced to marry him if she ever wanted to leave it again. That or hope she could swim for the mainland. Across the Aegean Sea. In October.

"That wasn't the silent treatment," she said now, stretching her legs out in front of her as if she felt as carefree and relaxed as he apparently did.

He shook his head in that way of his that reverberated inside her like another press of his strong fingers against her skin. "I don't understand why you bother to lie when you must have realized by now that I can see right through you."

"I merely ran out of things to say to you," Mattie said

loftily. "I imagine that will happen quite often. Yet one more sad consequence of a forced marriage like ours—a lifetime of boredom and silence while stuck together in our endless private hell."

His lips twitched. "It's not your silence I find hellish."

She nodded as if she'd expected that. "Resorting to insults. Quiet little threats. This is what happens when you blackmail someone into marrying you, Nicodemus, and we're not even married yet. I did try to warn you."

"There's no reason to resort to anything quite so unpleasant," he said silkily, leaning back in his chair. He tossed his pen down on the polished wood surface, and then the heat in his gaze made the narrow walls of the plane seem to contract in on her—or perhaps that was nothing more than the wild drumming of her pulse. "I'm sure we can find any number of things to do that don't require words."

Mattie rolled her eyes. "Veiled sexual threats aren't any less threatening simply because they're sexual," she said. "Quite the opposite, in fact."

"Is that why you're turning red?" he asked lazily. "Because you feel threatened?"

"Yes."

He shook his head again, slower this time. "Liar."

She reminded herself that just because he was right it didn't mean anything. He didn't *know* that he had this insane effect on her. He only *hoped* he did.

"I'm assuming you have some idea of how this works," she carried on, because now that she'd started poking at him, the idea of returning to that heavy silence was stifling. She was afraid it would crush her. "Now that you're in the process of isolating me from everything familiar, as most men like you do."

"Men like me," he said, and there was a dark current in

his voice that was either laughter or something far more treacherous, and she felt the uncertainty, the edginess, everywhere. "Are there many? And here I'd considered myself a special snowflake—almost an American, I'm so remarkably unique."

"It's a typical pattern," she assured him and smiled kindly. "Run of the mill, really."

"If you're attempting to shame me into releasing you," he said drily, "you have seriously misjudged your target."

"No one is *actually* shameless, Nicodemus," she said, and her voice softened somehow—lost that cool, mocking edge. She had no idea why. "No matter what they pretend."

"Perhaps not," he agreed, shifting slightly against his seat, though he never took that hot, hard gaze from hers. "But you don't know me well enough to even guess at the things that crawl in me and call my name in my darkest hours. You wouldn't recognize them if you did."

There wasn't a single reason that should take her breath away, or why her stomach should flip over, and so Mattie told herself it was a patch of turbulence, nothing more.

"You seem to want to make this a squalid little transaction," he said when she didn't throw something back at him, and she couldn't read the expression on his face then. He lounged back in his chair, propping his head up with one hand, and looked at her. Just *looked* at her. As if her layers of clothes and even her skin were no barrier whatsoever. As if he could see straight through to what lay beneath. "As painful and as horrid as possible."

"It is what it is," she said. "I have no idea how these barbaric arrangements work. Will you check my teeth like I'm a horse? Kick my tires like I'm a used car you bought off the internet?"

Something sharp and hot, a little too much like satisfaction, flared in the honeyed depths of his dark gaze, and his harsh mouth pulled into a very dangerous curve.

"If you insist," he said, lazy and low.

Mattie went still. She felt her eyes widen and could see from that gleam in his gaze that he saw it.

For God's sake! the hysterical part of her—currently occupying almost every part of her save her big mouth—shrieked. *What is the matter with you? Don't* challenge *him! Stop this right now before it gets out of hand!*

"Oh, I'm sorry," he practically purred, reading her much too easily. Again. "Was that yet another example of your mouth getting you into trouble? It's either lying to me or provoking me, I notice. It does make me wonder what it would be like to put it to better use."

He was right, Mattie realized. If he was truly the man she'd been treating him like he was, she'd be significantly more respectful and careful around him, wouldn't she? The truth was, she knew he wasn't. She couldn't believe that he'd really do this. She *didn't* believe it, even though she was currently suspended somewhere over the ocean on her way to Greece.

Granted, he was doing an excellent job of acting like a scary, overwhelming, my-way-or-the-highway barbarian, but she'd known this man for years. More important, her father had genuinely liked him. Had even considered him a good match for his only daughter. She simply couldn't make herself believe that Nicodemus would honestly *force* her to marry him.

Much less any of the other things he wasn't *quite* threatening to do, that were pressing into her so hard now that she was certain they'd leave marks.

"I wasn't kidding," she said, and she stood up then, uncoiling herself to stand there in the aisle before him. She opened up her arms and spread them wide, as theatrically as possible. "I'm sure the third richest man in Greece—"

"That's rather less of a salutation than it might have been once," he pointed out, that cool amusement in his gaze. "I can't tell if you mean it as compliment or condemnation."

"—doesn't buy one of those crotch-rocket motorcycles of his without making sure it lives up to each and every one of his exacting standards," Mattie continued as if he hadn't interjected anything.

She'd seen him on a Ducati once, roaring up a winding country lane in France to a weekend party in a friend's chateau she never would have attended if she'd known he'd be there. She'd escaped shortly thereafter, but she'd never been able to get that image out of her head. A powerful man on such a sleek and dangerous machine, like lethal poetry etched against the backdrop of vineyards turning gold in the setting sun, as if they'd been doing it purely to celebrate him.

She glared at him and held her crucifixion position. "Well? Here I am."

Nicodemus's dark eyes glittered, and he didn't move, yet Mattie felt as if he'd leaped up and yanked her to him. She felt surrounded, smothered. And lit on fire.

He raised his shoulder in that profoundly Mediterranean way of his, then dropped it lazily.

"Go on, then," he said, his voice *this close* to bored, though his gaze burned through her, churning up too much heat and that dangerous hunger she'd been denying for years now. "Strip. Show me what I've chased across all these years and bought, at last."

CHAPTER THREE

MATTIE GAVE UP her charade of even, calm breaths. She stared at him—and he only smirked back at her.

Because he didn't think she'd do it, she realized. He thought he'd push her the way he had outside that club in London—until she broke and ran.

Not this time, Mattie thought icily. If he wanted to act like the kind of man who bought wives, she'd act like the kind of woman who could be bought.

She dropped her arms and shrugged out of the long red sweater jacket she'd been using as much like a blanket as a coat. She tossed it on the leather bench beside her, then kicked off her short boots.

Nicodemus said nothing.

Mattie pulled her cashmere V-neck up and over her head, aware as she did it that a fair swathe of her belly was exposed as she stretched her arms over her head. She thought she heard him mutter something, but when her head was free again he was still right where she'd left him, still watching her as if this was the safety demonstration on a commercial flight and about as entertaining.

So she peeled off her tight T-shirt, too, and refused to allow herself a single shiver of response when his gaze dropped to move over her breasts and the burgundy-colored bra she wore. She didn't move a muscle on the outside—

but her stomach pulled itself into a tight, hard little ball and she could hardly breathe around the fire of it. She stood there, so hot and so long she was sure her skin matched the bra, and still, he took his time returning his gaze to hers.

"Do you like the merchandise?" she asked coolly.

"How can I tell?" he asked in a similar tone. "It remains covered. Surely not an attack of modesty, Mattie? Not after that topless shot that so entranced your adoring public two summers ago?"

"There's nothing wrong with sunbathing topless on a yacht in the middle of an ocean," Mattie said, and only when she heard her own voice did she realize how defensive she sounded. "I thought I was alone. Am I supposed to live my life wrapped up in a shroud on the off chance there might be a helicopter above me?"

"Perhaps you could simply pay slightly more attention to how you display your body," Nicodemus suggested, with a hint of steel in his voice. "Particularly now that it's mine."

He watched her for a moment, and she felt too obvious, too exposed. He was right. It was silly. She'd worn dresses to banquets that covered less than what she was wearing right now. Why should this feel so much more intimate?

She decided she didn't particularly want to explore that line of thought.

But she'd started this. She'd push it all the way to the finish. She'd push *him*.

"Do you have any other awkward, pathologically possessive remarks to make?" she asked, nothing but brisk politeness in her tone. "Do you perhaps feel the urge to fire up your company logo and brand it into my skin?"

That curve of his harsh mouth. That bright, hot gleam in his dark eyes. That languid, offhanded way he lounged there, as if he was something other than the most physically powerful man she'd ever let this close to her.

She swallowed, hard. Betraying herself. Nicodemus smiled.

"I'll let you know," he said, and then he inclined his head in a regal sort of way that was as infuriating as it was strangely attractive, silently bidding her to continue.

Mattie despaired of herself. But she leaned over and pulled off her socks then stood again and shimmied out of her skinny black jeans, kicking them out of her way when she was done. And then she stood there. In nothing but her bra and panties.

And told herself—over and over again—that it was like a bathing suit. It was fine. It was *nothing*.

Nicodemus's gaze was so hot it hurt. But he still didn't move.

"I can't tell if this is modesty or a dramatic pause," he said after a moment, his voice insultingly bland. "But it bores me."

For the first time, a little trickle of fear dripped down the length of her spine, and it occurred to Mattie to wonder who was pushing who.... But she only lifted her chin up then reached behind her to unclip her bra. She pulled it from her body slowly, exposing one breast and then the other, and then she dropped it. He watched, a kind of fierce concentration stamped over his strong face. So she hooked her fingers in the sides of her panties and tugged them down to her knees, then let them fall the rest of the way to the floor so she could move them aside with her foot.

Then she was standing naked in front of Nicodemus Stathis, the bane of her existence, who was now her fiancé. Who would soon be her husband, if he had his way. Her mind shied away from all of that. The terms themselves. The reality.

And she was still completely and utterly naked.

Which was really not the best time to question the decision-making that had led her to this point—so Mattie held her head at a belligerent angle and waited, as if she was perfectly comfortable hanging around planes in the nude with infuriating men.

Nicodemus let out a low sound that wasn't quite a laugh, and then he stood up. Mattie's mouth went dry and for a stark, spinning second her mind blanked out.

He was too big for the plane—*for the world,* she thought wildly when she could think again, and certainly much bigger than he'd seemed when she'd had her clothes on—and he only took a single step closer then braced himself on the ceiling above them and left the rest of his lean, powerful body angled away from her. Looming and not looming at the same time.

It didn't make him any less dangerous. Mattie didn't feel remotely safe. But she didn't dare examine what she felt too closely.

He frowned down at her, and it occurred to her that she should have paid more attention to the things he'd said before. About how little she knew him when they both knew he'd studied her very closely indeed over the past decade. It put her at a distinct disadvantage.

That and the fact she was naked.

"Why are you standing there?" She only blinked at him in confusion, and he made a spinning motion with one long finger. "Turn, please."

She told herself he only wanted to humiliate her. To break her. And she was still holding out hope that he wouldn't take this as far as he could. That this was all some kind of extended practical joke. Or, if not a *joke,* precisely, that he wanted to teach her some kind of lesson for rebuffing him all these years. He'd back down. He had to back down.

But that meant she couldn't.

Mattie turned, and she took her time doing it. She even put her hips into it, so it was a little bit of a show—

Then she felt his hands on her. And froze.

It took her a moment to understand that it wasn't a random touch, or even a particularly sexual one. He was tracing the delicate tattoo that flowed over one hip and up her side to cradle the lower edge of her ribs.

"It's a phoenix," she blurted out, and hated that her voice was so quiet and so rough. Like this was getting to her—his too-warm hands on her skin, his terrifying and intoxicating closeness, her ill-conceived nudity.

"I know what it is," he said, his tone curt, and she couldn't see anything she recognized in his face when she turned the rest of the way around to face him. "What I don't know is how it applies to the charmed life you've always led."

Mattie had no intention of ever telling him. Or anyone.

"Nicodemus—" she started, but he shook his head.

And she had no idea why she fell silent. Why she obeyed him when everything inside her was a blistering, shattering scream.

"And that cursed belly ring," he muttered, still in that short, dark way, and she steeled herself when he reached over and tugged on the little silver ring, gently enough. So gently it shouldn't have seared through her the way it did, burning a path from her navel to the molten core of her. Making her *melt*.

She managed to keep herself from making any sound, but his lips twitched again and she was sure that somehow he knew, anyway.

He shifted closer, and her heart exploded, pounding at the wall of her chest like it might break free, and that was the least of her worries. She was too hot, too cold. Her breasts ached then *hurt* when he brought his hands up beneath them, spanning her waist, holding her. *Caging* her—

"Nicodemus," she started again, and she couldn't contain her panic or her need, or keep either from her voice. She hardly recognized herself.

"Is this what you wanted?" His voice was gruff and dark, shocking her with the force of it. "Next time, the little dance isn't necessary. You can simply ask."

And then he leaned in, as if she'd begged him to do it and he had all the time in the world, and took her mouth with his.

It was better than he remembered.

Much better.

Mattie tasted like smoke and heat, some kind of perfect whiskey that was all woman and only her, and Nicodemus felt knocked sideways. Drunk for the first time in more years than he could count.

He let go of the sweet indentation of her waist and sank his fingers deep into that glossy hair of hers, widening his stance so he could pull her off balance to sprawl across his chest. And they weren't in London this time. There were no bouncers nearby, no fear of exposure.

Nicodemus could finally take his time.

He could test this angle and then that one. He could taste her again and again, kissing her with a fury and a longing that took him over, making him wild and desperate and intoxicated with every drugging slide of his tongue against hers.

Mine, declared that primitive voice inside him, the way it had done so many years ago at that fateful ball. And ever since.

And she was perfect.

That spill of thick, beautiful, dark hair that fell around her shoulders and felt like raw silk against his palms. That rangy body of hers, so tall and taut, with her proud, rose-tipped breasts to the inviting swell of her hips. She made his mouth water. Even that damned tattoo he'd ordered her not to get stamped into her pretty skin suited her, as delicate and mysterious as she was, in a swirl of bright colors he longed to taste.

And that belly ring that made him think of long, hot nights and the sweet undulation of feminine hips.

He'd never wanted another woman like this. Not even Arista. He'd never *wanted* like this.

That sent a chill spiraling through him, and it was the only thing that penetrated the delirious, pounding need that threatened to take him over there and then. He pulled his mouth from hers then ran his hands down the silken length of the arms she'd wrapped around his neck, continuing down the perfect line of her spine to cup that sweet, delectable bottom in his palms. Her eyes were closed, those sooty lashes a distraction. Her lush mouth tempted him, full and slick from his. Her breasts pressed against him and he marveled, once again, at how right she felt in his arms. Not so short he had to stoop, not so slight he was afraid he might break her. *Perfect.*

Nicodemus thought he might die, then and there, if he didn't get inside her. If he didn't taste her. If he didn't *do something* about the thing that howled in him, fanged and clawed and desperate for more.

He ordered himself to set her aside, to hold off, to wait until he had every last bit of the power he was after, but Mattie shifted against him and made a small, needy sound in the back of her throat—

And he was only a man. He could only take so much.

He lifted her arms from around his neck and guided her toward the leather couch along one wall of the jet. He sat her down then knelt between her legs, shouldering her knees apart so he could see every part of her.

"Wait," she said, her eyes fluttering open then, sounding as breathless as she was flushed. "Are you—?"

"Hold on," he ordered her, bending down to her, inhaling the rich scent of her arousal, the sweetness of her skin.

"Nicodemus." But her voice was so insubstantial, a token protest at best when she was still open and arched before him, and he was so close. *Too close.* "I don't—"

"I do," he muttered, the way a religious man might utter a fervent prayer.

And then he simply worshipped her. He pulled her long and lovely legs over his shoulders, wrapped his hands around her hips and buried his face in her heat.

The way he'd longed to do for a thousand years. More.

She made the most beautiful noise he'd ever heard, something like a gasp and a scream at once, and Nicodemus growled against the slick, hot core of her. She tasted sweet and wild. Like honey. Like *his.* He could feel her quiver beneath his hands, and he licked his way into her, teasing her and tasting her, until he felt her hips begin that lush dance against his tongue.

"Oh, no," she moaned, but even as she said it, she raised her hips to meet his mouth. She threw her arms over her face, hiding right there in plain sight, and he was too lost in the exquisite pleasure of tasting her at last to do anything but let her.

And then she was crying out his name, tense and even more beautiful as she bucked against him. She sobbed out words he didn't understand, almost as if he was bringing her to this delectable edge against her will when he could taste her need—

Until she shattered. Into a million pieces the way he'd always dreamed she would, long and loud and calling out his name.

All mine, Nicodemus thought with a deep satisfaction

that felt like something else. Like a truth he didn't know how to name—so he didn't try.

Not here. Not yet.

Mattie hated herself.

It took her a long time to open up her eyes. When she did, she found she was curled up on the leather couch, her sweater jacket draped over her like a blanket and Nicodemus sitting beside her with his long legs taking up the whole of the aisle and an air of smug confidence she didn't have to look at his face to see. And he was turned, she found when she dared sneak a look, anyway, so that he could watch her with those stark, too-incisive, dark eyes of his that seemed to burn straight through her to all the places she most wanted to hide.

She pulled in one breath. Then another, just as shaky as the first. And she still didn't understand how she'd allowed this to happen. How had he *done* that? It was as if he'd used her own body against her—and in that moment, Mattie couldn't think of a single thing that frightened her more.

She shoved her hair back from her face with one hand, using the other to keep the sweater in place, which she didn't need that small gleam in his gaze to tell her was absurd, at this point.

Ruined, she thought then. She felt utterly ruined. Wrecked from within, like a stranger inside her own skin.

The silence stretched out, filling the jet, drowning out the sound of the engines, not comfortable in the least.

And beside her, Nicodemus radiated that heat and menace that made him who he was: the most dangerous man she'd ever met. She'd always known he was exactly that—and now he'd proved it. His dark eyes tracked her, and she was afraid to look too closely—afraid of what she'd see.

"Is this what it takes?" he asked in a quiet voice that

seemed to crack her foundations deep inside her. "This is what I must do to see behind all the masks you wear?"

She was terrified that he really could. She was terrified of what had happened here, full stop, especially because she could still *feel* his mouth against that most private part of her. She could still *feel* the aftershocks. The lush, impossible wave of joy and pleasure that had rent her in two. She shook her head—once, hard, as much to snap herself out of this fugue she was in as anything else—and found she was scowling at her lap.

"I doubt there will be a repeat of that unfortunate demonstration," she said, but her voice lacked its usual force even to her own ears. "Once was enough."

"Once," he said, and his voice, by contrast, was alive with fire and that sharp edge that sliced deep into her, "is by no means enough. That was only the beginning, Mattie."

"I said I'd marry you," she heard herself say, as if from some far-off distance. She didn't recognize that voice that came out of her mouth. Soft. Pleading. As if he'd licked her into a different person—and she was deeply afraid he really had. "That doesn't mean you can claim marital rights like some eighteenth century relic. I'm not sure you can even really call me your *wife*, since you're essentially purchasing the title."

"Look at me."

She didn't want to do that, and she couldn't understand, then, why she did it, anyway. She felt much too raw, like her heart was a throbbing thing that might rip her wide open in a moment, and yet she looked at him. Because he'd told her to. And she bit back something she was terribly afraid was a sob when he reached over and brushed her hair from her face.

With devastating gentleness.

"Are you afraid of me?" His voice was softer than it

had been a moment ago, but Mattie couldn't allow herself to melt into that the way her body wanted to do. The way her body *did*. She couldn't let herself topple over into the way he was looking at her. She couldn't let this happen. She couldn't risk this kind of thing—this kind of softness.

Mattie knew what came next. First the softness, the intimacy, the love. Then loss. And all that darkness ever after.

"Why would I be afraid of you?" she asked, her voice a bitter little scrape against the taut thing that hung between them, against that softness making his eyes gleam like gold. Against the darkness she hid away inside her and yet held before her like a shield. "I love it when men I don't want spirit me away on private planes and then put their mouths wherever they like on my body. It's my favorite thing."

"Ah, Mattie," he said quietly, and if he'd been someone else, if she'd been someone else, she might have thought he truly cared about her then. That she was something different, something more, than a long-sought trophy he aimed to put high on the shelf of his choosing. "I don't know if it's your favorite thing or not. But it just became mine."

Something swelled in her then, making a new, hectic kind of heat prickle all over her exposed skin and, worse, lodge behind her eyes with too much dampness. Mattie didn't know what she'd do if she actually cried in front of this man. She didn't know how she'd survive any of this—how she'd possibly remain intact when he had all of this shocking power over her—but particularly not if he saw her cry.

"I don't want this," she gritted out at him, so desperate to keep the tears from spilling over that her hands clenched into fists, and her fingernails dug deep into her own palms. "I don't want any part of this. I never have, and you know it."

She didn't know what she expected. Not that long, oddly

shattering look Nicodemus gave her then, that she might have called *hurt* on a less-dangerous, less-inscrutable man. Not another brush of his hard fingers against her cheek, making a different sort of heat warm to a glow inside her.

"You know it," she said again, more insistent, and his mouth moved, pulling to one side.

Like he knew her better than she did. "So you have said."

Mattie moved, jerky and strange, as if she was a marionette someone else was operating on very stiff strings. She found her panties and pulled them on, feeling immediately better. Her bra. Her jeans. Her T-shirt. As if it was all armor-plated instead of merely from Barney's, and could keep her safe from this man. As if anything could.

Nicodemus only leaned back against the leather sofa and watched as she pulled on her V-neck sweater and then stamped her feet into her boots.

"I didn't mean for that to happen," she said when she was clothed and felt somewhat more like herself than she had before.

"I know what you meant to do." Still that too-dark, too-painful look. "Perhaps in future you'll listen to me. When I told you it was impossible for you to shame me, I meant it."

"Then you are a far worse creature than I imagined," she said. "Wholly irredeemable."

"If you say so," he said. He rubbed his hands over his face. "Your problem is that you expect these pronouncements to wound me." And when that dark gaze of his met hers again, it seemed to slam into her. Another gut punch, hard and deep. "You're a decade too late. I've watched you for too long. I know that you'll say and do anything to try, even now, to escape the inevitable."

"Maybe you should ask yourself why you're so dead set on marrying someone who wants to escape you," she pointed out. "Why a man who could have any woman chooses to buy one, instead. All to become president and COO of a company that isn't even his. Don't you think that's a bit sad?"

It was as if the longer she wore her clothes, the more she reclaimed herself. Or the more she could pretend she couldn't still *feel* him in that betraying softness at her center, so hot and wet even now, pulsing with that destructive need that could destroy her. That would, if she let it.

That already has, something whispered.

"Is this where you appeal to my reason?" His mouth was harder then. Lethal. And she could still taste it. "My good side?"

"Or the part of you that doesn't live in the Stone Age."

"But where you are concerned, I do." His voice even sounded like stone, as if to underscore the harsh way he said that and the way his dark honey eyes gleamed, all menace and certainty. "I don't mind the dance, Mattie. Twist yourself into as many convoluted shapes as you like. Try out all your last-ditch attempts to save yourself. Keep going. See what happens."

"I refuse to believe you're really going to force me to marry you," she threw at him. Accusation and desperation, rolled into one.

"I'm not." That tug in the corner of his mouth, not quite a smile. Not anything that pleasant. "I didn't drag you from your apartment in handcuffs. I didn't kidnap you. No one made you come with me. Just as no one will make you recite your vows."

Mattie was shaking again. Why couldn't she make it stop? How had she managed to completely lose all her self-control? She crossed her arms over her chest, but that only served to make her far too aware of her breasts, which still ached. For him, she knew. Always for him.

"You're splitting hairs," she said. "And you know it."

"No." And his voice was no less stern for that gentle look he aimed at her. "I am a very simple man. I keep the promises I make. I don't have to force you to do anything. I don't *want* to force you. I told you before—you're free to do as you like. You always have been."

"Free to have you hunt me down all these years? Free to have you make nasty little bargains with my brother that you know I'd have to be a selfish monster to refuse?"

Nicodemus didn't quite shrug. "Freedom is never without cost."

"And what was—this?"

She jerked her chin in a hard little gesture that she hoped encompassed what had happened right here on this plane. She certainly didn't want to think about it, much less let those images chase through her head, or move like wine in her veins. She didn't want to feel the aftereffects, all those leftover flames still dancing just beneath her skin.

She didn't want to admit that he'd knocked down a lifetime of her defenses that swiftly, that easily. With her participation and help, no less.

"I thought you wanted me to take you for a test drive, Mattie," he said, horribly, and even laughed when she scowled at him. "Was that not enough of a test? Should we try a higher gear?"

"I," she said very distinctly, very deliberately, "would rather throw myself out of this plane right now."

"That would be unfortunate," he said, without sounding in the least concerned she'd try. "And undoubtedly painful, before your inevitable death."

"I don't want to have sex with you." Her voice was much too strident.

As usual, Nicodemus didn't do what she'd expected he might. He only shook his head at her as if she was a child.

"That is a lie," he said quietly. "As I think you must know I am well aware, having tasted what you want right here."

"Are you going to manipulate me into that, too?" she demanded, uneven and too loud. "Are there more hideous consequences if I don't lie down and take it the first time you order me to do it?"

Nicodemus blinked. "I can promise you that there will never come a day when I will order you to *lie down and take it,* as intriguing as that image might be."

"Don't avoid the question."

Nicodemus studied her, and, not for the first time, Mattie had the prickly sense that he saw all the things she'd spent her life working so hard to conceal. All the things she'd shoved aside, hidden, buried deep.

"No," he said, and he didn't break that uncompromising gaze. "I'm not going to force you. I'm not going to manipulate you."

"I wish I could trust you," she said.

"I've never lied to you," he said, in that same inexorable, impossible way, as relentless as an incoming tide. "You can't say the same. I suspect it's you that you can't trust."

She rubbed her hands up and down her arms and moved to sit in one of the comfortable chairs across the aisle, pulling her feet up beneath her in as close to the fetal position as she could get while still upright.

"I have no idea what you mean."

"Mattie." He might have been laughing again. She could see it in his eyes , could hear it, rich and thick and entirely too beguiling in his low voice. "I don't have to force you or manipulate you or strip off my clothes in a clumsy little challenge, do I?" His smile then was beautiful, truly. Stunning and shattering at once, and it poured into her, through her, like light. Like a nuclear blast. Like a death knell, and she knew it. "I only have to touch you, and you're mine. You've always been mine. Perhaps it's time you admitted it."

They arrived on his island a little before noon the following day after a helicopter ride from a private airfield outside Athens, and it took every shred of control Nicodemus had left inside him to keep from simply tossing Mattie over his shoulder and ravaging her the moment they stepped inside his villa. Exactly the way he'd told her he wouldn't.

This has been a very long game, but the end is in sight, he reminded himself fiercely. *Don't lose your advantage now.*

She had to come to him, one way or another. She had to surrender. She had to be complicit in his triumph over her, or he wouldn't truly win her at all. He knew this as well as he knew his own name. On some level, he supposed he'd always known it.

Nicodemus had bought this island not long after seeing Mattie for the first time at that damned ball of hers, flush with his own burgeoning success and sense of purpose. He'd planned to remake the world in his image and to a large extent, he'd succeeded. He'd built the vast, sprawling villa in the intervening years, making it as much a monument to his own growing power and influence as to the stunning views it commanded from the top of the rocky hill that made up the bulk of the small island, tucked away in a sleepy part of the tourist-heavy Cyclades islands.

It was the kind of house he'd dreamed of while growing up in a crowded flat in the port city of Piraeus outside Athens, mired in his father's strict rules and then, afterward, the mess of his father's lies. It was a house filled with light and art and the sea, not the clamor and struggle of the busy, working-class neighborhood of his childhood.

Quiet elegance and wealth were evident in every last detail, from the dizzyingly high ceilings to the recognizably famous canvases he'd installed on his walls. All it needed was the perfect gilded lily of a woman to live in it with him, as glossy and as bright and as expensive as the view he'd worked so hard to claim as his own.

Not any woman, he knew. He'd tried simply glossy and pedigreed once, and it had brought him Arista, who had wanted his money and his power and his prowess in bed, but not his ring or his name. It had taken him much too long to see her true face, to understand what it had meant that her family sneered at him and his lower-class roots. Mattie was different—because he'd always seen her true face. He'd known from the start that she was lying about her aversion to him. He'd held her in his arms in that ballroom and felt her tremble even as she'd denied him. More than that, claiming her meant claiming a place deep in the bosom of her family. He knew exactly how highly her father had thought of him, because Bart Whitaker was a self-made man who'd married above his station, too.

It was as if Mattie had been crafted specifically for him.

And now she was here. Right where he'd wanted her for a decade. Standing in his house, contained by the walls he'd designed and built himself, the last component of his dream come true sliding into place with a *click* he thought was nearly audible.

Few things in life were as good in fact as they seemed in theory, Nicodemus knew from painful experience, but this—*she* was one of them. He didn't know what surged in him then, some wild concoction made of equal parts lust and satisfaction and *at last,* and he simply stood there in the foyer and let it beat through him. As simple and as poignant as joy.

He watched her as she turned around in a circle in the

great room that opened up in front of him, that too-pretty face of hers unreadable in the bright fall sunlight. She tipped her head back, as if to bask in all that sunshine, but then she caught him looking and stopped. Hid. Again.

Because there was always another game where Mattie Whitaker was concerned. Always another lie.

It was good he remembered that now, he told himself sternly, before he forgot himself entirely and did something foolish. Like pick her up in his arms and swing her around, as if she'd come happily and willingly to this marriage. As if this was some kind of love story.

His own sentimentality should not have surprised him. It was nothing new. This was the culmination of his last remaining dream. He'd already achieved all the rest, one after the next. Mattie was the last thing he'd wanted that he hadn't yet had. The very last. It was his own burden that he also wanted her to be *real*.

"I would ask you if you like this place," he said, aware of the chill in his voice and doing nothing to modify it, because better she should hear that than what lurked beneath, betraying him completely, "but it doesn't really matter, does it?"

"Apparently not." Her dark eyes met his, then moved away again—too quickly, as if she feared what he'd see if he looked too closely. Or perhaps he only hoped that was why. "If you say so." Her mouth shifted into something far more recognizably bitter. "Is this how you prefer I address you, Nicodemus? As submissively as possible? Should I curtsey?"

"There is very little submissive about you, Mattie," Nicodemus said with a great patience only slightly marred by his clenched teeth and the rigid way he held himself too still. "Especially when I can hear you choking back your temper as you speak."

"A natural reaction to my circumstances, I'd imagine," she retorted, her arms crossed tight over those beautiful breasts of hers, and it didn't help that he now knew what they looked like when they were taut with need. He knew how she tasted, and it might very well be the ruin of him. "I'd see about forming a support group, but I suspect the taking of war brides went out with the last century. If not well before."

"This is the history of the world," he said, with what he thought was admirable patience. He thrust his hands deep in his pockets so he'd keep them off her, and roamed across the marble floor in her direction, the room in blues and whites with hints of darker woods as accents, and Mattie's glossy black hair a startling midnight in the middle of it. *Perfect.* "We aren't doing anything particularly new, you and I. People have always done things like this, for the same reasons, all throughout the ages."

"You mean *women* have always *been forced* to do things like this," she corrected him, but he was closer now, and her voice wasn't as strident as before. He saw the remains of all that exuberant heat still there in her lovely eyes, and he wanted to taste her again more than he wanted his next breath. But he only waited, and watched her pull in a long, ragged breath. "Women are forced to bend, or kingdoms break. Women are made to surrender, or nations and corporations and *men* fall apart."

"Consider this a history lesson, if you must. If that makes it easier for you. More palatable."

She glared at him. "And what about what I want, Nicodemus?"

"What about it?" He shook his head when her glare deepened into a scowl. "We both know that you aren't as opposed to this as you pretend. Did we not prove that in scorching detail at thirty-thousand feet?"

"You're wrong. Again. Why am I not surprised?"

"Have I beaten you?" he asked, his voice a lash in the vast room, and she jolted slightly, as if she felt its edge in long, red stripes against her skin. "Abused you in some way?" She looked as if she was about to speak but he kept going. "There are a lot of men who might have taken that impromptu strip show on the plane as an invitation to indulge whatever appetites they liked."

"Didn't you?" she accused him, and he laughed.

"Remind me, in future, never to restrain myself where you are concerned." He shook his head. "Particularly when you take it upon yourself to get naked in inappropriate places."

"I didn't want that!" she hissed at him, with as much force as if she'd have preferred to scream it. Her hands were clenched tight. She was rigid and obviously angry and Nicodemus's curse was that he found her beautiful. Distractingly so. Even—especially—when she was attempting to defy him. "I didn't want any part of what you did."

"This I could tell by the way you screamed my name as you climaxed in my mouth," he said with arid impatience, and she flinched as if he'd slapped her.

"I thought you would stop." It was a harsh whisper.

"Because I always have before?" The laugh he let out then was devoid of humor. "Then you've learned a valuable lesson. Don't test me again." The look on her face was mutinous and miserable at once, and so unnecessary when they'd come this far already—but he bit back the more earthy reaction he had to it. "Your body doesn't tell the lies you do, Mattie. It's significantly more honest."

"Just because my body has some insane chemical reaction to you doesn't mean *I* want to indulge it," she threw at him. "The world doesn't work that way."

"Yours does," he said flatly. "The sooner you accept

that, the happier you'll be." She made a sound that was as close to a growl as he'd ever heard her make, and he really did laugh then. "This is like your very own, personal fairy tale," he told her. He swept an arm through the air, inviting her to truly take in her surroundings. "Blue sky, perfect Greek sea, a little castle on a hilltop, and all of it yours. All you have to do is marry a man with whom you have all of this inconvenient chemistry. No glass slipper required. You should look a bit happier."

She turned slightly to look out at the view, through all the sweeping glass that let in the glory of the Greek islands on three sides and all that sunshine from above, but her mouth pressed into a flat line.

"You're thinking of Disney fairy tales, I think," she said, those dark eyes fixed on Kimolos, the nearest island, as if she was calculating how far it would be to swim to it. "This feels a bit more Grimm Brothers, where everything ends in pecked-out eyes and a river of tears."

He waited until she turned toward him, which took a few tense moments, and when she did, he only shook his head, slowly. A dark scowl like a thundercloud rolled across her lovely face, ferocious and fierce. It only made him want her more.

"I'm pleased to see that you've accepted the reality of the situation with such grace," he said smoothly. "And while we're on that topic, I'll show you to our room so you can get settled."

She blinked. Went entirely too still, the way he'd known she would. "*Our* room?" she asked.

And Nicodemus smiled.

CHAPTER FOUR

THREE DAYS LATER, Mattie dutifully mouthed a set of vows that might as well have been gibberish for all they resonated in her, high on a rocky cliff with a view of nothing but the deep blue Aegean Sea and the next island over, which Nicodemus had informed her boasted a population of less than a thousand souls and the only nearby ferry to Athens.

"Should you wish to swim for it," he'd drawled that first night when he'd installed her in the bedroom he'd claimed they were to share, with its stunning view of the shifting sea and the green hills of the other island, "you should know that it's several miles and there's a vicious current. You could wind up in Tripoli by morning."

"And wouldn't that be a shame," she'd sniped back at him, because she was incapable of biting her tongue at the best of times—and especially when facing him over the wide, vast expanse of the giant bed his amused expression had told her he had every intention of sharing with her. "This close to the wedding of the century."

Nicodemus had only laughed and left her there, to seethe and plot and try her best not to fall apart.

Mattie still didn't believe this was real. That this was really happening.

Not when Nicodemus had looked her up and down in

that dizzying, glassed-in great room of his obnoxiously perfect villa earlier today, his mouth crooking slightly as he took stock of the dour gray dress she'd opted to wear for the occasion.

"Are you in mourning already?" he'd asked, that rich amusement making his voice deeper, darker. It had washed through her like another devastating lick of his talented tongue, and with the same explosive effect. She'd tried valiantly to fight it off, though his expression indicated she hadn't been particularly successful.

"It seemed appropriate," she'd replied coolly. "It was the only one I could find on such short notice that screamed *forced to the altar*. Don't you agree?"

Nicodemus had only laughed. *At* her, she'd been well aware, the way he'd done a great many times since that day in her father's library. Since her eighteenth birthday, for that matter. Then he'd taken her by the arm and led her over the smooth stones toward the priest and the two members of his household staff who were standing in as witnesses to this quiet little tragedy out on his covered marble terrace.

Mattie had told herself that none of this was happening. That none of this was real. That none of it *mattered*.

Not when Nicodemus took her hands in his. Certainly not when he recited his own vows in that powerful voice of his that seemed to echo deep in her bones, however unreal the words seemed to her. Not when the priest spoke in English and then in Greek, as if to make certain it took. Not when one of his staff took a series of photographs that Mattie was sure she didn't want to see. Not when Nicodemus pulled her close to him to press a coolly possessive kiss to her mouth, more matter-of-fact than anything else.

Not that her treacherous body had cared how he kissed her, so long as he did—and she hated that she couldn't lie to herself about that. That the proof was right there in the rowdy, insistent pounding of her heart and the blistering heat at her core, telling her truths she didn't want to accept. Especially when he left her there on that achingly lovely terrace to escort the priest and the two witnesses back into the villa, as if it had never crossed his mind that she might consider jumping from that cliff, to swim or to drown or to be swept off to Tripoli with the next tide, to escape him by any means necessary.

It was no more than another nightmare, she thought, and she was well-acquainted with those. *That didn't really happen.* But even as she thought it, she looked down at her hand at the heavy set of rings that he'd put there, sliding one on right after the next. A square-cut diamond raised high above two sapphires next to a ring of flatter diamonds around a platinum band. The kind of rings reality show "housewives" wore, she thought uncharitably, though she knew that wasn't fair. They simply weren't the sort of hushed, restrained rings her mother had worn all those years ago, the sort Mattie had always imagined she'd wear herself one day.

Not that Nicodemus had asked what she'd wanted. And the rings he'd given her still fit perfectly, she noticed, no matter how she scowled at them.

The October afternoon was cool, or maybe that was her. Mattie had never been one of those wedding-maddened girls, forever imagining *her perfect day* and flipping through bridal magazines in the absence of a groom, but she'd always imagined that at least one of her parents would be there when it happened. That neither of them was alive to know she was married, much less to have witnessed it, ached—and ached deep.

And while she'd known that this situation with Nicodemus was part of a much wider bid to retain control of the family company and all the high stakes that implied, Mattie really had imagined that Chase might have made it from London to watch her sacrifice herself for his benefit, rather than sending her an underwhelming text with his apologies.

Then again, she and Chase hadn't been close in a long time. And she'd always known whose fault that was.

It was a good thing she'd frozen solid, she thought then, because if she hadn't, she might have been tempted to indulge that great, heavy sob building up somewhere inside her. And that might wreck whatever little of herself she had left.

"Reflecting on your good fortune?" Nicodemus asked from behind her, and Mattie congratulated herself on managing, somehow, not to jump at the sound.

"Something like that," she said, as coolly and unemotionally as she could.

Down below, she heard the roar of a motor before she saw the small boat take off in the direction of the island of Kimolos a few miles away. She frowned when she saw three figures on the deck. The priest and both witnesses, clearly, which meant she was alone here with Nicodemus.

Alone. And married to him. *Married.*

Mattie turned, very slowly, to face the man who stood behind her, his hands deep in the pockets of the loose-fitting tan trousers he wore. His crisp white shirt highlighted his olive skin, the contrasting beauty of his dark eyes and almost wild hair, and though it didn't cling to him at all, it still somehow emphasized his powerful chest. He should have looked anything but elegant. But somehow, on him it all worked, and brought out his power and his ruthlessness instead of undermining it.

There was something different about him then, she realized. Something even more dangerous than before. It made the tiny hairs on the back of her neck and down her arms prickle in uncomfortable awareness. It was almost as if—

But then she understood. *He'd won.* Just as he'd always promised her he would.

Her throat was dry. Too dry.

And Nicodemus Stathis was her husband.

"Come inside," he said, his gaze as dark as it was patient, and that made something very deep inside her shudder.

"I'm fine right here."

It was a profoundly stupid thing to say. It made her sound like an infant and she knew it the moment the words passed her lips. Nicodemus's hard face softened, and that only made everything worse.

"You're afraid that if you come inside with me, that means we'll immediately consummate this marriage," he said after a moment. His head canted slightly to one side, as if he was imagining it, sending a fist of need punching into her belly, then clenching tight. "Does it happen on the marble floor, in your half-terrified, half-longing fantasies? Up against the wall beneath the paintings? Sprawled out across the couches, to really settle in and take our time?"

"I don't think anything of the kind." But she did. She really did, and his scalding-hot images didn't help matters, not when she knew how he'd hold her, how he'd tease her and torment her. How he'd take her places she'd never dreamed she could go. "We've shared a bedroom the past two nights and you haven't attacked me. I'm not afraid of you."

His mouth moved into that mocking little crook. "Of course you're not. That's why I've found you sleeping in the guest suite one night and on that sofa in the solarium the next. Because you are so unafraid."

Mattie had no intention of telling him about the nightmares—the screech of tires, that endless singing, that empty stretch of road—that had ripped through every night for as long as she could recall, torn it and her apart. It was why she'd never shared a bed with anyone.

And while she might have realized pretty quickly that first day that fighting with Nicodemus on the topic of separate bedrooms was futile, that didn't mean there weren't ways around it. She'd done what she'd always done before when faced with unacceptable sleeping arrangements, whether here or in boarding school or wherever she found herself along the way: she pretended to sleep where she'd been put, then snuck away to somewhere her inevitably violent awakening wouldn't attract any notice.

"You 'worked'—" and she crooked her fingers in the air to hang quotation marks around that word "—both nights until dawn. What do you care where I slept?"

He studied her the way he did much too often—the way that made her wonder yet again how she'd failed to realize that he'd spent these long years figuring her out while she'd only been focused on avoiding him. And worse, made her remember what it had been like to wake both nights to find herself lifted into his strong arms then carried through the house against the sweet torture of his magnificent chest. *Safe,* a rebellious part of her whispered. Like when he'd placed her back in that huge bed in the master bedroom that he made feel so tiny and so crowded when he slept beside her for an hour or two, his arms around her like he could fight off whatever came their way.

These are not helpful thoughts, she told herself sternly.

"I care that you continue to be disobedient when I've made it fairly clear that there will be consequences for disobedience," he said, so silkily she nearly missed what he'd actually said. "But you should ask yourself why—if

I knew I had to work all this time, and I did—I insisted you sleep in the master bedroom at all."

"If I cared as much about sleeping arrangements as you seem to do," she said icily, "I would have asked you."

"Because I know you far better than you think I do," he answered for her, those dark honey eyes gleaming hard, his voice even darker, even smoother, confirming a whole handful of her worst fears. "And everything with you is easier if it is introduced slowly, and in stages."

She really, really didn't want to think about that, and everything it implied. About their history. About him. About what was going to happen here, between them, if he had his way.

"I'm not a headstrong mustang you can break with a few muttered words and a carrot," she snapped at him. "You're definitely not a cowboy, and this isn't the Wild West."

"I think you should consider the fact that if I was happy to allow you to get naked on a plane, I'm unlikely to stand much on ceremony on my own island, where no pilot or air steward lurks a few feet away," he replied, that voice of his lethal. "If I want you, the fact you're standing outside is hardly going to put me off."

"Thank you," she gritted out. "That's very comforting."

"If you want me to comfort you, you need only ask, Mattie." He paused, his dark eyes searching hers, and that soft thing in them again that would be the undoing of her. "Just ask."

And that was worse. That hint of emotion in his voice, of something like understanding. *Sympathy.* It choked her, black and thick and terrible.

"What if what I need comfort from is you?" she asked, her voice a jagged little bit of sound, hardly there at all with the sea crashing into the rocks below and a few hardy seagulls cartwheeling in the air around them as if it was still summer. It matched that almost-smile he aimed her way, that sent a bolt of something a great deal like sorrow arrowing through her. As if she'd already lost something here.

"Come inside," Nicodemus said again. It wasn't a request.

If you can't be in control, Mattie's father had always said, *you can at least be practical.* So she gathered herself together as best she could. She kept her spine straight and her head high, and she marched through the open glass doors like she was proceeding straight off a plank into shark-infested waters.

He slid the doors closed behind her. Mattie heard the *click* when they shut like a gun to her ear. She walked to the seating area nearest the great windows and sat down in an armchair with great deliberation, so Nicodemus couldn't sit next to her. He watched her, his mouth twitching again as if he could read her mind as easily as breathe, and then went to the bar tucked into a cabinet to the side and poured two flutes of champagne.

"Take this, please," he said when she only glared at the glass he brought over and held out to her.

She felt numb, but she took it, staring at it as if it was poison.

"Eis igían sas," he said. When she frowned up at him, he lifted his champagne in a toast she was certain was mocking. "To your good health."

"I'm not sure good health is anything I should be aspiring to, in my situation," she said crisply. She set the flute down on the vast, glass-topped table before her with a decisive *clink* without so much as tasting it. "It seems to me that a tidy little virus that will carry me off with a minimum of fuss is what I ought to be hoping for. It might be my only escape."

"I'm sorry to tell you that with great wealth comes immediate access to the best physicians across the globe," Nicodemus said, seeming perfectly content to *stand* there, tall and dark and *her husband*. "I'd make certain you were cured."

"Exactly how long am I to be trapped in this marriage?"

"You should have paid better attention earlier. Until death," he said quietly, and there was something in the way he looked at her that made that heavy knot low in her belly flare to life again, hot and needy. Longing and betrayal at once. "Forever."

"*Until death* is not the same as *forever*."

"Then yes, Mattie," he said in a mild tone that made her feel like a tantruming toddler. She supposed it was meant to do exactly that. "You may have all the freedom you could possibly desire. In the grave."

"Wonderful." She treated him to a tight, fake smile. "Well. This has been delightful. Every girl dreams of being hurriedly married across the planet from all the people she cares about. And half in a language she doesn't understand. If you'll excuse me, I think I'll take a nap to recover from the thrill of so much fairy-tale glamour at once."

"You've taken quite a few naps since we arrived here." He moved then, draping that absurd body of his on the nearby couch, at an angle to her, and her heart kicked into a higher gear. "I wonder why?"

"Jet lag?" Mattie supplied tartly. It wasn't as if she'd slept during those *naps* she'd claimed she'd needed, of course. She'd been keeping as far away from him as possible.

"Perhaps." His long fingers toyed with the delicate crystal he held, and she remembered, with startling accuracy, the feel of those fingers dancing across the skin at her side, tracing the sweeping lines of her tattoo. "Or perhaps you are merely trying to avoid the consequences of the past ten years, to say nothing of what happened on the flight over."

"You talk a lot about these consequences," Mattie said in as unbothered a tone as she could manage. "But I already feel humiliated. That happens when one is forced into a marriage she doesn't want. What's a little in-flight entertainment on top of that? I hope you filmed the whole thing and are planning to upload it to YouTube. Sixty million page views and a host of vile and insulting comments are about the only thing that could make this any worse."

"That's more your province than mine, I think," he said, his dry tone reminding her of that unfortunate video a "friend" of hers had uploaded when Mattie was twenty-three and very drunk. "I've never graced the internet without my knowledge, as far as I'm aware."

"Do you own the internet, too? Or just every person who might post on it?"

"I'm so pleased," he said after a moment, "that none of this has dulled your sense of drama."

Mattie found that her hands were in fists again, stuck in the voluminous dark gray skirt of the dress that had seemed like such a good idea when she'd packed it in New York, and now felt nothing but childish. Just as he'd accused her of being, directly and indirectly, a thousand times. It made her heart ache and her head pound today.

Being near him made her feel as out of control and panicky as it ever had. As perilously close to losing herself and all those tightly held spiked things she carried in the deepest, darkest part of her. Worse, now, that he'd kept so many of his promises. That he'd won.

That he kept winning.

"Did you send your staff away with that priest?" she asked. Her voice was quieter. More raw. Too telling by far.

And she thought he heard that, because he studied her for a long moment without speaking.

"I did." She didn't understand that particular light in those honeyed dark eyes of his. She didn't want to. "We are very much alone, though there will be deliveries to the dock each morning should you require something. Do you?"

"A ride to Athens?"

His lips crooked. "Other than that."

"I don't know what you want from me."

"You do." He smiled, and she told herself the chill that snaked down her back was fear, not anticipation. Never that. "Everything, Mattie. I want everything, as I've told you from the start."

She shook her head. "That was all a game. A dare stretched out across the years. Stupidity." She broke off and tried to find the right words, or, when that failed, *any* words. "This is different. It's not a game anymore. I don't *want* this, Nicodemus."

He leaned forward to put his empty glass on the table and then sat back again, and she still couldn't get that raggedness inside her under any kind of control. She still couldn't do a thing about that wild red tide that rose inside her, as relentless and unstoppable as he was.

And he simply sat there, unmoved and unbothered, as if everything between them was unfolding according to his plan. She supposed it was, and that made her feel even more trapped, even more hunted, than before.

"I don't believe you," he said, with that remarkable, maddening calm. "But even if I did, it's done."

"I did what you wanted," she gritted out. "I married you. Why can't that be enough?"

Again, that smile, much too knowing. Much too dangerous. "You know why."

Mattie didn't mean to move. She had no intention of doing anything but continuing on as she was and hoping that somehow poked holes in his smooth, impenetrable armor....

But instead, she simply *burst*—reaching out and slapping her full glass of champagne with all of her might and an open hand. It flew through the air, spraying the amber liquid all around and then smashed into pieces on the white marble floor some six feet away.

And for a moment, the only sound was her own harsh breathing and the drumming of her pulse in her ears.

Nicodemus's too-calm gaze tracked the arc of the champagne glass, stayed on the shattered glass rather longer than it should have then finally cut back to her.

"Ah, Mattie," he said. Soft. Lethal. And something like kind, which made it that much worse. It told her exactly how much trouble she was in, on the off chance she couldn't guess. "You really shouldn't have done that."

Nicodemus decided he was enjoying himself, after all.

"You're going to clean that up," he told Mattie, who had her chin set at that mulish angle that he found far more amusing than was wise, and all that murder in her eyes. "But first, of course, there must be punishment."

"Punishment," she repeated, as if she'd never heard the word before.

"It's what happens when one throws temper tantrums," he said. "As you would have realized had your father not shipped you off to stuffy British boarding schools for half your life and treated you with benevolent neglect the rest of the time."

She stiffened, and her lovely, dark eyes flashed with outrage. "You're insane."

Nicodemus smiled and settled back against the couch, lazily at his ease.

"I'm feeling benevolent myself, as this is our wedding day," he told her, injecting a note of magnanimity into his voice, purely to watch the fireworks in her gaze. "So I'll give you a choice. Either you subject yourself to the task of my choosing, or I spank you."

For a moment, she didn't react. Then his words clearly penetrated. She flushed hot. He saw the pulse in her neck leap as she jerked back against her chair.

"You can't *spank* me!" But there was that note in her voice, and that heat in her eyes, and he wondered what images she was playing with in that complicated head of hers. If they matched the ones in his.

"Can't I?"

"You can't simply…do whatever you want!"

"By all means, Mattie, complain to the local authorities." He nodded toward the windows and the sea beyond. "It's a bit of a swim, as I've said, but I'm sure you'll receive a perfectly warm welcome in Libya when you come in with the tide."

"Don't be absurd!" she snapped.

But he could see that she wasn't as sure of herself as she'd been in all their previous encounters, and that amused him more than anything else could have. Perhaps it had dawned on her that for all the years they'd played their game of cat and mouse, she'd relied as much on the fact they were in public while they danced around each other as she had on his restraint. And now they were stranded here, together.

This was his home. His rules. His game.

"Act like a child and I will treat you like one," he told her after a moment, when he thought he could have heard her heart thumping if he'd only stopped to listen. "I'm not your father, Mattie. I'm far more proactive. I'm not going to spoil you on the one hand, ignore you on the other and hope for the best."

A best that had included Mattie's well-photographed "wild phase," which still irritated Nicodemus more than was warranted or, he was aware, fair. A best that had also included making no provision for his own children in the event of his own death. What had Bart been thinking?

"You're not really going to *beat* me." She'd reverted to that bored tone of voice again, but he could see the hectic sparkle in her eyes.

"It's not a beating if you end up begging me for it, I don't think. Certainly not if you enjoy it. Though you can call it that if you like."

"I won't submit to something like that, obviously," she said coolly, though her gaze was anything but. "It's barbaric."

Nicodemus smiled, and he realized it was with actual fondness, which should have terrified him. It should have brought back his history with Arista and all the red flags he'd ignored that first time. But instead, he filed it away and concentrated on the woman before him, whose outrage had thawed the frozen shell she'd been wrapped in since their wedding ceremony. *Another victory,* he thought.

"Is it?" he asked then. "If I reach between your legs, will I find you as desperate for me as you were on that plane? Wet and needy and mine already?"

She did nothing for a long moment but breathe, trembling where she sat, all fists and fury and that sizzling lightning just beneath it, blinding him. Tying him in knots. Making him nothing at all but greedy.

Soon, he promised himself. *It will be soon enough.*

"I'll clean up the glass," Mattie said in a low voice. "But there will be no spanking."

"Not today, then," he said, relaxing back into the sofa. "I understand. Trust takes time."

She looked at him with loathing—or what would have been loathing, had he not been able to see that spark of need in her dark eyes. Not only for sex, he thought—which was one of the reasons she got beneath his skin. All the *more* that lurked in her, that called to him. She got to her feet stiffly and started toward the mess she'd made, and he let her walk a few steps. He doubted she knew how she looked in that dress. Not at all like a widow or a wraith as she'd obviously intended. The gray suited her, made her flashing eyes and glorious hair something like glimpses of clear sky through lovely clouds, and he wondered why any bride wore white, instead. But then, not every bride could possibly look like his.

God help him, the ways he wanted this woman. Only the fact he'd held on to his composure for so long already allowed him to keep doing it.

"Stop," he said when she'd moved far enough into the center of the room, and though she scowled at him when she turned to look back at him, she obeyed. And he liked that as much as if he truly was the barbarian he knew she thought he was. "Stand right there."

He simply studied her, watching as her scowl deepened. And then, moments later, as she shifted from one foot to the other, in some mixture of impatience and anxiety, and he wanted to taste both.

"What now?" she asked tightly. "Aren't menial chores and threats of physical abuse enough for one day?"

"Don't move," he ordered her. "I told you there were two options. And if you are as adamantly opposed to my spanking you as you've claimed, that means you've cho- sen the other by default."

"Is it really necessary to play these dictatorial games,

Nicodemus?" she asked, and there was something more than her usual provocation in her voice then. Something real. Raw.

"I don't know. I asked myself a similar question many times over the past ten years. Do you have an answer?"

"I wasn't playing games. I didn't want you. I don't."

"That's what I thought you'd say." He smiled. "You seem very fidgety, Mattie. Almost nervous."

"You obviously want me to be nervous," she snapped.

"Perhaps you should be. Perhaps it's past time you took this seriously."

And he could see that she was as nervous as he could hope. Finally. But it wasn't as simple as nerves. There was that longing beneath, that need. And that other, electric current that looked a great deal like anticipation.

He'd spent a long time learning how to read this woman. It was finally paying off.

"You used to tell me how much you liked to dance," he said when he could see it had built in her to a fever pitch, and he wasn't sure what she'd do next. "Do you remember? Every time you explained to me why it was necessary for you to spend *quite* so much time falling in and out of clubs."

She clenched her hands tight, then opened them.

"Yes." He hardly recognized her voice when she finally spoke. "I like dancing. Is that another manufactured crime you can claim you need to punish me for?"

"Then dance." It was a dare. A command. He waved a hand, taking in the vast, empty room, nothing in it or the whole villa but the two of them and this bright, greedy thing that grew tighter between them with every breath. "For me."

"I...what?"

But she swayed where she stood, in unconscious obedience, and it sent a spike of pure need straight through him, deep and hard. She might not know how much and how deeply she wanted him. She might not be able to admit it. But Nicodemus knew. He'd known since that very first dance they'd shared all those years ago now.

How much different would all of this be—would *they* be, he wondered, if she'd allowed him to claim her then? If she hadn't led him on this merry chase across the years?

"Pretend," he invited her, and it was as if the space between them shrank. Disappeared. "Pretend you want me so much it's like a fist in your gut, making it hard to breathe. Pretend you desire me almost as much as you fear me, like a terrible flu you worry might carry you off. Pretend you can claim a little bit of your power this way, by beguiling me and seducing me." His gaze was hard on hers, the way he wished his hands were. "Do it well enough, my sweet little wife, and perhaps you won't be pretending. Do it better than that, and perhaps we won't need to call any of this *punishment,* after all."

CHAPTER FIVE

INSTEAD, MATTIE FLED.

She ran through the sun-bathed halls of the villa, past the awe-inspiring paintings she refused to look at too closely for fear they would tell her things about their owner she didn't wish to know. She ran all the way to the master bedroom and that huge bed she didn't want to share with him, and then she locked herself in the bathroom.

Like a child. Again.

And then she waited there, her heart pounding so hard she could feel its staccato rhythm when she swallowed, for Nicodemus to storm in on her. For him to pound on the door, rage and shout on the other side, even break it down before him—

But he did none of those things. She couldn't even tell if he'd followed her wild dash through the house or if he was still sitting where she'd left him, that harshly seductive mouth of his crooked to one side and his low voice urging her on.

Pretend you desire me almost as much as you fear me.

Mattie didn't have to pretend when it came to Nicodemus, and she was terribly afraid he knew that, the way he seemed to know everything else.

She still didn't understand *how* he knew. How he'd always known.

The shadows lengthened. The bathtub was a grand affair, set high on its own dais with a wide window facing the slumberous expanse of the sea, and Mattie curled up there, taking an austere sort of comfort from the rigid porcelain beneath her. She watched the sun sink toward the horizon, then disappear in a blaze of brilliant reds and oranges. She watched the stars come out, only a few as twilight stole the bright colors of the sunset away, then too many to count as nighttime fell in earnest.

She fell asleep eventually, then woke in her usual state of tumult and desperation, the nightmare clinging to her as she tried to fight her way free of its sinewy grip. The crash. The horror. The hours trapped in that backseat with her face pressed into the leather and Chase holding her there, both of them shaking—

Mattie wiped her eyes, waited for the same shaking to pass in the present, then fell back asleep.

And when she woke in the morning, the light was pouring in, dazzling her, so it took her a few critical moments to realize that she was no longer in the bathtub. She was in the big bed in the master bedroom and Nicodemus— *her husband*—was stretched out beside her.

Just like every morning since they'd arrived here, only this time, Mattie had no memory of him carrying her from the bathtub to the bed. She could remember nothing but the nightmare. How had he moved her without her knowledge? Had she told him the truth while she slept? And what else had happened that she couldn't recall?

Mattie jackknifed to sitting position, tearing back the covers to make sure she was still wearing her sour version of a wedding dress. She made no attempt to hide her sigh of relief when she discovered it was still on, as were the bra and panties she'd worn beneath.

"Let me assure you," Nicodemus said in that low,

amused voice of his that seemed to wind through her, setting her alight, especially when it sounded as sleepy and as *close* as it did just then. "If anything of that nature had happened, after all these years, you would not have to check."

She swallowed, feeling much more fragile than she should have. She cast around for her outrage, her fury—but there was only that same old panic he always kicked up in her. Simmering there inside her, more mellow, somehow. Or more resigned.

Almost as if it wasn't panic at all, but something else entirely.

"So I am to have no privacy whatsoever," she said, her gaze trained on her lap. The yards and yards of gray that had failed to protect her.

"I apologize," he said in that arid way of his that was no apology at all. That mocked the very notion of an apology. "Were you comfortable in the bathtub? My mistake. You looked cold and underfed. And I think you were having a nightmare."

Mattie went cold. Her mind cleared. No one had ever been near her during one of her nightmares, and she certainly couldn't let it happen again. What if she told him what had happened? What if he knew what she'd done?

She felt ill at the very idea and didn't want to think about the contradiction there.

"No privacy," she said crisply, as if reading off a list. "Spankings presented as reasonable resolutions to conflicts. Threats issued. Told to dance for your pleasure and to perform chores at your command." She stared at him. "You'll understand if somehow, I found the bathtub more inviting."

"You made a mess, princess." His dark eyes probed hers, and for once she couldn't find any laughter lurking there, only that implacable iron that made her shake down deep inside, and she couldn't lie to herself and pretend it was fear. It wasn't. "I had every intention of making sure you cleaned it up."

"Oh, right," she replied. "You mean that in the broader sense, I gather. I'm supposed to spend this sick joke of a marriage paying penance for not racing into it sooner? That's the mess I made?"

He was quiet, and that wasn't any good. It allowed Mattie time—and she didn't want time. The morning sun spilled over him like a radiant, clinging lover, bathing his perfect form in too much light to bear. The trouble was—had always been—he was flawless. He wore nothing but a low-slung pair of boxer briefs this morning, and in truth, he had nothing to hide. Every inch of him was stunning. The taut, lean muscles in his arms, his flat pectorals and ridged abdomen, those tough, strong thighs. He was dusted with dark hair that thickened and then disappeared beneath his boxer briefs, and she told herself she didn't notice the rest of him.

Certainly not the part of him that stood ready, huge and impatient and barely contained, right where she absolutely refused to look.

"You've been crying," he said gruffly, and for a dazed moment she didn't understand what he meant. He reached over and ran a thumb beneath one of her eyes and she jerked her head away. "Why?"

She blinked, oddly off balance. "I can think of a thousand reasons."

"Pick the one that's true," he suggested, still in that rough way that, perversely, made her imagine he cared. She hated that she wished he did.

And Mattie couldn't tell him the truth. Her nightmares were her business—and anyway, she told herself, he didn't really care, no matter that note in his voice. He only wanted to make certain she had nowhere to hide.

"It doesn't matter what I say." She shifted away from him. "You've already decided that I'm a liar. You decided it a hundred years ago, so why should I bother saying a word?"

"Or you could try not lying."

He rolled toward her, closing the distance she'd put between them and propping himself up on one elbow, and she could have done without that play of all his beautiful muscles beneath his sleek skin, *right there* in front of her. She could have done without the unearned, unwanted, terrible intimacy of this. It felt like a great and awful weight, pressing down hard on her chest, like he was holding her down with all his obvious strength when what was far, far worse was that he didn't have to.

"I've been bartered off to save a company, as if I were nothing more than a collection of shares in human form," she said instead of any of the other things she could have said. "A spreadsheet with legs. Anyone would shed a few tears."

But his dark eyes only lit up with all that golden amusement, sending a shiver straight through her.

"This could all have been very different," he said lazily. "If you had married me the first time I asked, I would have treated you like you were made of spun glass, not shares. I would have worshipped the ground you walked upon. Bent the whole world before you, to service your every whim."

Worried that if she tried to get out of the bed he'd reach over and stop her, which would involve touching her—and she had no idea what she'd do then—Mattie pushed herself back until she was leaning against the headboard, curled her knees beneath her and tried to stare him down.

"I was eighteen," she said, not sure where that urgency in her voice came from when she'd wanted to match his nonchalance. "I was a kid. I had no business thinking about getting married and you shouldn't have asked. The only reason you *did* ask was because you wanted an in with my father. Let's not pretend your heart was involved, Nicodemus. It was your wallet first and then, when I refused you repeatedly, your pride. It still is."

He reached over and pulled the hem of her dress between his fingers, and she bit back the rebuke that hovered on her tongue. What did it matter if he touched her clothes? There were far worse places he could put those clever fingers of his, and she knew that all too well now.

"Perhaps I simply wanted a Whitaker as my wife, and all the shares and spreadsheets that go along with that. Sadly, you are the only one available."

"I'm told I have distant cousins in Aberystwyth. I'm sure one of them would have suited you fine." She scowled at him when he laughed. "And I don't think you should try to get too much mileage from the term *wife*."

He shook his head at her as if he knew exactly where she was going with that. "Did you knock yourself on the head in the bath? That was an actual wedding yesterday. All very legal, I assure you."

"That might have been a wedding, but this isn't a real marriage," she insisted, surprised to hear how loud her voice sounded in all that dizzy Greek sunshine that filled the room. "In the real world, marriages don't involve threats and promises of high-ranking positions in corporations as some kind of twisted dowry. You're going to be COO and President of Whitaker Industries, Nicodemus. Those are the titles you care about. *Husband* and *wife* are just words."

He moved then. He reached over and hauled her to him, rolling with her until she was beneath him, he was pressed between her thighs and braced above her, and she could do nothing at all but gape up at him.

She thought she was having a heart attack, but it kept *pounding* like that, jarring and huge and whole-bodied, and it took her long, shuddering moments to realize that this *was* living through it. That it only felt like it was killing her.

That if it killed her, that might be better, because everything that was happening to her right now—everything he was *doing* to her—she was all too aware he could *see*.

"Does this feel real, Mattie?" he asked roughly, his gaze on her mouth. "Marital enough for you? *Real?* Because neither your father nor your brother are in this room. It's only me and you and your heart has gone mad inside your chest. I can feel it."

"That's panic," she threw at him. "And a little bit of revulsion."

But she made no attempt to fight him off. No attempt to roll out from under him, or to dislodge the sleek, solid weight of him from on top of her, from that place where he rested against her as if they were already joined. And she knew, somehow, that if she'd tried any of that, he'd have let her go at once. She didn't try.

You can't let this happen! cried that voice inside of her, the way it always did—but this time, she knew on some deep, feminine level she'd never accessed before, was for completely different reasons.

This wasn't some overeager boyfriend she had to placate and put off. This was Nicodemus.

This was *Nicodemus* and she couldn't even manage to pull her gaze away from his. And that profound failure to act told her things she didn't want to know about herself— that and what felt like a slow-motion detonation from that molten-hot place between her legs outward, making her burn from her navel to her fingernails. Making her nothing but heat and wonder and that thing she liked to tell herself was fear. Pounding, driving, consuming fear that wasn't *fear* at all.

Nicodemus did nothing but gaze down at her, fierce and demanding and still. And Mattie wasn't afraid of him the way she knew she should have been, because *she* was the one who closed the distance between them. *She* lifted her lips toward his. *She* found she was begging with every part of her except her voice—

"First you must ask," he told her, his gaze a dark fire and his voice like gravel. "Out loud, so there can be no mistake."

"Ask?" She hardly understood what he'd said, much less what she'd repeated. As if she'd never heard the word in her life. And all she could see was that beautiful, harsh mouth of his, bold and hard and so deliciously close to hers—

"I'd prefer it if you begged," he said, low and rough and needy, but absolute. Implacable. "But if you ask nicely, I'll let it slide. Just this once."

And then there was a very long moment where Mattie couldn't think of a single reason why she didn't do exactly that. Not one single reason.

She opened her mouth—but then reality asserted itself inside her, blinding and brilliant, bringing with it a kind of desperate reason, and she didn't care if he saw all of it in her eyes. Intimacy with this man meant losing herself first, and then losing him. She'd known that for years. She knew it the way she knew he'd wanted her, always. Deep in her bones. Immutable and irreversible. A simple, searing truth.

"I'm not going to ask you nicely," she promised him, though her voice shook. "And I'm certainly not going to beg. That might be your conception of marriage, but it certainly isn't mine."

"I thought this wasn't a real marriage," he murmured,

all silk and fire. "No need to fight for equality in a sham like this, is there? Just surrender, Mattie. I promise you, you'll like it."

She believed him. That was why she scowled at him again. Harder.

"No begging," she snapped. "Unless you plan to get down on your knees and try it yourself?"

His hard mouth crooked. "I hope you're prepared to suffer." He was so big, hard and gorgeous and almost entirely naked as he pressed her to the bed yet kept the bulk of his weight on his arms on either side of her, as if he was the only thing protecting her from what they both wanted. "Because that's the only way I'll touch you again."

"You're touching me now, I can't help but notice."

"Splitting hairs won't take the ache away, Mattie," he all but crooned at her, as if he knew how badly she already did. As if he could *see* all the ways she longed for him. "It will only draw this out."

He laughed, and it was that same dark victor's laugh, but this time it rolled through her differently. Because his mouth was so close to hers, maybe. It swept inside her like an inexorable wave, and she didn't know if she wanted to weep or scream or betray herself entirely and beg the way he wanted her to do.

Anything to get him to touch her again without her having to ask—without her having to thereby prove that he was right about her.

She hated herself for that twisted little thought.

"Let me go," she whispered then, furious at both of them, but he only laughed again, in exactly the same way.

"I don't know why, when you obviously want me as badly as I want you, you go to these lengths to deny it. But none of that matters."

"Because you've seen the error of your ways and are

setting me free from this absurd pseudo-marriage?" she asked with all the bravado she wished she felt.

He leaned in and nipped at the soft place beneath her chin, punishment and seduction at once, and Mattie could do nothing but jolt and then shudder. Showing him too much, she understood. Proving herself the liar he already thought she was.

The liar she'd proved herself to be again and again and again. Every time he touched her, she lied.

"Pick a new strategy, Mattie," he told her, and then moved up and off her in a breathtakingly smooth shift of athletic grace, giving her an unwanted object lesson in all of that divine, stunning strength of his. "The problem with this one is that I'm bored with it."

"Heaven forbid I *bore* you," she snapped out. "You've blackmailed me, threatened me and manhandled me into this sham of a marriage—but all of that pales in comparison to *boring* you. A fate worse than death!"

"You dance too close to the edge again and again," he said as if she hadn't spoken. "You treat me to your sharp tongue whenever you feel like it, you run and hide when I return the favor, then you repeat the pattern ad nauseam. All without any consequences, until now."

Nicodemus was standing then, by the side of the bed with the morning sun casting his face in shadow, but she had no trouble seeing that gleam of honey in his gaze. That dark *knowing* thing behind it. She felt it everywhere.

Worse than his mouth on her. Deeper. Infinitely more destructive.

"Without consequences?" she asked, her voice shakier than she liked. She raised up her hand with its heavy rings. "What do you call this?"

His mouth curved. "I can do this for another decade if I have to, and I'll still win. It's entirely up to you."

* * *

He was right. She was going about this all wrong.

Mattie came to that conclusion in a near-violent rush while she stood in the spacious shower, her hands braced against the lovingly crafted stone wall and her head tipped back, letting the water fall down on her like rain. She'd spent all this time treating Nicodemus like he was an unfightable force of nature, some impossibly powerful creature made of myth and magic, when the truth was he was a man.

Just a man, like all the rest.

And when she put her wildly beating heart aside, when she shoved off the things he made her feel against her will and the very real fear that she was already coming undone because of him, she knew that she'd been playing this the wrong way from the start. Because he'd taken her breath away when she was still eighteen without even trying, and she'd forgotten the simple truth she'd known even then: men were easy.

Men were creatures of simple needs and impulses that could be directed and finessed and yes, used. Fathers, brothers, boyfriends—it was the same thing, really, if different tools. Mattie had learned that a long time ago in the glare of cameras usually wielded by men, none of whom were immune to the judicious application of a little bit of feminine charm. It was easy to flirt or flatter her way out of trouble, to misdirect, to indulge in a little sleight of hand. It was easy to change the conversation from the things she didn't wish to give up to other things she didn't much mind surrendering.

Mattie hadn't been able to do much about her guilt. But a little bit of charm had gone a long way with Big Bart, especially because she'd been willing to move back to the States and under his thumb. And if she could charm her father, who she'd hurt so terribly twenty years ago, she knew she could charm anyone.

If she wanted to gain back any of the ground she'd lost in these explosive few days, Mattie needed to treat Nicodemus like any other man she'd ever known. Mortal. Manageable.

She started by dressing for him.

Mattie tried to remember every single thing he'd ever said to her about her appearance—all of it negative, generally, and delivered in that withering tone of his—and dress around it. She ended up in a soft, cocoa-colored cashmere sweater that was airy enough for the Greek sun and warm enough for the hint of autumn chill beneath it. She layered it over a pair of white trousers and left her feet bare in a touch of feminine vulnerability. She twisted her hair back into a casual chignon with a few strands left loose, and when she was done she looked a good deal more like the kind of woman Nicodemus had always seemed to think she should have been than she usually did. The kind of woman she might have been naturally had she not felt compelled to dress in dark, moody colors and clothes he found inelegant to convey her defiance every time she saw him.

And then she squared her shoulders, reminded herself how many times she'd done something like this before when she'd needed to appease one of her boyfriends who'd grown too demanding and went to find him.

He was only a man, she reminded herself again as she moved through the villa. No matter how he made her feel. No matter that he'd somehow managed to make her forget herself completely almost every time he touched her. No matter that he'd taken a piece of her no one else ever had.

None of that mattered. She had to even this playing field, or she'd disappear.

He sat with his laptop at the gleaming counter in the

expansive, light-filled kitchen on the lower level of the villa, a Greek coffee steaming at his elbow. She hesitated in the doorway, assuming he'd heard her approach the way he always had before, though he didn't glance her way.

And for a moment, she forgot about her strategies and her plans. She forgot what he was or wasn't. What she could or couldn't do. Because he was staring off into space with an unguarded, wholly un-Nicodemus-like expression on his face. Not fierce, not hard. Not myth or magic.

She couldn't categorize it. She didn't recognize it.

Mattie only knew it made her throat feel too tight.

But then it was gone as if it had never been, and all the dark steel she recognized as pure Nicodemus returned. He shifted slightly in the high stool, frowning at the screen before him.

"Has the funeral ended so soon?" he asked mildly enough, making her wonder exactly when he'd seen her there in the arched doorway when he still didn't bother to look her way. "I expected to see you draped in shrouds and mantillas for at least the next week."

"I suppose I had that coming," she agreed in a soft voice, and that made him look up and focus on her, those dark eyes narrowing immediately.

He's just a man, she reminded herself as that look seared into her. *He can't read a single thing in you unless you let him. He doesn't have the slightest idea what you dream about.*

And if she redirected his attention, he never would.

She walked into the kitchen as if she was unaware of that faint frown between his eyes and settled herself gingerly at the counter with him. Not across from him as she would have done before, but on the stool next to his, the way she would have done if he was someone else. *Right* next to his, and it was hard—almost too hard—to keep her head in this game instead of losing her cool.

He was so big, so solid. Sleek and fierce and this close to him, she felt him—all that dark, restless power, all his stark ruthlessness—like an electric hum beneath her own skin.

"Still," she continued in the same soft voice once she was seated, ignoring all the rest, "I thought you'd appreciate that I've attempted to dress more to your taste."

He trained his simmering dark gaze on her, and she felt simultaneously very small and very exposed. Instead of striking out, she let it show. Men liked softness and small, helpless things. They liked to feel large and mighty. She'd watched this same scene play out a hundred times.

He is the same as all the rest, she chanted to herself, like that could make it so.

"By that I assume you mean that I should applaud the fact you're actually wearing something attractive?" Nicodemus asked silkily. "Rather than displaying your wares to any and all who venture near or wrapping yourself in the sartorial equivalent of a cocoon? What a gift, indeed."

It actually hurt to gulp back the sharp retort that appeared on her tongue, but Mattie did it. Men were all about pride and fury. And they were all brought low by lust. Nicodemus was no different, despite the fact his barbs struck harder. Deeper than anyone else's ever had.

"Nicodemus," she said, as calmly as she could. "Maybe we can stop all of this. Maybe we can just…talk."

"Talk." He shook his head as if amazed. Then he shut his laptop with a quiet slap that made her think of ferocity restrained. "You want to *talk.* All these years later."

She shrugged and let her sweater slide down one shoulder as she did. "I want to start over."

His gaze moved over the exposed curve of her shoulder,

then he aimed it at the ceiling and made a sound that was somewhere between exasperation and laughter. He crossed his arms over his broad chest—happily covered in a soft shirt now, though with too many buttons left undone for her peace of mind—and regarded her with that darkly honeyed gleam in his eyes that promised nothing but trouble.

"Let me guess what this is. You think that you can charm me into dropping my guard with you, because your usual games and stunts aren't working." He sighed. "And I've never seen your charm except from a distance, and always aimed toward others, so who knows? This might be an excellent plan."

Mattie ordered herself to breathe. To think before she spoke. To *stay calm*—because God knew she'd spent ten years completely out of control around this man, and what had that ever gotten her? Married against her will and trapped on an island in the middle of nowhere, that was what.

Adapt or die, she snapped at herself. *Right now.*

"I want to get to know you," she said, and she even smiled. It was easy if she simply *pretended*, as he'd suggested. Though Mattie doubted he'd intended that she should pretend he was someone else. Someone far less… *him*.

His gaze was far too shrewd. "Whatever for, I wonder?"

She turned toward him and extended her hands out in front of her, making sure she almost touched him—but didn't. It was a gesture of supplication. Of something like surrender.

"Because there's no one here but you and me, Nicodemus, and as you've pointed out several times, you know me already. I think it's time I stop fighting this and return the favor, don't you?"

He shifted in his stool so that he was more standing than

sitting, and facing her completely. He was so tall. Dark and beautiful, and she had to do this. She had to wield the only weapon she had or he'd tear her wide open, sift through her hidden places and see everything. She had to put them back on common ground—any common ground at all—or she'd lose herself. For good.

And she couldn't risk him finding out the truth.

"What do you want, Mattie?" he asked softly.

You on a platter, she thought, but did not say. She would get there. She could wreck him, too. She was sure of it. Chemistry went both ways, surely.

She took a deep, ragged breath that she didn't have to fake, and then she reached over and put her hands on his rock-hard thighs. He didn't appear to move at all, but she felt him tense beneath her. And he was so hard. So absurdly perfect in every way it made her feel something like drunk.

"I'll ask you again," he said, in a voice gone fierce and hot and lethal. "What do you want?"

She slipped from her stool and stood too close to him. Not quite leaning into him, but not losing contact with him, either. Then she slid her hands to the waistband of his trousers and felt him turn to stone beneath her palms.

"If you truly did fall and hit your head, you should tell me now," he said in that dry way of his that she was afraid would be the death of her, because he might make her laugh and that would make this all much more difficult. Much more *real.* "Before I assume the worst and have you treated for a concussion."

And Mattie understood, then, in a sudden flash that made her wonder how she'd missed it before, that she had far more power here than she'd imagined. That he was as off balance as she was. That perhaps he always had been, and she'd never noticed. She'd never *allowed* herself to notice. She told herself she could use that—and ignored the sudden hollow place in the vicinity of her chest.

She didn't speak. She shifted closer and let her hands drift down, until she could cup the bold length of him through the fabric of his trousers. He didn't groan. He didn't push her away. But he was hot—*so hot*—and he let out a very long breath as if it hurt him.

As if she did.

"Mattie." His voice was brutal. Clipped and hard. His hands came up to wrap around her upper arms, but he didn't move her off him. And his touch was gentle, belying the tension she could feel in every part of him. "What the hell are you doing?"

She tilted her head back and looked up at him through her lashes, testing the length of him against one palm while he shook slightly, very slightly, and scowled back at her.

"I don't know," she told him.

But she did know. She'd never felt anything quite like this before, like every time she stroked him and felt him tense, the same shudder he fought to conceal worked its way through her. She felt molten, wild. And she'd hardly done anything yet.

She thought he was at the edge of his control and she didn't know what might happen if he tipped over, so she moved quickly. She unzipped his trousers and reached inside, freeing him, holding him in her hands at last. *At last.* He was velvet and steel. Hot and silken to the touch, and so powerfully male it was difficult to breathe.

And she didn't know who was shaking more at that point, her or him.

That was as terrifying as it was thrilling, and she didn't want to examine it. His eyes were so dark now they looked like the small hours of a long night, and he was muttering in Greek, almost beneath his breath, oaths and invocations. Curses and prayers, if the look on his face was any guide.

"Mattie." Like her name was another curse, a heftier one.

She sank down to her knees, never breaking eye contact with him, never letting go. He was big and heavy everywhere, hotter than should have been possible, and she forgot that this was supposed to be a weapon. *Her* weapon. She forgot what game she was playing, or why. She wanted to taste him so badly she thought she'd do anything, say anything—

"What is this?" he asked, his accent heavier than she'd ever heard it, his voice thick, but he didn't push her away. He didn't stop her. His chest was rising and falling too fast to mistake, and the sight made her feel almost as needy, almost as molten bright and greedy, as he'd made her feel with his mouth.

"An apology," she whispered, which wasn't what she'd meant to say and had more truth in it than she liked, and so before she could think about it or betray herself further she leaned forward and took him deep into her mouth.

CHAPTER SIX

HE WAS DYING.

Or dreaming—but Nicodemus had had this dream a hundred times before or more, and it had never, ever been this good. *Never.*

Mattie's mouth was so hot, her tongue so delicate and wicked at once as she licked him and tasted him. Tracing patterns, then taking the whole of him deep inside. She moved as she knelt there before him, the culmination of a thousand fantasies and far better than any of them, rocking slightly as if she really was dancing for him, at last, and he died.

Again and again, he died, and she kept going.

Nicodemus was no fool. This kind of sudden reversal made no sense, especially not from Mattie. But he couldn't seem to care about that.

And it would take a far better man than he was to do anything about it now.

He sunk his fingers deep in her thick hair, loosely holding on to her as she tormented him, as she worshipped him. Letting her build the fire in him higher and higher, letting her take him, letting her have him any way she pleased.

Mine, he thought with every stroke of her wicked tongue. *Finally mine.*

And when he fell off the side of the earth and shattered

into a thousand pieces, he shouted out the glory of it in words he knew she couldn't understand.

When he opened his eyes she was still on her knees before him, those marvelous eyes big and wide and focused only on him. Another trillion dreams shattered by a far better reality, he thought. Her lush mouth was swollen slightly, and there was that flush across her cheeks that told him she was as affected by this as he was. For a moment he only stared at her, this woman who had haunted him for so long.

This woman he still didn't understand at all.

Then Nicodemus tucked himself away and zipped up his trousers, the fire still roaring inside him. He wanted to haul her to her feet and bend her over the counter. He wanted to lick his way into her heat again, then lose himself in it, until they were both as shattered as that glass she'd thrown.

He wanted all of her. Here, now.

But he'd waited so long—and he couldn't trust her sudden capitulation. He reached down and slid his hand along her jaw, holding the side of her face, the soft satin of her cheek warm against his palm. Something like tenderness, but with so many lies between them.

Always the lies. Always so many damned lies.

"I think I like you kneeling, princess," he said, not wanting to face that yet. "I may make it a daily requirement."

She didn't like that. He could feel it in the way she quivered, could see it in the way her pretty dark eyes narrowed. But she didn't throw something back at him the way he could see she wanted to do. She stayed there, passive and accommodating and not at all the Mattie he knew.

Not that he was complaining. Not at the moment. Not when he was still breathing hard.

"Wasn't that…okay?" she asked, with breathy concern.

But he could see the calculation in her eyes, and it helped bring him back to reality.

"You don't listen," he told her coolly. "I've told you before—I don't care how I have you. I'm not that proud. If you want to kneel down before me and pretend it's an apology instead of a manipulation, I won't stop you." He shrugged. "I didn't."

He was impressed with how she held herself so still. "I don't know what you mean."

"This kind of about-face would be suspicious in anyone, but is especially so in you." She started to move, and he shook his head, made his voice harsh. "Stay where you are."

"So you can indulge your domination fantasies?" She rolled her eyes. "No, thank you."

"This is not a fantasy." He smiled, enjoying the fury in her gaze because that was the *real* Mattie behind whatever sugar-coated, undeniably hot game she was playing out. "This is a fact."

He was fascinated by the way her face changed, one emotion after the next and none readable. Eventually, her shoulders dropped. She let go of the ripe tension drawing her body so tight, blowing it out in a long sigh that drew his attention back to her mouth, which he knew, now, could make him her slave. Easily. And then she smiled at him in that way she had before, so that the exquisite little dent beside her mouth revealed itself anew.

As if she was made entirely of sunshine and sweetness.

He didn't believe it, of course. But it made that heat flare again inside him, pooling in his groin with as much force and need and hunger as if he'd never let her use her mouth on him in the first place. As if he'd never found such sweet release.

"I'm sorry," she murmured. "You make me feel—" She

shook her head, as if she couldn't bring herself to name it. "I don't know how to react to it."

"That may be the most honest thing you've ever said to me." Her hair had tumbled down from the little twist she'd put it in, thanks to his hands and the madness of the way she'd brought him over the edge like that, and he brushed the silken mass of it back from her face. "But I doubt very much that's why you're saying it."

"Fine." She settled, relaxing her bottom on her feet, looking less like she was kneeling and more like she happened to be doing some kind of yoga near him. "You're the expert on me, or so you keep telling me. So what terrible, underhanded reasons do I have for doing what I just did? Maybe you can explain why you did the exact same thing to me on the plane. Will our reasons be the same?" Her mouth curved, challenging him. "Or will you decide, the way you always seem to do, that I'm devious and motivated only by plots and schemes and deceit while you—and only you—are nobly called to action by nothing more than the purity of your intentions?"

"I might be less sarcastic, were I on my knees," Nicodemus observed.

That curve in her mouth deepened, her eyes were bittersweet chocolate with that blue besides and still seemed like sunlight next to the glossy midnight fall of her hair, and he knew that this could go on forever. That it would.

It made him inexpressibly sad.

They'd been sniping at each other for a decade, and there was no end in sight. Playing power games, raising the stakes. He'd forced this marriage and she'd only today touched him for the first time entirely of her own volition—and not, he understood and hated that he did, because she'd been overcome with the longing to do so.

He'd told her he didn't care how she came to him, and

on some level, that was true. But it was also true that there was a restlessness in him, like an uneasy winter wind, and a howling expanse inside that he didn't want to admit was there.

Finally, everything was exactly how he wanted it. Everything was in its rightful place. He had every single thing he'd ever desired—and yet this was still nothing more than an echoing, cavernous house filled with *things*. The world in his pocket, the woman of his dreams at his feet with his rings on her finger, and he was still as entirely and utterly alone as when he'd realized what Arista really was all those years ago. What she'd really wanted from a low class man with high class aspirations and too much money too fast.

How was this any different?

He realized, then, the depths of the fantasy he'd built up around Mattie Whitaker. The things he'd imagined she could do, the magic she could work, and why? Because she'd been the prettiest thing he'd ever seen when he was twenty-six and so far away from the ugly little place he'd come from. Because, as she'd accused him, he'd wanted that access to her father and to Whitaker Industries. Because he'd wanted *her* and had convinced himself that he'd already learned his lesson with Arista. That he'd never repeat those mistakes.

Nicodemus was, as he had always been, the king of the damned. A lie his father had told and nothing more. And the worst part was that he knew he wouldn't change a thing he'd done to get here. Not one thing. Not even this.

Especially not this.

"Are we going to stare at each other forever?" Mattie asked, her voice easy but those dark eyes of hers intense. "Or is it that you don't have an answer?"

"I have an answer." He thought he sounded far smokier,

darker, all the way through, but she didn't seem to notice any difference, and why would she? She didn't know him. No one ever had, and he understood then that no one ever would. Especially not this woman he'd made his wife, a word she'd claimed was meaningless, anyway. He believed her. Finally, he believed her. "I doubt you'd like it."

Nicodemus dropped his hand from her face and when she rose to her feet in a lithe sort of ripple that made all sense desert him for a beat of his heart, then another, he didn't object. She reached over and helped herself to his coffee, swirling the traditionally thick mixture around in the cup before taking a dainty sip.

"This is about control, isn't it?" she asked. But it wasn't really a question, and he found he was preoccupied with the fact that the soft, airy sweater she wore matched the darker parts of her eyes. "You're obsessed with making sure I don't have any."

"No," he said. He wanted to be the coffee cup she pressed to her lips. He wanted to lick the little bit of moisture away when she lowered it. He wanted her to *want* him, and not because she thought she could leverage it. Maybe that was all he'd ever wanted. More fool, him. It was Arista all over again, and he wasn't twenty any longer. He had no excuse this time. "This is about lies. It always is. And I'm afraid you've miscalculated."

She raised her eyebrows at him, but didn't speak, not even when he reached over and traced a path along her delicate jaw, over that little dent that made him foolish with longing, then on down the elegant line of the aristocratic neck she'd inherited from her titled English mother. Then he found his way along the collarbone that led to her exposed shoulder. Her skin was so soft, so warm. She was still so pretty, as gleaming and lovely in his house as in her father's.

And she was no more than what he'd made her inside his own head. A stranger with a perfect face. One more critical mistake in a long line of them.

Another damned lie and this one all the worse because he'd told it to himself. For years.

"I've known for a long time that everything you said to me was untrue," he said after a moment, and he wasn't playing up that dark note in his voice then, like grief. That was what this was. What he'd lost. "But your body, I believed. I told myself it whispered the truth no matter what you said."

The more dramatic papers claimed she'd lured him into this marriage, that she was a siren who'd enslaved him with her infamous charms, that she was her brother's instrument sent to bring him to heel. He watched her now and wished that any of that were true. That he could fool himself for a little bit longer.

"My body and I are not separate entities," she said, grittier than whatever too-sweet voice she'd been using, but at least that was real. At least that was *her*.

"And now I know it," he said quietly. He dropped his hand and stepped back, away from her, the way he should have done when she'd come to him in the first place. The way he should have done ten years ago when he'd found himself drawn to yet another pointless, pretty little heiress who would never do anything but look down her nose at me. "Which means there's not a single thing about you I can believe, Mattie. And from this moment forward, I promise you, I won't."

That shouldn't have hurt her, given how deliberately she'd played out this scene, and it certainly shouldn't have sat on him the way it did, so heavy and dark he thought it might crush him, but there was no mistaking the ravaged look on her face then.

"I wouldn't have—" She stopped, and he got the impression she'd surprised herself by speaking. "Nicodemus, if I didn't want—"

But she didn't finish. Her expression was equal parts misery and resignation. What he would have called longing, before, when he was still clinging to all his fantasies. When he'd still imagined that this was a game he could win.

That she was.

"Nothing's changed," he said . "I finally see this for what it is."

"A mess?" she supplied bitterly, and he smiled.

"Just another lie," he told her. And he'd had his fill of them so long ago, hadn't he? How had he done this to himself? "But it's our lie, Mattie, and there's no escaping it now."

He knew he had to leave her there in the kitchen before he made himself a liar, too. Before he forgot what he was doing and lost himself in her, instead, that gorgeous deception she'd offered on her knees with a smile. That marvelous deceit he wanted to believe more than he wanted his next breath.

More than he wanted anything.

Nicodemus didn't know how he made himself walk away. Only that he did.

"If I had known that you planned to work through our honeymoon, such as it is," Mattie said in a very bored tone, lifting her gaze from the tablet computer, where their wedding pictures were splashed across all the tabloids, and glared at Nicodemus's profile as if it was *his* fault she looked besotted and in love in every one of them, "I might have brought my own along."

Nicodemus had his laptop open before him on the glass-topped table between them, his smartphone in his hand,

and he didn't bother to look over at her. As if they'd been unhappily married for years, Mattie thought darkly.

"Your work?" he asked, perfectly politely. "I was unaware that you had more than a passing acquaintance with the term."

And that right there was the problem. He'd been nothing but *polite* since that scene in his kitchen almost a week ago now. Nicodemus was scrupulously courteous. Unerringly distant. And that gleaming thing she'd taken entirely for granted, she only realized now that she couldn't see it, was gone from those dark eyes of his.

He insisted she sit with him. Sleep in that bed with him whenever he was in it. Eat all her meals with him. He was still attempting to *gentle* her, like she was an obstreperous cow. But the Nicodemus she hadn't realized she'd come to know—and, on some level, depend upon—was gone.

Mattie hated it.

"You know perfectly well that I work in PR," she said now. "I can think of at least three occasions in the past five years you've referenced it directly."

She was curled up in a corner of the sofa in the great room while Nicodemus sat in one of the armchairs, leaning forward now to tap at his keyboard. He still didn't look at her. Not even to point out that none of the references he'd made to her career were positive.

"You do not *work in PR*," he said when he finally deigned to answer. That harsh mouth of his didn't curve the way it would have, once. There was no hint of that rich laughter in his low voice. "You get paid to attend parties with the paparazzi in tow. You get paid more to call up your equally rich, bored and pointlessly famous friends to come along with you. You raise the profile of already sensationalized events by your exalted presence. Is that PR? Or a slightly more sanitized version of prostitution?"

Ouch.

"The tabloids claim you've stolen me away and married me without Chase's permission, because you're business rivals fighting over the company like a couple of wild dogs." She eyed him. "Making me the bone in this scenario."

The old Nicodemus would have smirked at that. This one didn't bother, and Mattie hated that she felt it like an acid inside her, eating away at her. Leaving nothing but gaping holes and a kind of hollowness behind.

"They also claim you've been secretly in love with me for years." He kept typing whatever it was he was typing, ruling his world from a distance and not sparing her a single glance as he spoke. "That your father opposed our relationship and only now can we be together, the Romeo and Juliet of the business world. Or that you're actually the conniving power behind Chase, and this union was all your idea to throw off your father's creditors. I'm not sure which version I find more laughable."

HAS MATTIE BEEN FAKING IT ALL ALONG? screeched one article, which had hypothesized that Mattie was actually some kind of corporate Mata Hari, slithering from one rich man to the next while hiding herself in plain sight as a vapid tabloid train wreck. She thought that one might actually be the most insulting of them all.

"I thought the witnesses to our wedding were household staff with the odd smartphone camera," she continued, changing the subject slightly from the obnoxious headlines that showed no signs of abating as the days passed. "Imagine my surprise to discover that one was a photographer so talented he made that sad little exercise look like a romantic moment."

"You're a far better actress than I ever gave you credit for," Nicodemus said, and he did glance over at her then, but she saw nothing on that fiercely beautiful face of his but impatience. "But then, why shouldn't you be? It's not like you know anything about reality."

"Like you do, you mean," she retorted, and waved a hand around them to indicate the sprawling villa and the stunning views in all directions. "Because this is reality."

"The difference is that I earned this." His cell phone buzzed and he frowned at it but didn't answer, and Mattie hated how she clung to that. Like it meant something. "I built this. I came from nothing and believe me, I remember what it was like to have no reason to live but dreams that someday, it might be better. I don't imagine you can say the same."

"Everybody's had to fight, Nicodemus," she said, and she was horrified at what she heard in her voice. That rawness. That telling darkness. The memories that came with it, and then the guilt. Always the guilt. "Everyone. Even someone you find as useless as me."

He looked at her then, but it was different—so damned different—from the way he'd studied her all these years. She didn't understand why it made a clawing panic rise inside her, making her chest tight and her throat hurt. She didn't understand any of this. She only knew that she'd played her best weapon and won—but lost something, too. Something she hadn't realized she could lose. Something she certainly hadn't realized she'd miss.

And suddenly, she was afraid to hear what he might say next.

"Is it in your grand plans that I continue to work?" she asked languidly, as if she wasn't affected by any of this at all. "When we get back to New York, I mean. Does your great and glorious male dignity demand that I become some kind of housewife, instead? I read an article that claimed you've abducted me against my will and hypnotized me to force me to act against my brother. Just FYI. There could be questions if I don't turn up at the office."

"I don't believe you possess any of the skills I might require in a housewife," Nicodemus said, and there was the faintest hint of his dry humor there. It made Mattie's heart kick at her. "Can you cook? Clean? Do a single thing you're told?"

She settled back against the couch. "A man of your wealth has a housekeeper for all that, surely."

"Yes, and my housekeeper obeys me. *She* is a gem without price."

"So am I to perch on your arm and be decorative?" Mattie asked. "That sounds delightful. Very intellectually stimulating, I'm sure. What will we tell the tabloids? What new stories will they create? That you took me to Greece to lobotomize me?"

He ran his hand over his face and for a moment—just a moment—looked tired. Sad, even. It reminded her of that unguarded moment she'd stumbled upon that day in the kitchen, and, like then, she didn't know what to make of it. Or of her own response, which was outsized and strange. *Unwieldy.*

If she could, she thought—if she was someone else—she would reach over and try to soothe him with her hands. She scowled down at her fingers, clenched around the tablet with too many tabloids and still sporting those too-bright rings he'd put there, as if they'd betrayed her.

"You can do whatever you want, Mattie," Nicodemus said, and she hated everything about this. That she felt caught up in whatever this new thing between them was, tighter and harsher and so much narrower. That she hurt—and more for him and that light she missed seeing in his eyes than anything else.

She didn't dare ask herself what that meant.

"And if I want to leave you?" she heard herself say, because she couldn't stop.

"Anything but that," he said, his voice harsh, and when his phone rang again he swiped it up from the table, though his dark eyes stayed on her. "We'll suffer in this together. I know I already made that clear."

And then he directed all of his attention back to his work, and Mattie knew she had no one to blame for that dark and heavy thing squatting on her chest but herself.

That night they worked together in the kitchen, putting together one of the simple meals they'd been living on here. A fresh salad. Homemade pita bread warmed in the oven and placed in a basket. A plate with a hunk of feta and tangy local olives, drenched in a gold-green olive oil. Lamb that Nicodemus had prepared matter-of-factly and quickly on the grill, then placed on the plates Mattie carried out to the table on the terrace.

It occurred to her as they settled across from each other that they'd developed their own rhythm in these past days. That this was what married couples *did*, this quiet dance of shared food and a laden table. Candles against the cool October air and no need for conversation.

It occurred to her that despite everything, despite what she'd done to avoid it, this was the most intimate she'd ever been with a person she wasn't related to.

The insight was like a slap to the head and she sat there for a moment, staring at Nicodemus in dismay. Because this was precisely why he was doing all of this, she understood. Even if he was angry with her, he was still creating bonds between them that had nothing to do with their decade of games or that sexual tension that burned between them even now. He was making this—*him*—a habit.

This was exactly what she didn't want. What she couldn't allow.

"What now?" he asked, reaching out to drag a soft square of the pita bread through the olive oil, then popping it in his mouth. He sat back in his chair as he chewed, but the way he looked at her was anything but indulgent.

"I think it's time you explained to me what happened the other day in the kitchen," she blurted out. "Most men would be transported with delight if they received an unsolicited blow job."

Was that a muscle that twitched in his jaw? Or did she only want it to be because it indicated she still affected him? How could she know her own motivations so little?

"I am not most men."

"Obviously." She sat much too rigidly in her seat, and found that her appetite had deserted her. She shoved the perfectly grilled lamb around on her plate. "You've been punishing me ever since."

"Don't be so dramatic." He seemed unperturbed, and continued to eat with every appearance of contentment. "Punishment can take many forms, but none, I think, involve whiling away your days on a beautiful island with nothing to do but relax."

"That depends on the company."

"Here's the thing, Mattie." His gaze flared into something else. Something so blisteringly hot it robbed her of breath. "I've done all this before. The pretty girl. The endless, circular lies. I already know how it ends."

She didn't like that flare of prickly heat that washed over her, because she knew exactly what it was, and she'd never been jealous of anything before in her life. *Damn him.*

"Are you trying to tell me that I don't measure up to your ex?" she asked tautly. "They say comparison is the thief of joy, Nicodemus. Maybe that's why you're so grumpy all the time."

He looked like he wanted to bite at her, and she shouldn't have thrilled to that.

"I don't find all the insults and digs and snide remarks amusing anymore," he grated at her.

"Why not?" she asked, and she didn't know how she dared. Or why her voice was so tiny when she did. "I thought you knew how it ends."

"What I thought was a game we were both playing was something else entirely to you," he said with a quiet menace that rolled through Mattie like a seismic event, and paled in comparison to that look in his dark eyes. "I wasn't lying. You were."

"But what if I'm not?"

She hadn't meant to say that. She didn't even know where it came from—and yet it was there between them, stretched out prone on the small table, surrounded by the flickering flames of the candles and the rich Greek night all around them.

"There are always consequences," he said after a moment. "In this case, I don't believe a single thing you say. You wanted to manipulate me and you were willing to go as far as possible to do it."

"You're one to talk," she managed to reply, though her eyes felt glazed and she was half-afraid the rest of her had turned to stone. "Where do you think I learned how to use sex as a weapon in the first place?"

"You're such a liar." It came out somewhere between wonder and despair, and she'd never heard him use that tone of voice before. It tore at her. "You lie to my face about things I know are not true. I was there. I've never *used* sex. I've simply admitted the attraction I feel and occasionally acted upon it. There's a difference."

"Because you say there is!" she threw at him. "That doesn't make it so!"

"I've been dreaming of getting my mouth on you for years," he growled at her, looking much too dangerous for a man who still appeared to do no more than lounge there across from her. "I didn't ask you to strip for me, Mattie. You did that."

"But you were happy to take advantage, of course."

"I'm not going to have this argument," he told her then, that colder note of impatience back in his voice. Shifting, she thought, from potentially emotional husband to unamused CEO in an instant, and she loathed it. "Because we both know you know better—and that I wasn't the one playing games."

"Nicodemus—"

"Eat your dinner," he told her. He picked up his own fork and speared a piece of lamb with barely repressed violence.

"This is fake," she gritted out, and was surprised to discover that her hands were in fists in her lap, and her throat was so tight it hurt to speak. "This is nothing but a game of make-believe. We might as well be the tabloid stories they make up about us. How is this any better?"

"This is a marriage," he retorted, all of that ferocity in his voice , and darkening his gaze, and she was sick enough to exult in that, because at least she'd reached something in him. "Our marriage. You should count yourself lucky I've decided it should be so goddamned civil."

Nicodemus woke in a rush.

He didn't need to reach out to the empty mattress beside him to realize that Mattie wasn't in the bed. He knew immediately. But his hand moved over the spot she normally occupied—as far away from him as she could get and still technically be in the same bed—and he found it cold. Utterly devoid of her heat, telling him that she'd slipped away again. She always did.

He swung his way out of the bed and onto his feet, not bothering to turn on the lights. Outside, the moon was flirting toward fullness, creating a rippling path across the dark water, and Nicodemus was furious.

He would have asked himself what the hell was wrong with him, but he knew. It was always Mattie, always this same woman lodged in him like a pebble in his shoe. Or a knife in his side, if he was more accurate, and he had no idea how he was maintaining his control. If it didn't bother her so much when he went cold and distant, he acknowledged to himself in the predawn quiet of his empty bedroom, he would have broken already.

So maybe he played as many games as she did, after all.

But it was this particular game of hers—this nightly ritual—that he thought might drive him to the brink of madness.

Every night she deserted their bed. Every night he would either wake to find her missing or come to bed after another round of irritating international conference calls to find she wasn't there. Every night he would hunt her down, find her sleeping somewhere else in this sprawling place and sometimes muttering and thrashing in a way that suggested anything but sweet dreams, and carry her back with him.

Every single night, and they never discussed it.

Nicodemus assumed it was her last gasp of rebellion, and on some level he couldn't help but admire her hardheadedness and persistence. But it wasn't admiration he felt tonight as he failed to locate her in any of her usual spots. She wasn't in any of the guest suites. She wasn't in the great room, the solarium or on the leather couch in his office. He went through every room of the villa without finding her, and it was only when he stood near the wall of windows outside his private gym and indoor lap pool that he realized she'd escalated things and left the building.

He thought she might be the death of him one of these days, he really did.

Nicodemus let himself out into the cold night, the October wind and the watching moon piercing him as he walked across the flagstone patio that made a ring around the outdoor pool that he'd need to close for the season soon. He felt the coming winter in the stones beneath his bare feet, and he felt like a caveman when he wrenched open the door to the pool house and saw her there, where she shouldn't have been.

She was in a ball on the summer chaise in the corner, and for a moment, he thought she was awake and speaking to him—

But then he saw the tears. And the look of abject terror on her face.

She wasn't speaking, he realized. She was crying the same word over and over and over.

Nicodemus didn't hesitate. He wasn't *civil*. He simply closed the distance between the door and the chaise in two strides. He picked her up, blanket and tears and all, and cradled her in his lap.

She was ice cold and distraught and she wasn't, it finally dawned on him, awake.

So he simply held her. He rocked her gently, murmuring old words he half remembered from a childhood he would have said had held no softness of any kind. He smoothed her hair back from her face and let her sob into his neck.

And he pretended he would do the same for any woman he encountered, any person at all. That he would feel this same sense of immensity and something very nearly like awe that she was letting him hold her, this same ache that she was in pain. This same pounding understanding—like his own heart in his chest—that he would fight off anything that threatened her, even if it was inside her own head.

Slowly, the sobbing subsided. Her breaths came smoother, slower. And Nicodemus knew the moment she came fully awake and aware of her surroundings, because her whole body went tense.

"You're all right," he told her quietly, glad it was so dark in the pool house. Glad there was no chance she could see the expression he was afraid he wore much too plainly on his face. "I'll keep you safe."

He chose not to investigate how deeply and wholly he meant that.

"What—what happened?"

Nicodemus had never heard her stutter, he thought then, nor sound so terrified. Not his Mattie, who careened through the world like Don Quixote but with a far sharper tongue. He rubbed a hand over that aching thing in his chest, then smoothed it over her hair again—but she was awake now, and she pulled away.

And he had no choice but to let her.

"Do you have these nightmares often?" he asked as she scrambled up and out of his lap like she was on fire, then wrapped herself in that blanket as if it could protect her. From him or from whatever dire thing stalked her dreams? He couldn't tell. "Is that why you creep out of our bed every night? You've been upset before, but not like this. You usually quiet down when I hold you."

"What?" Her voice was sharper then, but no less panicked. More so, he'd have said. "What do you mean?"

"You were having a terrible nightmare," he said slowly, aware from the taut way she stood and the sudden spike of tension in the room that he'd stumbled into something here. Something important. "You were sobbing. Screaming, I think. The same word again and again."

"How strange," she said, and though her voice was cooler then, he could hear all the panic and the leftover nightmare beneath it. "I must have eaten something that disagreed with me."

Another lie, Nicodemus thought, but he couldn't summon up the usual fury at that sad little truth. She was so brittle; she was acting so tough—but she hadn't faked those desperate sobs. She hadn't faked those tears that he could still feel against his collarbone, the night air turning his dampened skin cold. Like proof.

He stood and saw the way she jerked her chin back, as if she had to fight herself to stay still. He wished, then, they were different people. Or that they could start this whole thing over the way she'd pretended she wanted to do that day in the kitchen. He wished that he could trust her—or that she could trust him, even a little, with who she really was.

He wished this hadn't all been set in stone so many years ago now.

He didn't touch her, though he wanted nothing more. But he didn't think he'd stop at a mere touch, and that was the last thing she'd allow. He could almost *see* the defensiveness prickle around her, like she'd grown spikes where she stood.

"I don't think it was food poisoning," he said after a moment. His voice was matter-of-fact in the dark room. "You were crying out for your mother."

She made a sound like she'd been socked in the gut. "My mother?" she asked, much too softly. "That doesn't make any sense. You must be mistaken."

"No, *agapi mou*," he said, and he was only distantly aware that he'd called her *my love*. It hardly seemed important, though some part of him registered it would be.

Eventually. He reached over despite himself and wrapped a strand of her black hair around his finger, pleased that it retained a small bit of her warmth. Wishing he could, too. "All you said was *mama*. Over and over again."

CHAPTER SEVEN

WHEN SHE WOKE up it was morning, and Nicodemus was gone.

For a moment, Mattie blinked at the side of the bed where he normally sprawled, all of his masculine perfection on mouthwatering display. But then her memory caught up with her in a sickening rush, and so did her headache.

She felt hungover, though she knew she wasn't. Dreadfully, hideously hungover, from the pounding at her temples to the desert where her mouth should have been. And there was panic like a stomach cramp, deep in her belly, growing more acute by the second.

A shower—long and hot and almost punishing—didn't help. Neither did sneaking down to the kitchen and fixing herself a huge mug of coffee to stave off the fog in her head. Mattie crept down the long hall that led to Nicodemus's office and stopped when she heard his voice from within. Powerful, commanding. Certain.

"I've already signed the papers," he was saying, and Mattie imagined boardrooms all over the world filled with corporate disciples in three-piece suits, leaping over each other to do his bidding. "I will be forced to view any further delays or dragging of feet as hostile, am I clear? *Endaxi.*"

His voice lulled her into a false sense of security, like

he could handle anything—even her, and she knew she couldn't risk that.

She slipped back down the hall and climbed back up to the master bedroom. It took her only a moment to locate her things in the vast walk-in closet, and she pulled the cigarette packet out of the bottom of her purse with a small sigh of relief. The packet had crumpled on the side and the three cigarettes that remained within were bent almost to breaking, but that hardly mattered. She pulled one out, then rummaged around for her lighter.

She didn't go out on the balcony that wrapped around the master bedroom on three sides. Instead, she retraced her steps through the villa and then continued on into the long wing where all the guest suites were. It was there, at the farthest point of the house, she snuck out onto a little patio, found a small iron bench not directly visible from inside and indulged in her filthiest habit.

Mattie pulled her legs up beneath her and tipped her head back, letting the chilly air and the warm sunlight battle it out. Slowly, surely, she felt better. The cigarette tasted stale, but that didn't matter. It wasn't about the taste. It wasn't even about smoking.

It was, if she was honest with herself, purely about reminding herself that Nicodemus couldn't control this. *Her.* That he didn't know her, no matter what he'd thought he'd heard last night. That she still had whole parts of herself she was keeping at bay, keeping hidden, that he couldn't reach no matter how many meals they shared or nightmares he soothed away. That he cast the illusion of safety, but it was only that: an illusion.

Because that had to be true, or she was well and truly lost.

And if there was a growing part of her that wanted to simply surrender to him, to lose herself in him, to see if someone as strong and formidable as he was could help her carry the weight of all her secrets—

"Don't be an idiot, Mattie," she said out loud.

"I am afraid it is much too late for that."

She jumped against the iron bench and swiveled to see Nicodemus standing there in the French doors that led to the guest room. Tall, dark. Grim.

And furious.

Mattie looked at the cigarette as if she'd never seen it before, then looked at him. *That will be your last cigarette,* she remembered him saying so long ago in her father's library. Her heart was wild against her ribs. But she couldn't back down. She'd already given too much away.

So she held his dark gaze while she put the cigarette to her mouth again, took a long drag and then blew the smoke out. At him.

For a moment, everything stopped. The world on its axis. The air around them. *Everything.*

Then Nicodemus threw back his head and laughed.

It was the last thing Mattie expected; it filled the morning with its golden, infectious sound, and maybe that was why she didn't think to move when he closed the distance between them, rounding the bench to stand in front of her.

And then it was too late. He leaned over her, trapping her against the high back. He plucked the cigarette out of her fingers the way he had once before, and this time he stubbed it out beneath his foot. Then he caught her where she sat with an arm on either side of her, bringing his face dangerously close to hers.

There was a fire in his dark gaze. And it lit her up with what she chose to call fear, though that molten thing down deep in her core knew better.

"Was I unclear?" he asked in a mild tone at complete odds with the fierce look in his face. "Because I remember telling you that smoking was unacceptable. Did I dream this conversation?"

"I never agreed to obey you, Nicodemus," she said, amazed she had the power of speech when he was so close and so obviously furious with her. "You simply decided I should, the way you've decided any number of things since the day we met." She didn't know where she got the courage—or foolishness—to shrug like that, like he bored her. "And you're welcome to decide whatever you like, but that doesn't mean I have to agree with your decisions. Much less follow them like gospel."

He looked at her for what felt like a very long time. And then he smiled.

"Thank you," he said, almost formally.

She was almost afraid to ask. "For what?"

"For making this easy."

She didn't see him move. He only shifted, and then she was in the air, unable to make sense of what was happening to her until the soft curve of her belly hit the rock hardness of his shoulder. He was already inside the villa and moving swiftly through the guest wing by the time she registered that he'd simply picked her up and thrown her over his shoulder.

Mattie fought. She kicked at him and beat at his back with her fists, and he only laughed and smacked his hand down on her bottom. Hard.

Then he tipped her upright again and dropped her. She cried out in the instant before she bounced in the center of their bed. *His* bed, she corrected herself furiously, desperately scrabbling to catch herself and sit up—

To see Nicodemus standing there at the foot of the bed, his arms crossed over his chest and his eyes like stone as he glared down at her.

"We've had a week of lies and strained civility," he said,

and there was nothing cool about his voice. Nothing measured or *polite*. "Now we do this my way."

"This has all been your way already!"

"Mattie," he said, harsh and certain and more like steel than she'd ever heard him. "Be quiet."

She told herself she wasn't obeying him. That she was simply trying to calm her racing heart, stop her ragged-edged gasping for breath. She told herself that *if she'd wanted to*, she would have screamed at him. But whatever the reason, she fell silent.

Nicodemus could have been carved from marble.

"What do you suggest I do with a woman who acts like a disobedient child?" he asked, his voice a low rasp.

"I take it that's a rhetorical question?"

He ignored her. "It doesn't take a psychiatrist to figure out that you have Daddy issues, Mattie. The question is, do I play that role? Is that what it will take?"

Her jaw ached. That was how she realized she was clenching her teeth.

"I," she bit out, so angry it was like a living thing clawing its way out from within her, "do not have *Daddy issues*. The only issue I have is you."

"This is what you need to understand," Nicodemus said in that ruthless way that made something shiver through her, settling low in her belly and becoming a pulse of heat, mixing with that anger and changing it into something she couldn't recognize. Or she didn't want to recognize. "I will win. No matter how long it takes, no matter what I have to do, no matter what games you play. I will win because winning is what I do."

"You don't get to order me—"

"It is time for you to stop running at windmills," he told her in that same ruthless way. "We are not living in your world, where you can order everyone around and have them dance to your tune. We are in mine. And I find my interest in indulging these tantrums is over."

She couldn't speak for a long moment. There was that terrible yearning deep inside her, too deep and too dark. It would eat her whole, she knew, and what would be left of her on the other side? What would happen when he got what he thought he wanted and really, truly knew her?

Why did she want to find out when she knew she'd regret it?

"The fact that you think you have the right to expect obedience is a problem, Nicodemus," she said, scowling at him, hoping she could bluster her way through this the way she always had before. "The fact that you think you can manhandle me? Also a problem."

He was dressed all in black today, she couldn't help but notice. A black T-shirt that strained over his muscled arms and black trousers that clung to his narrow hips and showed the faintest hint of his olive-toned skin at the waistband. He looked like he could singlehandedly take down a terrorist cell if he felt like it—which meant cowing her should be the work of a few moments. The idea made her limbs feel like liquid. Hot and slippery when she wanted to be strong.

"And the fact that you call anything I do that you don't like *a tantrum*," she continued, her chin rising up as she refused to let herself look away from him, "is certainly a big problem, as well. It's wildly condescending, for a start."

"Here is what will happen," he said in a perfectly calm, conversational tone, as if there was no tension in the air, no beating, throbbing, white-hot *thing* wrapping tighter and tighter around them both. "I told you I was going to spank you. You had the option to dance for me, instead, but you chose to run away, as usual. Leaving me to clean up yet another one of your messes. Also as usual." He smiled faintly. "Did you think I had forgotten these infractions?"

"Is this boarding school all over again?" she demanded, still going for the bluster even as that hot, slippery, *yearning* thing made her worry she might turn into a puddle on the bed. "Will I get detention for smoking that cigarette? Will I have to write lines? Scrub the floors?"

"I have something significantly more corporeal in mind."

"You say you want obedience but you didn't like it much when I actually got on my knees, did you?" she snapped at him, telling herself that fire in her was fear, not desire. Because she didn't want to be fascinated by this. She wanted to be afraid. "And I'm not calling you s*ir*, by the way, no matter how many shades of crazy you show me."

A careless shrug. "You made your body fair game in this little struggle of ours. Why shouldn't I do the same? I think we'll do this my way and see what you call me when I'm done. You might be surprised."

"If you spank me," she told him, low and fervent, "I really will let that current sweep me off to Libya. I mean it, Nicodemus."

"Note to self," Nicodemus said mildly, sounding completely unimpressed with her threat. "Tie wife to the bed."

He moved then, putting his knee on the mattress as if he meant to crawl toward her. And everything seemed to slide sideways in a dizzy sort of shift. The world went red. Mattie thought something blew up inside her—knocking out reason. Knocking out everything save that grinding, expanding, whole-bodied *desire* for anything and everything he might give her.

She panicked.

Mattie dove for the side of the bed, already envisioning

her escape. Into the bathroom, where she could lock the door and, if all else failed, crawl out on the roof and try—

But he simply reached out and caught her with one large hand around her hip, yanking her back into the center of the bed.

"Be still," he told her.

So instead, Mattie fought.

She flailed and she kicked, she bucked and she twisted, and she was lost for what seemed like a very long time in the haze of it. But then the fever seemed to lift, and Mattie had to face the unpleasant realization that, as ever with this man, she'd only made it all that much worse.

Because he hadn't fought back. He'd simply pinned her to the bed with his superior strength. And waited.

She was out of breath. Nicodemus was impassive.

He was stretched out above her in absolutely the worst position she could imagine. His chest pressed against hers, flattening her breasts in a way that made her simultaneously hot and very, very worried. His hips were flush against hers, his legs on the inside of hers, and he made no attempt at all to hide the fact that he was hard. Ready. Aroused.

He was so strong. So perfectly formed. Beautiful even when he held her down, his fingers threaded with hers, her arms up and over her head and flat against the mattress.

"You're only making this worse for yourself," he told her.

And she was sick, she decided, because she didn't want to fight him any longer. She wanted to melt into him. She wanted to shift so that his hardness pressed more directly against the core of her. She wanted to lift her mouth and press it against his. She *wanted*—and she knew that it was more destructive by far than anything he could do to her.

"Nicodemus." But she was whispering, and even she

could hear the longing in her voice. And the fact she didn't demand that he release her.

"You claim you won't surrender to me by choice," he said, in that firm, relentless way that made a rush of heat wash over her, turning her restless and liquid and *yearning* beneath him. "And yet it has been obvious to me for some time that surrender is what you need above all things. Think about it. You, completely out of control. No manipulations. No schemes. No plotting. Just your bare bottom and my hand. Imagine what we can learn from an interaction so elemental?"

It took her long moments to realize that she was shaking, over and over, as if something had gone loose inside her and could no longer be contained. As if he was already doing the things he'd painted so vividly. As if she was already that far gone. That lost. As if she could truly surrender the way he wanted her to do. The way she wished she could do. She shook, hard and deep.

But she didn't say no.

"Or," he said, in that dark, low way, "you can tell me one true thing." His gaze locked with hers. "Just one. The truth, Mattie, or my hand. Your choice. But I'll have some kind of surrender from you, either way."

And that was when Mattie realized what she had to do.

Because it was the only thing she had left. And she didn't know why she'd been avoiding it for so long. As Nicodemus had taught her too well in this last fraught week, there were intimacies much more shattering than sex. The world was filled with one-night stands, bedpost-notchers and all kinds of people who used sex to hide from intimacy, not to enhance it.

She could do it. She should have done it long before now. She should have realized it was the only possible way she could get the upper hand with him.

Mattie swallowed, hard. She searched his face for any give, any softness, any sign that he was something other than this: hard, demanding, implacable. But it was the Nicodemus she knew staring back at her, and the sheer, startling *rightness* of that—of him and of this decision she'd made so effortlessly after all these years of agonizing—washed over her. It made her remarkably calm for someone who was pinned to a bed and literally trapped between a rock and a hard place.

But it also made it easy. Or maybe that was because it was him.

Maybe, a small voice whispered inside her, *it's always and only been him, and you should have admitted it a long time ago.*

Mattie didn't want to think about that, or all the things it could mean.

"One truth," he said, as if he thought she wasn't going to answer him. "That's all it will take to clean the slate. Can you do it?"

She pulled her fingers out of his, faintly surprised when he let her. Then she reached up and slid her palms along his hard jaw, letting the sensation crash into her. She liked the fact he hadn't bothered to shave in days, that his skin was rough to the touch. She liked that gleam in his dark eyes. She liked that she was closer to him now, almost too close to bear.

"I want you," she whispered.

And Nicodemus froze.

For a shimmering moment, everything was taut. Stretched thin on the edge of a knife—or maybe that was him, holding himself above her, her words like a shout ricocheting within him.

Nicodemus didn't ask her to repeat herself. Not because

her words were burned into him, though they were. Not even because he knew he couldn't possibly hear her over the racket inside him, the clamor of his heart and the shout of his blood in his veins.

But because he had never seen that look on her face before, in her pretty eyes. Wide open. Clear. Determined, perhaps, and more than a little anxious. Bright.

True.

It moved over him like a wave. Like an ocean's worth of tides, dragging at him, blessing him or condemning him, and Nicodemus wasn't sure he cared which. He reminded himself that Mattie was a liar. That like the only other people who had ever meant anything to him, she would lie to him as easily as she breathed. That there was no point in believing her now, when she was only telling him what she thought he most wanted to hear.

When she was right.

She moved then. She slid her hands from his face and wrapped her arms around his shoulders, and then she shifted her hips against his, dancing for him again. Making him wish that this once, he could believe her.

"Nicodemus," she whispered. "I always have."

And he was still only a man, despite everything. He was as weak as any other. Perhaps even as weak, in his own way, as the man he'd always hated the most—his father. And Mattie Whitaker had been crawling in him like an itch for all these years, whispering his name in his darkest hours whether she knew it or not, and promising him exactly this in every last one of his favorite fantasies.

How could he resist her?

He stopped trying. He simply dropped his head and crushed his mouth to hers, and who cared what came after? If she proved—the way he assumed she would, because she always did—that even this was a lie?

For the first time in his life, Nicodemus didn't care.

She tasted like fire and longing and all of the wildness that had swirled between them all this time. He kissed her again and again, glutting himself and losing himself at once, feeling that lush, lithe body of hers pressed against him, soft where he was hard, tall and long and perfect.

Mine, he thought, reveling in the word, in her exquisite warmth in his arms and that pounding, beating, hungry demand inside him, spurring him on, making him half crazed with need.

Her hands traced shapes down his back, tested the heft of his biceps, then found their way to his hips. Everything was the heat of her mouth, the glory of her taste, the maddening slide of her body against his. He pulled back to peel off his shirt and she made a soft sound of distress.

Nicodemus thought he might very well eat her alive.

He threw his shirt away, then tugged hers off. He peeled the skintight black denim from her endless legs, feeling as delirious at the sight of all that lovely flesh as he had been when she'd done this for him in midair. He reached out and traced her phoenix tattoo again, attuned to the soft sounds she made, the way she caught her breath and then let it out hard as he leaned in close and licked his way over the riot of color.

He took his time. He settled in and followed every line, tasting every part of that magical, mystical creature she'd inked into her skin. When he was done, she was shifting and rolling beneath him as if she couldn't help herself. As if she was as needy and insane with it as he was.

But it wasn't enough.

Nicodemus pulled her bra down, one cup at a time, so he could worship each of her breasts in turn. He remembered the thrust of her nipples, the sweet rose of them, but this time he savored each one. He used his tongue and his lips and even the scrape of his teeth, until she was thrashing against the mattress and muttering what sounded like his name. Or perhaps it was an endless stream of something very much like a plea.

Either way, it moved in him like the finest music.

He shifted then, following a meandering path down her abdomen until he reached her pierced navel and could admit, at last, that he liked it. He more than liked it. It made her even sexier, something that he'd have thought impossible. He wanted her—all of her, all of these bright colors and sexy rings—entirely to himself.

The possessiveness wasn't new. But the simple beauty of her surrender, her body wide open beneath him, quivering for his touch—made him feel like a god. He would do anything for this, he understood then in a way that might have worried him had he allowed himself to consider it, and yet at the same time he doubted he'd ever drink his fill of this woman. He couldn't see how he'd ever come close.

Mine, he thought again, the way he always did, though this time it felt darker. Hotter. Much more intense.

Because it felt like truth, at last.

When he reached the dainty lace thong that stretched to contain her femininity, her fingers dug into his hair. Hard.

"No." He only watched her, though he went still, however difficult it might have been. "I want you," she said again, even more beautiful this time because her voice was so ragged, and he knew he'd done that to her. "Inside me, Nicodemus. Please."

"Be certain," he told her, still crouched over her, his mouth a scant inch above that sweet, hot core of hers he longed to taste again. But he didn't care what she did or what she said, what she let him do at the moment or what she held in reserve, as long as she didn't stop. *Please don't stop.* "This is one among many things you can't take back."

Did he imagine her eyes darkened then? But it didn't matter, because she was moving, rising to her knees to take off the bra he'd only shoved out of the way, then wiggling out of her panties, as well.

"I don't want to take anything back," she said huskily, her eyes never leaving his.

And he believed her. God help him, but he believed her.

He reached out and tugged her closer, so they were kneeling together in the center of the bed he'd always imagined would be theirs one day. She kissed him with a passion and a wonder that echoed in him, making him that much wilder, that much closer to losing control.

He sank his hands into her hair and held her where he wanted her, where he could plunder her mouth while her hands worked between them, pulling open his trousers and freeing him. When her hands closed around him, he groaned, resting his forehead against hers. He was too hard. It had been too long. It had been forever.

Still, he let her test the length of him in her palms. Once. Twice. But at that third slide of rough silk and all that ferocious, impossible hunger, he pulled her hands away.

"But I want—"

"You already told me what you want," he told her, gruff and dark, "and you won't get it if you keep that up."

And perhaps he'd gone completely delusional, after all, but the smile she gave him seemed to fill the whole room. And him, too, kicking through the shadows that lurked inside him and letting light into the darkest places—

This was the real danger, he knew. It always had been. *He wanted to believe.*

Nicodemus stretched out on his back, kicking his trousers off as he went, and pulled her down beside him. Then he pulled one of those long legs of hers up over his hip and took her mouth again, feasting on her as his hands roamed.

One anchored in that thick, sweet-smelling hair of hers. The other moved lower, making its way to her core.

Where she was molten hot, wet and soft, and there was no doubt at all that she wanted him. That this was real. That whatever she might be lying about still, and he was sure she was because she always was, it wasn't this.

This was real. This was true.

This was finally happening.

Nicodemus stroked his way into her, finding her shockingly tight and incandescent all around his gentle entry. She shuddered against him, and he tried another finger beside the first, twisting his hand so that every time he rocked into her, he pressed hard against that jutting center of her need.

And Mattie went wild.

She thrust against him. Her hips were like lightning and he didn't want to contain it—he wanted to glory in the storm. He held her mouth to his as she moaned, holding her when she would have pulled back, feeling her tighten everywhere as she melted into his hand. Feeling her shudder and twist, hearing her make the wildest, sweetest noises imaginable, until she choked out something that sounded like his name and catapulted straight over the side of the world—consumed in all that glorious fire while he watched, fierce male satisfaction and that terrible need pouring through him, setting him aflame.

"You are mine, *agapi mou*," he told her then, pulling his hand from her clenching heat and shifting her over to her back even as she shook and cried out in his arms. "You have always been mine."

And then, at last, he slammed his way into her, hard.

He felt the tightness, then the tear as she gave way. Felt her go rigid even as she cried out, and no longer in anything like passion.

Impossible, he thought.

But the sound she'd made was sheer pain, threaded through with shock. Her eyes were dark and glassy, and her hands came up to slam against his chest, and he didn't think she knew she hit him, much less that hard—

She was a virgin.

CHAPTER EIGHT

IT HURT.

Mattie only realized, as that strange, overstretched full-ness went on, as the burning part felt like it might drown her and her thighs felt like someone else's, with so much of him hard and prodding and huge between them and *in* her, that she'd convinced herself it wouldn't. Not after all this time.

Not with him.

Dimly, she realized that he was much too still. That it could only mean that her fantasy of him not even notic-ing had failed to come true. That he had, indeed, noticed.

And worse, stopped.

"It's okay," she said in a bright sort of voice that even she could hear sounded strained and awful and much too loud. "It can only get better. Right?"

She gave an experimental roll of her hips and had to suck in a breath, because it wasn't better. It was…pierced and heavy and *full.* Much too *full,* and so much more *physical* than she'd imagined.

"Even here, you find a new way to lie to me," he gritted out, his voice a scrape of sound and painful to her ears. "When I'd have told you it was impossible."

He did not sound remotely lighthearted or amused, or *darkly thrilled,* all of which she'd imagined as alternate scenarios to him simply failing to register it at all.

And it still hurt.

"I didn't lie," she told him, surprised that she could speak when *so many things* were happening to her, *in her,* far too many to process—and yet none that looked anything like what she'd seen online and in all those movies. She even managed to sound faintly offended. "You never asked me if I was a virgin."

He was still holding himself motionless, stretched there above her, every inch of him managing to *bristle* somehow, as if she'd betrayed him. She didn't like the tiny little tremor that moved through her, like something in her agreed.

"How?" He bit it off in a dark voice so filled with storms that Mattie shivered again, and hated that he was right there. That he saw it. The way he saw everything.

"The usual way," she said, shifting beneath him, trying to find a comfortable way to lie there with a man *inside* her. "Which mostly involved never doing this."

She could *feel* his gaze boring into her, burning her, accusing her.

"You are twenty-eight years old. *Twenty-eight.* I would sooner expect to see the face of God appear on the side of a dinner plate than a twenty-eight-year-old virgin."

"It's not like there's a law that everyone has to lose their virginity at a certain age."

"No." His voice then could have stripped paint. "But there is something called reality. To say nothing of your very public relationships, all conducted in the glare of a thousand cameras."

"What happens in front of the cameras is theater and misdirection, Nicodemus," she said hurriedly. "A game. You know that."

"You mean lies."

"That's not the word I'd use."

His fingers tapped at her chin, which was when Mattie realized she'd been frowning at the center of his neck this whole time.

And when she finally saw his face, she almost gave in to that hectic heat that threatened to spill over from her eyes. He looked drawn and furious at once. Something like wounded, and haunted around the eyes.

She had done that to him, she knew, though she shoved that aside and concentrated on the fact that once again, Nicodemus was not like other men. He wasn't like anyone else she'd ever known, and she hated that acknowledging it made her feel that much more raw.

"How?" he asked again, his voice far more clipped.

It occurred to Mattie then that she hadn't thought this through—mostly because she'd assumed that she was so old that none of the usual virginity concerns would apply. She certainly hadn't anticipated having to defend something she'd hardly dared admit to herself had even been happening all these years, that seemed that much more silly and pointless now, when it *hurt* and he was looking at her like she'd *done something* to him.

"Why am I not surprised?" she flared at him. "Give the man a blow job and he has an extended temper tantrum. Give the man *virginity*—which I believe some women sell for astronomical prices on the internet, by the way, so prized is it in this modern age—and he acts like it's some kind of communicable disease. My God, Nicodemus. What's the matter with you?"

"You are an idiot," he retorted, in a tone she'd never heard him use before. "I begin to believe it is entirely on purpose. A willful and deliberate course of action you choose to cause the most harm."

"I'm not an idiot," she retorted, stung, which only made her feel like one.

"Did you want me to hurt you, Mattie?" he gritted out. "Is that was this was—a carefully orchestrated scene to make certain I would feel nothing but guilt and regret and make you my victim, at last? Congratulations. You have succeeded admirably."

He moved then, and she realized he was about to roll off her. About to end this whole strange experience—and that shot through her like a bullet, clearing out that terrifying rawness that hovered within her like a fragile thing and leaving only a desperate flare of fury in its wake.

"Don't you dare!" She,tightened her legs around him as if that could keep him where he was, that or her sheer panic that if she let him go, she'd lose him forever. She opted not to consider why that would bother her so much. "If you stop now, all it will ever be is this. Painful and weird."

"You have no idea what you're talking about," he told her bitterly, though he didn't pull out of her. He'd stopped moving away, just as she'd asked. And she felt a deep relief she hadn't earned, and wasn't certain she even understood. "As you have demonstrated, going so far as to hurt yourself in the process."

She realized her hands were on his chest, balled into fists, and she opened them, spreading her fingers wide and soaking in the heat of his skin, that chiseled perfection that was only Nicodemus. She felt his heart thundering there, under one palm, and became aware, then, of the way he breathed. Harsh. Like this hurt him, too. Experimentally, she moved her hips against his.

She couldn't claim it felt *good*. But it didn't make her want to cry, either.

"Make it better," she ordered him, and his dark eyes widened slightly, in a kind of shock he hid almost as soon as she saw it. And then, behind that, she saw that heat she recognized.

Male. Primitive. Fire and need.

She wanted that back.

"What makes you think I can?" he asked, but there was less of that grimness in his voice, she thought. Less of that impenetrable darkness. And she clung to it.

"Because you've already proved that you can."

Mattie didn't know why she was whispering. She knew only this. Him, still and strong above her, holding himself off her with his fists dug into the mattress. She wanted him lower. Closer. She wanted him to *do something* with this strange yearning inside her, somehow physical and emotional at once. Twined and nonsensical, but all his fault.

Deep inside her, she felt him twitch, and it made her break out in goose bumps, all the way down her arms. She shuddered.

His dark eyes narrowed.

"And if I do this," he said then, as if he was choosing his words carefully, "what do I get in return?"

Mattie frowned at him. "An orgasm, presumably. Unless something goes horribly wrong. Isn't that what you usually get out of it?"

She thought she saw a glimpse of that dark, honeyed gleam, that amusement that she thought was only hers, and it made that fullness in her—that quivering stretching place inside her that he still claimed—seem to shudder, too. It wasn't quite heat, but it didn't hurt. Not as much as before.

And then, when he shifted against her—once and then again, in a lazy sort of almost rhythm that made her freeze, then relax, then let out her breath in a rush—she realized that he really did know what he was doing in ways she couldn't possibly have imagined.

"This isn't about orgasms, Mattie," he said softly, with an undercurrent of pure, male confidence. "Orgasms are what happen when chemistry and skill unite. That isn't in question here."

"That," Mattie said very seriously, "is not at all what I've read."

His mouth curved then, and she felt it everywhere. In the places where their bodies clung together. In the core of her, where his quiet little movements were making her feel soft again, and warm. In that raw heat that was too much for her eyes to hold, she was sure of it, and might at any moment overflow and betray her.

"You are killing me," he whispered. "And I may kill you yet myself. But first, I see I must show you the difference between reading and living."

He bent his head and licked one of her nipples, and she could feel his smile against her skin when it responded to him at once, pulling taut in a way that drew a rippling sort of line directly from his mouth to her core. A line and with it, a kind of fire.

"You will enjoy the lesson." He used the edge of his teeth on her other breast, and she found she was shifting against him again, around that relentless hardness inside her, and it felt a whole lot better. "Then, princess, we will talk."

He rolled his hips on hers, somehow hitting her right in that needy little button that only he had ever managed to find, much less use to such effect, and she suddenly realized *why*. Why it was all connected. Why she felt him *everywhere*. Why they were built like this, so oddly and so perfectly, so obviously for each other.

Nicodemus pulled out, then thrust back in, slow and steady, and it all made a glorious kind of sense.

"Keep doing that," she whispered, amazed to find her voice was shaky, "and we can talk all you want."

He laughed then, long and low, and that, too, was its own blaze inside her.

Mattie didn't know when it all changed. One moment she was counting all the things that *weren't* painful—and then the next, she couldn't count, because it was all too much. It was fire and glory. It was beautiful and wild. It was a perfect storm of pure insanity, and Nicodemus was orchestrating it all.

His hands, his mouth. That lazy and yet somehow demanding rhythm he chose, rocking them both closer and closer to something *huge*. Mattie had had an orgasm before. She'd even had more than one with him. But she understood, somehow, that the place they were headed together was different. Immense and life-altering. Too intense to survive—

"Nicodemus—" But she didn't sound like herself, and he laughed again, as if this was all part of his plan. "I can't—"

"You will," he said, his mouth at her ear, and then he really began to move.

And Mattie felt it everywhere. She felt it curl up from some dark and wondrous place inside her she'd never known was there, spreading out like a brushfire until there was nothing but him, nothing but the way he moved and the way she met each thrust. Nothing but this beautiful light they made together.

Nothing but love.

An alarm rang in her then, but she ignored it, too far gone to care.

"I can't," she said again, but this time her voice was a sob and she hardly knew what she said.

"You must," he told her, so dark and so sure. And she believed him. "Now."

And then he reached down between them and pressed down hard just above her entrance, never stopping that delicious rhythm of his, and Mattie exploded. Shattered into nothing but slivers of that same great light, cast out to the heavens.

Shattered into nothingness, but not before she heard him shout her name, and follow.

It was not until the night fell again outside that Nicodemus finally left her, and even then, it very nearly proved impossible.

She was so warm. Pliant and perfect as she lay against him, her face in his neck and her breathing solid and even. A perfect fit, even now.

But he made himself do it. He pulled away and sat up on the edge of the bed, almost wishing she would wake as she'd done so many times before, tempting him back to her side so he wouldn't have to think. Wouldn't have to consider what to do next. Wouldn't have to accept what he already knew he would have to do.

It had been a long day.

A very long day, and all of it moved in him, slow and sweet, making him want her anew when he'd have thought it impossible. He'd finally explored every inch of her delectable body. He'd taken her again and again, even after he'd thought she must surely have had enough—but all she had to do was whisper that she wanted more in his ear and his self-control deserted him.

He knew how she tasted now, everywhere. He knew what sounds she made when she was close and what cries she let out when she was feeling frustrated and deliciously greedy. He knew how she threw back her head, how she went liquid and wild then burst into flame.

And he was the only man who knew. The only man who had ever touched her like this, had her, claimed her— and Nicodemus knew he was every inch of him caveman enough to revel in that. His possessiveness roared in him, almost drowning everything else out.

Almost.

"Is this the talking part?" she asked from behind him, her voice husky in the shadows.

He could have said no. He could have simply turned, swept her into his arms again, lost himself in her the way he wanted to do. He could have put this off for the night, for the rest of their time here. Forever.

But he didn't. He couldn't.

"You are a liar," he said, and this time, it wasn't that same accusation. It was a simple statement of fact, and he heard her shift against the sheets behind him.

"Does this qualify as pillow talk?" she asked. "Because if so, I think you suck at it."

Delivered in that way of hers that made him want to laugh, and he understood that this was why she was so dangerous. Even more dangerous than he'd thought she was when he'd only longed for her from afar. Unlike Arista, who had only ever been what he'd projected on her, Nicodemus *liked* Mattie.

He liked her wry humor. He liked how profoundly unafraid of him she was. He liked how willing she was to mock them both, as if all of this was simply a game they were playing instead of so terribly real and important it made him ache inside. He liked a thousand things about her that had nothing to do with how pretty she was, or how terribly he craved her, or his merger with her father's company and the work he'd do with her brother in the coming months.

Yet none of that mattered, because she couldn't stop lying and he couldn't live with it. He'd had more lies in his life than he could bear. And he couldn't help noticing she hadn't denied it.

"That wasn't meant to be anything but a simple truth," he said then, shifting around so he could look at her. "It's the central core of who you are, Mattie. You lie. Always. About everything. Even this."

She frowned at him, though her mouth looked vulnerable, and he had to steel himself against reaching for her.

"You can't demand that someone let you into their private thoughts. That takes time and—"

"Why did you save yourself for me?" he asked her, swift and brutal.

Her frown deepened. "It was an accident."

"That's a lie, even as we sit here discussing lying." She flushed, confirming it as surely as if she'd openly admitted it. "Let's try again. What are your nightmares about?"

She looked miserable then, and he wanted that to be enough. He wanted that to matter. But she swallowed, looking down and moving her hands beneath the sheet she'd pulled over her so he couldn't see them. He didn't need to see; he knew she'd made them into fists.

He knew too much about her now. That was the trouble.

"I had one nightmare," she said in a low voice, and she couldn't even look at him. "And you woke me."

He felt like he was cracking open, breaking apart. Like that final lie was the last nail into a sheet of glass and it shattered everything.

"I thought I could reach you," he said quietly. "I thought it was all a game and you'd stop playing it when we were here, alone. All this time, I thought that beneath everything, this mattered."

She lifted her dark eyes to his, and they were bright with tears he had no expectation she'd ever shed. He couldn't even be certain they were real, no matter how much he wanted them to be.

"This does," she whispered. "This matters."

"Then tell me one true thing, Mattie," he said, more urgently than before. "One that isn't a trap. One that doesn't take us down your little rabbit hole of lies within lies until we are nothing but twisted into knots. *One thing.*"

"You know everything that matters," she said instead. "I'm here, aren't I? This all happened. I saved myself for you, and what does it matter why? What more do you think you need to know?"

He shook his head , and the battle to keep himself from touching her became pitched and nearly violent. He stood, moving away from the bed to slap on the lights that lit the room with a golden glow—but it was better than all those shadows. All that too-intimate darkness, where he was too likely to imagine he saw what he wanted to see instead of what was.

Mattie sat in the center of the bed, wrapped in his sheets, blinking in the sudden onslaught of light. And he still longed for her, despite everything. He was still as hungry for her as if he hadn't spent an entire day indulging that appetite.

He understood, then, that this would never change. That she'd had this hold on him since the first and always would. That he loved her as he'd loved no other, and it still didn't matter.

He never did learn his lessons.

"My father was a strict, grim man," he told her, though he didn't know why. But then, he didn't want to leave her in any doubt as to his motives. "He came in and out of our flat in a dark cloud, and my mother rushed to appease him, no matter what he did or said. For a long time, I didn't understand why his moods were the only important ones in our home."

He studied her as she sat there, her eyes wide and fixed

on him. "No smart little interjections, Mattie? I'm surprised."

"You never talk about your past," she said simply. "Only what you own."

He accepted that as a hit, though he wasn't certain it was meant as one. It stung, nonetheless.

"As I grew, my father took an interest in my character." He folded his arms over his chest and stared at her, though what he saw was that crowded little flat and the angry man who dominated it with his temper and his cruelties. His ability to find fault in everything. "He could smell lies on me, he told me. And when he did, he took it upon himself to beat them out of me."

"So we are both liars, then," Mattie said, and he thought her voice was warmer than it should have been. Warmer than made any sense.

"He was given to great lectures he punctuated with his fists," Nicodemus continued. "He had very distinct ideas about what was wrong and what was right." He smiled, not nicely. "Needless to say, I was a grave disappointment to him in all ways."

She let out a small sound that was something like a sigh. "It's hard to imagine you subject to someone else's whims. Much less a disappointment to anyone."

Nicodemus didn't want to continue with this. He wanted to explore that soft note in her voice, instead. He wanted to pretend none of this mattered to him. He wanted to bury himself in her and let that be enough. It almost was, after all.

Almost.

He wanted more than *almost*. He'd accepted *almost* for the whole of his life. From his parents, from Arista. From Mattie. He couldn't do it any longer. He wouldn't.

"Luckily, my father did not stay with us all the time," he

said, instead. "Often he was gone for weeks. My mother would tell me he was away on business, and that he loved us very much, as if she thought I needed soothing, but the truth was, I preferred it when he was away. The only time my mother ever hit me was when I said so out loud."

"I don't mean to overstep," she said quietly. "But I can't say I'm forming a positive impression of your parents."

He saw his mother's stunningly beautiful face, those flashing black eyes and that lustrous fall of hair she'd spent so many hours brushing and curling and tending. He saw the creams she'd only used when his father wasn't there, the drinks she'd favored while alone that were liberally laced with the alcohol she otherwise only served his father. He could picture her, pretty and breakable, staring out the windows as if looking for ships at sea—though they hadn't had a view of the sea from their flat. And the only one who ever came to visit them was his father.

"One day when I was twelve, I decided to follow my father when he left us," Nicodemus said then, because he couldn't seem to stop. "I don't remember what brought this on. I'd like to think he'd given himself away somehow but I suspect the truth is, I was twelve. I was bored. He had come less and less that year, and the less he came, the more it upset my mother. She coped by drinking and spending her days further and further away inside her dream world."

"Who took care of you?" Mattie asked.

He smiled. "Did your father take care of you himself while running Whitaker Industries?" he asked. "I imagine not."

"We had a series of excellent nannies," she shot back, tilting her chin up as she did, reminding him of all the ways he couldn't have her. "And a fantastic housekeeper that Chase and I consider a member of the family."

"My mother did not work, though she told stories of

when she'd cleaned houses before I was born. There were no nannies or housekeepers. I took care of myself." That look on her face made him feel something like claws inside his chest, so he pushed on. "But that day, I followed my father. I followed him up into the hills where the houses were bigger. Prettier."

Nicodemus found himself moving without meaning to do it, ranging toward the windows and pausing there, his back to the bed, because he wasn't sure what he'd do if she kept looking at him with all that softness in her gaze. He didn't know what would become of his conviction, his purpose. Of him.

"And when I peeked in the windows of the big house he'd gone inside," he said quietly, as much to the sea as to the woman behind him, as much to his memory as anything, "I found he had a whole other family." There was no sound from behind him, not even a breath against the air in the room. "I didn't understand at first. I couldn't make sense of it. There was a woman, three children. One was a boy who looked about my age. And they all called my father *Babá*."

He had never said that out loud. And even now, he refused to admit that it tore at him, like knives into flesh. That he could still feel such an old betrayal so keenly, even after all these years.

"That is the word for *Dad,*" he clarified. And he heard her then. She breathed out, long and hard, like she hurt for him, and his curse was, he wished she did.

"I don't know how long I watched them through their big windows." He remembered it being a long time— months, even—though he supposed that could have been the vagaries of memory, playing tricks on him. "I went back day after day. And watching them, I learned to want. I wanted all of it. The parties that seemed to bore them.

The fancy toys they never seemed grateful for. The great big house with whole rooms they didn't enter for days at a time, if at all."

He turned back to face her then, leaning one shoulder against the wall to the side of the window. She hadn't moved. She still sat where he'd left her, more beautiful now than any woman had the right to be. Her hair was a tousled mess, tumbling down her back in its midnight glory. Her mouth looked ravaged and her eyes gleamed with emotion. And he wanted her. God, how he wanted her. The way he'd always wanted her. The same way he'd wanted that other life he'd glimpsed through his father's windows.

He should have known better then. He did know better now, and still, here he was. It was as if he'd learned nothing, after all.

"The next time my father beat me for my supposed lies, I asked him about his." Mattie frowned, as if she could see what was coming in that small, sharp-edged curve of his mouth he allowed himself. "I knew it was a secret, but you see, I had no secrets of my own. He'd seen to that. So it never crossed my mind to consider the reasons secrets like his might be better kept hidden."

"Nicodemus," she said softly, like she could see straight through him to his guilt. His lingering fury. "Whatever happened, you were a child."

"I was twelve," he corrected her. "Not quite a child, not where I grew up. And certainly man enough to receive the vicious beating my father gave me for questioning him, following him, calling him out. I was his sin, you see. The living, breathing emblem of his betrayal of his wife with the low class servant girl who had cleaned his house. He was very self-righteous when he told me that he had come to us all these years purely in an effort to wash the stain from my soul. To help me become a better man, because left to my own devices, I'd no doubt become a whore like my mother." Nicodemus didn't look away from Mattie as he said this, laying out the history he never spoke of so matter-of-factly. And he didn't crack when she winced at that ugly word. "He made me thank him as I lay there, bloody on the floor. And then he walked out the door and he never returned."

"Never?" Mattie asked, shock coloring her voice, her gaze. "But he was your father!"

"Worse, he stopped supporting us," Nicodemus said. "That meant I had to leave school to work wherever I could, and it meant my dreamy, useless, fragile mother had to work in the factories. Thread, mostly. And it killed her."

Mattie didn't say his name again, but she made a small noise that sounded almost too rough, too raw. It made him want to touch her, hold her, almost more than he could bear.

"When I went back to my father's great big house on its sparkling hill, to ask him to help once my mother had collapsed, he had me arrested."

It was amazing how remote he could sound, he thought. As if these things had happened to someone else. But he could still feel his father's security guards' hands on him, his father's foot against his neck, as he was held facedown in the dirt. He still remembered the stink and the din of that grotty cell.

"While I sat in jail, my mother died. And when I got out, Mattie, I dedicated my life to making certain that no one would ever use their wealth or power to get the better of me. And that no one would ever lie to my face again. I was sixteen, and I maintained this position for at least a couple of years. And then, when I was twenty and full of myself and all the new money I'd made running construction sites, I lost my head over the boss's daughter."

"Nicodemus," she said in that thick, ragged way that he feared would be his undoing.

"Her name was Arista and she was much too pretty," he said. "It blinded me. She took my money and my adulation and she liked what I could do for her in bed, but when it came time for her to marry she chose a rich boy from her social circle and laughed at me that I'd expected anything else. I was something stuck to the bottom of her shoe, nothing more. I thought I'd learned my lesson, at last."

She looked at him for a long time, and Nicodemus wished things could be different. Wished all of this was different. And wishing had never led to anything but trouble.

His smile felt bitter. "And then I came to the States and I saw you. And you were everything I ever wanted, Mattie. More than I dared dream. Your father treated me better than my own ever had, and I could see all that heat in your eyes when you looked at me, and I knew you were the one I wanted. You and no one else."

She jerked slightly. And when her gaze met his again, it was something more than troubled.

"You wanted a pretty girl you saw dancing at a party," she said, very carefully. Very distinctly. "I could have been anyone. I could have been that girl in Greece. You didn't know anything about *me*. You still don't."

"I love you," he told her, because there was no point pretending any longer, and it didn't matter, anyway. "And everything you've ever told me is a lie."

Her breath caught, then came fast, like that flush across her cheeks and the upper slopes of her breasts. Her mouth opened, but she snapped it closed, and he saw a whole world of misery in those bittersweet eyes of hers.

Still, she said nothing. But then, had he expected anything else?

"And when I tell you I cannot abide liars, Mattie, I mean it. I mean this. I mean you."

Everything had gone too dark, despite the golden light that made the room seem so cheerful, so bright. Too raw. Too stark. And she looked at him like he'd broken her heart. Like he'd torn her in two.

It said terrible things about him, he knew, that he wished he had. That he wished he could. That he wished she felt something for him when he knew—*he knew*—that would only make this that much worse.

"Tell me the truth," he said then, his voice final, and he could see she heard it. "I won't ask again."

It was as if a thousand words fought inside her, pushing at her throat and making it feel tight, turning into the tears that pricked at the back of her eyes, running over her skin and into her veins like some kind of poison—but Mattie knew she didn't dare open her mouth. She didn't dare try to speak.

She knew, somehow, that she wouldn't stop.

And the idea of that—of spilling her guts the way Nicodemus had done, of letting out all the brutal things that had lived inside her all this time—swelled in her like a terrible wave.

She couldn't do it. She would rather he hate her forever for the things he *thought* he knew about her than tell him the truth and see it right there on his face. Unmistakable and real.

Mattie fought back a wave of panic and crawled to the edge of the bed, then onto her feet. Only then did she let the sheet drop, and was rewarded for that with the sharp sound of Nicodemus's indrawn breath.

"Don't play these games with me," he warned her. "You didn't like how it ended the last time you tried to manipulate me with sex."

But he didn't move from where he stood near the window, and that was what she focused on.

I love you, he'd said, and the words tumbled around and around inside her, picking up mass and speed with every second until she thought they were all she was. That and all the things she *couldn't* say in return.

She moved closer to him, feeling that pull, that electricity that called to her whenever he was near. And now she knew what it meant. What it was promising.

"Mattie." He took her hands in his when she would have put them on his bare skin, and his face was grim again. Dark and forbidding, and that thing inside her that she'd always thought was broken because it only ever responded to him pulled taut. As attracted to his darkness as his light. Attracted, no matter what. "Just tell me the truth. Any truth, damn you."

But she couldn't do that. She didn't know how.

All she'd ever done with Nicodemus was fight. Fight and lie, just as he accused her. It hadn't been a strategy—it had only ever been survival.

And so, she told herself, was this.

She melted against him. She turned her head to kiss her way along his strong forearm, amazed when she felt him shudder. She tipped forward until her breasts pressed into his chest—and she smiled when he let out a stream of dark, evidently filthy Greek.

He let go of her hands.

And Mattie told him all the truths she knew in the only way she could.

She loved him with her mouth, her fingers, her cheeks against the expanse of his abdomen. She loved him the way she understood, now, she always had. He'd cast his shadow across the last ten years of her life, and she finally understood why.

Why she'd waited. Why she'd had boyfriends but had never felt right about taking that last step with them. Why she'd run so hard in the opposite direction every time she'd seen Nicodemus.

It was *this*. The things he wanted were uncompromising, exhilarating. The things she felt were the same.

Too much. Everything.

She couldn't open herself up like that. She didn't dare.

But she could give him this.

Mattie showed him what lurked in her heart, what she'd never dare say aloud. She lavished him with all the beauty and terror and sweet, hot need he'd introduced her to so expertly. She led him to the bed and crawled over him, leaving no part of him untouched. As if she could press all the things she felt directly into his skin. As if she could tattoo him with her own mouth.

As if this was better than the truth he wanted.

And then, finally, when everything had tightened beyond bearing and both of them were desperate, she climbed on top of him, wincing slightly when she took him deep inside her.

"This is too much," he gritted out, even now, when she knew he was pushed to his limits. "You are new to this."

Mattie only held his gaze. And then she began to move.

She built her rhythm slowly, carefully, and then, when she was more comfortable, she picked up her pace. His hands gripped her hips as he met her, thrusting hard and deep and beautiful.

And this, she thought and had to bite her lip from saying, was better than simply true. This was truth itself and this was *right* and surely, he must feel it. Surely, he must know all the things she felt, yet couldn't say.

Surely, he must understand how desperately she loved him.

This time, when the fire built and built until it finally

burned them both alive, they flew off that glorious edge together.

But when Mattie woke from a shockingly uninterrupted sleep, it was another perfect gold and blue morning outside the windows, there was a servant bustling around in the kitchen downstairs with unwelcome efficiency and cheer, and Nicodemus was gone.

CHAPTER NINE

NICODEMUS'S ENTIRE LIFE mocked him.

There were the papers he'd signed in a grim fury the day he'd returned from Greece to merge the Stathis Corporation with Whitaker Industries, despite that burning thing in him that had wanted nothing more than to fly to London and punch Chase Whitaker in the face, because Chase was the closest thing on the planet to Big Bart. He still didn't know how he'd managed to keep himself in check. How he'd returned to Manhattan and his office there without causing any international incidents, such was the temper he'd been in when he'd left his island.

There was the brownstone in New York's West Village he stood in now, that he'd bought and painstakingly renovated years ago and had been calling *home* when his real home should have been in Athens near his own headquarters. There was even this damned mood he was in, black and dangerous like the autumn storm outside the windows, pelting the city with the same bitter cold he felt inside himself.

It was all about her, and he felt it like one of her mocking little laughs, lighting him up and ripping into him at the same time.

You have to put this behind you, he ordered himself.

Over and over again. But it didn't seem to work.

The sad truth was, everything he did and everything he'd done for years revolved around Mattie Whitaker, and the fact he hadn't noticed it even as he'd done it galled him. The fact he'd never seen her for what she was ate at him. At first, perhaps, it had been unconscious. He'd wanted a woman *like* her, he'd told himself. And he'd admired her father, the first man who'd ever treated Nicodemus as something other than a trashy upstart. The man who'd encouraged him to educate himself and had given him the tools to do it.

But at some point along the way he'd stopped pretending. And now he was married to a woman he couldn't trust, tied up in a thousand legal knots with her family business, and completely screwed.

Literally as well as figuratively, he admitted darkly, and let out some rendition of a laugh.

And she'd been a virgin.

He still couldn't believe it. He still couldn't handle all the implications of that—the one thing she couldn't fake or lie about. He didn't know what was worse—his absolute disbelief, because her virginity meant he didn't know her as well as he'd thought he did, or that primitive part of him that simply wanted to claim her as his, now and forever.

It stood to reason that now he finally had her, now that he'd made her his in every possible way, he didn't see how he could let himself keep her.

Another blustery autumn night had fallen over Manhattan, blanketing the city with a thick darkness that looked almost soft from inside the office he'd built on the second floor of the brownstone, despite the rain that still pounded down, making the trees along the city street bend and sway.

And Nicodemus ignored the insistent beeping from his laptop that indicated one incoming email after the next.

He ignored the buzzing of his mobile phone. He stared out at the cold, wet dark and tortured himself.

One scalding-hot image after the next, as relentless as the freezing rain outside, and as brutal.

Mattie kissing him, using her mouth all over him, beguiling him and enslaving him. Mattie sitting astride him, the most beautiful creature he'd ever beheld, riding them both into all of that white-hot wonder.

Mattie, Mattie, Mattie, the way it had been since the moment he'd seen her in her long-ago ball gown, sparkling so brightly she'd eclipsed the whole of the world.

And that was when the truth of things hit him, making him feel something like sick.

After all this time, after all the effort he'd put into never, ever becoming a man like his father, he'd neglected to recognize that it was his other parent's influence he should have guarded himself against.

Because he was no different from his sad, discarded mother, was he? She'd taught him how to pine. How to spend years longing for someone who would never return the feeling. Arista had been a mere practice run. He'd built a whole life around his hopes and dreams about Mattie.

"How can you consider taking him back, after all of this?" Nicodemus had railed at his mother in those terrible days after that last scene with his father, when his mother had still maintained her vigil and her beauty regimen as if those things were sacred rituals that would bring him back. "How can you weep for him?"

"The heart is more forgiving than you imagine," his mother had told him, humming to herself as she'd combed out her hair. "And far more resilient."

And he'd hated her for it.

He could admit that now, after all these years had passed. After he'd exacted his revenge when he'd gutted his father's company and stripped him of the better part of his wealth. After he'd gone on to far outshine the man who had ruined them both. God, how he'd hated her. He'd hated her almost as much as he'd loved her, in that same helpless way, so unable was he to fix what was broken in her or save her once his father had abandoned them.

"He is never coming back," he'd told her when she'd ended up in the hospital and had insisted that he dress her in something nicer than a hospital gown, in case his father deigned to stop by when Nicodemus had known full well he wouldn't. "He doesn't care if we live or die."

"Love is not always a straight line, Nicodemus," she'd replied in that reedy voice of hers, so thin even he'd known, at sixteen and before the doctors had taken him aside to confirm it, that she hadn't had much time left.

And the guilt he'd felt over how much he'd hated her obliviousness, her dogged optimism, her reckless belief in one so deeply unworthy of her notice, had led him to approach his father that last time.

His reward for that had been a month in jail, and his mother had died alone.

Nicodemus couldn't shake aside these old ghosts. He felt as if he was that twelve-year-old boy again, miserable and astonished, with his face pressed to the gates of a fancy house high in the hills above Piraeus. He'd done exactly what he'd set out to do then. The houses. The expensive toys. Whatever he desired was his—precisely as he'd dreamed when he'd first seen the true life his father led. When he'd understood that he and his mother were the dirty secrets.

But he'd forgotten—or chosen to ignore—that the heart that beat inside his chest was softer.

As foolish and as suicidal as his mother's had been.

"You must stop this," he ordered himself, only aware

that he spoke out loud when he heard the resounding silence that followed his words.

He cursed beneath his breath, pushing back from the desk, ignoring his ringing phone. Ignoring the hours of work he had left to do today. Ignoring everything but that darkness inside him that he wished he could excise with his own two hands.

He wished. He still wished and that, Nicodemus understood, was his problem. Perhaps it always had been.

He had to decide what to do with Mattie now. It occurred to him, standing in yet another home he'd made with every expectation that she would live in it with him one day, that this was the first time in a decade that he'd had any doubts. He'd always known exactly what to do with Mattie Whitaker. He'd always had a plan. That plan had changed in its particulars over the years, but essentially, it was always the same: isolate the two of them from the rest of the world and let their insane chemistry do the rest.

He'd always imagined that would be enough.

But now—he'd tasted her innocence. He'd seen truths in her beautiful eyes that she'd refused to speak out loud. He'd soothed her in her restless, broken sleep and he'd held her in his arms as she'd cried. He'd watched her rebel, and he'd watched her surrender, and he couldn't have said which part of her he liked most.

He'd loved her from afar for ten years. He loved her even more now.

And it still didn't matter.

He couldn't trust her. He didn't believe her. She was made entirely of secrets and lies, and he couldn't do it. He knew where it led. *Exactly* where it led. He'd already done this, more than once.

Which meant that somehow, after all these years and all the things he'd done to get them here, the lives he'd built for them to live in and the dreams he'd been fool enough to think he could indulge, he had to find a way to let her go.

"You must have done something," Chase said over the phone, with what sounded like sheer irritation in his voice. It made his British accent that much more pronounced.

It made Mattie want to reach through the phone and slap him, all the way across the Atlantic Ocean in his London office.

This is your beloved big brother, the only family you have left in all the world, she cautioned herself. *None of this is his fault,*

None of this is your *fault, either,* she replied to herself staunchly—though she imagined that depended on which of her faults was under discussion. And with whom.

Mattie took a deep breath as she stood in her same old living room on the Upper West Side, now its usual size without Nicodemus looming in it to shrink the dimensions around him. His absence lanced into her, a sharp and searing pain, no less bearable for the fact it wasn't anything new, and she deeply regretted returning her brother's call.

"Would you like a point-by-point analysis of how I executed my duties as Nicodemus's arranged bride?" she asked, her voice almost as clipped as his, and her accent had gone American years ago. "I should warn you in advance. Some parts get a little bit naked. That's what happens in marriages whether they're arranged or not, or didn't you know?"

It was easy to keep her voice cool and even. Or arch and brittle, more accurately. Because ever since Nicodemus had left her to make her own way home from his island, Mattie had felt…nothing. Not when Chase called. Not when the papers speculated about her and her marriage. Not at all.

She was a polished piece of glass, she told herself now. Hard and smooth. Impervious to harm.

"I don't need this bloody headache," Chase muttered.

It was almost under his breath. And Mattie therefore *almost* pretended that she hadn't heard it. But there was that raw thing inside her that felt like a poisonous snake, coiled tight and ready to strike, and Chase was setting himself up as the perfect target.

"I apologize that the marriage you pushed me into for business purposes has turned out to be less than blissful," she said in that same bright and hard tone. "You'll remember how thrilled I was about it in the first place. Who could possibly have predicted that this might happen?" She pretended to wait a beat, as if considering the question. "Oh, right. I did."

Chase sighed at her sarcastic tone. Mattie's fingers clenched so hard around her phone receiver that it hurt, her rings biting into her flesh, and it wasn't her brother who she was angry at, she knew. He had nothing to do with all the things that had happened between her and Nicodemus on that island—all the things she couldn't tell him. Or anyone.

All the things she wasn't entirely ready to admit to herself, even now.

"I spoke to Nicodemus not three days ago and he gave me no indication that there was anything wrong with your marriage," Chase said, sounding impatient, which made that thing inside her pull tight. Coil harder. "In fact, you didn't even come up."

"Oh, I see," she gritted out. "That must mean that I hallucinated the past month of my life, then."

She heard the sound of papers rustling, and then a keyboard tapping, and it filled her with a completely unwarranted fury that Chase could simply…go about his business while she was nothing but stuck.

Not that she'd entirely admitted that to herself in the week or so since she'd returned home from Greece. She hadn't allowed herself to think such a thing while tossing herself back into the life she'd left behind here and wanted so desperately to believe still fit like a glove.

But that didn't make it any less true.

"Although, now that I think about it, he did seem particularly focused on business," Chase said, almost grudgingly. "He's usually a little more friendly. Only a little."

Mattie waited, but Chase didn't offer up any other details. She realized she was clenching her teeth, and forced herself to stop.

"Thanks," she said mildly, though inside, she was so terribly raw and too hot and shattering into jagged little pieces. "I'll write you a note, shall I? And the next time you see him or talk to him, you can give it to him, and we can all pretend we're in grade school together."

"Mattie—" Chase began.

"I don't want to hear whatever you're about to say," she told him, and there was nothing smooth or glass-like about her voice then. She only wondered how she'd held it together so long. "I did what you wanted me to do, and you couldn't even do me the courtesy of showing up to witness it. And I only called you back today because I thought you should know the state of things between Nicodemus and me. Foolishly, I was worried that it might affect the business. I'm delighted to hear that while Nicodemus may have broken a promise or two to *me,* all is well where the company is concerned." She laughed, and it was not a nice sound. "As ever, that's all that matters."

"It's not all that matters." Chase sounded tougher than the brother she knew. Harder. Colder. "But it's the only thing we have left. And if that doesn't mean something, Mattie, then I don't know what does."

It's not the only thing, a tiny voice whispered inside her. *It's a company. It's not us.*

And Mattie realized then that she was miserable. Pure and simple.

She let that unfortunate truth trickle through her, filling her up until she hardly recognized herself, as if it had changed her from the inside out. Altered her. It made her want to throw her phone across the room and watch it break into pieces. It made her want to curl into a ball and cry for days, as she'd only done one other time in her life.

She'd been a liar for most of her life because there was one truth she couldn't tell. And she wondered why she'd never noticed that keeping that secret had changed her. Turned her inside out. Made her the kind of woman who could look at a man she loved and be too afraid to admit it, even to herself.

That thudded into her. Like a sledgehammer. Like Nicodemus's heartbeat beneath her palm. Like one more true thing she couldn't tell him, couldn't say out loud, couldn't let herself believe.

"Do you think about that day?" she asked Chase, because they were what was left. The company was incidental. Or it should have been.

His silence told her he knew exactly what day she meant. And more, that he did think about it. But they hadn't spoken of it. Not in twenty years. Not since it had happened.

And she didn't want that guilt anymore, the guilt that had always convinced her that it was her fault they had this distant, strained relationship. That it was her fault they were like this.

"I get that you're upset, Mats," Chase said after an uneven moment, when there'd been nothing but that heavy silence between them that she wasn't sure he'd break. "But I don't see any point in revisiting old ghosts. Particularly those ghosts."

"I'm guessing that means *you* don't wake up every night of your life screaming, then," she heard herself say, as if from a far-off height. "Calling out for her again and again."

"What is the point of this?" And she'd never heard him sound like this, not in years. Like there was something raging beneath his skin, too. "What is there to be gained? I'm sorry that you still have the nightmares, I am. But dragging ourselves back through this swamp is only going to—"

"I don't understand why we lied about being there," she whispered, because she couldn't seem to stop now that she'd started. "What was the point of *that*?"

"You were eight years old," Chase said succinctly. "I was thirteen. I don't think we remember the same things. We did her a kindness. As well as us."

"I'm not eight anymore, Chase. Tell me what you remember."

"Our mother died in front of us," he said, and she couldn't identify what she heard in his voice then. Pain, yes. That same horror she still felt herself. Grief and fury and then something so much darker beneath it. "On the side of a road. But you and I are safe. I don't know what else you want."

"I want the truth," she said, and maybe it shouldn't have surprised her that her legs were too shaky, that she had to sit down. That the world felt as if it was breaking apart all around her, and she wasn't sure she wanted to know why.

Or maybe she was afraid she already did.

"Leave it, Mattie," Chase told her, his voice hard again. He sounded like a different man entirely today, raw and grim, and it changed everything. It changed her. Or maybe it was Nicodemus who had done that. "There are some stones it isn't worth turning over."

And she wasn't surprised when he claimed he had another call and disconnected moments later. She sat where she was for a long time.

Mattie had been protecting something she didn't fully understand since she was eight years old. She'd been held hostage to those memories. And the only way she'd figured out how to do that and carry on living was to hold herself at a distance from anyone and everything that ventured near. Let nothing and no one close, she'd reasoned, and they couldn't know her. Or hurt her, the way she'd been hurt the day they'd lost her mother.

Or learn things they shouldn't. Things so terrible that her relationship with her father and with Chase had never recovered after that awful day.

But Nicodemus had never been one for distance, until now. She shook her head slightly, as if trying to clear it, and understood that was part of what was happening to her. Why she felt like an empty echo chamber. Why she was so miserable.

He wasn't there.

For ten years, Nicodemus had always been there. If not right in front of her, then nearby. She'd known it. She'd expected it—perhaps even come to depend on it. He'd made certain she did. He'd been a fact of her life, like the weather, like the inevitability of fall into winter. He'd been relentless. He'd been *Nicodemus*.

He'd pushed and pushed, and he'd made it so very easy to push back—

Mattie didn't know what to do with herself now. Not when she'd given him everything, more than she'd ever given anyone, and it still wasn't enough. Not when she'd pushed back the way she'd always done and he'd walked away instead, leaving her with no choice but fall forward on her face. Leaving her where she landed on the ground.

Leaving her, at last, the way she'd always claimed she'd wanted him to do.

After everything, it shouldn't have surprised her so much that he was right. She really was a liar.

Glass, she told herself frantically as she felt all of this surge inside her, so close to bursting out. She was smooth and she was hard all the way through and she was *glass*—

But what she felt was broken.

Mattie waited for him in the decidedly sleek and modern waiting room of his Manhattan office, high in one of those Midtown buildings that housed everything from doctors to lawyers to international multimillionaires like Nicodemus in varying shades of lush, dark wood and understated gilt edges.

"Mr. Stathis may be some time," the gatekeeping receptionist said pleasantly enough from behind her fortress of a high, curved desk, if not for the first time. "He doesn't encourage walk-ins."

"Mr. Stathis will see me," Mattie assured her with a grand sort of bravado that she did not feel at all. Also not for the first time.

"I really do need your name, ma'am," the woman replied, her professional smile showing signs of strain.

"I'll say it once more." Mattie raised her voice so that all the people around her pretending not to listen to this interchange—business associates of Nicodemus's, she could only hope, waiting for their meetings with his various staff members and capable of all kinds of gossip should he ignore her for too long—could hear her. And recognize her, she had no doubt. And wonder. "Just tell him there are consequences to his behavior, and they are sitting in his lobby."

The woman's lips all but disappeared, she pressed them together so hard, but she didn't say another word.

And Mattie waited. She used her smartphone to page through tabloid articles heralding the quick end to her hasty marriage and did her best to look as relaxed and confident as she wanted to look—as she'd dressed.

Once again, for him. Killer heels not suited for New York City sidewalks in the wet, slippery fall, a pencil skirt that made poetry of her long frame and a silk blouse that wrapped around her torso lovingly yet failed to show anything a possessive Greek husband might find objectionable.

At least, Mattie fervently hoped he was still both of those things. Possessive and her husband. Or this meeting she'd engineered was going to be significantly more devastating than she was prepared to handle.

But it was still a very long time before a sharp, expectant sort of silence descended over the waiting room, like the fall of an ax. Mattie sat a little straighter in her chair, but she didn't look up. Not while she heard a low, quick conversation in a voice she knew all too well, one that made her whole body shiver into immediate goose bumps. Not when she felt a very familiar dark glare sear into her flesh from across the room, making it difficult to sit still.

Not until he was looming over her and she had no choice whatsoever but to crane her head back and look up that mouthwatering length of him, packaged to extremely gorgeous effect in one of the dark suits he favored that made him look like he really was king of the goddamned world.

He wasn't smiling. His eyes were cold—colder than she'd ever seen them before.

And both of those things hurt in ways Mattie hardly knew what to do with.

"Are you pregnant?" he asked. Not at all gently, or even politely.

She didn't blush. She didn't look around to see if any-one had heard. She knew Nicodemus well enough by now to know he never would have said that if anyone was lis-tening.

Or she hoped she did.

"No," she said, very calmly, which wasn't at all how she felt.

"Then I fail to understand what *consequences* there could be that require not only my presence upon demand, but your theatrical appearance here at all."

If he was having trouble with all of that subzero wind chill that dripped from his low voice and oozed from every taut, unwelcoming line in his body, he certainly didn't show it.

Trust only went so far, Mattie decided, and snuck a glance around him to see that—as she should have ex-pected, because he might be furious with her but he was still Nicodemus—he'd dismissed the receptionist and cleared the room.

"I'm not happy with you," she informed him.

Something in his hard jaw twitched. "I will cry my-self to sleep over that, Mattie, I promise you. But in the meantime, I have a company to run and a merger with an unpleasant family company I regret already to oversee. I left your histrionics and your lies in Greece for a reason."

"And I slept with you," she retorted.

He hadn't expected that—she could see it in the way his dark eyes widened slightly, then narrowed. He frowned at her, and there was something wrong with her that she saw that as a kind of progress. Better than all that ice, anyway.

"Thank you," he said, in such frozen tones she almost missed the fact that his accent was heavier—also a good sign. "But my memory works perfectly."

"I'm twenty-eight years old and I've never slept with

anyone but you," she said, and she pushed up out of the chair then, so she could face him. So he wasn't towering over her, especially not with the shoes she had on. So she could look him in the eye, the way that had always made her feel so strong and so weak at once. Today was no different. "You gave me one night and then you disappeared."

His stunned pause was so brief that she almost missed it.

"I'm reliably informed that is the plight of many a young woman in this dark, dirty city," he told her, with all that menace and ruthlessness in his voice, in the way he looked at her, and her curse was that it moved through like a long, low lick of heat. "You should count yourself lucky I didn't make you walk home from Greece."

"I waited a long time to have sex," she said, keeping her chin high and her eyes on him. "I want more of it." She felt more than saw the way he caught his breath at that, but she had no trouble identifying that flash of murder in his dark gaze. "And I'm married to you, which means that if I head out for the bars like so many young women in this big, bad city, I'd be committing adultery."

"That," he said, his voice a mere rasp of darkness despite the bright lights all around them, "and I'd kill you."

Mattie smiled. "So you see my predicament."

He stared at her for a long time. Too long. Then he reached over and wrapped his hand around her upper arm, sending a bolt of that wildfire straight through her. There had to be something wrong with her that even a touch like that made her melt—but she didn't care. She was too busy reveling in it.

"Once again," Nicodemus said in that same dangerous tone that was wreaking havoc with her nervous system, "you play with things you cannot possibly understand."

"Play with me or I'll play with whoever I want," she countered, fairly bursting with all of that fake bravado, because it was the only thing she'd been able to think of that would push him enough, and quickly. "Those are your choices, Nicodemus, though you claim I never give you any."

His hand tightened around her arm, and he hauled her, gently yet inexorably, around the side of that fortress of a desk that was currently missing its gatekeeper. He towed her down the long hallway, while his employees leaped from his path and did a terrible job of pretending not to stare, until he reached the great, big office in the far corner.

It had a long, deep view of the city along the outside walls, and when he closed the door behind them, they were trapped there together. A wall on one side to block them from prying eyes and the canyons of Manhattan right there on the other.

He let go of her, but she could still feel his fingers and the heat of his skin, like brands into her flesh.

"I don't know what I'm going to do with you," he told her, his accent under control again, but this time she sensed how hard it was for him to maintain it. "But it will not involve bargaining for sex like an animal."

"Not like an animal," she protested mildly. "Unless, of course, you think that's fun. I'm willing to try anything once. Even spanking. I think."

He shook his head and leaned against the massive granite desk that should have fallen through the floor beneath it, so gargantuan did it look, and yet somehow it suited him. He ran his hand down his front as if to straighten the tie he wore that didn't require any straightening, and it would have been easier if he'd glowered at her.

But he didn't. If anything, he looked sad and tired, the way he had before, and like then, it made her heart clutch inside her chest.

"I don't want to play games with you anymore," Nicodemus said quietly. Too quietly. "For too long, I thought this was all a game, and that I knew how to win it in the end, but I was wrong. I'm not accustomed to that. It might take some adjustment."

She'd expected temper. Accusation and heat. Not this.

But she didn't know how to do anything with this man but push back.

"Does that mean divorce?" she asked in her same nearly flippant tone, so at odds with the one he'd used. "Or no divorce? I can't keep track. Though the fact you ran away from Greece rather suggests the latter, if I had to guess. You're usually far more direct."

"I did not *run away*," he corrected her, his dark gaze narrowing with a temper he didn't let color his voice. "I had work to do, and let's be honest, Mattie, though I know that's a stretch for you. You can't give me what I want."

If he'd shoved a red-hot fire poker into her chest, he couldn't have hurt her more, and she couldn't control how stricken she felt. He saw it and shook his head as if it hurt him, too.

"I'm not trying to hurt your feelings," he said after a moment, his voice a fraction less cold. Less painfully precise. "Perhaps it was never fair of me to want the things I demanded of you. I don't know. Maybe you were right when you said any pretty girl would have done. I can't take any of that back. But I can stop chasing a person who doesn't exist."

This was worse. This made the misery she'd felt without him pale and wither away, and she had no idea what that was that swamped her then in its place. Only that it felt too much like despair.

"And what am I supposed to do?" she asked, and she didn't understand why she sounded so muffled and squeaky at the same time until she felt that heat trickling down her cheeks. She was crying. After all this time, she was crying in front of him without a nightmare to blame it on, and she didn't even care.

Nicodemus looked hewn from stone, propped up there against that granite desk with the city laid out at his feet. His gaze was dark and troubled, but he didn't move.

"I don't understand," he said after a moment, and there were too many undercurrents in that voice of his, too much Mattie knew she couldn't comprehend. "I thought you would rejoice at this. You've wanted me to leave you alone for years."

"But you never did," she said, or sobbed, and she didn't care which. How could she not care? After all these years so desperate to keep him from seeing any hint of vulnerability? But all she cared about was him. "You were always there. You were always pushing at me, and I got used to it. To you. What am I supposed to do when I push back and there's nothing there?"

He stared at her then, for so long that she thought she'd almost reached him—but then he shook his head. Once. Hard. Like he was waking himself up.

"I don't want to spend any more time than I already have, loving someone I made up inside my head." He looked tormented as he said it, torn apart, and it made Mattie feel like she was falling to pieces herself. "I know where that ends. I know what it looks like. I can't do it. Not again."

He'd gotten louder as he said that, more the Nicodemus she knew and less that creature made of stone and blame and judgment, and it was absurd how very nearly giddy that made her then, a dizzying hope like a great, bright beam of light inside her.

"That's a lie," she said, wiping at her cheeks and then holding his incredulous, thunderstruck gaze with hers, brave suddenly, because she recognized this. "And I would know. You're afraid."

CHAPTER TEN

"I BEG YOUR pardon?" His voice was a harsh warning, but Mattie ignored it.

"You heard me," she said, forging on. "What happened to the Nicodemus who told me that our marriage would last forever? Babies and no divorces?"

"I also told you there would be no secrets," he bit out. "But you can't do it. You prefer to play your games, trying to manipulate your way out of anything honest with sex."

"So do you."

In the silence that fell between them then, Mattie could hear her own heart, catapulting itself so hard against her ribs she worried it might break right through. Slowly, very slowly, his dark gaze fixed to hers, Nicodemus straightened from his desk, and she was reminded how very dangerous he was. How lethal when he chose.

"You know you do," she said. "Any game I might have played with sex, you've played yourself. The fact that you think you had different motives doesn't change anything. It's the same game."

"It most assuredly is not."

"This has been the same pattern from the start. You push, I push back. Around and around we go, and we've been doing it for years. You had no reason to think anything would change when we went to your island—but then it turned out that I wasn't who you thought I was. And if I was a virgin, you couldn't stay up there, all warm and comfortable on your moral high ground."

"You can twist this any way you like, Mattie," he said in that same harsh tone. "That doesn't make it true."

"There are a thousand ways we could have handled this marriage," she said, searching his face for the man she'd glimpsed in Greece, the man who'd been discarded by his father and had still made so much of himself. The little boy he must have been once, who'd made himself into a king of sorts, by the force of his own will. "It could have been a team effort. But instead, you threatened me and crowded me. Gloated about your victory over me."

"You're unbelievable." He took a step toward her, then appeared to think better of it and stopped. "Are you truly standing here today, claiming that had I approached you differently you would have—what?" He shook his head in amazement. "Come to this marriage dancing and singing?"

"I don't know," she said. "But I do know that you couldn't risk it. How could you possibly pretend to open up to me and then retreat like this if I was interested in a real partnership? That might make you something less than the upright and honest one here, and then what would happen?"

She couldn't help the bit of sarcasm that snuck in there at the end, and she saw him register it with a scowl.

"Let me guess," he said, witheringly. "Somehow, this is all my fault, yes? Isn't that where you're headed?"

"Not at all." It was hard to keep her head up high, her gaze on his, but she did it. "You *wanted* me to respond the way I did. Because that way, you get to be the martyr, and I'm still the spoiled brat who even managed to remain a *virgin* to spite you."

"Then why?" And there was nothing controlled about

his voice then. Nothing concealed in his expression. She could *feel* the kick of it. "If not for spite—for another point in this endless game?"

"Why do you think, you idiot?" she hurled back at him, and she threw her hands up as if she wanted to hit him or encompass all of Manhattan or maybe because she couldn't stand still. "Because of you!"

Nicodemus stared at her, his beautiful wife and this warrior creature who'd taken her over, making her lovely cheeks flush and her bittersweet eyes glitter wildly. She looked perfect in her stunningly feminine clothes, from head to toe his living, breathing, fantasy—and she'd just called him an idiot.

"What do you mean, because of me?" he asked, because he couldn't process any of this. It was like he was learning English all over again, and missing half the meaning.

"I mean, because of you," she said, and her voice was a little too thick and too uneven. "You were always there, weren't you? Since I was eighteen. And how could any of the boys I dated compete?" He only stared at her. "Whatever I felt for you, Nicodemus, it was consuming. I spent more time worrying about how to avoid you than I did about the boys I was supposed to be in love with. It never seemed right to take things any further when you were always there, lurking around in my head or at the next party. Always *so sure* that I'd end up with you."

"Careful, Mattie," he said, unable to do anything about that dark thing inside him that colored his voice, bitterness and confusion and all these years, all these long years, "or I may be tempted to think you care."

"That's what I'm trying to tell you," she snapped back at him. "Obviously. Since I'm standing right here, in your office, after you left me on a Greek island half a world away." She was scowling at him now. "Why else would I be here?"

"Sex?" he supplied acidly. "As you mentioned in the reception area?"

"Right," she said, her voice so dry it hurt. "Because after waiting twenty-eight years to have sex, it makes perfect sense that I'd suddenly want to whore it up all over Manhattan. Like it's a faucet I can turn on or off and *oops!* You left it on! Like it had absolutely nothing to do with you at all." She looked so furious for a moment that he wouldn't have been at all surprised if she'd swung at him. Instead, she crossed her arms over her chest again, which didn't help him at all, as he already found those perfect breasts distracting. "You really are an idiot."

"I let that slide once," he bit back at her. "Don't push me."

"That's the only thing I know how to do!" she shouted at him. "And God knows, Nicodemus, it's the only thing you ever respond to!"

He moved toward her then, but she backed away, her eyes stormy as they fixed on him.

"Don't touch me," she ordered him. "That confuses everything."

He recognized the things that flowed through him now, though he couldn't quite believe any of them. Triumph, yes. Hope, which was harder to stomach. That same old wild desire—and he knew too much, now. He knew that the reality of her trumped his fantasies, and then some.

"You wanted honesty," she was saying, still watching him too intently, as if all of this was hurting her. "You can't cut it off in the middle because it doesn't fit the story you've already told yourself about how this would go."

She'd backed up all the way to that wall of windows, and stood there, bracketed by another perfect autumn afternoon in New York City. The light was tipping over toward gold, and it poured over her, making her look like something out of a dream.

His dream, he realized. He'd had this dream.

He stood and waited though he thought that it was perhaps the most difficult thing he'd ever done.

"My mother died when I was eight," she said, and for some reason, Nicodemus felt a chill go through him. "But you know that already."

"Of course," he said, not sure why he felt so uneasy all of a sudden. "Lady Daphne was in a car accident while your family was on holiday in South Africa. It was a tragedy."

"It was a tragedy," Mattie said in a whisper that wasn't at all soft. "It was my fault."

Nicodemus only watched her. She swallowed hard, her gaze on his like she was searching for condemnation. She must have seen something on his face that encouraged her, because she cleared her throat and continued.

"I was in the backseat with Chase. Mama was in the passenger seat in front, talking with the driver. I was singing. Chase told me to stop. They all told me to stop. And I hit him."

Her eyes darkened, and he realized that this was her nightmare. This was what he'd found her reliving that night in the pool house.

"I'm sorry," he said quietly, when it seemed she'd gone somewhere inside her head. "But I don't understand how you could have caused a car accident from the backseat."

"I hit Chase," she said again, and it tore at him, how she said that so matter-of-factly, as if, inside her head, she'd conducted whole trials and found herself guilty again and again. "And he teased me, and I hit him again. They told me to stop and I didn't. I was too mad. And then I hit the driver and everything…flipped. And then we were on the side of the road and Mama—" She shook her head instead of finishing that sentence. "It was my fault, Nicodemus. I hit the driver and made him lose control of the car. He died, too."

"Mattie," he said softly. "It was an accident."

"Nothing was the same afterward," she whispered. "No one could look at me. Chase, my father. We all pretended, but I knew. They even made us lie about what had really happened." Her eyes welled up then. "And every time I told someone that Chase and I weren't in the car, that it had happened to her while she was on her own, it made it worse. I did this horrible thing. I ruined my family and killed an innocent man. And yet I was protected."

He couldn't hold himself back then and he stopped trying. He crossed to her, pulling her into his arms and holding her the way he'd always wanted to hold her—the way she'd only let him the night he'd found her sobbing and in the grip of her internal terrors.

She shook against him, and he held her so he could look down at her, at those pretty eyes slicked with tears again, at all that guilt and misery he understood, now, had been behind all of this from the start.

"And you wanted me so badly," she whispered. "But I knew you wouldn't, if you knew."

He shifted so he could cup her face in his hands.

"There is nothing you could do to make me want you any less," he said gruffly. "Much less this revelation that when you were a child, you acted like one. There was a terrible accident. You survived."

"What kind of person kills their own mother, Nicodemus?" she asked harshly.

"Me," he said after a moment. "I'm as guilty of it as you are."

Her face flushed. "It's not the same."

"Yes," he said. "It is. If I was a child who couldn't be held responsible for what followed my recklessness, so were you. Maybe it's time we both forgave ourselves."

Her eyes searched his. She took a deep breath that he could feel move through him, too.

"I'll try if you will," she whispered.

And then, at last, he kissed her.

It wasn't until the second kiss, that sweet fire, that easy press of his mouth to hers, that Mattie realized she hadn't truly believed he would ever kiss her again.

When she felt him smile against her mouth, her neck, she realized she'd said that out loud.

"I should have kissed you at that ball a hundred years ago and spared us both all this wasted time," he muttered. "And all this unnecessary guilt."

Mattie lifted her head then and opened her eyes, and couldn't quite fathom what she saw on that hard, fierce face of his. Shining openly from those dark eyes. It lodged in her chest. It melted all that hard, cold glass inside her as if it had never been.

"You gave up on me," she said, very seriously. "On us. Don't do it again."

His smile deepened. "My version of giving up involved signing a major merger with your family's company and returning to the city where you live." His fingers moved near her temple, playing with a strand of her hair, and the look in his dark eyes made her want to cry again. "I don't think you have to worry."

"I never sleep through the night, Nicodemus," she said. "Never. But I did that night in Greece. And when I woke up, you were gone."

"I don't want any more of these games we play," he told

her, and the words were like a song inside her, buoyant and melodic, sweet and perfect. "I only want you."

"You can have me," she promised him, and these, she understood then, were her real vows. These pierced straight through her, leaving tangled roots in their wake. Binding her to him forever. No witnesses. No pictures for the hungry tabloids. Only the two of them. And the truth. "But I want the same in return."

"I'm yours, Mattie," he told her, and he pulled her close again, lifting her up as if she weighed nothing and holding her there, like she was a miracle. Like this was, this thing between them that finally made sense. That meant everything. "All you had to do was ask."

"I love you," she said softly, threading her arms around his neck and smiling down at him as if he was the whole world. Because he was. He was hers. "But to tell you the honest truth, Nicodemus, I think I always have."

She kissed him then, and there was nothing between them but light.

And the love that had been there for all those years, waiting for them to notice it.

The summer sun poured in through the high window, and Mattie woke slowly, letting the gold of it warm her and run all over her like her husband's clever hands. She reached out to feel for him across the vastness of that great, Greek bed, and woke further when she heard his low chuckle from beside it.

"Do you miss me already?"

She opened her eyes to find Nicodemus standing there in nothing but a towel, and smiled at him, feeling lazy and happy.

"Always," she said. "You should have taken me with you."

It was amazing what a full night's sleep could do— much less three years of the same. Three years of learning how to love this man as he deserved. Three years of learning how to let him love her back.

The best three years of her life.

"The last time I attempted to take you into the shower before you were ready, you acted like it was an attempt on your life," he reminded her. "You've become appallingly lazy, princess."

"I have," she agreed with a grin. "And so demanding."

She crooked her finger at him, letting the instant gleam of dark honey in his eyes warm her.

Nicodemus crawled across the bed to her, taking her mouth with that marvelous ferocity that made her sigh against him while everything else turned molten and hot.

"I love you," she whispered when he pulled back marginally, and smiled when he kissed her again, harder and deeper than before.

"I love you, too," he replied. "Which is why you'll understand that I cannot tolerate any secrets between us. Was I unclear on this in the past? I feel certain I wasn't."

"I have no idea what you're talking about," she lied. "I'm a model wife. What more could you ask? I'm the perfect decoration."

"The decor does not normally start its own PR firm and find itself too busy to tend to its primary purpose, which is standing about looking pretty," he pointed out, shifting so he could take her in his arms and roll them both, until she was on her back and he was sprawled out beside her. "You've become entirely too professional."

"I apologize." She wasn't sorry at all, and the little nip he gave her, at the tender place beneath her ear, made her laugh. "I know you preferred it when I was pointless and spoiled."

He propped himself up on his elbow so he could look down at her, and she loved him so much it felt like a wave that crashed over her, again and again, bathing her in its sweetness. Its goodness. She loved the smile he wore so often now and that gaze of his that was always more honeyed than grim. She loved how well she knew him and how, astonishingly, he'd come to know her, as well.

Intimacy, it turned out, was worth all the trouble it took to get there. All the fear and all the pain. That sensation of being turned inside out, vulnerable and exposed, was only the beginning. Every day it deepened. Every day it got worse.

And better. So much better. So exquisitely, miraculously better.

"Tell me," he said, grinning down at her. "Because I already know."

"Then why must I tell you? Surely, your psychic powers are their own reward."

"Confession is good for the soul," he said, letting one big hand travel over her warm body, heating it as he went, from her tender breasts to the bright phoenix that flirted with the curve of her belly that wouldn't stay trim much longer. "Especially yours."

"Maybe you should spank it out of me," she suggested, taking his hand in hers and holding it where it rested, hot and right, above the place far within where their baby already grew.

"How kinky you've become," he said, pretending to chide her. "Spanking was meant to be a punishment, Mattie, not a pleasure."

"Liar," she teased him, and he grinned back at her.

"I love you," Nicodemus said, his gaze another vow, and it warmed her all the way through. "You and that baby, who you should have told me about weeks ago."

And then he made her pay, in the delicious way only he could.

The way he always did.

The way she knew—as she knew the sun would rise in the morning, as she knew she'd loved him a lifetime already, as she knew this child of theirs would be a little boy whose father would never, ever lie to him or leave him— he always would.

* * * * *

MILLS & BOON®

Power, passion and irresistible temptation!

The Modern™ series lets you step into a world of sophistication and glamour, where sinfully seductive heroes await you in luxurious international locations. Visit the Mills & Boon website today and type **Mod15** in at the checkout to receive

15% OFF

your next Modern purchase.

Visit **www.millsandboon.co.uk/mod15**

MILLS & BOON®

Why not subscribe?
Never miss a title and save money too!

Here's what's available to you if you join the exclusive **Mills & Boon Book Club** today:

- ✦ *Titles up to a month ahead of the shops*
- ✦ *Amazing discounts*
- ✦ *Free P&P*
- ✦ *Earn Bonus Book points that can be redeemed against other titles and gifts*
- ✦ *Choose from monthly or pre-paid plans*

Still want more?
Well, if you join today we'll even give you
50% OFF your first parcel!

So visit **www.millsandboon.co.uk/subs**
or call Customer Relations on **020 8288 2888**
to be a part of this exclusive Book Club!

SUBS_2014

Snow, sleigh bells and a hint of seduction

Find your perfect Christmas reads at
millsandboon.co.uk/Christmas

1014/MB506

MILLS & BOON®

Why shop at millsandboon.co.uk?

Each year, thousands of romance readers find their perfect read at millsandboon.co.uk. That's because we're passionate about bringing you the very best romantic fiction. Here are some of the advantages of shopping at www.millsandboon.co.uk:

* **Get new books first**—you'll be able to buy your favourite books one month before they hit the shops

* **Get exclusive discounts**—you'll also be able to buy our specially created monthly collections, with up to 50% off the RRP

* **Find your favourite authors**—latest news, interviews and new releases for all your favourite authors and series on our website, plus ideas for what to try next

* **Join in**—once you've bought your favourite books, don't forget to register with us to rate, review and join in the discussions

Visit **www.millsandboon.co.uk**
for all this and more today!

MILLS_WEB